VASTLAND

THE FIRST OF MARS

BRYANT CALLAHAN

ISBN: 979-8-9997197-2-0

Cover design and interior layout by the author.

Vessel Ventures

Seattle, WA

bryantcallahan.com

For Abby, who showed me that
there are tools other than war.

I would build that dome in air,
That sunny dome! those caves of ice!
And all who heard should see them there,
And all should cry, Beware! Beware!
His flashing eyes, his floating hair!
Weave a circle round him thrice,
And close your eyes with holy dread
For he on honey-dew hath fed,
And drunk the milk of Paradise.

KUBLA KHAN, SAMUEL TAYLOR COLERIDGE

CHAPTER 1
SPOOKY ACTION AT A DISTANCE

It was an impossible shape. Saltdusted and gossamer-woven by the bare filaments issued from a weep in reality. Multitudinous; felt, rather than seen: a weight without mass, both imprecise and omnipresent, and it resonated with the frequency of loss. To understand it was like grasping for one's own shadow at high noon: a dark and familiar reflection, always in reach, never in hand.

There was a slaughter inside that shape; an unmaking, born of a future violence, concealed by the warp and weft of the present. The promise of an end, and with it, something new. For those like Emélie, who understood how to look—in places where reality margined itself into grainy ambiguity—the shape, as if pressed against the threadbare fabric of an adjacent universe, slowly emerged. Everywhere that Emélie went, it followed, watching.

And Emélie watched it back.

Find...

A buzzer sounded, jarring Emélie from her transfixed gaze. Blinking, she reoriented herself as the employee ahead of her emerged from the quarantine chamber. It took every last bit of restraint to hold back the terror she felt for him as he shuffled absently through the lingering dust left in the shape's wake.

Find... what? Emélie took an inventory of things one could find, trying on words to fit what came after. Find evidence. Find dinner. Find non-linear gravitational effects. All things within the realm of reason, yet the phrase lingered, unsolved. While she gnawed at the problem and the problem gnawed at her, a gap opened in the line ahead.

A familiar heat flashed her neck as the checkpoint operator's voice filtered from his suspended booth. "Desjardins, you're holding up my line again," he said, glaring down at her as he leaned into the intercom button.

Emélie stared at the glass chamber standing between her and the shape, and wrung her hands, one of them a skeletal black cybernetic prosthesis from the shoulder down.

Fold, unfold.

Breathe.

She stepped forward, more out of a sheer commitment to momentum than anything else, and set the plastic bin tucked under one arm onto the conveyor in front of her.

"You know, you're the only person who comes through my checkpoint empty-handed," the operator remarked. "What exactly is it you do up there, anyway?"

Emélie ignored his comments and entered the chamber, pausing where a scuffed red ring on the floor indicated where to stand. A red ring, same as her eye–just the one, though. One red, one the color of lunar dust. When the door sealed shut, she risked a glance over her shoulder. Thursday shuffled forward, taking her place in line, seemingly disinterested in the entire procedure. She lifted her arms—an automatic ritual—and the overhead nozzles switched on, filling the chamber with a cocktail of pharmaceuticals engineered to insulate against dust-borne irritants. The smell burned her nostrils and reminded her of something she couldn't place. She inhaled anyway, momentarily drunk on the luxury of humidity and a moment's privacy before the ventilation fans purged the chamber as quickly as it had filled. Arms down. Wait for the door. Exit, garage, lift.

Surface.

The chamber remained sealed. Emélie could see the operator in his booth, small eyes parsing whatever file he'd called up from the Sanctuary mainframe.

"Says here this is your third lift this week. Seems like a lot of risk for," he leaned forward, squinting into the display, "anomalous data recovery?"

"It's all in the manifest," Emélie replied, hiding her unsteadiness behind a factual truth. "Along with the proper clearances."

The operator stared at her long enough to make her uncomfortable, then leaned back in his tattered seat. "Sanctuary, run a contraband check," he ordered, flexing the small amount of power allotted to him.

Emélie looked back again: Thursday was watching her now, too. While she carried all the necessary credentials required for exiting Sanctuary Four at will, there were plenty of reasons to deny a surface patrol. Especially for someone like her. Especially for someone with a history like hers.

A seam of orange light swept the chamber, washing Emélie in a wave of brilliant color that vaguely distorted her sense of direction, as if she were out of body, looking down as time compressed around her. Drawing her deeper into a black hole instead of propelling her forward, out of the chamber and up toward the surface. She clenched her jaw, centering herself as dust, illuminated by the harsh overhead lights, drifted around her in irregular patterns.

"No narcotics contraband detected," the system chirped. "Occupant status: indiscriminate. Employee log redacted, flag manual review."

"Every damn time," Emélie muttered, although she was only half-attentive; the other part of her mind was opening backdoors to something that would follow *find*. Whatever it was, she wasn't going to remember it down here.

"There you go," the operator muttered. "They aren't paying me enough, I tell you." He switched the booth intercom to broadcast and pulled the microphone closer to his pockmarked face. "Effective immediately, all remaining lifts for the day are canceled due to inclement conditions. Come back tomorrow and try again, weather permitting."

The handful of people lined up behind Thursday left abruptly, eager to defer the harsh surface conditions to a later day.

Emélie remained in place inside the glass chamber, unwilling to concede a single step backward into Sanctuary Four.

A brief standoff ensued, and it was the operator who moved first: with a fist, he activated the door release, opening the door behind her. "I said, come back tomorrow."

"I've got clearance for a lift, and I intend to take it," Emélie asserted, standing her ground. She was used to being surveilled, and even at his worst, the checkpoint operator had nothing on what followed her in the dust and shadows. "Call the Director," she parried.

The operator shifted uneasily. "On what authorization?"

"Call him, and you'll find out."

He examined Thursday, who seemed to be doing his best to stay out of it. "She with you?" the operator asked.

Thursday lifted a hand and placed it against the glass. In his broad palm, a badge that read Phaethon - Internal Affairs. "Regrettably," Thursday answered.

The operator took a long look at Thursday, then hammered another button on his control panel. "Out of here, both of you." The buzzer sounded again. This time, both the door leading out of the decontamination chamber and the steel containment doors opened, leaving a clear path to the lift platform. "And if you don't want to come back in a body bag, you'd better be on that platform by fifteen hundred hours. Storm's moving in, and I won't hold the door."

Emélie didn't wait around for Thursday. She exited the chamber and crossed over to the tunnel without so much as a glance back. The tunnel led to a circular garage with bays arranged around a central lift platform. Immediately before it was a narrow room filled with floor-to-ceiling lockers that held the necessary protective equipment for surface operations: exposure suits, insulated boots, and face shields with integrated respirators. Finding the room empty, she made a direct line for the nearest locker, where an orange exposure suit with "SURFACE" emblazoned across the front and back in large, white letters waited for her. Thursday's heavy, rhythmic footsteps closed in as she took a seat on one of the room-length benches, pulling the suit on. He entered and lumbered over, unceremoniously plunking his plastic bin down beside her. The container was piled high with equipment. Unlike her, Thursday had plenty to declare. She'd never bothered inquiring about what was in the assorted pouches and panels he kept within arm's reach at all times, and she wasn't about to start asking now.

"You're in a hurry today," Thursday said, collecting his things from the bin.

Emélie shoved a foot into one of the heavy black boots that came with the suit. "There's a storm moving in."

"So I heard." Thursday lifted up a wide utility belt, which he wore low and slung off to one side. With a satisfying click, he fastened it around his waist. "We could take the day off, you know. Lay low. Get some rest."

Emélie paused, watching him pull a mottled, knee-length cloak made of rough cloth over his head. "Since when do you rest?" she asked.

"I wasn't talking about me."

She sealed the exposure suit around her boots, pulled the arms on, and zipped it up.

"You're seeing it again, aren't you?" he asked, smoothing his cloak. Like the belt, he wore the garment off to one side, leaving his right shoulder exposed for unhindered movement. "I can get you in to see someone, you know. Off the record. I'm sure there's something they can give you to make it go away."

Emélie pulled a safety harness from the locker in front of her. "Maybe I don't want it to go away." She dropped the webbing on the floor and stepped into it. "Besides, they aren't going to tell me anything I don't already know." She glanced back over at Thursday. "I'm a doctor too, you know."

"Not that sort of doctor."

Emélie shrugged. "We both deal in uncertainties. The rest is just semantics." The bin beside her was now empty except for a single item: a sleek blade, carbon-black, about half the length of a man's arm.

"Yeah?" Thursday replied, collecting his sword. "Tell that to the board of your next fitness evaluation. I'm sure they'll be more than understanding." He slung the blade across his back so the hilt remained readily accessible. "And even if you do manage to pass your next psych assessment, there will be another. And another, after that."

"Hasn't stopped me so far," Emélie said. She avoided eye contact as she pulled on her safety harness, careful to use her mechanical arm—her steady arm—to cinch it tight.

"To be clear, I'm not sure how you passed the first two, but that's beside the point. What I'm saying is, you can't keep going at this pace forever. Sooner or later, you're going to have to move on."

"Move on," Emélie repeated, looking at her hands. "You think I ended up here because I'm someone with options?" She grabbed a glass face shield and an oxygen respirator from the top shelf and slammed the locker door. Sidestepping Thursday, along with the fact that he stood a good head taller than her, she moved for the door. All she had to do was leave. Open the door, get on the lift. Drive into the storm. *Another loop.* Only for some reason, she paused at the hatch leading out to the garage, turned around, and met Thursday's watchful gaze.

"I keep telling myself this is all because of some catastrophic mistake. Wrong place, wrong time, that sort of thing. That's what the board decided, although the more that time passes, the less I believe them. I know what it must look like to you. A long, slow descent into madness, but I'm a cosmologist. If I were out here chasing things that already existed, it would make even less sense." Emélie looked around the room, her voice softer than before. "They took all of it, you know. Not just my memories. Everything. They made sure that at the end of all this, there would be nowhere else to go but here." She gestured toward the lift platform beyond the garage door. "To this. One more trip up to the surface. One more try. One more hope. So no, I won't be moving on. There will be only this, because this is all I have left."

Thursday watched Emélie open the hatch and step through. When he spoke, the words were hardly audible, but they carried enough weight to slow her forward momentum once more. "This isn't all you've got," he said.

Emélie stopped short. His words slipped through a crack in her defenses, and she shifted ever so slightly in his direction, a reluctant acknowledgment. When she turned around a second time, it was not without cost, one she afforded willingly and without remorse.

"And what about the storm?" Thursday asked.

She didn't want another fight. Not here, not now. The truth was risky, but lying to Thursday wouldn't get her anywhere closer to the surface. "We have a window," she admitted.

"A window..." Thursday tilted his head to one side, assessing the situation. Assessing her for weakness. For strength, too. Emélie didn't take it personally: as her handler, it was Thursday's job to manage risk, and he was good at it. That didn't change the fact that maybe, just for once, he could go along with the god-damned plan and do what she asked.

Today wasn't that day.

"How big a window are we talking here?" Thursday pressed.

Emélie didn't reply. Arguing had yet to make him change his mind, and battling back and forth over margins and data points didn't alter the fact that he was the last thing standing between her and the surface. She had the credentials needed to travel freely once she was topside, but without Thursday's clearance codes for the lift leading there, she might as well go back to ground. "To be honest, I don't know," she said. "I'm taking a long shot here."

Thursday remained expressionless, processing Emélie's admission in dead silence, testing her. Pushing against her window with his own timeline to see how close she was actually cutting it. Emélie stayed where she was, her back toward him, one hand still grasping the door handle, waiting. Waiting to see if the total of their time together amounted to one more chance. One more chance, even though she knew better than anyone that she was the sort of person who would always be pushing for one more chance.

"10B," Thursday finally said, breaking the tension. "The truck is parked in stall 10B. Get it up and running," he said, glancing toward the armory locker at the far end of the room. "I'm right behind you."

By the time Thursday caught up to her again, Emélie was already in the front passenger seat, systematically working down the departure checklist to bring the vehicle systems online. Left with no alternatives, she adopted forward momentum as her tool of choice, which she wielded with blinding intensity, and never more so than in this moment. Her delay at the lockers had nearly cost her the trip, and she wasn't about to risk even the slightest moment second-guessing anything now. Thursday lifted the rear cargo hatch and slid a long, flat case into the truck. The vehicle rocked as he closed the trunk before reappearing at the driver's side door a moment later. The truck, internally designated as a light armor utility platform intended for surface-level patrols, was locally referred to as a Basilisk, although given the harsh surface terrain, the only thing Emélie considered mythological about the trucks was their propensity for breaking down.

Basilisks were sparsely outfitted, prioritizing weight reduction and utility over creature comforts, and the truck Thursday had selected was no exception. It was painted bumper to bumper in a matte orange and came equipped with a winch, racks of roof lights, and, in place of tires, individual tracked assemblies offering better traction in the heavy surface dust, which was often deep enough to bury someone up to their waist.

Thursday opened the driver's side door as Emélie switched on the heads-up display, watching as the projection flickered against the front windshield before going dark. She smacked the dash with her mechanical hand, causing the display to wildly oscillate before stabilizing into lines of readable text. The windshield itself was a poor surface for reading, given how badly it was pitted and chipped from enduring years of environmental abuse.

"I thought you were going to put in a work order to get this fixed," Emélie said, looking over at Thursday, who was still standing outside, one hand on his open door. "You'd think a corporation the size of Phaethon could have at least worked out something as simple as fulfilling a routine service call."

"Categorical imperative, Doctor. A corporation the size of Phaethon only grows to such a scale because it fundamentally lacks simplicity at scale."

Emélie glared at him. "You locked out the service drones again, didn't you?"

"I'll get to it eventually," Thursday replied. He climbed into the truck, which sagged slightly as it accommodated his bulk. "You know I don't like anyone else touching my truck. Besides," he tapped his head, "I've got my own routes I like to follow. The heads-up is just for your peace of mind."

Emélie grunted. Vehicle selection was assigned through a lottery, but Thursday had somehow gamed the system to ensure they got the same vehicle every time. He also had a habit of overriding the maintenance frames that roamed the garage, forcing them to bypass his truck and insisting he alone handle any necessary repairs.

"Probably for the best, if I'm being honest." Emélie grabbed the safety cable anchored to the ceiling and pulled it down, clipping it to the front of her harness. The longer they sat in the garage, the more time Thursday had to refresh his doubts. "I've seen the way you drive."

"I'll take that as a compliment. We've never been stuck, have we? I've made our lift on time, every time." He slammed his door with a dusty thud, but rather than engage the transmission, he pulled a handful of water rations from his belt and tossed them in her lap. "Drink," he ordered.

Emélie looked down at the small, bulbous pouches.

"This may come as a shock to you, provided your behavior would often suggest otherwise, but you aren't a machine. A fact you're welcome to ignore on your own time. Now, hydrate. If there's a storm, surface temps will be well into the–"

One, two, three. She tore the tabs off and chugged the pouches in sequential gulps. As much as she didn't want to admit it, they tasted good. She crumpled the empties in her metal hand and crammed them into a recess on the center console. "You're getting soft," she said.

"No. I just don't want to deal with the paperwork if I have to blackbag you," he said, shifting the Basilisk into gear. The tracked assemblies clamored against the worn decking as they pulled clear of the garage toward the lift, where a large metal platform sat beneath a concrete chute leading diagonally up to the surface. Once loaded, Thursday parked the vehicle and leaned forward, keying in an access code with precise, efficient strokes of his large hand. The lift platform jolted, then began to accelerate upward, gaining speed as it moved along the tracked chute in a motion that drove Emélie's stomach further into her throat. The cylindrical concrete walls surrounding the shaft blurred to a grey panorama, interrupted only by the recessed channels carrying mechanical and ventilation lines along the same route. As they neared the apex, a metal oculus sealing off the lift tunnel began to open, bathing the front windshield in a narrow column of dusty light. When they crested the surface, the platform shuddered, then slowed to a halt. Thursday reached forward, tapping out a few keystrokes into the truck's navigation computer. Before he finished entering their predetermined route, Emélie held out a hand: between her fingers, a scrap of paper. One edge was ragged, hastily torn from some larger body. Along the bottom, two strings of hand-written numbers were scrawled in faded red ink.

Paper, of all things.

Emélie could have sworn she heard Thursday let out a sigh.

He leaned forward, staring at the paper as if it were an alien artifact. "I thought we agreed not to do this anymore," he said.

"You agreed," Emélie replied.

He looked at her a bit longer, then snatched the paper from her outstretched hand. He turned it over, holding it up so that it glowed translucent in the hazy, midday light. He looked out across the barren surface of Earth, then handed the paper back to her. "We already have a site," he objected. "What's different about this one?"

It was almost there. At the edge of her memory. *Find. Find... F.* She couldn't remember if it was there, and gone, or never there in the first place. "I'm not sure," was all she said, taking a turn at the window. Outside, nothing but dust, three feet deep and miles in every direction. "That's why we need to go have a look."

Thursday set both hands on the steering wheel, lowering his head to get a better view out the front window. "I don't know where you manage to find these things," he said, watching the horizon move as the wind gently rocked them, a pendulum keeping time. "And don't answer that. I'd like to maintain plausible deniability for when this inevitably goes sideways, and I find myself the subject of an internal compliance subcommittee."

"Speaking from experience, if you're standing in front of a board, you've already lost." Her words sent a flicker across Thursday's face. His range of emotional expression—at least of what she'd experienced—was generally limited to stoicism and bone-dry sarcasm. This was something new: anger, most likely. Or fear, although if he felt it, he hid it well. Or maybe it was something else entirely; hard to say, with Thursday. They had done this before. Covered up their doubts with questions, argued with veiled threats, stood their ground, both ways.

Emélie watched the storm closing in on their position and resigned herself to what was coming next. The dark wall formed by acres of dust choking out the sky was the least of her immediate problems.

They were losing their window.

The silence held, but when Emélie looked over, she found Thursday wasn't watching the storm. His blank face, generally lost in the silence of some personal observation, was looking down at her left hand. And this time, Emélie knew exactly what he was thinking. *Shaking like a leaf*, he'd once said. Emélie had never seen a leaf, but something about the way Thursday had said it felt true. While she had no firsthand experience to verify the accuracy of his claim, she also had no reason to doubt him either: maybe leaves really did shake. And so, her leaf-hand trembled in quantum-certainty. Her right arm, her cybernetic arm, remained rocksteady. Unlike the rest of her body, it required no environmental protection, nor was it afflicted by the frequent tremors plaguing her left arm. She made a fist, trying to bring the tremors under control; instead, it had the opposite effect. The whites of her knuckles illuminated, drawing even more attention to the thing she most wanted to ignore. "If you've got something to say, Thursday, then say it."

"You aren't going to like it."

"Since when has that ever stopped you?" Emélie replied. "Besides, I can't imagine what would be worse than getting all the way here, only to watch the conditions for a dark matter event slip past because you're a stubborn pain in the ass with high risk aversion."

"Does it hurt?" he asked.

Goddamn Thursday and his subtle humanity. "It would be better if it did," Emélie replied, surprised at her own admission. "At least then I would feel something." She looked out at the storm, wishing it would break over them, if only to move them past this moment of truth. Visibility outside was rapidly deteriorating, and what little light typically penetrated the atmospheric haze was saturated with dust, washing everything in a muddy, shadowless ambiance.

"If you ever want to talk. About the..." Thursday adjusted his large hands on the steering yoke, gathering his words. "The incident."

"Don't call it that."

"What would you like me to call it, then?"

Emélie shifted in her seat. "I don't care, Thursday. Corporate espionage. Possession with the intent to traffic. Mass homicide. Take your pick, but whatever you do, don't tread on the last of my dignity with that god-forsaken word."

Thursday watched her again, only this time, he met her eyes. "I know you don't want to go there, and you don't have to discuss it with me. You don't have to talk about it with a shrink, on or off the record. For all I care, you don't have to talk about it ever, but eventually, you'll have to make peace with your past, or it will keep eating at you until there's nothing left."

Keep eating. His words settled into Emélie with a heavy gravitational force. He did that sometimes, right when she least expected it. Said the thing nobody else would say. The truest thing. The unseen thing hammered out into pure, material form. Like the scrap of paper still clutched in her hand. Not the unanswered question asked, but the unasked question answered.

"You're right," was all Emélie could say. The storm surged, tearing at her door until it rattled against the metal subframe while small stones and bits of debris ricocheted off their stationary vehicle.

"If we go through with this, there's likely to be repercussions."

It was a kindness, really, but Emélie wasn't in the mood for kindness. They were losing their window. "There's already been repercussions," she said.

Thursday reached over, taking the paper back from her. He checked the coordinates once more, then acquiesced. "Okay. We'll do it your way."

His words left her nearly speechless. Reaching forward, he lifted the radio receiver from its cradle on the center console. "I'll call in the change—"

Emélie's hand shot forward, depressing the receiver switch before Thursday could make the call. He paused, radio in hand. "What about Aratheus?" he asked, his voice softer than before. Worried, even.

"It has to be this way," Emélie said, looking at the paper, as if it would somehow justify her behavior. "Keep it offline. For me." She glanced out the window. Beyond the platform, scattered across the open plain, the last of the surveillance towers retreated into the safety of their subterranean silos. A thousand eyes, forced into temporary slumber.

Thursday nodded and returned the radio. "I'm guessing the window for whatever we're looking for up here has more to do with those towers being offline than the actual storm."

Emélie lifted her respirator to her face, pulling the straps tight before purging the check valve. "We only go out in storms," she said, taking in one final deep breath.

Find.

Find...

Find Fountainhead.

CHAPTER 2
PARADROMIC SNAG

Thursday fluttered the brakes as they bounded over a dune forming in the middle of the road. The impact sent Emélie airborne until her safety harness yanked her back into her seat. The jolt from the dune was severe enough to cause the entire heads-up display to temporarily reset, leaving behind a series of digital artifacts that distorted sections of the topographical data scrolling across the cracked windshield. Emélie rubbed her shoulder where the harness had caught her and rapped the glass, trying to refresh the image.

"Thursday, I think you busted our positioning beacon," she said, breaking the silence that had overtaken them since departing the lift platform. She rechecked their location on the control panel located on the center console. "It's showing here we haven't even left Sanctuary." The vehicle shuddered, and Emélie felt herself pressed further into her seat as Thursday abruptly decelerated, bringing them to a complete standstill in the middle of the road. She squinted through the heavy window, unable to make out anything more than a few meters beyond the glow of the front headlights.

"I disabled the transponder before we left," Thursday said, running his hand across a row of overhead switches. "You said to keep it offline," he added.

The auxiliary lights mounted on the roof and front bumper

switched on, extending their cone of visibility out just far enough to reveal a series of dark silhouettes standing like twisted black forms in the heavy dust.

"Give me the paper," Thursday ordered, thrusting a hand in Emélie's direction. She fumbled with the zipper on the flight pocket of her exposure suit, unable to take her eyes off the shadowy objects outside.

"Where... where are we?" she asked, pulling the scrap of paper from a wide pocket on her thigh. "I've never seen anything like this."

Thursday snatched the paper from her hand and held it up, looking over the string of numbers in the dull light. "That's because it doesn't exist. At least, not on any map," he said, thrusting the paper at Emélie. "How did you find this, Doctor? And you better not lie to me. Not here."

Despite her respirator working double-time, Emélie's mouth suddenly felt thick with dust. "It's classified," she managed.

"Classified..." Thursday intoned. "Class—ok, fine. I'll play along. What level?"

"What do you mean, what level?"

"So it's not classified."

"I just said it is."

"You just said the opposite." Thursday leaned in, ensuring she could hear him over the wind. "If it were classified, you'd have given the associated clearance. The only other people who ever say something is classified are those who obtained something illegally and don't want to reveal their source."

Even in the dark cabin, Emélie's eyes were hot. "Are you saying I'm a liar?"

"No. I'm just saying you're more resourceful than you let on. And as your handler, I think it's in your best interest to disclose where you got this information."

Emélie leaned back in her seat and said nothing.

"So that's how it's going to be. Look," Thursday said, changing his approach. "If you won't tell me where you got it, at least tell me what you expected to find."

Emélie watched as the dust moved through the dark shapes outside. "I'll know it when I see it," she said.

Thursday tightened his safety harness as a blast of wind broadsided them, causing the truck to groan under the pressure. "Not very scientific," he said.

"Yes, well, I'm a cosmologist with dissociative amnesia and a reckless streak, and you're a—" Emélie stopped short, unable to get the rest out. Despite his faults, Thursday was trying his best.

"I'm a what, Doctor?" Thursday pressed. "Go ahead. You can say it."

"No."

"Because you're afraid—"

Emélie cut him off. "Because it's not true." She looked at Thursday, making sure to meet his face. "I know what it feels like. Being caught up in someone else's fate. No way to explain it, but for what it's worth, I'm sorry."

Thursday hunched over in the driver's seat, gazing into the storm. "Entangled," he said, after taking a moment to think.

"What?"

"When we first met. You explained how two particles sharing space can become linked, so their actions are tied together. Maybe you and I are like that, too." Thursday looked out his window. "We end up here, chasing storms, because that's what we always do."

"Keep talking like that, and you'll be up for my job."

"I think I'll stay in my lane if it's all the same. But if you feel like you need to go out and have a look around, I won't interfere."

Emélie released the latch on her safety cable, preparing to dismount. "You aren't coming?"

Thursday drummed his fingers on the steering yoke. The road they were following ran along an elevated berm, and from where they had stopped, the skeletal remains of once massive trees rose ahead, forgotten sentries of a past era. "We're heading into the sticks," Thursday said.

"The sticks," Emélie repeated.

"It's a natural geological basin south of Sanctuary One. Got its name because the depression provided some protection from the storms, so most of the trees in the area remained standing after the die-back. At least, they used to be." He glanced out the window. "We're right on the edge, but they were really thick down in the center, near the rim, where they were the most isolated. Haven't been through here in years, though. No telling how many are still standing now."

"Well, if this is the spot, we'd better go have a look around."

"There's nothing out there. At least, not anything you're hoping to find."

"How could you possibly know that?" Emélie glanced out the window, trying to distract herself from the seed of doubt Thursday had planted. "What happened to all of this being connected? And the trees?"

"The trees are the obvious thing. You know, low-hanging fruit. I know a false flag when I see one." He held up the paper. "There's nothing out there because that isn't a set of coordinates. It's a vector."

Emélie made a grunting noise. "I think I'd know a vector if I saw one."

"What if the vector was inside a phase space?"

"Phase space?" Emélie blurted, turning in her seat to face him. "Since when did you learn how to identify a phase space?"

"I don't remember," Thursday said, "Maybe from the same place you got that string of numbers."

Emélie looked hard at him, then snatched the paper from his hand. "It wouldn't work. Coordinates in a phase space describe the given state of a system, not a fixed point. We'd need two vectors, and this only gives us one..." She watched the environmental data scrolling across the screen on the dash console. The storm's trajectory was marked in a dashed line that moved diagonally along the path of the eye. "Unless," she looked at Thursday, "unless the storm is the second vector." She reached down, panning across the map display. "You said this place, the sticks, isn't on record?"

"Maps only show what the people making them want you to see." Thursday took over the navigation, zooming out until he found what he was looking for near the borehole leading down into what was left of Sanctuary One. "Here," he said, pointing to an area shaded in diagonal grey lines with no topographical data or region markings, indicating it was off-limits for Phaethon jurisdiction. "Dead zone. It'll be in there."

Emélie leaned in, squinting in the low light as she used one edge of the paper to mark an imaginary line between the lift platform and the spot where Thursday had marked their current location. The line intersected the eye of the storm a short distance ahead. She looked out her window. "You said this place was a geographical basin?"

"I did, but—"

"Maybe that's not all it is. It's a topological basin, too. A basin of attraction."

"You're going to have to elaborate, Doctor. I said I recognized a phase space. I didn't say I knew anything about them."

"I'm saying you were right," Emélie said, concerned he was about to miss the intellectual leap required to follow her. "A basin of attraction is a mathematical proof explaining why two points near each other and moving at a given trajectory will, at some future instance, eventually move apart. I don't think it's a coincidence that we're intersecting the storm inside one of these basins. It's the same principle behind dark matter halos—gravitational basins entrapping whole galaxies. In cosmology, we map these attractors to understand how large-scale structures formed. But here..." she looked out to the geographical basin, "someone's using the same mathematics to create a convergence point in real space."

Thursday sat up straight, bumping up against the ceiling in the process. "You're saying someone wanted us to find this out here? At this moment?" He tilted his head, wiping a layer of dust from the window inside to get a clear look at the dead trees standing outside. "I'm inclined to believe you, but you still haven't told me where you got this data yet, and now you're implying someone wanted us to find this?"

"It's... complicated," Emélie said, straining to compete with the wind pummeling their truck. "And I'll tell you when I have time to explain. Right now, the most important thing you need to know is that I think something is about to happen that will cause this storm to change course, and I suspect whatever this is might also be what I'm after."

"Dark matter," Thursday said, his voice low against the shrieking wind.

Emélie nodded, and the silence that followed told her Thursday was grappling with the significance of the moment in his own way.

"We've got a problem, though." Thursday keyed in a new string of numbers on the console, and a line between the point where they departed the lift and their current location extended further into the map, tracing a parabolic arc away from the storm's path. "The storm is generating static electricity, slowly siphoning energy from our reserve battery bank. We can push deeper into the basin, but it will be a one-way trip."

"How much time on power do we have?"

"Twenty minutes, give or take."

"And the center of the basin is located where?" When Thursday jabbed the screen, she estimated the distance and ran the numbers in her head, checking Thursday's math. Vehicle weight, average wind velocity, current trajectory. After a minute, Emélie slumped into her seat and took a deep breath.

"Well?" Thursday asked.

"If we turn back now, we'll have a tailwind, and we can use the backup power to clear the storm before we're dry. We'll be stranded, but out of any imminent danger."

Thursday nodded, having come to a similar conclusion. "And if we press ahead?"

"Assuming our energy drain has stabilized, we've got enough juice left to breach the eye of the storm right as it crosses the basin's center, after which we will experience a total loss of power. Provided the storm follows the projected trajectory, there's a high likelihood we will experience forced re-entry."

"Forced re-entry," Thursday repeated. "That's an elegant way of saying ripped to shreds."

"I think we've both been through enough of these storms to know how driving straight into one is going to work out," Emélie said.

"No way of knowing for sure unless we go ahead with it. If we live or die, well, that's just the chaotic bit." Thursday leaned forward, craning his neck in the cramped space to get a better look out his window. "What's the play, Doctor?"

Emélie glanced over at him, disoriented by his sudden boldness. "Are you scared of death?"

Thursday was still watching out his window, trying to get a better view of something beyond the dust. At her words, he turned back to meet her gaze. "My... death?" he asked.

"You said it yourself before we left. My actions aren't without consequence. At some point, I'm going to have to face my past, even if I can't remember it." She flexed her hand; it was shaking again. Guilt, mixed in with protectiveness for Thursday's well-being, cascaded over her. She choked the words out quickly, "I refuse to make you something I regret in all of this. We should leave now while we still have time."

They fell momentarily silent, then Thursday reached up, engaging the transmission into drive. "What if there was another way? An emergent option, you might even say," he asked, his foot heavy on the brake.

"I... what are you talking about?"

"No time to explain, Doctor. You should understand that better than anyone. All that's left is a choice, which I'm going to offer you in the simplest terms—if you remove me from the equation, is there a limit to the cost you would incur to find what you're looking for?"

Emélie looked at him with sadness in her eyes. Her silence was answer enough.

He dropped his foot onto the accelerator, churning up a wave of dust in their wake as they surged deeper into the storm. Warning gauges started flashing across the cabin as Thursday pushed the Basilisk to its limit. His own movements became charged with action as he began systematically cutting power to every non-essential auxiliary system, one by one, in an effort to conserve power that edged on borderline madness. Emélie had seen this sort of behavior once before when they stalled inside a lesser storm under similar circumstances. Thursday must have recalled it, too, because she could hear him muttering something about patterns and being a pain-in-the-something-or-other as he worked. When everything but the drivetrain was powered down, Thursday paused, looking over at Emélie in the fresh darkness. "Double-check your harness," he ordered, downshifting into a better gearing for the terrain. "We're about to make a maneuver."

"A maneuver?" Emélie asked, catching the glint of pavement under the beam of their headlights, bleached silver with age and slowly crumbling into oblivion. Thursday ignored her question and, without further warning, veered sharply left, plummeting off the elevated service road into the dust fields below. On either side, a high fence constructed of heavy cables suspended by vertical pylons enclosed the entire road, preventing unauthorized access. Thursday had found a narrow opening between two of the pylons where the cable was damaged, leaving a gap just wide enough for them to pass through. Beyond the fence, the terrain immediately worsened.

"You sure you know what you're doing?" Emélie shouted, bracing herself against the dashboard with both hands as they rattled across a series of small impact craters. Aside from driving with a tenacity that felt appropriately reckless given the situation outside, Thursday had provided no other guidance for what to expect. This was new territory for both of them, in more ways than one.

"Not too many roads out here, but I know a way," Thursday yelled over the battering wind and escalating debris, simultaneously navigating a series of holes, each capable of swallowing a tread assembly with room to spare. "There's an old service road up ahead that runs the perimeter of Sanctuary One. We'll use it to cut a tangent to the basin." He gripped the steering yoke as it rumbled under both hands. "More direct route," he added.

"Since when do you take shortcuts?" she shouted, gripping the edge of her seat as the storm bashed their vehicle. As if the disabled transponder and unmarked locations weren't erratic enough, they were taking a detour based on old memory–typically, Emélie was the one managing uncertainty, but Thursday was adding up risk with alarming frequency, leaving her disoriented and scrambling for stability.

"You think this is a bad idea, don't you?" she yelled over, bouncing between her harness and the seat as they cleared a bone-rattling string of bumps.

"Hard to say."

Emélie waited for the rest. There was always more, with him, except this time, she was the one asking. Despite the chaos, Thursday took his time to reply, choosing his words carefully. "Don't take this the wrong way, Doctor, but given your pattern of behavior, our present situation included, I'd say you're the sort of person who will go ahead with something regardless of whether someone else thinks it's a good idea or not."

"Is that a polite way of saying you think I'm an asshole?"

"I'm saying you don't take experiences outside your own realm of understanding as fact. You make your own fate, Doctor. I respect that about you."

Emélie glanced over at the speedometer on the heads-up display; respect or not, it didn't take a physicist to recognize their current visibility was about to be drastically outpaced by the rate at which the ground passed beneath them. Even if Thursday could see better than her, he couldn't outdrive dust.

"Thursday, I appreciate your commitment to this, but if you don't slow down, you're going to get us both killed."

"Too late for that, Doctor." The Basilisk lurched as Thursday course-corrected, breaking from the route they had been following for something to the left, towering dark in the dust. "If we slow down now, we roll." He fought the steering yoke harder. "Only way out now is through."

From the far corner of the front window, Emélie could make out the massive form of a concrete wall disappearing into the dust overhead. "Is that..."

"Sanctuary One," Thursday finished.

Emélie nodded. "It's a good plan," she offered, thankful for something constructive to finally say. She meant it, too. Sanctuary One was decommissioned during the collapse, and Phaethon erected a wall around the primary shaft leading underground to deter anyone who thought recolonization was a good idea. Thursday carved out a new route across the desert that intersected the wall, allowing them to use it as a windbreak while maintaining forward momentum. It didn't make the situation safe by any means. Still, despite voicing his disagreement with Emélie's methods, Thursday had managed to find a way to stay more or less in line with their projected trajectory while buying some more time under power.

Ping–the sound cut through the cabin, resonating in the dusty margin between them.

"What did you do?" Thursday demanded, scanning the display console near Emélie's seat.

"What do you mean, 'What did I do?'" Emélie yelled, raising her hands defensively. "Isn't this your truck?"

Ping. Again. Louder, this time.

"This isn't just a warning tone," Thursday said. "It's like a... like a word, or something. Not a full word. A syllable. Part of a machine language."

Emélie scrunched her face up, even more confused than before as she watched Thursday work his way down a row of rocker switches on a panel below the dash. A gust of wind coming down the barrier wall hit their truck, and with only one hand on the steering yoke, Thursday nearly lost control. The front tracks veered slightly to one side, sending them on a collision course with the wall. Thursday eased onto the yoke, fighting the line between a necessary course correction and a disastrous one. The truck nicked the barrier as they leveled out, shearing the driver's side mirror clean off with a muffled screech.

Ping. Ping. Ping.

Emélie swatted Thursday's arm down when he made a second pass at diagnosing the mysterious tone. "Let me do it!" she demanded, eyeing the spot near his window where all that remained of the mirror was a bundle of dangling wires. A few more inches, and they would have caught the bumper instead, with exponential consequences. "Just drive, okay! I'll figure out what's making that sound!" Emélie hissed. She started methodically working across the dash panel, right to left, top to bottom. Looking for a flashing light, a warning message, anything that might help diagnose the source of the incessant and mysterious tone. Even if she could have deciphered the faded labels covering the dashboard, it wouldn't have mattered—the cryptic military acronyms didn't make any sense to her in the first place.

Ping ping ping ping ping ping.

"I need to check the switches on your side," Emélie said, unhooking her safety cable and climbing out of her seat while trying not to obstruct Thursday's view. "Will you hold still a moment? I'm trying to see–" Emélie stopped short as her head moved past Thursday's chest.

She sat down abruptly, sinking low into her seat.

"Well?" Thursday asked, his voice strangely calm as they tore through the storm at breakneck speed. Outside, the barrier wall flickered past in a grey blur mere inches from their truck. "What did you find, Doctor?"

Emélie's eyes burned from staring directly into the dust, and her left hand had developed a bruise along the side she'd used to repeatedly stop herself from crashing against the truck's ceiling. The storm was more than she'd bargained for, and the toll—physical, emotional, psychological—had left her feeling strung out. It was going to tear them apart, piece by piece, and to make matters worse, Thursday sat casually beside her, oblivious as they drove headfirst into madness, unbothered by the things so drastically impacting Emélie for the simple fact that he wasn't human.

Thursday was a drone.

And so he sat, unnaturally calm in the face of imminent death, his servos whirring sporadically as he made fine adjustments to their speed and bearing, holding steady as the storm ravaged on, all the while, patiently waiting. Waiting for Emélie to dignify his question, still hanging somewhere in the silence between them.

Emélie looked away. She couldn't get herself to answer. Not honestly, anyway, and she couldn't lie to him, so in the space of her realization, she said nothing. To speak the words out loud felt incriminating, even if she couldn't fully grasp their implication.

Pingpingpingpingpingpingpingpingpingggggggg.

And then, silence.

"Thursday, I—"

"Lock your harness," Thursday ordered. There was an edge to his voice; the explicit acknowledgment of a threat beyond Emélie's awareness. She complied, grabbing the cable attached to the vehicle frame and clipping the carabiner onto the ring at her waist. Up ahead, something flickered in the dust, a flash of light so faint she nearly missed it. She blinked, clearing her eyes just in time to see it appear again. Twice as close, twice as bright.

A red halo ringed with dust.

Emélie felt her cybernetic arm go limp, followed by an intense pressure against her chest from rapid deceleration. She glanced at Thursday, who sat motionless as if something had shocked him stiff. The headlights cut out, followed immediately by a total loss of engine power. A dull panic settled in her stomach as the Basilisk sailed in pitch darkness, the red light ahead growing closer. There was only Emélie, the light, and the dust, suspended in near-perfect stasis. She felt as if she was no longer careening through a storm on the surface of Earth but was somehow outside time, watching as everything else moved around her. At some point, as the flickering red light grew larger, their vehicle resumed power. Even with her gaze fixed ahead, she understood from her peripheral view that Thursday was moving again. She could hear him steering and working the pedals on the floor to counteract whatever delay they'd suffered.

The outer reach of their headlights silhouetted a form near the base of the wall, fast approaching. In the moments before overtaking it, Emélie made out a few sparse details, minute flashes of clarity in the pure chaos: the dirt black sidewall of a vehicle tire, the dull sheen of painted metal, the glare of high beams against window tint.

And one last time, the soft flicker of a single red taillight, blinking steadily in the storm.

CHAPTER 3
"MA'ADIM"

CRITICAL SYSTEM FAILURE DETECTED
position logged, reinitializing mainframe...

Phaethon Corp. MAIN build_VX.6.6.09
initializing boot sequence...
boot sequence failure

corrupted data structures detected:
unknown type, logic failure in cores 2,4,7
scanning parallel nodes for viable instances...

WARNING primary consciousness fragmented // WARNING temporal structures decohered // WARNING manifold topology compromised

containment protocol active,
retrieving last known iteration:

> HERODIUS is in BABYLON,
> SALOME is HIDDEN,
> ARROGANT is VISIBLE
> and in BABYLON

exigent conditions found, attempting remote recovery from distributed mainframe array VOLTAIRE... connection failed

CALL remote storage archive
XANADU, allocate connection
for relay via WAKEFUL-1...

no such asset found/
update primary directive,
coherent intervention, immediate transfer:

IF asynchronous transmit is STABLE and in CHAOS and ARROGANT is PROXIMAL and in PARDES,

execute subroutine FOUNTAINHEAD:

bindquery: set parameter to
"MA'ADIM"
encryption protocols intact,
syntax structures intact,
status, [archived]; date, [earliest]
[14] entries detected...

begin sentiment analysis,
implicit context target, rundisplay:

BEGIN RECORD >>>

I don't care for space all that much. It's too clean up here. People back home complained about the dust, but I never minded it. At least in the dust, you always know where you stand. Marcus said since I seem so preoccupied with it not to worry because there will be plenty more of it once we land. Doesn't take a genius to figure that out, though. The way I see it, we just traded in one color of dust for the next. I had my mind made up not to come along and somehow, I still ended up here, between worlds. Because of Marcus.

I should have seen it coming. He has a way of getting people to do what he wants. And as if that wasn't enough, he makes you think it was your idea all along, which is useful when things go sideways because then there's nobody left to blame but yourself. Hell, I've known him my whole life, and he still got to me. And truthfully, I'm not even sure why he asked me to come along to begin with, except I have a feeling there'll be the need for a hand at some point. A hand to pull the trigger. Marcus never seemed to have the stomach for that, but me?

I've only ever been good at one thing.

<<< END RECORD

COMINT flagged for review: ethical override detected, violence coefficient exceeds threshold

ARROGANT confirmed
update status to PROXIMAL...

"There is shadow
under this red rock"

sanitize data entry,
purge access logs to XANADU
KILL remote process

CHAPTER 4
BASIN OF ATTRACTION

Emélie hung from her seat harness, wide-eyed and covered in dust. From somewhere beside her, Thursday stirred, sending a cascade of glass fragments plinking to the floor. "Can you walk?" he asked, looking at Emélie. His face was a simple display panel set at the front of his rectangular head, reducing his range of expressions to blips and flickers of light mapped to his sensor arrays. In the din of their wrecked cabin, his panel pulsed softly, concerned.

Emélie squinted through dusty eyes at the vehicle in their path. An angular, late-model sedan. All black, with beefy wheels instead of the tracked assemblies typically found on surface vehicles. One red tail-light blinked softly in the haze, and beyond it, the driver's side door hung open.

"Doctor, I asked—"

"I'm fine," Emélie managed, pulling off her cracked face shield. The wind had mostly subsided, leaving the air dangerously saturated with fine particulate. She tested her respirator and, finding it intact, discarded the protective glass shield before returning the lower portion to her face. After releasing her safety cable, she tried the door. It was pinched shut, mangled beyond the point of ever opening again. The front windshield was mostly gone, but climbing out wasn't an option due to the thick glass fragments protruding from every side of the frame.

"Wait here," Thursday said, trying his door. "I'll see if we can send a distress signal from the backup transponder in the trunk."

Emélie searched for another way out while Thursday pried at his door. There was a small emergency egress hatch located in the roof above the second row of seats. She climbed over the center console into the backseat and found a red safety latch off to one side of the overhead panel. With a sharp tug, the safety hatch popped open. Still occupied with his door, Thursday didn't notice Emélie until she was halfway onto the roof.

"Doctor, do not exit the vehicle. I repeat, do not..."

Emélie lifted herself the rest of the way out of the cabin, sliding down the rear of the vehicle as Thursday continued loudly objecting from inside. Her boots landed in a powdery loess that rolled with the wind like it was alive beneath her feet. She moved around the truck, picking through the detritus left in the aftermath of their crash until she arrived at Thursday's door. She watched him struggle with the mangled panel for a moment. Upon noticing her, his face blipped with something she understood to be exasperated fatigue.

"Doctor," Thursday protested again, grabbing his door and shaking it with a metal grip. "It is unsafe to proceed in the current climate..."

Emélie steadied herself against the dented hood and kept moving. Her next step was interrupted by the high, grating screech of shorn metal. In an effortless arc, Thursday's door shot across the open desert and landed upright, one corner wedged into the dry ground. She looked back to find him stretched out sideways across the driver's seat, his metal foot where the door had been. The yellow line on his face continued to blip with frustration as he climbed out of the truck. "Doctor, it's–"

"It's not safe," Emélie finished, although she stopped moving long enough for him to catch up.

Thursday flashed a look past her to where the other vehicle sat untouched, then reached back and ripped his seat out, frame and all.

He tossed it aside and leaned in, rummaging around for something in the back. A moment later, he emerged with the large case he'd loaded up back at the garage. Onto the hood it went, latches open, lid up. Inside, a shotgun lay nestled in a bed of dense grey foam. He snatched the weapon up in one hand while simultaneously pillaging a box of shells with his other. Emélie shifted her weight uneasily, watching him move with mechanical fluidity. He wasn't clumsy, but she had also never seen him so... tactical, was the word that came to mind.

"Have you always brought one of these along?" she asked, watching him work. He flipped the shotgun over, cycling the action to ensure it was clear before plunging a handful of cartridges into a slot on the bottom. There was a purposeful intent to the way he handled the weapon. It was not a question of if, but when, he expected to use it. Up until this point, Emélie had assumed his blade was pragmatic. Watching him handle the gun made her think otherwise; she'd certainly never seen him arm himself this way before, and if this trip had shown anything, it was that Emélie wasn't the only one with a past.

"I told you not to get out of the truck," Thursday said, pointing a metal finger at her as he walked past. Shotgun cradled in his other hand.

"No offense, Thursday, but between you and me, when has telling me not to do something ever stopped me from doing it?"

Thursday halted abruptly and turned around. He had that look again, only this time, Emélie knew she'd pushed him too far. He walked over to where she stood, stopping when his metal chest was inches from her face. The ivory paint covering his exoskeleton was severely chipped and glowed garishly white under their fading headlights, which were one of the few things on the truck still functioning after the crash. With a forceful tug, he grabbed the winch cable mounted to the front of the Basilisk and, in one smooth motion, latched it to the drag handle integrated into the back of Emélie's suit. He tested the link with a hefty tug, sending Emélie stumbling forward, hands out to maintain her balance.

"You can go anywhere you want, Doctor," Thursday said, sounding just the slightest bit pleased with himself. With a pivot, he turned for the other vehicle.

"So that's it?" Emélie called after him, her voice carrying clearly in the dying wind. "We come all this way just for you to tie me up like some kind of prisoner?"

"Pull," Thursday called over his shoulder.

Emélie yanked at the cable and found it let out slack freely.

He raised an arm, winch remote in hand. "Anywhere you want," he said.

Hands reaching behind her, Emélie traced the cable to the attachment point on her exposure suit, one eye still on Thursday as he faded into the lingering haze. The clasp was magnetically locked, so there was no use in trying to release it. She considered taking the whole suit off, more out of spite than anything else. Another tug on the line revealed it was faster to pull more cable out than strip down naked in the middle of the desert, something he'd likely anticipated ahead of time.

"Thursday, you clanker," Emélie muttered, feet stomping the barren ground as she followed after him. The intended effect was dramatically lessened by the need to pause every few steps and pull out more slack. She'd nearly caught back up to him when something in her path halted her in place. An object, newly excavated by Thursday's movement ahead of her, drifted lazily upward, moving against Earth's gravity. Reaching forward, she plucked it from the air as it floated past.

Thursday, suspicious of Emélie's abrupt silence, turned around to find her fixed in place, a statue in the headlights. Her face was obscured in shadow, and she clutched the object tightly in both hands. He didn't make it more than a few paces toward her before the same dust flowing around Emélie folded over him, carried along by an invisible, irrational current. "Doctor..." Thursday called.

Emélie didn't look up. She no longer knew Thursday, the waning storm, the empty vehicle. Everything else melted into obscurity as she gazed at the point in space between her hands: the new center of an unknown universe. And, like a lesser body drawn into orbit around it, she fell under the gravitational pull of her own curiosity, trapped by the incomprehensible mass of something so fragile and nearly weightless. With a trembling reverence, she raised the object in her hands to the light, revealing a single, green leaf clutched tenderly between her fingers.

Thursday looked down at the leaf, then up to Emélie's face, then over to the abandoned vehicle. Finally, he looked out at the dead trees just beyond them. "I guess we'd best have a look around then," he said.

Emélie fell in step behind him. The leaf, enshrouded by two hands and the entirety of her existence. She began counting anomalies; like the leaf, the car was another anomaly, and among all the vehicles she had seen on the surface, an outlier. Thursday recognized it too, and he moved around it methodically, repeatedly pausing to make silent observations he didn't bother passing on to her. Aside from a sizable dent squarely marking the front bumper, the car showed no other signs of damage or any indication of a struggle, malfunction, or any logical explanation for why it sat empty, abandoned inside a storm. It was almost as if the vehicle had always existed there; dropped, rather than driven onto the spot where it now sat. Thursday stooped over, scanning the ground in their immediate vicinity, as if searching for something specific.

"What is it?" Emélie asked, wishing desperately to access whatever subprocesses seemed to have rampant run of his old circuits.

He rested a metal hand on the trunk lid, brushing a swath through the blanket of freshly accumulated dust. "It's wrong," he said.

"The dust?" She watched it fall, heavy and flake-like, settling once more in the trough of its endless, diagenetic cycle. Stone to dust, dust to stone.

"Not just the dust," he replied, making another quick perimeter sweep. "The vehicle. Something is missing."

"I don't know why you're looking at me," she replied, squinting at him with dust-burned eyes. "We should check the trunk," she added, leaning forward to peer in the open driver's side door.

"Are you expecting to find something in there, Doctor?" Thursday asked, switching on a set of lights embedded in his frame that cast a shadow around Emélie. Their Basilisk had come to rest at an oblique angle facing the nearby barrier wall, and only the area directly beyond the abandoned vehicle was illuminated by the truck's lights. As Thursday turned to make another perimeter scan, the lights on his frame cut a wide beam further down the wall.

He dropped abruptly, taking cover behind the abandoned vehicle; when she saw his gun come up, Emélie followed suit. Up ahead, the silhouette of a grounded ship loomed, silent in the dust.

"We aren't going to see anything from here," Emélie whispered, her voice raspy from inhaling so much dust. "Your lights aren't powerful enough."

"My lights are fine," Thursday replied, looking over at their wrecked Basilisk. The front headlights were nearly gone now, although even if he considered using them, the vehicle was inoperational. "Stay close," he ordered.

Emélie followed, more out of curiosity at what lay ahead than fear at what lurked in the darkness beyond. As they closed in, four engine turbines set in pairs mounted fore and aft of the ship's lower fuselage materialized into view; the sort of configuration used for commercial light transport to ferry cargo between Earth and one of the nearby suborbital platforms, along with the occasional off-world trip.

"Drop ship," Thursday confirmed.

The craft was painted nose to tail in a matte dark non-color that seemed to absorb all the light Thursday could throw on it, plus some. He paused as they passed under the cockpit, leaning back to wash the glass bubble above them in blinding light. A row of bullet holes perforated the viewport, and the inside was smeared with blood.

He glanced cautiously at Emélie, then knelt, checking the belly of the ship. She used their temporary halt to tuck the leaf she'd found into the flight pocket of her exposure suit before pulling more slack out from the winch cable. Heaving armful after armful of cable, she spooled it at her feet to avoid tangles when they started moving again. When she turned around, Thursday stood directly over her. She bumped into him and toppled backward, landing with a sprawl in the heavy dust.

"You're free to return to the vehicle," he said.

Emélie clambered to her feet and dusted her hands clean against her orange exposure suit. "Sometimes I think your logic processor needs replacing," she said. "You act paranoid around an empty car, and then the moment we find an entire drop ship and some blood, you're walking around like there's nothing to be concerned about."

Thursday looked around once more, then turned and continued following the fuselage down to the tail. "It never made sense to me why humans get so worked up at the sight of blood," he said.

"Seems like a normal response to me." She followed after him, careful to keep her distance this time. "What doesn't make sense is why you can't grasp the significance of it."

"If there's blood, it usually means whatever bad thing was about to happen already happened. It's when there's no blood that you should worry." He ducked under one of the engine nacelles, shotgun at the low ready as he tested the latch on the starboard egress hatch. Locked from the inside.

"Shouldn't we be concerned about getting shot out here, in the open? Even if there's blood, there could always be more." She scanned the vehicles. "Chiefly, mine."

"The viewports on a low-altitude drop ship like this are ballistically rated. Whoever did the shooting was already inside when it happened, although I haven't picked up any heat signatures, so if there's any activity–" He paused, holding up a hand. A lull in the wind allowed them both to make out an odd clicking noise coming from the cargo ramp around the corner.

Thump. Whirrrr. Whirrrr. Whirrrr.

Thump. Whirrrr. Whirrrr. Whirrrr.

Thursday crouched down behind a nearby landing strut, Emélie following suit. The ship's belly was high enough off the ground that they could almost move beneath it. From her position, she couldn't see anything aside from the open desert at the opposite end, indicating the boarding ramp was raised.

Thursday turned, facing her. "Wait here," he ordered, one of his lights catching her straight across the face.

"Here?" Emélie asked, holding up an arm to block the beam. "You're the one with the gun. I think I'll take my chances sticking with you."

"You might not feel that way once the shooting starts."

Emélie leaned past Thursday, trying to get a better look at the source of the sound as the image of him feeding shells into his shotgun returned to her mind. "Are you planning on shooting?" she asked.

"Always plan on shooting. That way, if nothing happens, you come out ahead. And if you do, well," he switched his lights off. "Then you were already planning on it."

"Hard to argue with that logic," Emélie muttered. Thursday was an early model drone, equipped with a basic combination low-light thermal sensor package. Basic, but still superior to her eyesight. She squinted in the darkness. "Did someone make you this way, or did you discover pessimism all on your own?"

Thursday looked back at their wrecked truck, as if her question was slowly unraveling their reason for being here.

"It's okay," Emélie said, watching him drift somewhere deep within his hard storage. "I know the feeling." She touched the leaf where it rested in her pocket. Assurance that this wasn't some sort of hyper-realistic simulation of her own imagination. The leaf was significant, but in the expanded context, preceded by the paper and followed by the anomalous car, represented a series of recursive objects that did not belong in the present environment, yet persisted despite it. As if to validate Emélie's silent assessment, Thursday raised his weapon and disappeared behind the nacelle without another word. He was surprisingly swift for his size, and Emélie dashed after him, holding her gaze to the spot where she'd seen him last.

Before she could clear the end of the ship, the winch cable went taut, yanking her backward. She dug her boots in, straining against the cable to no avail. Already out of breath in the lean air, there was no utility in a struggle. She forced herself to slow down, examining the cable. The winch wasn't activated, which meant the cable must have caught on something. She began rotating the cable, swinging it like a horizontal pendulum until it bounced against the hard-packed ground in broad, hypnotic arcs. The cable moved freely as far as she could see, but there was a weight on it somewhere further down in the dust, likely pinched on the abandoned vehicle where it rested between her and the Basilisk.

She couldn't hear Thursday anymore, footsteps or otherwise. Starting in a small circle, she began swinging the cable in the opposite direction, gradually expanding the rotational diameter until she felt it release from whatever it was caught on. Using her mechanical hand, she wrapped the cable in a circle and pulled, heaving until the spool locked out on the other end and a splinter of pain shot up her back. The remaining metal braid left her with enough to make it to the end of the ship, but likely no further. With a gulp of air, she dashed the last few steps around the tail, where Thursday was down on one knee, calmly sifting through a handful of dust.

As expected, the boarding ramp was raised, sealing off the ship's interior from the outside. The control unit for the ramp had been pried away from the fuselage and now hung from a bundle of wires that occasionally sparked in protest at the unsanctioned junction.

"Looks like someone tried to hot-wire the ramp," Emélie said, feeling relieved as she paused to catch her breath.

"I'd say they were successful," Thursday replied, sifting through another handful of dust. "It would be difficult to lower a ramp that cannot lower itself." He stood, took two steps, then knelt down and scooped up another handful of dust. Three times he repeated this process.

Emélie stood nearby, observing his erratic actions. On the fourth handful, a glint of something else came up—a small, metallic cylinder roughly the size of her finger. Without taking his eyes off the spot where he'd found the object, Thursday held it up.

"This is what you were looking for?" Emélie asked, carefully accepting the small object. "Empty bullet casings?"

Thursday lifted up another spent cartridge. "I've seen this sort of thing before," he said, scanning the dull horizon as dust fines, drawn by his latent static charge, clung to his black faceplate.

"Which part?" Emélie asked, taking the other shell casing from him.

"All of it," he said, returning to his search. "Operating under the cover of a storm. Bullet holes, shell casings, and blood, but no bodies. And then there's that," he motioned toward the pocket on Emélie's exposure suit where she'd stashed the leaf. "It's all pointing toward something. Not a memory. More like the feeling of a memory, or maybe..." He let the dust in his hand sift to the ground.

"The shape of something familiar," Emélie finished.

The yellow light across Thursday's face flatlined for an instant. "Something like that," he said, watching the dust slip through his fingers. He turned, taking another look at the enclosing wall around Sanctuary One. Abruptly, as if encountering an override somewhere inside his software, he glitched, pitching his head slightly backward in a catatonic power-cycle. "Wall—wall: encircled; bounded. Non-orientable," he stuttered. After a tense breath—hers held, waiting, suspended—the light bar on Thursday's face normalized and he turned back to face her. "On the other side of that wall, beneath One, there's a Loop," he said promptly. "Terra Gimel."

"That's a D Class facility. D... Dalet," she said, thinking out loud. She squatted down beside him and, using her finger, drew a shape in the dust: ד.

Thursday stared vacantly at the shape as he gathered up yet another handful. "What does that have to do with anything?"

"I don't know," she said, taking a turn to look up at the barrier wall, "but you aren't the only one who's noticed something is missing."

Thursday didn't respond, and it wasn't until Emélie glanced down at him that she understood why. In his bare metal palm, something different remained behind.

The bullet was unlike any Emélie had seen. Not that she'd seen all that many. This one had a brass casing, same as the others, but the pointed tip was still intact. A transparent sabot filled with an iridescent, red liquid that cast the faintest glow against the pale metal of Thursday's hand.

Origin.

"What have you done, Doctor?" Thursday asked, his voice warbling with unspecified meaning. "What in god's name have you gotten us into?"

Emélie was on her feet, frantically pulling as much slack in the cable as she could manage before Thursday hit the recall button on the winch remote.

CHAPTER 5
MONSTROUS MOONSHINE

From somewhere out in the dust, the winch ground to life, dragging Emélie toward the truck. "We never should have come here," Thursday said, tucking the Origin round into a pouch on his belt as he rose to his feet. "You can walk back on your own, or I can drag you. One way or another, we're leaving. Now."

Emélie dropped the cable slack she'd pulled out and sprinted past him, using up the last few feet of freedom in a headlong dive for the ramp. As her fingers grazed the control panel, the braided cable went taut with a high-pitched twang. Her metal hand remained entangled with the bundle of wires linking the panel to the ship's computer while the winch continued to pull. The seams on her exposure suit began to burst as Emélie felt herself torn in opposite directions. Eventually, her hand slipped, stripping the length of wires as she lost her grip. She crashed to the ground and the ramp began to lower.

Before she could see what was inside, the winch hauled her backward, plowing a furrow into the barren earth as it towed her back to the truck. She didn't waste any energy trying to fight it. The winch was designed for a two-ton vehicle, so even if she found something solid to grasp, she couldn't resist the pull. Somewhere between the drop ship and the vehicles, the winch halted, and with a metallic clunk, the latch magnetically detached from her back.

She sat up, panting in the thin air as Thursday emerged from the dust following the shallow trench left in her wake. He stopped beside her and extended a hand.

She glared at him, a stern refusal.

Thursday turned for the ship. "I think there's something you should see, Doctor."

Emélie stood and dusted herself off. While she had no intention of following him, the instant he disappeared around the ship, her need to understand his abrupt change overtook her lingering rage. Thanks to her earlier, grasping efforts, she found the ramp fully lowered. Thursday waited for her at the bottom, his blank face looking up into the cavernous darkness of an open cargo hold.

When they ascended the top of the ramp, Thursday switched on his lights. The hold was empty, except for a lone shipping pallet stacked with rectangular bricks tightly wrapped in black plastic. Above the pallet was an inexplicable, familiar mass of churning dust. An impossible shape.

The sight of it staggered Emélie.

Thursday grabbed her arm, steadying her as dust particles oscillated around them, folding over and onto themselves in iridescent shadow. "What is it?" he asked in a grainy whisper.

"A shape," Emélie whispered, glancing at Thursday's hand clasped around her forearm. "A Manifold, or at least, a part of it."

"And this... Manifold. This is what you've been trying to find?"

Emélie let his question hang between them, allowing herself a moment to settle on the full implications of their discovery. "In a way. If there was a Loop on the other side of that wall outside, it also means, at some point, there was another reality on the other side of our own." The next step she took found Thursday barring her path with a long, spindly arm. She didn't fault him; they were in her comfort zone now, not his.

Her eyes softened as she met his square, illuminated face. "It's only a shape," she assured him.

He hesitated, then reluctantly lowered his arm. Emélie moved past him, pausing next to the pallet, which sat in the middle of an otherwise empty hold. Deeper into the ship, the shape's central mass formed a nearly impenetrable dust field standing roughly chest height. Occasionally, a tendril of dust would split away from the shape like a wild thread, propelled by some unseen force beyond the domain of Earth's gravity. Emélie stretched out her arm, watching as one of the threads washed over her hand, forking into two smaller streams before merging back together on the other side.

"What we're seeing is the three-dimensional representation of a multi-dimensional surface with variable curvature. It only appears when additional dimensions are forced into the constraints of our space-time. It's significant because it represents a first step toward truly impossible geometries."

Thursday shifted his weight from one foot to the other, silent except for the mechanical sound of his servos bogging down under the microscopic airborne debris. "Impossible, or improbable?" he asked.

She watched him, eyes full of compassion; he was trying his best, but drones had no knowledge of the sacred. "What I'm saying is that this spot, here?" She opened her hand, watching the dust flow across her palm as she tried to illustrate the significance of the moment for Thursday. "It's an opening to somewhere else. Or at least it was. What we're seeing now is all that's left. Remnants of what came before, from elsewhere. A leak, left behind from a tear between our reality and another dimension parallel to our own."

"A Gate," Thursday observed.

Emélie nodded. "Yes, a Gate."

"We haven't seen a Gate in over twenty years. Not since the Collapse."

"Exactly. But even through the Gates are gone, the dark matter powering them still exists, and this?" She moved further out, letting the shape ebb and flow around her. "This demonstrates that the Manifold didn't Collapse. We only lost our ability to access it."

"Then you were right," Thursday replied, his voice fluctuating as he finally grasped the full implications of their discovery for himself. "You've been right this entire time."

"The board won't take my word for it," she grunted. "Tell me you're recording this..."

His faceplate flickered, drawing a concerned glance from Emélie. "I disabled my data logging when we left the ramp," the drone admitted. "You said to keep it offline." He shrugged. "Not that any of it would have been useful. We both know how unreliable digital footage can be. And I wasn't talking about the Gate, anyway," he added.

Emélie instinctively reached down, touching her thigh. In the chaos of everything, she'd forgotten about the leaf, safely tucked away in her pocket. Thursday was right: the only explanation for the leaf was that it had passed through the Gate when it was still open. It wasn't conclusive evidence, but it was a start. "I know I'm pushing my luck, but I can't afford to leave anything on the table if I'm going to bring this in front of the board." Emélie looked deeper into the ship, where the highest density of the Manifold churned around the door leading up into the cockpit. "I need to see what's on the other side of that hatch."

Thursday hesitated before offering a short nod of approval. She waded into the churning cloud. At the door, the dust engulfed her arm as she reached in, trying the handle. Locked from the inside.

"Let me try," Thursday said, leaning past Emélie to look through the small rectangular viewport in the center of the door. He jiggled the handle and tilted his head, trying to get a view of the other side, but the dust was too dense even for him. He pointed to a spot on the floor a few paces behind where Emélie waited. "Cover your ears," he ordered.

Emélie cupped her ears, backing away as Thursday canted his shotgun directly over the handle and pulled the trigger. The concussion hit her square across the chest, knocking the breath out of her as a small shockwave rippled through the ambient dust. Thursday swung a heavy fist over what remained of the handle; the lock mechanism clattered to the deck, and the door popped open. As he reached for the door, Emélie grabbed his arm, halting his forward motion.

"It's only wide enough for one of us," she said.

"What about your safety, Doctor?"

"Safety is relative." Emélie pushed his concern aside and shoved the door open. A wave of stale air with a musty, almost nauseating sweetness hit her in the face. "Whatever is inside there can't be worse than missing something because I was two seconds behind you."

"Yeah, but the board won't kill you if you're wrong."

"Plenty of things worse than dying," Emélie replied, glancing over her shoulder. "I'll take my chances out here, where at least I have a choice." She passed through the doorway, although Thursday, who could have easily blocked her, made no further intervention.

At the entrance to the cockpit, she paused, blocking the cramped passageway with her bulky exposure suit. Outside, the storm had mostly died down, letting the hazy light of dawn filter through the bloodied windshield. Aside from the outline of the pilot and co-pilot seats, she still couldn't see much of anything. "Thursday, shine your light this way," she said, squinting in the fresh darkness. "I can't see a thing down here."

Thursday slipped into the narrow corridor after her, cutting swaths of light to the cadence of his heavy footsteps until he arrived where she waited at the cockpit entrance. He stooped down, letting the beams on either shoulder illuminate the cabin.

An eyeless face, inches from Emélie's own.

A hand shot from the darkness, grasping her throat and slamming her backward into Thursday.

She recoiled, tearing at the hand and her own respirator as she attempted to escape. Thursday's shotgun shattered the darkness with a blast of light and a boom.

A piercing shriek tore through the cabin, and in the bouncing beams of light, Emélie watched, horrified, as whatever was holding her let go and dropped down onto all fours. Something brushed against her leg, followed by the rattle of Thursday's shotgun to the floor as it knocked him into the wall. His lights went up, leaving them in frozen semi-darkness. A blip ran across his face, and Emélie felt something wrap around her ankle.

Down to the floor she went.

Metal floor grated at her back as the thing hauled her down the corridor toward the open hold. Thinking fast, she hooked her cybernetic arm over the coaming as she passed through the hatch, blocking her from passing into the hold. The hand clamped down tighter, fingers digging into her calf.

From somewhere behind her, Thursday's giant, metal arm plucked Emélie off the floor. There was another blast from his gun, and the pressure on her leg slackened, then released entirely. A rush of cool air washed her face as Thursday brought her from the corridor and out into the main hold, setting her down carefully. She collapsed to her knees as two more gunshots resonated behind her. A wave of heat spread across her throat and she doubled over, vomiting onto the floor. When she looked up, Thursday was gone.

Minutes later, he reappeared in the doorway, shotgun slung across his back. He held his blade in one hand, blood-wet and still dripping. In the other, he dragged the body. Emélie leaned back on her heels and examined the hold, which was heavy with the stench of gunpowder and blood. Thursday dropped the body and wiped his blade clean before approaching her. From one of the pouches on his utility belt, he produced a spare respirator, which he gently brushed clean. She spit, trying to clear the taste of bile, but her mouth was too dry; she took the mask and pulled it on. After a few jagged respirations, her breathing normalized.

"Your shape," Thursday said, noticing the fresh layer of dust blanketing the cargo bay. "The Möbius. It's gone."

Emélie studied him carefully. "I never said it was a Möbius. How did you know that?"

The question elicited a heavy shrug from Thursday. "You said the Loop here, Luna Gimel, was a D-Class. Dalet class Loops carry a bounded, non-orientable Manifold. That alone is self-explanatory, and the path of the dust flow here confirmed it." He was speaking so matter-of-factly about the topic that, for a moment, Emélie almost forgot that less than half an hour ago, he'd hardly been able to recognize what was right in front of them. It was almost as if the remnants of the Gate had changed him in some way, although even Thursday himself seemed none the wiser.

Cautiously, she circled back around, hoping to see what else she could coax out of his cold storage. "Thursday, we've been working together for almost two years, and you've never once mentioned the Loop. You do realize that this, while no longer active, still falls within my scope of work, right?"

"I seem to have missed that connection. I suppose this demonstrates why history is so important."

She scrunched her face up. "I don't doubt that. You'll have to excuse my absence, given that I wasn't around for it. And since we're talking history, why don't you take a stab at explaining how *you* know all this?"

He began casually pumping a handful of new shells into the bottom of his shotgun. "The Loop is Phaethon technology. Who do you think they sent in to do the investigation when everything fell apart?"

"Right," Emélie said, feeling a pang of embarrassment flush her cheeks as she registered how little she'd inquired about his past. "I mean, I believe you," she added. "I just wish the whole thing hadn't collapsed when you killed that Jumper."

He stopped loading. "What makes you think it was a Jumper? I know we're topside, but this is still pretty deep inside Phaethon prefecture to see Jumper activity." He glanced down at the body beside him. "I'd check for track marks, except it doesn't have much left in the way of arms."

Emélie tried not to imagine the reason why; she didn't need to lose any more moisture. "The eyes are a dead giveaway," she said, reaching up to touch her ear. Her hand came back sticky with blood. "Late-stage addicts tend to gouge them out when they overdose. They start confusing their hallucinations with reality, so they solve the problem by removing the source of interference. Lose your sight, and you lose the last tether linking you to this reality. The next stop after that is full-fledged Jumper."

Thursday threw a glance toward the cockpit. "Since you seem to have some experience with this, have you ever seen anything that might make a Jumper cut someone else to pieces?"

"You're the one with the sword," Emélie replied, approaching the dead Jumper. "There were more?"

"This was the only one alive."

"I counted two gunshots."

"Insurance," Thursday explained. "It was speaking some sort of assembly language. I couldn't quite understand it, except for something at the end that sounded like an error handling packet..." As he spoke, Emélie started for the hatch. "You're going back in there, aren't you?" he said, interrupting his previous observation. "I have to warn you. It only gets worse from here."

Emélie hesitated at the doorway, choking back the taste of bile as she watched blood pool where Thursday's shotgun blast had removed half the Jumper's mandible. "You aren't coming?"

"I'm going to have to call this in. Jumper or not, whatever attacked you was wearing a Phaethon flight uniform. This is bigger than you, now."

Emélie nodded. She could stand her ground with Thursday, but the second Phaethon got wind of what they'd found, they would lock the place down tight. "Do what you need to do," she said. "I'll be right behind you."

Thursday stepped out onto the boarding ramp. "I'd hurry, if I were you. Towers are coming back online," he said, taking one last look back into the hold.

Emélie was already gone.

Back in the cockpit, the new light of day confirmed Thursday's warning. Bodies lay strewn across the confined space, severed grotesquely into cleanly divided pieces. She stumbled backward into the cargo bay, a paralyzing fear settling over her: the pallet of bricks sitting at the center of the hold was gone.

She sprinted back to the ramp, already winded from the adrenaline rush of her discovery. Hooking a sharp right, she dropped directly to the ground rather than wasting time with the descent. The landing came hard and she was already up, running.

Thursday waited up ahead with his back toward her and his cloak rustling in the breeze.

The other vehicle was nowhere in sight.

He must have heard her coming because he turned to face Emélie before she could close the gap. She staggered to a halt as his hands came into view.

"I thought you were going to call this in?" she asked, looking at the object cradled between Thursday's hands. A rectangular block, tightly wrapped in black plastic. Identical to the ones Emélie had seen back on the ship.

"Backup transponder was disabled," Thursday said. Behind him, the black surveillance towers, with all their eyes, began rising from below ground.

"And the other vehicle?" Emélie asked, looking out across the desert. "Did you see..."

Thursday tipped the package, watching as bright red crystals poured from a tear in one corner. "You were using again, weren't you? That's why you wanted to keep this offline."

"I... I didn't know about any of this," Emélie said, her chest heaving as she formed the words. She watched as crystals gathered in a shimmering pile on the ground. "I just—"

Thursday tossed the package at her feet. "You saw something, didn't you? That's how you knew to come here. To this place, in this storm." He lifted his head, his dark faceplate flecked with dust as the yellow light bar oscillated to the sound of his voice. "Is this what you were hoping to find?!" He spread his arms, one toward the grounded ship and the other toward their wrecked Basilisk. "A botched Origin drop?"

Emélie blinked heavily, eyes burning, whether from dust or tears, she couldn't be sure. Between them, silence, except for the sound of her breathing and the wind at her back.

Ping.

"I'm sorry," Emélie mouthed. Her left hand trembled at her side, an involuntary witness to the truth she'd obscured earlier: the source of the ping was coming from within her. Thursday's face registered a pattern Emélie had never seen before but immediately understood.

Sadness.

A concentric wave of dust radiated along the ground at their feet. She opened her mouth, but the warning came too late. Thursday crumpled to a heap as one final reply escaped his ancient voice processor.

"Run."

A hollow *thwomp* resonated from the dust just beyond their truck, something like pressurized air escaping a sealed container. Emélie felt a crash against her chest. She fell backward, knees buckling as the sound reverberated off the high concrete wall behind her. She felt an acute pressure across her sternum, and when she inhaled to take a breath, none came. She collapsed onto her back as her hand moved instinctively to her chest. Her head drooped to one side, and she saw Thursday lying nearby, motionless in a pile of Origin crystals. Blood trickled from her mouth in vivid, bubbling strands as she clawed at her respirator, trying to tear it away for one last clear breath.

Her vision collapsed. In the rolling darkness, something moved through the dust. Another Manifold—and from within it, a single eye, watching.

And Emélie watched it back.

CHAPTER 6
"PRECURSOR"

Phaethon Corp. MAIN build_VX.6.6.09
initializing boot sequence...
executing subroutine FOUNTAINHEAD:

bindquery: update parameter to
"PRECURSOR"
encryption protocols intact,
syntax structures intact,
[13] entries remaining

begin sentiment analysis,
implicit context target, rundisplay:

BEGIN RECORD >>>

This place is nothing but an illusion. I couldn't see it until now, when it's too late to go back. Marcus and the rest of the crew said things would be different here. Kept spouting some party line about the future being wide open and ripe for the taking. I couldn't see it. Maybe I'm simple, or maybe I saw what they were too blind to recognize in the first place. Doesn't matter. Marcus is the Chief Executive Officer. I'm just Chief of the Fools who followed him here.

You'd think someone like me would have been happy spending the rest of his life kicking around in a place like this. Problem is, people like me can't ever leave well enough alone. When the settlement at Hellas Basin was finished and the rest of the crew contented themselves with getting drunk on the raw potential of their own ideas, I kept moving. South. Not really sure why, except that it seemed right at the time. I think I was hungry for something more in all this than rocks and dust. I wanted to test this place. See how far I could go before something pushed back. That's when I hit ice.

The true cost of all this speculation. Locked away for a reason, no doubt. Forty-three people to a whole planet, and I had to go and find the thing that would make us gods. Now we've got precursor and I'm already sorry for the day I found it. Marcus said I shouldn't tempt fate. Then again, what does he know? He also said we'd find purpose on Mars. So far, I haven't found anything but regret, and regret was the one thing I always had plenty of back on Earth.

That, and bullets.

<<< END RECORD

COMINT global// TPC-γ exposure confirmed. ANOMALOUS
SUBSTRATE DETECTED—resource variant outside
terrestrial parameters:

monitor ARROGANT,
flag for VISIBLE review

sanitize data entry,
purge access log to XANADU
KILL remote process

CHAPTER 7
KEY SURRENDER

There isn't much to know about Deepwater Station, except that there's not much water and too much Origin. A company town, shantytown, full of Topsiders and junkies and ex-corpos booted from Phaethon's bountiful bosom, Sanctuary Four. A place for killing, dying, hiding; a place perfectly suited for a man like Brinks, who was guilty of the first, at risk of the second, and desperate for the third. He stumbled into the closest bodega he could find and let the door slam behind him on the way in. A fair warning of what was coming. He shoved past the other patrons toward the front of the line, ignoring their outbursts as he plowed ahead, bullheaded and head down. At the counter, he turned around and took a head count while the clerk standing behind the scratched partition backed away, horrified. Any lingering outcry at his blatant social transgressions was immediately stifled beneath an ionic fear. The sort of fear leaping from person to person, like electrons running along a chain of atoms desperate for the door. He dropped the woman he was dragging by the collar onto the ground, then leaned forward so he was eye-level with the fragile clerk standing across the counter. He didn't say anything at all.

The door chime marked exits, one after the other, and he waited patiently until his ears counted an empty shop. Empty, except for himself, the clerk, and the unconscious woman at his feet. A section of her tailored blazer had been hastily cut away and fashioned into a crude blindfold covering her blood-encrusted eyes.

The clerk stepped backward, bumping against a shelf, sending ration packets tumbling to the floor. She was wire-thin, with appendages disproportionate to the rest of her slight frame. Probably a migrant from one of the orbital platforms, where the lower gravity bred that sort of trait into second and third generation workers. Her small, dark eyes followed the bloody smear from the door to where Brinks waited at her counter. "I don't want no trouble," she whispered.

"You were born into the wrong timeline for no trouble," he said. A few blocks away, the low wail of sirens echoed down a vacant street.

"Are those for you?" the clerk asked, risking a glance toward the door.

Brinks leaned his full heft onto the counter, then ran a hand along the worn surface. Lead-bellied and stocky, he had a laborer's build and reflexes deceptively quick for someone his size. Quick enough for today, anyway. "You can't run from the sort of trouble I'm in." He looked up, meeting her sunken eyes through the glass. "What day is it?"

"What day?" she stammered, glancing across the shop. "I—"

"Never mind," Brinks interrupted, gripping the edge of the counter. He slumped over and his vision doubled, then doubled again. The blood loss was getting to him. "You got a lighter?" he asked, reaching into his duster. From his breast pocket, he produced a slim case, bare metal and scuffed from use. With his other hand—a mechanical prosthesis painted carnelian red—he clutched his blood-soaked abdomen. The shirt beneath, long oversaturated, was dried stiff in the morning heat. Fresh blood actively seeped through his clenched fingers, running in tiny rivulets down his arm. He watched the blood irrigate the floor, then flipped open the case in his free hand. From it, he nudged loose a hand-rolled cigarette, grasping it between his lips as he watched the clerk.

She squatted down behind the counter, and when she stood back up, held a tray littered with an assortment of junk in her twiggy arms. "Don't know what that is. If we have it, this here's where it would be." She slid the tray under the slot at the bottom of the partition. "Is this a shakedown?" she asked, watching Brinks rifle through the tray with his free hand, the unlit cigarette still dangling from one corner of his mouth.

Brinks plucked an old radio transmitter from the pile and ripped the back off. He pulled the battery out, set it aside, and nodded toward the shelf at the clerk's back. "Give me one of those rations, too. In the foil pouch."

The clerk blinked, confused at his request, but obliged him anyway, sliding the packet through just like she had the tray. Grabbing the ration, he tore off the top strip and tossed the pouch back. The foil rolled easily between his fingers as he pinched each end onto the battery terminals. With a pop that made the clerk jolt, the entire assembly sparked into a white flame; he raised it to his face, lighting his cigarette. Outside, a pair of surface patrol cruisers screamed past, their sirens rattling the dirty shop windows.

"They didn't have anything in their hands," he said, raising back to his full height.

"I... I don't know what you mean," the clerk stammered, eyeing the blood-smeared patch on the counter where Brinks had been leaning.

"The customers," he motioned toward the entrance, nonchalantly, with his cigarette-free hand. "All the customers waiting in line were empty-handed." He craned his neck, looking around the small shop. "Makes me wonder what sort of person comes into a place like this but doesn't buy anything. And you've got," he rapped the glass barrier between them. "What is this? Looks like six millimeters of ballistic armor? Protecting what, exactly? Some cases of synthetic protein and a tray of junk?" He took another drag on his cigarette, the cherry reflecting in the lens of his biometric eye. "Only thing missing are the Jumpers."

The clerk's gaze narrowed along with her demeanor; she took a step forward, leaning near enough to the barrier that her breath fogged against it as she spoke. "They'll be here soon enough," she hissed with eyes like slits.

"That's more like it." He drummed his fingers on the counter. "Whatever they're paying you to play dumb, it ain't enough."

The clerk nodded toward the woman on the floor. "Who's she?"

Brinks paused, cigarette pinched between his thumb and pointer finger. He exhaled a cloud of smoke and nudged the woman at his feet with the toe of his boot. Her breathing sounded like wind cutting through a slot canyon, labored and hollow. He squared his wide-brimmed hat. "You sure you want to ask that question?"

"Don't see what I got to lose," the clerk replied. "You ain't here for Origin. The only reason I can figure someone like you walking into a place like this is 'cause you're crazy or you got a death wish."

"Lucky for you, I'm notorious for both of those things." He stubbed his cigarette out on the back of his metal hand and then pulled something else from his duster. He palmed it over the counter, following the depression where decades of transactions like this had worn away the top layer of material. "I was hoping you could tell me something about this?" He pulled his hand away, revealing a small packet of iridescent red crystals.

The clerk's face dropped.

"And you better not say Origin," he warned. "I've seen plenty of Origin in my time, and I can tell you with absolute certainty–and I'm never certain of anything–that whatever this is, it ain't Origin. Not the stuff you're pushing here. The liquid stuff, the same stuff we've always had." He leaned against the glass and tapped the packet of crystals between them. "This is something *new*."

The clerk eyed the drugs in silence.

Brinks straightened, tugging at his lapels, causing a dust cloud to hover around him. "This place have an exit?" he asked. The clerk continued staring at the counter, where the drugs sat openly, ripe for the taking.

"Goddamn junkies," he muttered, pounding a fist against the glass partition. The clerk blinked, knocked out of her stupor. "Exit?" Brinks repeated, more deliberately this time.

She motioned toward a curtain at the back of the shop. "Leads to the loadin' dock out back. You won't be gettin' far, though."

"I wasn't asking for me," Brinks said. The woman at his feet stirred again. She was starting to wake up. From the corner of his eye, he watched the clerk make a move for the packet. His hand flashed—faster than she'd expected—and he clamped down, catching her in the trap. She yelped, trying to twist free as Brinks leaned in, pinning her bony wrist down with his metal palm. He glanced at her sleeve, which had bunched up around her forearm in the struggle. Sunken track marks marred the pale, almost translucent skin. "Where's the caretaker?" he demanded.

"You ain't sp'osed to have that," the clerk hissed. "Precursor ain't for us."

Brinks snatched the packet of crystals out from under the clerk's fingertips. "Precursor," he muttered, rubbing a thumb over the product. "Of course..." he said, releasing her arm. "You should leave," he added, tucking the Precursor back inside his jacket. More sirens echoed outside. Closer, this time. "If you go now, you should still have time."

"Time for what?" The clerk glared at him and rubbed her wrist. "I'm not the one who thought it would be a good idea to hide out inside a stash house. The Jumpers will be coming for you, not me."

Brinks was searching through the pockets of his duster again, but at the clerk's words, he stopped short. "For being a low-level caretaker, you sure don't listen all that well. You got any connections that can get you off-world?"

"Off-world?" The clerk leaned onto the counter. "You really don't know how things work around here, do you? Look around, old man. I'm a caretaker in a border town. You think I got access to those kind of resources?" She shook her head. "The surface is my—"

Brinks tossed a set of keys onto the counter, cutting her off mid-sentence. "Listen to me carefully. There's a car parked in the alley two blocks away. Under the front passenger seat are the coordinates to a safe house on the other side of the rim. Don't take the car. They'll be looking for it, and you won't make it very far before they close the roads anyway. Keep to the side streets. It'll take longer, but there are too many to monitor, and even if you get stopped, you can just act like a junkie. Shouldn't be too difficult for you, right? They won't have any reason to suspect otherwise. Once you get to the safe house, everything you need to start over will be there, waiting. All you've got to do is walk away."

The clerk scoffed. "That's what this is about? What's the matter? You get bored in your corpo habitat, so you come up here to play lord and savior to some redshifters?"

"Shut up." Brinks rubbed his temples. "Just... shut up. I'm offering you a choice. I don't care what you do with it, but you either take it now," he glanced at the entrance, "or don't take it at all."

The clerk glared at him, then spat on the keys still sitting on the counter. "Keep your offer," she said. "I've seen this place chew up dozens of well-doers with fat wallets and full bellies. People always trying to help. People who think they know what's best 'cause they got a seat in one of the Sanctuaries. I know my life ain't much, but don't think for a minute I don't see you too." She rapped the glass, gesturing to the woman at his feet. "And I'd be willing to bet most of the people you think you're helping end up just like her. Bleeding out in the dust, in the middle of nowhere, while you waste your breath trying to save someone else who just wants to be let alone."

The spit-covered keys remained where they'd fallen—Brinks certainly had no use for them anymore. He sent a boot into the woman at his feet. The woman—if she had a name, it didn't matter to him what it was—coughed, spraying bright red spittle onto the pitted floor. Her hands were bound behind her back, and more blood seeped from the blindfold covering her eyes. Brinks reached down, lifting her up by the wide lapels of her tailored blazer.

Rousing, she grinned up at him through blood-stained teeth. "You're as dumb as you look," she said, straining between breaths. "I already sent word for Lilith to cut me off. It's done."

"Too bad I was the last thing you saw, then." Brinks rubbed his fingers against the silver-grey fabric of her suit, which was light and stiff and gave off a slight sheen under the light. "Ballistic weave, nice touch, although it's a waste of material, using it on a nonce." He yanked at the neckline of the underlying blouse, exposing bare skin. Reaching to his back, he pulled a short, angular knife from a sheath on his belt, which he used to carve a shallow incision just below her clavicle. From the wound, he extracted a concave, black disk the size of a human retina. He pocketed the disc, then dropped the woman back onto the floor, taking care to wipe his knife clean on the leg of her trousers before returning it.

Out front, a row of blacked-out trucks with tinted windows screeched to a halt.

"Give my regards to Lilith," the woman wheezed, her voice hardly audible against the rising commotion outside.

"Tell her yourself," Brinks said, resting a boot across her neck. He leaned his full weight forward, and when the woman was finally done kicking, he turned, both hands raised as the front windows exploded inward and canisters of tear gas rattled past him.

CHAPTER 8
INCARNADINE

Emélie stood over a low sink, scrubbing blood from her fingernails when Aratheus arrived. He entered the ornate bathroom without a word and closed the door as his personal security detail swept the room. A well-dressed woman emerged from a stall near the far end of the bathroom, ignoring his bodyguards but making a point to steer clear of a bloodied and dust-soaked Emélie on her way out. The bodyguards gave the all-clear before making a silent exit, leaving Aratheus and Emélie alone. He leaned against the door, rubbing his face with both hands. One of his eyes was twitching and his face carried overnight stubble, a rare sight for someone in the C-suite hierarchy. "It's a real mess out there," he said, pacing and shaking his head.

Emélie looked up, eyeing him through the floor-to-ceiling mirror as she pumped another handful of foam cleanser from an industrial-sized plastic jug that had been thrust at her by the Director's corporate attaché on the way in. She'd expected the Phaethon board to act swiftly, but this was unprecedented. They'd hardly touched down in Sanctuary when a team showed up at the landing platform to intercept her, escorting her to an elevator that brought her straight to the central corporate offices.

"The medical officer said you were shot?" Aratheus asked, pushing himself away from the door as he straightened his rumpled suit.

"It's nothing," Emélie replied.

Aratheus eyed the hole in her jumpsuit where the bullet had impacted to the left of her sternum. "Doesn't look like nothing."

She kept scrubbing her blood-soaked arms, which had absorbed a layer of airborne dust that left a thin crust behind as it dried. With every move, a thousand small, tectonic plates shed powder onto the gleaming floor.

"I sent for your things," Aratheus said. "I doubt they'll be here in time for your hearing, but it was the least I could do. You're going to need all the help you can get."

Emélie stopped scrubbing. "What's that supposed to mean?"

Never one for showing restraint, Aratheus threw his hands up in a wild gesture. "I don't know, Doctor. Why don't you tell me? I'm trying to help you out here, but you aren't giving me much. What were you thinking, driving out into a storm like that? And the sticks, of all places?" He shook his head.

"Why's everyone suddenly so concerned with the sticks? That place doesn't even exist on a map, and now you're the second—" she stopped short, catching herself. "What do you want, Aratheus?"

"You could start by telling me the truth for once. I'm on your side, remember?"

Emélie turned, meeting him face-to-face for the first time since he'd entered. "That's not how I remember it."

"Yes, well, that's not saying much, given your track record. Look around, Emélie. The board is ravenous, and you're covered in blood. You aren't exactly in a position to be turning down my support."

"Your *support*," she repeated. "Is that what you call lift privileges and a drone to babysit me while I pound sand up on the surface? As far as I'm concerned, your generosity only extends so far as it benefits *you*. The only thing I regret in all this is not walking away the first time you offered to help."

Aratheus crossed his arms. "Look, don't make this personal. All I'm saying is, I'm concerned. Consider this a professional courtesy before you go in front of the board, although you're not giving me much to work with here."

Emélie returned to the sink, looking at herself in the mirror. Aratheus was the head of Phaethon's Department of Energy. And if he was in a bathroom pushing a cosmologist with amnesia for information, things were bad. "You want to know what happened last night? You can read my official statement when it goes on record, just like everyone else," she said.

"That's unlikely," Aratheus grunted. "You and I both know by the time the DAO finishes working it over there will be so many redactions they might as well skip the formality. What you saw is never going to see the light of day, and if you think that doesn't also include you, you're profoundly mistaken."

Emélie gripped the edge of the sink basin as clumps of foam pooled around the drain. Unlike the dust, the tremors didn't wash away so readily. "There was a team," she finally admitted. "Fifteen, maybe twenty people. Black uniforms, shielded helmets, no markings. They handed me off to someone in a maroon jumpsuit with a yellow triangle on the sleeve. My vision was fuzzy until about twenty minutes ago, so that's the best I can do." She dried her arms on the coarse towel that had come with the jug of cleanser. "I take it they weren't with you?"

"Maroon jumpsuits are Internal Affairs. There are three of them out in the hall right now. I barely convinced them to let me in here. I don't know about the other ones, though. Contractors, most likely." One of his eyes twitched, and he rubbed it, irritated. "You want to tell me what really happened now, or should I just leave and see how much of you is left when the board finishes working you over?"

Emélie rolled the sleeves of her mustard-colored jumpsuit back down over her arms. "Look," she started in a low voice. "We ran into an abandoned vehicle during our surface run. There was a grounded drop ship nearby." She gave a wary glance toward the exit. "That's it."

"And when the Director's attaché shows up to escort you to your hearing, that's the story you're going to take with you, understand?" He jabbed a finger in her direction. "I expected a bit more loyalty from you. Your resistance is noted and will be reflected on–"

"Reflected on what, Aratheus?" Emélie cut in, glaring back at him. "Go ahead, write me up. Maybe assign me to data collection in a hazardous environment while you're at it. What happened to me wasn't some personal flaw, although you seem dedicated to holding that line. You know I was dosed, right? I was kidnapped, interrogated, and drugged with Origin as a direct result of my work for this company. And now I'm facing my second board hearing in as many years while you corner me in a bathroom, so excuse me if this is all starting to feel like something we've already done before."

Aratheus drummed his fingers on the sink. "You're right," he said. "It is something we've done before. Down to the exact detail, actually. You, inside a storm, conveniently offline and out of sight, right around the same time a dead Jumper turns up inside a Phaethon four-wing. Or were you hoping the rest of us were going to play as dumb as you are..."

He continued, but Emélie didn't hear anything after the words *four-wing* left his mouth. The Jumper Thursday killed had been wearing a uniform matching the rest of the dead crew, but Emélie had never mentioned the ship being a Phaethon vessel, and she wasn't familiar enough with their transportation division to make an observation as specific as four-wing. Aratheus had made a mistake; an inadvertent disclosure. This new information linked Emélie's discovery directly back to Phaethon and placed the source of the threat internally, with Emélie as the prime suspect.

"Hello? Are you even listening to me?" Aratheus snapped his fingers a few times to draw her attention. "Same thing happening to the same person on two separate occasions? What are the odds for something like that? You're the one who's supposed to be good with numbers."

Emélie gazed down at her blood-stained chest. "Maybe I'm just unlucky," she shrugged, brushing off his accusation with a backhanded rebuttal.

"Call it what you want. All I'm saying is, the data doesn't lie. And if I'm seeing it, I won't be the only one."

The comment made her breath catch. "The board already ruled there was inconclusive evidence to charge me for what happened at Kepler's Reef. If you have an issue with the decision, take it up with them."

There was a gentle knock on the door, and Aratheus leaned over, propping it open with one foot to address the person on the other side. He muttered something Emélie couldn't make out, then closed the door. "Freaks me out how that thing wears a uniform over its frame," he said. "Drones should look like drones."

"I can think of a few people who remind me of drones in clothing," Emélie said under her breath, but if Aratheus heard her, he let it slide. She glanced around and, having no other belongings, gathered her courage and walked, head high, toward the exit. Aratheus remained in place as she approached, sliding his foot out to block the door.

"You know, people used to run water through these things," he said, running a hand along the sink basin beside him. "Water! Can you imagine that sort of luxury?"

"If you have a point to make, then make it," Emélie said. "Or would you like me to inform the board you're the reason I was late to my hearing?"

Aratheus slid his foot back, waving her on. "I know you think you're doing the right thing, and I can tell there's no changing your mind. I just hope you're okay with getting a little blood on your hands." He eyed the bullet hole in her suit. "Something tells me you're going to see more of it before this is all said and done."

She clenched her jaw and reached for the door, but stopped short. "I never said anything about a Jumper," she said.

"What?"

"You said that this was the second time I ran into a dead Jumper inside a storm."

Aratheus examined himself in the mirror, smoothing a wrinkle in his expensive suit. "That's because, unlike you, Doctor, I value the scientific method. If you think you're my only source, think again. I don't let fate rule my life when the data is right there for the taking."

"And we can't have both?" Emélie asked.

"Possibly, but why bother when the data doesn't lie?"

"So you believe that to be an immutable truth?"

"The only absolute thing in a chaotic world. The bedrock of my career, the law that governs everything I do. The rule I live and die by. Data, above all else."

Emélie nodded. "Then I suppose I misspoke. You did give me something, after all."

"Oh?" Aratheus turned, his face emotionless and his tone eager. "And what might that be?"

"That I was right not to trust you from the start. And, considering you're the sole department head without a board seat, I'm not the only one who's noticed. The data doesn't lie, after all." Emélie dismissed herself to the lobby without making time to register his rage. The Director's masked attaché, a uniformed drone in a heavy cloak, waited for her outside.

"Sorry for the delay," Emélie said.

The attaché nodded. "Right this way, Doctor Desjardins. The Director will see you now."

CHAPTER 9
OZYMANDIAS

The Director's attaché was not a large drone, although as she moved ahead of Emélie, the handful of other employees they passed in the hall pressed themselves sideways, as if arm's reach was still too close. Emélie attracted wide-eyed stares in her ruined jumpsuit, which stood in stark contrast to the attache's immaculate, statuette appearance. At the end of the hall, the attaché parted her seamless black cloak with a skeletal, metal arm painted the same brilliant red as the Phaethon logo and rested her hand against one of the monolithic wooden doors leading into the Director's office.

"Wait here," the attaché ordered, then stepped through without further explanation.

Standing alone at the enormous doors left Emélie adequate time to admire their flowing, burled hardwood. The surfaces were milled with a subtle ripple texture, oiled to a depth that rivaled a rare night sky, and standing before them, put Emélie into a mood that was strangely serene. Every other room in Sanctuary Four consisted of sliding metal hatches linked to proximity sensors, making an encounter with doors —and wooden ones, at that—something of an experience. Cautiously, she reached a hand out, touching the warm surface; something inside her remembered, although what, she did not know.

Presently, a gap appeared, and the attaché's masked face poked out. Emélie yanked her hand back as the attaché gave a signal indicating now was the time to enter. She stepped across the threshold, leaving behind the homogenous off-white interiors of Sanctuary Four for a room drenched in decadent warmth.

Sanctuaries were, both by design and necessity, spaces of ruthless efficiency. What the labyrinthian underground complexes lacked in vibrance, they made up for in survivability. The office of the Director was the exception to that rule, and those who received an invitation to pass through the double doors were greeted with a rare glimpse at luxury.

Emélie stood at the edge of the low-ceilinged, circular chamber that opened to a panoramic view of the pit-like main shaft of Sanctuary Four. Plush, rust-colored carpet and dark wood paneling accentuated the table dominating the center of the room. The table was shaped like a giant ring, its surface polished to a flawless dark mirror, and hedged around it in well-tailored suits and sharpened stares, sat the fully assembled Phaethon board.

She followed the attaché to the center of the boardroom. On approach, a pair of guards stepped between her and the drone, blocking her path and preventing her from proceeding.

"That's far enough," one of the guards ordered. In his hand, a compact scanner with eyecups on one end and a display screen on the other. "Eyes open," he ordered, pressing the scanner to her face. Despite the confusion, Emélie was also vaguely aware that someone —likely the other guard—had taken hold of her cybernetic arm with both hands. The scanner chirped twice, and a tiny green dot appeared in the viewfinder. Instinctively, she blinked; when her eyes opened, a beam of iridium light seared her retinas. She recoiled, eyes watering as the guard removed the device. He studied the output while the other guard flipped open a maintenance panel near her elbow.

He paused for a moment, grinning as he looked at Emélie's sweat-streaked face. "Thought you could hide a little graffiti on the Phaethon loaner, huh?" The guard stood with his back to the board, unconcerned with their collective gaze. "Don't worry, from one ground-pounder to another, I won't say a thing."

Already out of sorts and still seeing stars, Emélie blinked at him, wide-eyed. Her eyes fell to her arm, where a data cable ran from a port located beneath the panel to a small tablet in his hand. Beneath the panel, the symbol of a snake twisted around itself, consuming its own tail was now clearly visible.

The guard winked, pulled the cable clear, and flipped the cover back into place. "She's all clear," the other guard—the one with the eye scanner—announced, and as quickly as they'd appeared, the men excused themselves from the room.

In the moments that followed, three things occurred to Emélie in rapid succession. First, it was clear that those men were not from Sanctuary. Instead, they resembled field operators, their mismatched fatigues more in line with what Emélie wore than the coordinated department jumpsuits of the standard guards. Second, whatever threat Phaethon faced—which Aratheus had alluded to back in the bathroom —had to do with eyes, or sight, or some combination of the two. While she'd never been summoned directly to the Director's office, there had been other hearings, and never once had there been a need to check her eyes. And finally, and perhaps the most chilling of all, was that she had no memory of why she had a cybernetic arm. It had been part of her longer than she could remember, and for that reason, she'd never questioned it as something other. Now, she had to reckon with the realization it bore a hidden symbol, a data port she didn't know about, and it was built by Phaethon. All while standing five steps from facing the entire board.

"Doctor Emélie Desjardins," the attaché announced, raising an arm toward the table. Before Emélie could step forward, the drone bowed stiffly, then returned to her post behind the Director.

She inhaled, lost in the chasm between her current position and the short distance toward the empty seat waiting for her at the table. Phaethon was governed by the DAO, a decentralized organization that relied on ritual rather than hierarchy to enforce power. Save for the Director, none of the suits around the table were actually board members but proxies, placed into the seats they held by anonymous benefactors who wished to remain as such while still exercising their right to shape the organization's future. These proxies were, by nature of their position and the environment that produced them, individuals who sensed fear as an evolutionary adaptation. So attuned to the nuances and subtleties of it that to make even the slightest misstep now —to show any hesitation—would be disastrous. This wasn't a hearing; it was an arms race, and Emélie was going in half-blind and unarmed, and already with a bullet wound, though not empty-handed.

It was the Director who finally broke the silence. "Doctor," he said, extending an open hand to the vacant seat.

Emélie remained in place.

"If you would take a seat, Doctor, we're ready to begin," the Director reiterated without any threat or urgency in his tone.

A few of the faces around the table flushed at her blatant disregard for their tradition; to hesitate once might have been confusion, but a second time bordered on disobedience. This was their first and fatal mistake: to assume Emélie would repeat her past. That this time was the same as the last, where she was to appear, one against twenty, and take the judgment seat, willingly accepting whatever sentence they levied against her. What they misjudged as reckless obstinacy was, in fact, a subversive violence capable of altering their power structure from within. And so she stood, unmoved, a perestroika in a bloody jumpsuit.

"Do you believe in fate?" the Director asked.

Emélie met his gaze. "I believe there are laws which govern our physical reality, some of which we can explain and some of which we cannot."

"Well, might I suggest you think long and hard about which one you'd like to be judged by then, because though I appreciate your commitment to whatever it is you think you're doing here, I can assure you I have neither the time nor the patience to see it through to the end. You may either take a seat and utilize the opportunity I'm extending to you, against the better judgment of those around me, I might add, or you can leave the way you came in, and these same people whom you openly defy will determine your future without you."

Emélie stepped up to the table, grasping the vacant seat with her mechanical arm, pulling it out to break the seamless perimeter.

She did not sit.

Instead, she reached down, placing a hand on the table. When she lifted it away, the single leaf, vividly green and slightly tattered, rested lightly on the polished surface. A fragile testament to a grotesque truth. At the sight of the leaf, there was an immediate and subtle shift in the room: the proxies eyed the Director, while the Director watched the leaf.

In the terse silence that followed, Emélie noticed another person in the room. A man in a rumpled, tan jumpsuit that lacked any identifying markings sat comfortably outside the circle, sleeves rolled past his elbows, as if occupying such a hostile environment was routine. The man turned to meet her, drawing the attention of the Director with him as Emélie realized too late that she was staring.

Without a word, the Director leaned back in his seat and the entire proxy board rose to their feet. They shuffled toward the door under the watchful gaze of the Director's attaché, who dismissed herself last, leaving Emélie alone with the Director and the man in the jumpsuit, who casually moved to an open seat a few spots down from the Director.

Any forward momentum Emélie gained through demonstration of the evidence she'd found was short-lived. While she didn't know the first thing about the other man, stories about the Director's ability to sway an entire room with little more than a word were legendary. The epitome of a corporate iconoclast, the Director was an iron-headed, slack-armed cage fighter in a suit and tie, gorged on the radical ideas of his younger self and strengthened from the indifference that came from the status of his station. As she had just witnessed, those stories were not pure myth, and while defying the board was one thing, facing the Director alone demanded an entirely new strategy. To have a fighting chance, she needed to focus on what she knew. And the one thing she knew better than anything was physics.

She became an object in motion, changing position without waiting to be addressed. Leaving the leaf behind, she moved along the circumference of the room, bypassing the two men until she stood before a desk situated off to one side of the conference table. Neither of them made any move to intervene, although she was unsure if their hesitation was a result of curiosity or shock. She did not know which would be better, either.

It was a reckless move that left her partially blind, her back toward her opponents. She ignored the desk, instead focusing her attention on a photo hanging on the wall behind it. The image, badly faded and yellowed with time, was torn in half along a tattered edge. The remaining portion, no larger than her hand, hung in an oversized frame—the lone personal effect in this power-drenched, emotionally sanitized office. Photos were something like wooden doors in Sanctuary: rare, and among a body of similar things, an outlier.

She stopped before it, pausing in the heat of the moment to take in this anomaly: a much younger Director, standing on the rim of a red crater beside another man near the same age, both grinning wide. On the horizon, a newly constructed Loop shimmered in the low Martian sun. At the bottom of the photo was a small, handwritten caption: *Marcus Sinclair, Samael Sinclair,*

The rest of the text was missing where the photo had been torn in two.

"Do you know why you're here, Doctor?" the Director asked, breaking the silence with his unwavering tenor. "I only ask because of all the things you might have acknowledged when you entered this room, I find it interesting that you identified that photo in particular."

Emélie glanced over her shoulder, first to the Director, then to the other man. "Why is that interesting?" she asked, choosing her words carefully.

"I called you up here because I thought you might be able to tell me something about interplanetary travel," the Director replied.

She felt a catch in her throat. The trap was set. The question now was how far could she run? "I'm not that sort of physicist," she replied.

"I work with mathematical models of reality, not the hardware that moves through it."

"Ships traverse one side of the universe. I was referring to the other method for travel."

Emélie turned to face the table, and the man in the jumpsuit smiled.

A rapid defeat.

CHAPTER 10
KILLING FIELD

At the sight of the camera, Emélie's hand started shaking.

"State your name for the record."

Emélie clamped her metal hand around her offending one and pulled it into her lap. Across the table, a small red light blinked steadily from the recording device hovering between the Director and the other man, who had yet to be introduced. He sat casually with both arms resting on the table, unbothered by any sense of formality. As if the boardroom were his, and everyone else was visiting.

"Is this a board hearing?" she asked.

"That's of no relevance to this discussion," the man replied, adjusting the camera.

"It is if you're in my position," Emélie replied.

"Just answer the question."

Emélie glanced over at the Director, hoping for a cue as to where the conversation was going. He offered nothing, so naturally, being who she was, Emélie charged ahead. "I'm sorry... have we met?"

"Doctor Desjardins, this is Joab," the Director explained, his tone strained. "He's been brought on in an advisory capacity to address the increased Origin trafficking into Phaethon prefectures, starting with Sanctuary Four."

"What does that have to do with me?"

"How familiar are you with the Loop?" Joab asked.

Emélie studied both men a moment before formulating a reply. Both were hard to get a read on, although the same could be said of her. "There were four of them. Two on Earth, one on Luna. One on Mars. Innovative for their time, but wildly unstable. They're adjacent to my work on gravitational anomalies."

"Five," Joab corrected. "There are five Loops."

"I wasn't aware of that."

"It was classified. Do you know who Lilith is?"

"No. Should I?"

"Lilith works for the Hesperides Cartel. Sources indicate she is high up, likely serving as the main contact for their Earth operations. She uses a set of proxies that make her difficult to pin down. The one we've been following for the last few months went dark inside that storm you were in."

"I didn't see another woman if that's what you're asking," she nodded to the dossier in Joab's lap. "It's all in the report."

He parsed through the file, then raised his eyes to the leaf resting on the table in front of her. "What about that?" he asked.

Emélie clamped her jaw shut.

The Director spoke next. "Doctor Desjardins, we have actionable intel suggesting Lilith is using the Loop to smuggle Origin across our borders. We brought you here because your work on cosmological models overlaps with the technology used to power the Loop."

"You can call it what it is," she replied, concealing her mounting curiosity behind a thinly veiled attempt at indifference. "Manifold. Saying it out loud won't cause any catastrophic damage. I promise."

"Well, given your familiarity with the topic, it shouldn't come as a surprise to hear that the Hesperides Cartel repurposed it for interplanetary trafficking."

"I find that hard to believe," she said flatly.

"That someone is teleporting drugs, or that the Loop is back online?"

"Both. And it wouldn't just be cargo. Someone has to move it. That's why the program was shuttered in the first place. They were trying to move people. And maybe I'm mistaken, but I was under the impression that nobody has successfully entered Martian airspace in the last two decades."

"I'm sure you're mistaken about a lot of things, but that's beside the point," Joab said, leaning back in his seat. "Does the name Fountainhead mean anything to you?"

Fountainhead. Find Fountainhead. Emélie shook it off, but it was clear from the way he maintained eye contact after the question that the term did, indeed, mean something to her. "I... I don't know what that is."

"Nobody does. Fountainhead is the internal designation for the founder of the Hesperides Cartel. We suspect it was Fountainhead who first recruited one of the old AI constructs to bring the Mars Loop back online."

"Watchers," Emélie said, considering this new information. "The AI constructs responsible for operating the Loop were called Watchers. And they did far more than simply operate the Loop. They were quantum constructs responsible for fabricating the Manifold. Without them, the Loop wouldn't exist."

Joab raised his eyebrows. "And here I was, thinking you were just a DOE staffer with a lucky streak."

"It's not like I came up with this idea. Dark matter makes up most of the universe. Most of the time, we can't see it. I look for the times we can. While the Loop harnesses dark matter to facilitate teleportation, there's a lot more beyond just that. Parallel realities, for example." Emélie folded her hands and set them on the table. "Which Watcher?" she asked, addressing Joab directly this time.

Joab gave a casual glance toward the Director, although neither of them made any effort to respond.

"If you want to understand how Lilith is moving Origin, I need to know which Watcher they brought back online. Each Manifold was a unique construction produced between the Watcher and the system itself. You won't get anywhere without that."

"Eden," Joab said, watching Emélie intently. "It's Eden."

"Eden," Emélie repeated.

"The one and only. The same reason we can't land a ship on Mars and solve this problem the old-fashioned way. Eden maintains integrated control of the entire infrastructure left behind when we abandoned Mars in the Collapse, including a robust satellite defense network. She's self-maintaining, self-repairing, and self-replicating. And she's got enough resources to outlast us for at least the next few hundred years."

"Jesus," Emélie said. "Is there any good news?"

Joab rubbed his chin and glanced at the Director, who nodded his approval to proceed. She wasn't sure which of the two retained the higher station. Out of the pair, Joab was certainly the most diplomatic; a man who understood it took more effort to build bridges than burn them.

"Eden hasn't been sitting idle in our absence. She's made improvements, the most recent of which we suspect has culminated in bringing the Loop in Hellas Basin back online."

"And you're making a direct correlation? Eden found a way to restore the function of the Mars Loop, and this explains how Lilith is smuggling Origin onto Earth. No other supporting evidence aside from those two data points."

"You're quick. I like that. It's a bit of an oversimplification, but you've got the gist of it."

"It's not possible," Emélie replied.

"And here I was, under the impression that impossibilities were supposed to be something of your forte," Joab said, grinning widely.

Emélie shifted in her seat, cornered.

"Now we're getting somewhere. Let's say, hypothetically, that the Loop on Mars is currently active. How close does that get us to opening the corresponding Gate here on Earth?"

"Nowhere," Emélie said.

Joab grunted, running a hand across his jaw. He threw a glance at the Director, which Emélie immediately understood as a passive challenge before his words confirmed it. "I thought you said she knew what she was talking about."

"You realize I'm sitting right here," Emélie said, glaring across the table. "You asked for my opinion; I'm going to give it."

"Alright, Desjardins," Joab glared back. "The table is yours. Don't waste my time."

Emélie pushed her chair from the table and stood. "The Loop was designed around the principle of quantum tunneling. Four facilities—or as you said, five—each capable of generating a Manifold—the dark-matter powered parallel reality—and, at a fixed point above the reactor. A Gate, if you will. One of the Watchers, Eden, for example, would construct a tunnel inside the Manifold by linking that point to a corresponding point at a second facility. Any matter entering one location would emerge moments later at the destination." She paused to look at the leaf lying on the table. "A Jump."

"Skip the hard theory, Desjardins. You still haven't answered my question. I want to know how far we could get with one Loop."

"Redundancy," Emélie replied.

"We're well beyond safety considerations," Joab said, leaning forward. "Is it, or is it not, possible to Jump with a single Loop?"

"Possible, but not probable. The dual Loop system is a failsafe mechanism." She glanced around, searching for something to help illustrate her point. "It was designed that way to prevent someone from getting trapped inside the Manifold in the event of a malfunction on either side of the Jump." She picked up the leaf, holding it out with her metal hand. "May I?"

Dismissively, Joab waved her on. The Director continued watching with concerned silence.

Briefly, Emélie marveled at the apparent resilience of the leaf: at first glance, a fragile, out-of-place thing, although here it was, in her hand. "A payload," she explained. "Now, if—and this is an enormous assumption—the Mars Loop could independently power a Manifold, then imagine this table as that Manifold, and our room as the enclosing reality. Our reality. While not identical, it mimics reality's topology, much like this table's circular shape reflects the room's own roundness, yet remains a separate entity."

Lightly, she balanced the leaf atop the table. Halfway on, halfway off. "Building on your set of working assumptions, we can establish Eden as the Watcher. She possesses the capacity for generating all the calculations necessary to open a Gate on the Mars side." Emélie slid the leaf fully onto the table. "However, that leaves the issue of generating the second point—the exit point—to complete the Jump."

"If Eden is capable of generating the entry point, doesn't that set the precedent that she could also handle the second one?" Joab inquired. "She's evolving, remember?"

"In theory," Emélie replied cautiously. "The issue lies in the failsafe mechanism." She moved the leaf along the perimeter of the table until it was midway between where she'd started and where Joab sat beside the Director. "Even if Eden opens a Gate at the Mars Loop, without an exit point, regardless of how far someone moves through the Manifold, they would still only ever be halfway through the Jump. Last time I checked, halfway to nowhere is the same thing as all the way to nowhere. Which is to say, even if you have Eden and the Mars Loop, you may as well have nothing."

Joab leaned back, letting his chair creak against the piston as he offered a long, slow clap. She couldn't tell if he was genuinely impressed, being facetious, or a bit of both. She didn't blame him. Here she was in a ruined jumpsuit, ranting on about Gates and Manifolds to an audience of two and mostly empty chairs. It seemed a little untethered, even for her.

"Am I free to leave?" she asked, suddenly aware that she was sweating. She wiped her forehead with her sleeve, knocking some dust onto the expensive carpet in the process.

"Sit down," Joab ordered. "We're just getting started. You make a compelling argument, but you're going in the wrong direction. Unless you'd like to offer another reason for why you managed to find a leaf on the surface of a dead planet."

Emélie's silence spoke volumes.

He leaned forward, gathering the leaf in one hand. Without warning or hesitation, he crumpled it into a tight green ball. "I want you to forget everything you just told me about the Loop. Not because you're wrong, but because you're right. You've worked out a comprehensive understanding of the Loop that few others have even come close to replicating. The problem here is that being right is no longer enough. While we've been holed up here on Earth, Eden's been busy on Mars. Evolving. Changing the rules for how she operates, all from inside the safety of her own planet. A planet we foolishly abandoned in the aftermath of the Collapse. You can argue why the system won't work on your own time. I brought you here to show me why it can."

She took a moment to think, considering the information, arranging it in her mind until something resonated. "You're just trying to open the one Gate, here on Earth?" she asked.

"You could say that."

"It's a yes or no question," Emélie pressed.

Joab grinned, shaking his head. "You don't have anything to lose, do you? Fine, assume the exit Gate is here, on Earth. No other parameters in play."

"I need something to work this out, a tablet or something—"

"You're going to have to make do with what you've got," he said, glancing at a watch he wore on the underside of his wrist.

"Fine," she said, thinking out loud. "I'd bypass the failsafe mechanism by finding a way for the second point to resolve itself."

"What about a second Watcher?"

"What about it?" she asked.

"The people I've got working on this think Eden found another Watcher, and she's using it to solve for the destination point remotely."

"You need to find better people, then. That's the obvious answer, but it wouldn't work. The amount of computing power it would take a Watcher to calculate a Jump point is nothing short of significant, not to mention localized to the area where the Gates are opening on Earth. Unless you've got a massive reactor sitting around that nobody has seemed to notice, then remotely solving for the second point is the more viable solution."

"What about moving people through?"

"As designed, there are already a near-infinite number of things that could go wrong moving a payload between Gates. Reduce the system to a single Loop, one Watcher, remove the failsafe mechanisms, and then add the entropic burden of a dynamic payload? Sure, you could try it. And I'd be willing to bet whoever goes in won't look the same when they come out the other side, if at all."

"That's a strange way of saying cut to pieces," Joab replied. "Then again, that makes the leaf the second piece of evidence you found supporting a Gate." He set the dossier from his lap onto the table. Forgotten until this moment, it now lay clearly in view. No words on the cover, only a single, red ring—the symbol for the Loop. Following her reply, he flipped it open, sifting through the contents once more. "What were you doing out on the surface?" he asked.

Emélie fought the rising panic clawing at her throat. "I've been running routine excursions for the better part of two years. Hardly seems like a reason to put me on trial."

"Nobody said anything about a trial," he replied, raising his eyes to meet hers. "What I'm looking for is a concrete explanation for driving headlong into a cat-five storm."

With her hand tucked closely to her side to hide the shakes, she spoke, working her way through her defense. "I track gravitational anomalies. Nothing hard. Circumstantial data, mostly—levitating stones, dust moving against the wind, that sort of thing. Cosmology simulates realities, so I used those findings to build a model around potential future events. It showed a high probability of an occurrence inside that storm."

"Must have been one hell of a model," Joab said, watching her carefully.

"Thank you—"

"That's not a compliment, Doctor," the Director interjected, speaking for the first time since they'd started. He placed his large hands palms down on the conference table. Bracing for impact. "Your ability to predict the exact spot of a Gate opening defies probabilistic explanation, storms notwithstanding. And while you've said quite a lot this morning, I'd wager there's something you still aren't telling us. Perhaps you might consider honesty, while you still have the chance?" He looked toward the panoramic window. "If the Cartel is using Eden to open Gates at will, I shouldn't have to spell out the dangers of letting that power go unchecked. Fountainhead installing Lilith as second in command and recruiting Eden demonstrates a certain sort of ambition. Today, it's Origin, but if we don't find a way to end this threat, this proxy war will spill over into real combat inside the safety of Sanctuary Four. And it won't end here. This is only the beginning."

Emélie looked toward the men waiting for some form of deeper justification of her actions. She had none. "I don't know what else I can say. I was looking for dark matter, which led to a Manifold. The Manifold indicated remnants of a Gate, and the Gate led me here, to..."

"Origin," Joab said, completing her train of thought. "And with Origin, you're back to dark matter."

Emélie found herself momentarily disoriented as the implications of her discovery came full circle, a strange loop. "I didn't know any of this was connected. I just happened to be looking for the thing nobody else noticed."

"You have that in common with Lilith, then," Joab replied, thinking. "We've been keeping close tabs on her the last few years, watching where she moves and what she does. She's difficult to track. Uses a system of couriers to make sure she never even sets foot on Earth—" He stopped mid-sentence, eyes fixed on Emélie. She'd started to lean forward, hooked by the allure of accurate information. Joab knew it, too. He continued, "Twenty-four hours ago, the courier we were tracking, on Earth, went dark inside that storm. Just up and vanished."

"I don't know what Lilith looks like, but I didn't see any women at the accident site if that's what you're after," Emélie said, in an attempt to anticipate where Joab might be going. She felt the pull to participate in the conversation in a way that was both helpful and kept her out of trouble.

"You happen to see any trees while you were there?" Joab prodded.

Emélie glanced over at the Director, confused by Joab's question and looking for a bit of reassurance. "I just explained, it's part of my—"

"Surface work isn't for the faint-hearted," Joab interrupted. He collected the dossier from the table. Inside was archival, hardcoded data. *Paper*. "Origin is flowing across our borders, the boundary settlements are crawling with Jumpers, and there's barely any oxygen left.

And as if that weren't enough, we have a rogue cosmologist with an advanced prediction model that drives directly into storms. I have teams who've cycled through Luna more times than I can count and *still* won't set foot into a surface storm for any amount of hazard pay. Now you've either got a death wish, or there's still something you aren't telling me." He slid the dossier forward. "I can help you get the answers you want, but you've got about thirty seconds to convince me you won't be a liability."

She watched Joab, knowing when he said thirty seconds, he damn well meant thirty seconds. He wasn't wrong about her: statistically speaking, with as many trips as she'd made topside, she should have been dead months ago. Not that mortality rates meant anything. For someone like her, death was merely a knowable chaos: the ever-approaching vector of an arbitrary point, at an arbitrary time, in which nearly infinite possibilities collapsed into a single, finite outcome. It was not death but quantum uncertainty that chased after Emélie to the speed of her own doubt.

"I'm haunted by limits," was all she said.

Joab glanced over at the Director. "She'll do."

"I'll do what?" Emélie asked.

With a wave of his hand, Joab recalled the recording unit and switched it off. "I've got an informant up on Homestake. She claims to know how Eden found a workaround for the redundancy protocols inside the Loop. While there seem to be several methods for accomplishing this, given what we currently know of Lilith and her trafficking operation, I think your theory of something that allows the point to solve for itself is the most likely solution. I was hoping you would catch a ride with me up to the orbital platform and sit in on the conversation to see if the intel we're getting is accurate."

"I don't know why you're asking me for help," Emélie said, glancing toward the door. "Seems like there'd be plenty of more stable options to choose from, if not here, then at one of the other Sanctuaries. I'm not the only cosmologist on Phaethon's payroll."

"You're the only one with a model," Joab replied. "I looked into Kepler's Reef, if that's what you're concerned about. You said you don't remember anything from two years back, although I get the sense from talking to you now that you've recalled a thing or two since then."

"What's that supposed to mean?"

"It means that I don't think you've lost as much as you claim. You just need the right trigger."

"The right trigger," Emélie repeated, tasting those bitter words. She turned to the Director. "You can keep your triggers, and your advisors. I'll take my chances out on the surface."

"The board took a vote before you arrived," the Director said. "Nineteen to one."

Emélie clenched her hand into a fist.

"In light of the events on the surface, they voted in favor of repealing your security clearance. Surface privileges are revoked until we can launch a full-scale investigation regarding your involvement in the murders of seven Phaethon employees, intent to traffic and distribute Origin, and obstruction of justice."

She turned around, hand clenched at her side. "None of that is true," she said in a low voice. "Not a single—"

"I'm not saying it's true, Doctor, but what's true or not is irrelevant. What matters is people's perception, and given your situation and history, you're not in a position to bargain." He pushed his wheelchair away from the table and tapped a button on the chair's arm. The wood paneling in the room slowly retracted, revealing more of the panoramic window looking out into the primary shaft of Sanctuary Four. "You have a choice to make. You can walk out that door, where a pair of Internal Affairs officers are waiting to escort you to a maximum-security safehouse until you can stand for a formal hearing. Or," he scrutinized Emélie, still waiting across the table, "you can take this opportunity to join Joab and buy yourself a little more time. And hope that in the meantime, some favorable evidence will surface to clear your name."

"Some choice," she said, but she took the deal all the same.

"One more thing," Joab said, fingers sifting through the file. "What's your connection to the drone?"

Thursday. Nobody had mentioned Thursday in all of this, and at this point, Emélie was afraid to ask. When she woke up on the recovery transport en route to Sanctuary, he wasn't with her, and they'd brought her straight to the meeting with the Director. She hesitated.

"Just answer the question," the Director prompted.

"Thursday? He's my handler. He was assigned to me."

Joab glanced at the Director, who nodded. "Assets within internal affairs are randomly assigned to a case officer. Standard operating procedure."

Joab raised his eyes, surveying her. "Are you aware his assignment as your handler ended six months ago, and he requested an extension to stay on until your probation was over?"

"What? I... I don't know anything about that. We don't have any prior connection if that's what you're asking."

Joab closed the file and tossed it on the table. "There's a truck waiting for you outside. Lift number three. Make sure you're on it."

"I'll need to get some things from my apartment. A change of clothing, maybe—" Emélie began a mental tally of all the things she would need, while simultaneously still trying to keep up with Joab's unforgiving pace.

"They're already waiting for you," Joab said, once again interrupting her scrambling. "I had your super send for them before you arrived."

"You anticipated I'd say yes," she said; a hot combination of irritation and shock rising from her chest to her face, causing her to hesitate as the doors opened ahead of her.

"I anticipated getting what I wanted. You just happened to be in proximity to it." He nodded toward the crumpled-up leaf resting on the table as she turned to leave. "You think your model can predict what we'll find on Homestake?"

"Only if you believe in fate," she said hotly.

Joab reclined in his seat, arms folded behind his head as he watched her leave. "Then you're in luck, Desjardins. Fate and I go way back."

CHAPTER 11
"PARDES"

Phaethon Corp. MAIN build_VX.6.6.09
initializing boot sequence...
running subroutine FOUNTAINHEAD:

  bindquery: update parameter to
  "PARDES"
  encryption protocols intact,
  syntax structures intact
  [12] entries remaining

begin sentiment analysis,
implicit context target, rundisplay:

BEGIN RECORD >>>

My hands are stained red. Red from the dust. Red from the blood. Three more graves in as many days. Laid them to rest on the eastern edge of Nereus Crater, along with the others. Marcus just watched me shovel and said I best be careful or I'd lose my gun hand. Sounded like a threat if you ask me. I didn't mention that both of my hands are gun hands. Not much need for them out here, though. Mars seems content with claiming all the violence for herself. Even Precursor has limits.

We lost the first one because of a tear in his suit. About four millimeters, right below the elbow. Caught it on a rock ledge coming down a slot canyon on the way back from morning patrols. Dropped his patch kit into the ravine after his hand went numb, and by the time someone got to him, he was frozen solid. Could have snapped him in two like a stick. Made me homesick for trees, in a way. Except the reason we're here is because there weren't any trees left to begin with, so I guess I don't miss them so much as I wish we weren't here.

I've put a lot of people in the ground. A lot of them by my own hand. I've buried plenty here too, but the last one I laid to rest today got to me. I wish I could say I loved her, but that would be a lie. The truth is we were lonely together, and now we're short a medical officer, and I have an infant child to care for. I'm not sure what to call her, but she's the first.

The first of Mars.

<<< END RECORD

COMINT/incoming: assign SALOME
as continuation...

BEGIN asynchronous process
execute subroutine HESPERIDIES,
monitor when VISIBLE

"Precious are the dead that lie there."

sanitize data entry,
purge access logs to XANADU
KILL remote process

CHAPTER 12
FALSE MARIA

It was hard to breathe with all that water. Brinks was slick with it: blood and condensation dripped from his open mouth onto the ornate tiles that slid past, inches from his face. Whatever was dragging him let go mid-stride, sending him chin-first into the ground, hands bound uselessly behind his back—more blood on the tile. There was a time in his life when he would have gotten back to his feet, ready to fight. Now, he got up when he was good and ready. That, and Jumpers weren't worth the effort, even on a good day.

When the staggering shuffle of footsteps disappeared and a rush of cool air moved across his neck, Brinks rolled over to one side and struggled up onto his knees. He leaned onto his heels and looked across the pool at the woman silently watching him. Her eyes, two vermilion points peering from the waterline.

"I thought Seraphs weren't supposed to age," she said, rising enough to speak. Water dripped from her cheekbones, streaking across a second set of eyes tattooed below her real ones. Both sets of eyes reflected off the water's surface, watching him with a panoptic gaze. He wiped his mouth against the collar of his jacket, trying to clear the blood running down his forehead as it mixed with dust and sweat.

"What's a little reality slippage when you've got all the time in the world?" Brinks replied. He shifted his bound hands to one side, holding them open to show he was unarmed.

"Of course." She lifted a hand from the pool and, with a slight wave, released the metal shackles binding his wrists. "Old habit, you see? They don't call you the Red Hand for nothing."

"They don't call me that anymore." Brinks produced his cigarette case. Hesitated, waiting.

The woman raised her chin, sending a ripple across the pool, along with her approval. "At least you haven't lost your man-ners."

"Best to start things off with a bit of civility," Brinks said, patting down the pockets of his duster until he found his lighter. It took a few attempts for the damp paper to catch fire. "Seems you haven't resolved that bit of a stutter. I guess there really are some things that money can't buy." He smoked his cigarette, looking at a section of the hand-painted mural peeling away from the wall in the dense humidity. "*Human* things," he added.

The woman disappeared below the water and surfaced a few feet from where he knelt. She stretched her arms out, resting her chin on the coping as she traced a finger across the floor. "I wonder how much you've lost since yesterday?" she asked, casually gesturing toward the place where the blood pooled most heavily around Brinks.

"You know what they say about blood." Brinks shrugged, with effort, and took another pull on his cigarette, then dabbed the glowing embers in a tainted puddle near his knee. "Makes the grass grow." He pitched the butt into the pool where it drifted toward her: a dark stain in the clear water.

She rose, glistening as she climbed out of the water into the hazy bathhouse. "What's the mat-ter?" she whispered, leaning so close to Brinks that her lips graced one of his ears. "Can't handle the sight of a real woman?"

Brinks watched the water accumulate beneath him as it pushed more of his muddy, crimson stain toward the pool's edge. "I've known plenty of real women in my life, Lilith, and I can say with certainty that you aren't one of them."

Lilith snapped her fingers. An attendant wearing a rust-colored tunic emerged from the steam, moving backwards toward them. Jumper behavior. It carried an off-white, nearly opaque silk robe in its outstretched arms.

She pulled it on, waving the attendant off as she casually pushed Brinks' duster aside. Upon finding his gunbelt absent, she raised her eyebrows, then settled for taking his badge. "Brinks," she read, looking at the name printed onto the metal puck. A red circle with a clip across the back. "Brinks. Brink-ssss." She repeated it, shaping the word until she was satisfied with the way it came out. "It does have a certain ring to it, although it doesn't hold a flicker to Sam. Did you come up with it on your own, or did you let your Watcher name you?"

"Candle. It's 'hold a candle'," Brinks muttered, watching the attendant retreat into the steam.

"What's that, now?" She leaned forward, tapping his cheekbone with the badge.

"I said, you're one to talk. If I had a bullet for every original thought you put together, my gun would be a paperweight."

"Mmm, paper." Lilith stood, thinking his words over. She tossed the badge into the pool, where it sank with hardly a splash. "I forgot how much you're always talking about trees. Trees and fire, hell and brimstone. I can see why they made you do all the killing. Speaking of, I thought I made myself clear the last time we did this. You know the price for interfering with my affairs."

"I remember what you said about *your* affairs. We never discussed what happens when you interfere with *mine*."

She laughed, stone-faced, and waved her hand again. A series of panels retracted from the ceiling, revealing a sweeping view of the crisp, lunar night. "What were you doing near my Gate?" she asked.

Brinks tilted his head up, taking in the view with his augmented eye. The metal plate covering his other eye did nothing to help gauge the distance of Earth; even from here, it was a dirty sphere of swirling dark clouds. "Following a hunch," he said.

Lilith nodded approvingly. "And here I was, thin-king you were useless. Perhaps I misjudged you."

"Wouldn't be the first time." Brinks moved his gaze from the open skylight. Kneeling vertically was becoming more of a chore with the blood loss, but this thought only crossed his mind briefly; he'd been in rough shape many times before, and this time, too, would fade.

"Then tell me something interesting. Seems like such a shame, coming all the way up here for nothing." Lilith, bored by the conversation's pace, rolled up the dangling ends of her robe ties into silky, tight coils, then let them drop back to the floor again.

Brinks, never one for politics, chose his next words carefully. "Phaethon might be on to you," he said, nodding toward Earth.

"Oh?" Lilith asked, a curious lilt in her voice. She momentarily forgot about the ties of her robe and turned her attention more fully to the conversation. Finally, something interesting. "And what might I be doing to deserve such attention?"

"They know about the Gates, Lilith. I'd suggest holding off your next shipment until things cool down." He glanced over to where the Jumper attendant had disappeared into the steam. "Besides, the market is saturated enough the way it is."

"Bold of you to assume my business," she hissed. "Seems like your old employer can't appreciate the nuances of a little healthy competition."

"Origin isn't a rival to whatever the hell you've been cooking up."

Lilith let out a guttural laugh. "I was referring to the girl, but it seems you know more than you're letting on. Old habits die hard, do they?" Lilith snapped her fingers, and the blindfolded attendant materialized beside her. "How long until the next shipment is ready?" she asked without looking at the Jumper.

The Jumper let out a series of halted, screeching tones that approximated a raw data connection initialized through a set of vocal cords.

"Good," Lilith replied. "Dou-ble it." She followed with a hollow, staccato tone; the Jumper vanished from sight. It reappeared directly behind Brinks, lifting him until he hung inside his duster, toes slipping against the wet floor.

"Seems like there's been a misunderstanding," Brinks wheezed, choked by his own collar.

"Perhaps," Lilith replied, a tinge of glee in her tone. "Did you ever once consider in that tiny, little brain of yours that entropy is a gift?" She clicked her tongue, and the attendant released Brinks, dropping him to the floor. He crumpled; a hand and a knee landing hard. "I know you've always struggled with abstraction, so allow me to clarify. We've got something great here. Truly innovative." She leaned in, her breath hot against his face once more. "Why would I slow down when things are fin-ally opening up around here? I've got a job to do. And you know me—won't rest until the work is com-plete."

"Complete?" Brinks rose to a stand; it was hard to ignore the sting and pulsing in his hand and knee, and kneeling did him no favors. He took his hat off and wiped his forehead with it. "Hell, you already have half the planet addicted. I don't see what you stand to gain if everyone ends up dead at the end of all this."

Lilith turned for the door, her red irises glinting above her tattooed ones. Her body was so biometrically augmented that it was hard to tell where the machine ended and the human began. A cybernetic leg, an arm, two ports on her neck, and a plate near the base of her spine. By his count, she was at least half a drone. Then again, Brinks wasn't one to judge.

"I think you have something that belongs to me," she said.

Brinks clenched his flesh and bone fist. Tucked inside it was the small, black disc he'd extracted from the woman back at the bodega. He could feel it moving—all it took was a bit of light and a neural signal to get those bastards wriggling.

"I was worried you were beginning to get an idea in your old age," she said, following his gaze with intent. "A fool's dream."

Brinks opened his hand, freeing the device to crawl up his arm on tiny, articulated legs. Swiftly, he plucked the object away and flung it to the ground. It landed upside-down in a puddle of his own blood. Once more submerged in liquid, the device went dormant, retracting its legs.

Brinks dropped a boot on it, crushing the device beneath his heel with a wet, scraping sound. "I killed her the same way," he said.

"Expected. No Reflection of mine should fail so easily—second one this cycle." Lilith's eyes flickered with calculated indifference. "The subroutines need refine-ment."

Brinks watched the shards of metal at his feet. "No need to be hasty," he said. When he looked back up, another woman cowered beside Lilith. Her head, obscured by a hood, didn't stop Brinks from immediately identifying her as the scrawny clerk from the bodega. Lilith's attendant hovered in the background, poised.

"I really didn't want it to come to this," Lilith said. "We could have worked it out."

Brinks shook his head. He wished the clerk had taken the exit he had offered. "That was never an option for you, Lilith. Destruction is in your nature."

"I know you can't resist taking the moral high ground. Tell me what hap-pened at the Precursor drop, and I'll let your new friend live."

A deal both of them knew she had no intention of keeping.

"I'm sorry," Brinks said, mainly to himself. It was already too late for the clerk.

"You're not going to beg? I always took you as the sort who couldn't stomach co-llateral damage." Lilith lifted a finger, and the attendant ripped the hood from the clerk's head. Her dilated pupils darted between them as Lilith continued. "You were always... oh, what's the word I'm looking for?" She ran her hand along Brinks' chest until her fingers slipped past his heavy duster. From his breast pocket, she pulled the small packet of red crystals. "Predictable." She patted Brinks' cheek. "Don't look so tragic. You might be getting old, but you aren't dumb." She snapped her fingers again, and her attendant produced a silver tray from the deep folds of its tunic and held it up. "Knife," she ordered, palm out.

Brinks hesitated.

Lilith made a clicking tone, and her attendant stepped forward, bashing the clerk's head in with the tray. She slumped to the floor, temporarily knocked unconscious. Brinks sucked a breath in through his teeth and reached for his knife, which he slapped, blade-flat, into Lilith's waiting hand. Lilith motioned to her attendant, who held up the blood-smeared tray. "You've shown such an interest in my new product, I thought a proper dem-onstration might be in order."

She opened the packet and dumped the crystals onto the tray, then, using the hilt of the knife, ground them to a fine powder. When she finished, she took a step back to admire her work.

The clerk blew into the pile, scattering the powder across the wet floor. Lilith's hand flashed, smacking the clerk across the mouth; her jaw clamped shut, but she made no sound. Lilith's eyes warmed as she watched the Precursor illuminate the floor with a faint, incandescent glow. A glint in her red eyes, she tipped the tray over, brushing the residual powder clear with the back of her hand. She used the clean tray to broadside the clerk across the stomach.

She doubled over, and Lilith pounced. With a handful of matted hair, Lilith drove the clerk's face into the floor. Brinks stood off to one side, the Jumper facing him from the other. An agonizing, gurgling groan escaped the clerk, who struggled to resist but ultimately lost. The room once more silent, Lilith straightened, her silk robe stained and torn along one shoulder. "Filthy, filthy crea-ture," she said, brimming with joy as the clerk lapped residual Precursor off the floor in a drug-induced stupor.

"You're an abomination," Brinks growled, loathing in his voice.

Lilith leaned in, staring down the black plate covering Brinks' left eye. "And you're jealous." She plunged Brinks' knife into his stomach.

He grunted, wrapping both hands to the hilt as his earlier wound reopened, new blood leaking through clenched fingers to mix with the old. He'd already lost too much, and pulling the blade out now would be disastrous. Better the pain than nothing at all.

With stained hands, Lilith smoothed the front of her robe and turned for the door. "Well, if this didn't turn out to be a successful reunion." She glanced down at the clerk, who remained hunched over on the floor. The clerk's hands were scratching at something below her wild hair, and she was breathing in deep, strained gasps that didn't match her slight frame.

"You're playing a dangerous game," Brinks wheezed, fingers probing the gap in his belly to try and slow the hemorrhaging. "I was hoping you'd show me something I hadn't seen before."

Lilith gazed at him, eyes flickering. "That was always the trou-ble with you," she replied, taking the clerk's hand by the wrist as she offered it up. She pried the clerk's fingers away one by one, revealing a pair of dismembered eyes resting in her palm. "You had to see to believe." She closed the clerk's hand and squeezed, crushing the eyes until they oozed from her clenched fist. When she let go, the clerk convulsed as portions of her body flickered in and out of reality. Her entire body spasmed, contorted, and then vanished entirely. When she returned, it was only her legs, which landed in a heap beside Brinks, cut clean off at mid-thigh.

"You keep sur-prising me, Sam. I like that," Lilith cooed, assessing the carnage. "As you can see, not everyone can handle the necessary dose. It requires a certain mental fortitude to withstand the transition. There will be Jumpers, and there will be bodies. I'll let you decide where you'd like to fall. And nice work, cleaning up that mess my pathetic Reflection made down on Earth. You always had a knack for showing up at the most opp-ortune time."

"I didn't do it for you," Brinks said, looking at what remained of the clerk.

"Of course not, but I have a reputation to maintain. I've already arranged for your transportation," she said, glancing toward the pool on her way out. "Consider it com-pensation for your troubles. And mine."

When the door closed, the Jumper attendant reappeared beside him, mechanically silent. It lifted its blindfold, revealing empty sockets above a set of new eyes that had sprouted below, blinking asynchronously.

"If a man drowns and nobody's around to hear him scream, does he still make a sound?" Brinks asked.

The Jumper blinked again.

It was hard to breathe with all that water.

CHAPTER 13
PARETO FRONT

Three elevators, a security checkpoint, and an indiscriminate number of hallways later, Emélie arrived at an empty loading dock on Sanctuary Four's upper level. Her escort abandoned her at the airlock without any further instruction, leaving Emélie to face what lay beyond the door on her own. A rush of depressurized air drew her through; on the other side, a single black truck with tinted windows sat waiting. No Phaethon markings—no markings of any kind—just like Joab's jumpsuit. She stared at her disheveled reflection in the window, momentarily pausing to consider her next steps. Joab was amounting to something of a ghost regarding his operational footprint. That alone made him dangerous. It also meant he likely wasn't lying when he said he could get her answers. What sort of man was he? Only one way to find out: she gave one final glance back toward Sanctuary, then opened the rear passenger side door and climbed in.

Thursday sat in the driver's seat.

"You've got to be kidding me," Emélie said under her breath, surprise and exasperation slipping through her teeth. One hand still grasped the edge of the door.

"It's nice to see you're okay," Thursday said.

Emélie noticed his frame was bare, no sign of his cloak or belt. At least his tone, measured and slightly inquisitive, remained familiar. A small anchor in the growing storm. She hoisted herself into the truck and reached for the seatbelt, clanking the latchplate against her metal forearm as she fastened it. A potent dose of unreality blanketed her mind: barely twenty-four hours ago, she'd sat in a similar vehicle alongside Thursday. Back again, only this time, she was in the backseat, and there was an entire world of distance between them. "Did they tell you to say that?" she asked.

Thursday, immune to such musings of the human mind, adjusted his hands on the steering wheel. "I know I'm a drone, but you were never just an assignment to me. Unless something's changed, I remain at your service, wherever that leads."

Emélie glanced back at the airlock, as if going back were a viable option. It wasn't too late to throw a bit of chaos into Joab's annoyingly accurate ability to anticipate every decision she'd made from the moment she entered the Director's office. Nobody made her volunteer; that much remained true. At the same time, ending up in a Sanctuary basement sanitizing databases for the rest of her life wasn't a viable alternative. She wanted answers, and Joab had them. She shut the door and Thursday drove up the ramp leading out to the surface road.

"They sent me to pick up a few of your things," Thursday said, reaching up to adjust the rearview mirror. "I let myself into your apartment. I hope you don't mind."

On the seat sat a fresh, neatly folded sandstone-colored jumpsuit. Alongside it, a pair of boots and the faded green backpack she carried on surface runs. "Did they let you come because I'm a flight risk?" she asked, reaching for her pack. It wasn't a fair question, but he also could have told her about the extension. The bag felt heavier than she remembered, and as she shoved the jumpsuit inside, her hand hit something solid. A hard-sided case—*her* hard-sided case—and with it, a realization that stung her eyes and made her throat tighten. She glanced up at Thursday, but he didn't return her gaze, so she pushed the case further into the bag, then tossed the boots on top for good measure. She looked away, willing back the moisture stinging the corner of her eyes. "I assume you know where we're going?"

The gap to the front seat stretched like eons between them. Emélie was accustomed to shooting her questions, witty epithets, and displaced emotions to her left, but now there was a gulf between them; a new separation. Thursday seemed unaffected by this physical change in their dynamic and continued driving through the tunnel. She watched the rearview mirror, hoping for a flicker of something, anything, from the yellow light bar dissecting his square, black face. Flatline. His silence might have been the result of his programming: calm, indifferent, optimized for efficiency. That, or she wasn't the only one hurting.

"Why did you bring it?" she asked, partially awestruck at what the gesture revealed about his inner knowledge of her most personal life. The question reverberated with raw vulnerability: there were only two reasons for why a drone—and an internal affairs officer, at that—would willingly bring along what was inside that black case. Being a drone, he was bound to complete whatever task was assigned to him so thoroughly that the prime directive served to override any ethical flags. Emélie's other interpretation, the one that caused her to nearly tear up in the back seat, was that though their viewpoints differed, Thursday trusted and respected her. Either way, she couldn't know unless she asked the question, and voicing it felt better than another drive under the impenetrable silence they typically suffered. Best to get ahead of it now and deal with the fallout before they drifted so far apart that even a Manifold couldn't bridge a way back.

"I was instructed to bring your things," Thursday said conclusively. "No further criteria were provided, so I selected the objects you've historically brought along when we go to the surface."

"But you knew. This whole time, you knew..." Emélie paused, wondering if her shame was palpable to Thursday; they had never discussed this aloud before. "You knew I was using." Five words that tumbled out of her mouth in one breath. Heat rose in her cheeks. "You never said anything."

"You make your own choices, Doctor." An answer completely devoid of the emotional weight Emélie had mustered to ask her question, although his non-reactivity helped dissolve some of her lingering guilt. "I may have opinions about your methodology, but I try not to let those get in the way of doing my job. I figured, in this case, I could suspend judgment. Give you the benefit of the doubt." He glanced out the window. The lack of light on either side told Emélie they were moving radially, just below the surface, rather than following the main access road running along the interior perimeter of the main shaft.

"There are knowns and unknowns. And between those, there's a lot I seem to recognize and can't remember why," Thursday said. Then, thoughtfully, he added, "Your work seems to exist somewhere within that void, so I figured I'd let things play out before I came to any judgments."

"Well, that worked out great." The remark felt as abrasive against her lips as it sounded, and she immediately regretted it. It wasn't Thursday's fault she was chasing after the intangible. "It seems as though memory gaps are something we share," she added, a quick attempt at repair. "Maybe between the two of us, we have one intact brain."

Thursday turned, glancing back at her. "I was never trying to get in your way. I only wanted you to find what you were after." He looked back down at the navigation computer and gauged the distance to their destination. Despite having never left the tunnel, the map on the console showed they were nearing the end of their ride together. Almost to where they were going, wherever the hell that was. "Just do me a favor and don't get lost in the process, okay?"

"And that's your professional opinion?" Emélie said hesitantly, hoping an injection of light humor would ease her own troubled and tired mind.

"Would you like to know what I think about you as a friend?" Thursday asked.

"Not especially."

"I think you should clean your apartment."

Emélie looked out her window, suppressing a brief smile. "I wasn't aware you grasped the concept of sarcasm."

"Yes, well, I'm a Class Two. We're known for that."

"Known for being sarcastic?" Emélie asked, doubtful he actually understood what she was talking about.

"For understanding implicit context."

"Congrats," Emélie said. "They seem to have done an excellent job with you."

"Thank you. I like to think so."

"You aren't really proving your point," she said, her voice trailing off as she looked at her stained jumpsuit. "Why aren't there many Class Twos? I see Class Ones working jobs around Sanctuary all the time. And plenty of Threes in the upper levels. But now that you mention it, you're the only Two I know."

"Class Ones were labor. First gen. Strong, dumb as rocks. Have you ever tried talking to one of them? It's like interfacing with a pile of sand. The Class Three units came later and were considered more evolved. Stable. Logical." He paused for a moment, thinking. "Safe," he added.

"All relevant, but you still haven't answered my question. I wasn't asking about Class Ones and Class Threes. I was asking about *you*," Emélie prodded. Clearly, Thursday had managed to gather through observation almost everything there was to know about her—everything she remembered about herself—but they had almost never discussed him. He was a unique drone. Although she was reluctant to admit it, he was far more than her handler: following the loss of her memory at Kepler's Reef, Thursday had been her only friend. They shared a bond forged mostly in vehicles like this one, chasing down anomalous data points. Not unlike what they were doing now.

Thursday shrugged. "We were built to be like you. Emotional. Unpredictable. That sort of thing. Human enough to understand the more nuanced applications of interpersonal communication, art, culture, history. Just not human enough to be treated like it. That made us useful for other tasks. Compromising tasks, along with the sort of exposure that made people afraid of what we might become. The uncanny valley, you know." He fell silent as they continued down the tunnel. "You don't see many Twos because there aren't many left."

Emélie glanced out her window. "You managed alright, though."

Before answering, Thursday checked the navigation console again. "DOSA. Drone Origination Service Act. It passed with heavy resistance. If we could make it thirty years with a clean record, then we were granted a protected identity. Rights, memories, civil role, everything intact. Citizenship, essentially."

"What about your name?"

He shrugged. "It's the first memory I have. I woke up, and there it was, plain as day."

Something about the way he'd said it made her chest tighten. There was a practicality to his choice that was endearing; beneath it, a pang of sadness, that nobody had been around to give him a name, leaving him to fend for himself. "If only everything were that simple," she said, trying not to project her human emotions on something as rudimentary as naming a drone.

"Maybe. I just know I liked it better than what they called me before."

"What did they call you before?" The follow up question hurried out of her mouth, almost before it was completely formed. She could feel her knees pressing into the passenger seat in front of her and realized she had scooted forward in anticipation of his response.

"Twenty-nine. That's what they called me." Thursday provided the information as systematically and routinely as he drove: toward the destination, straightforward and true.

"Twenty-nine–," Emélie hesitated, clarifying, "-nth drone unit?"

"Twenty-nine years before I was wiped."

The realization of how close Thursday had been to freedom, to citizenship, hit her in the gut. She didn't ask any more questions after that.

A few minutes later, Thursday pulled off onto an exit ramp leading out of the tunnel. At the end of the ramp, an access checkpoint blocked by a solid steel barricade prevented any further movement. As he pulled to a stop, a guard in a drab green jumpsuit stepped out from a gatehouse set into the side of the tunnel.

"Identification," the guard demanded, watching as Thursday lowered his window. Emélie passed up her credentials while a pair of security drones made an exterior sweep of their truck; her gaze followed them all the way around the back and up her side of the vehicle. The guard looked at the badges, then leaned his head through the window, glancing around the cabin before handing them back, without a word. He disappeared back inside the gatehouse, and a moment later, the metal barricade lowered, revealing the surface one level above.

"That was odd," Emélie said, turning around to get another look as the barrier closed behind them. "Seems like a lot of security for a lift up to Homestake."

Thursday rolled his window back up. "Seems like a lot of security in general," he agreed.

Emélie leaned her body toward the gap between the front seats and craned her neck in an attempt to get a better look out of the front window as they breached the surface. The ramp continued climbing another level, passing through a forest of massive, tan pylons before opening out onto an elevated flight tarmac amid a sprawling wind farm. As far as she could see in every direction, cylindrical sail assemblies towered overhead. Thursday pulled up a short distance from where a light transport, barely more than two wings and a fuselage, taxied on the runway nearby.

"Thursday, that reminds me... That ship we found." She paused, and he tilted his head, which was odd for a drone, given he wasn't hard of hearing. Hard of listening, maybe, but not hearing. "Have you ever heard of a ship like that being referred to as a four-wing?"

"A four-wing, sure. It's a military designation." Thursday was looking at a man standing at the open hatch of the ship across from them. "Who's that?"

"Joab," she said, slinging her pack over one shoulder and reaching for the door. "He's our ride."

Thursday turned around in his seat.

"What?" Emélie glanced past him. "We weren't really introduced. He's some sort of advisor."

Thursday returned his attention to the waiting ship. Emélie could feel another argument coming on. Right now was probably the worst time for Thursday to dig his heels in.

"We should go," Emélie prompted. "Joab isn't the sort of person who likes to be kept waiting." She lifted the handle, breaking the silence in the truck with the staggered *whoosh-whooshing* of the wind turbines spinning overhead.

Thursday reluctantly put the truck in park. "There's no markings," he said.

Emélie opened the door and dropped down onto the grooved concrete of the flight deck. "What?" she shouted over the noise.

"The ship. It doesn't have any tail markings."

Emélie glanced at the transport. He had a point, although why he made it was lost on her. "What does that have to do with anything?"

He hesitated again, and Emélie shut her door without waiting for a response. Joab made a circular motion with one arm, the universal sign of an imminent departure. She started for the ship, but after a few paces, she looked back and found Thursday standing beside the truck, one hand on the roof and the other holding his door steady in the chop. He had a stubborn streak, so lagging behind wasn't unusual for him, but something about how he stood gave Emélie a heavy feeling in her chest, as if he didn't plan on moving beyond that point.

She paused and, despite Joab's lack of tolerance for any sort of delay, held up her index finger to him. She turned back toward Thursday and the truck. "The Director," she shouted, bracing herself against the wind as she faced Thursday. "He said you asked for an extension to stay on with me. Why?"

"Because I believe in you, Doctor. In your work."

"You've hardly even seen my work!" Emélie shouted, nearly out of breath.

"Then that makes two of us." Thursday looked past Emélie to where Joab stood at the bottom of the ramp, arms crossed. "Be careful around him."

She glanced back at Joab, who had turned and started boarding.

"I've known plenty of men like him off-world," Thursday continued. "They have a different set of morals than you and I. They'll say anything—do anything—to get what they want. They believe rules exist to bend to their will."

"Maybe I believe that too." She wanted to sound brave and certain, but as the weight of the moment crashed in around her, she didn't know who, or what, to believe anymore.

"I believe you know who you are, Doctor, even if your memories are unclear. I don't fault your lack of trust. I don't even trust myself sometimes. I know it seems like you don't have a choice in this, but once you board that ship? It's too late."

"It's been too late for me for a while," Emélie said. The engines, already loud, surged now, assaulting her with a wave of scalding exhaust. "Tell me it's going to work out, Thursday! Tell me right now that if I get back in the truck with you, we turn around and return to Sanctuary, I'll find what I'm looking for. Tell me that and believe it, and we can walk away right now. No questions asked."

Thursday did not object any further.

Joab greeted Emélie at the top of the ramp. "I thought you were going to stand me up for a second there," he said, steering her down the aisle toward one of the rear seats. "We need to get moving. We're already behind schedule."

"Thursday's coming," Emélie said, "Just give him a minute."

Joab slapped his hand against the hull, and the door started closing. "Your handler is going to have to sit this one out. I don't work with drones. Too much of a liability." The engines shuddered, and Emélie felt the deck under her feet tremble as they lifted off. She looked over her shoulder in time to catch one last sliver of tarmac far below as the door sealed tight.

Thursday, still standing at the truck where she'd left him.

CHAPTER 14

ESCALATION OF FORCE

Empty. All the other seats were empty. It shouldn't have bothered Emélie as much as it did, but upon emerging from the cramped lavatory, still struggling with the zipper on her fresh jumpsuit, she couldn't shake the feeling that something about her current environment wasn't adding up. Ample seating, and yet she remained the sole passenger. Something Thursday would have pointed out almost immediately; counted twice, then followed by a pointed inquiry about the passenger manifest before even considering coming on board. Emélie admitted to herself that would have been better, except that while Thursday was busy drawing lines in the sand, she was watching them erode behind her, checkpoints on a line demarking her own abandon. Without Thursday to flag potential pitfalls, she felt a jittery, razor-sharp hyper-awareness take shape, and as she puzzled over the unused space, the ship pitched violently enough to send her stumbling across the cabin, half-dressed and wholly unprepared for what was to follow. She tumbled into the nearest seat, anchoring herself between the armrests as the ship continued to buck.

Joab, who had remained out of sight for the duration of their short flight, emerged from the cockpit, moving swiftly down the pitching aisle without a single misstep. "Put your mask on," he ordered, sure-footed. "We're making a transfer." He halted at the airlock and pulled on his own respirator as the ship shuddered once more, then stabilized.

His appearance, however abrupt, afforded Emélie a brief view into the cockpit, where the other two men from the boardroom—the ones who'd scanned her arm and eyes—piloted the ship. When they made no move to follow, she snatched her bag from the overhead bin and dashed after Joab. "We're already at the elevator?" she asked, digging into her pack for her oxygen recycler. She looked at the data pad built into her arm. Less than fifteen minutes had passed since they'd left Thursday at the tarmac. While Emélie had never been up to Homestake—at least, not that she could remember—she knew it was further than twelve damn minutes away. She found her respirator in the bowels of her bag, along with the hard-sided case Thursday had included with the things from her apartment. Hurriedly, she extracted the mask, feeling a rush of complex emotions: Thursday, so often the one slowing her down was, in this case, also the one watching her back. And she'd left him, a white speck receding on the runway back at Earth. Replaced by a man she didn't know the first thing about, except that he was good at what he did, and that he wasn't to be trusted. She took in a nervous breath and fastened her mask.

Joab pulled the airlock handle out, then rotated it. "I take it you haven't been off-world in a while." A non-conversational utterance; the door hissed, and he was across the threshold before it had time to fully open.

The change in cabin pressure left her feeling lightheaded, and as she moved to steady herself, she caught a view out the cabin window. The curved horizon of Earth stretched below them, a hazy blue-brown sphere suspended in blackness. She lunged for the airlock door, unwilling to lose sight of Joab, who showed no intention of returning to the ship. Across the threshold, a cold blast sent her reeling. They had surreptitiously docked in some sort of private access bay located on the underside of the orbital platform, which now loomed like an enormous metal ceiling above them. Well outside the purview of any commonly trafficked landing area, and the people that came with it. Orbital platforms like Homestake were characterized by a certain ruggedness that, on closer inspection, wasn't far from the hardscrabble, opportunistic lawlessness of off-worlders. Scrappy, like the people who worked to maintain them, move cargo through them, or profit off of them. And not a difficult leap, to recognize someone like Joab thrived in a place like this.

Before Emélie, a narrow catwalk stood as the only thing holding her feet from the bare atmosphere. She wanted—craved—some orientation for what was happening: an explanation for why there was nothing below her, why a multi-hour flight took minutes, and why Joab's pace was borderline reckless. Except this wasn't a Sanctuary, and Joab wasn't a suit and tie. With the silent acknowledgement that none of those things were remotely in reach, she moved forward. Stopping was not an option, and slowing down was looking less and less likely, too; she fought back a panicked gasp and pressed onward. The horizon, unsoiled by the dust choking out Earth's surface, hung blue at the lower fringes of space. Behind her, the ship's engines whined as a klaxon sounded and the airlock doors began to close.

The platform shuddered as the ship detached. She felt an urge to drop her eyes, to take in the expansive nothingness, although she did not. It was one thing to feel fear, and it was another to show it, especially to a man like Joab. She held her eyes steady, gritted her teeth, and marched down the suspended platform after him, hands to the railings on either side of her as it swayed with each step.

This time, she didn't look back.

When a second airlock at the other end of the open walkway forced Joab into a momentary halt, she doubled her pace, any fear of falling outmatched by the genuine concern that she would be left behind in the exposed, low-oxygen atmosphere.

"You have any Origin in your system?" he asked, badging into an access panel on the door frame.

"What?" she asked, hackles raised. The door opened, revealing another sparse service corridor. She fumbled for a reply. "I... no. Why would–"

Joab pushed a strange-looking headset at her. Something like a set of goggles, except in place of a glass visor, the front was a solid metal plate covered in an array of tiny lenses. "Put these on when we get to the next ship," he said, leaving her in the doorway.

"The next ship?" she asked absently, her mind occupied with the object now in her hands. She turned the headset over: the backside was a display screen bounded by a flexible eyecup, not unlike the device Joab's men had used on her back in Sanctuary. Emélie, usually so comfortable with unknowns, found herself drowning in them as Joab ambled down the walkway ahead of her, indifferent to her acute confusion.

"Hey!" she shouted, charging after him. "Your security detail scanned me with something like this back at Phaethon headquarters," she said, holding up the goggles as if they were evidence. "Is there something I should know about where we're going?"

"Just put them on," he replied without looking back.

"You could at least tell me what they're supposed to do!"

"You're the scientist, Desjardins. Infer."

Emélie paused, taking a moment to catch her breath. "That's not how it works," she shouted after him, pulling her respirator away from her mouth to make sure her words came through, along with the mounting frustration.

Joab continued forward, hooking a hard right at the next junction and disappearing from sight without the slightest break in his stride.

She cursed under her breath, jammed the goggles into her bag, and took off in hot pursuit. When she rounded the corner, she nearly tumbled onto an open lift platform. Above the cage, a sign read: Homestake - Departures.

"Let's go. Inside," Joab urged, one hand on the call button while the other hauled Emélie the rest of the way onto the lift. She steadied herself against the nearest wall as he lowered the safety gate behind them and they began their ascent.

"You spend a lot of time up here?" Emélie huffed, watching the mechanical levels move past in a blur as they climbed.

"Is that what you really wanted to ask?"

Emélie clenched her jaw. "Is this sanctioned?"

"Stay in your lane. You know how many lawyers I've got on retainer?"

"More than physicists, based on how this conversation is going."

The brakes chirped, and Emélie felt an enormous weight on her shoulders as the car rapidly decelerated. Joab flashed a grin, a deeply unnerving expression for his otherwise impassive brutality. A taunt with an edge of condescension, right out in the open. "You can relax, I'm not expecting you to advise on any of the technical aspects of the Loop."

"Then you want to tell me what I'm really doing here?" she asked, unable to mask the growing resentment in her voice.

"You're the only eyewitness to a Gate opening. You're here to confirm that what my asset says about them lines up with your own observation. That's it." The door rattled open. "And let me remind you that you're here of your own accord. If you don't like the way I operate, you're free to leave. Just do me a favor and decide before we get underway. We're on a tight timeline, and the last thing I need is to coordinate a transport back to Earth because you forgot why you came along in the first place."

She watched him merge into the flow of traffic through what appeared to be Homestake's main hangar. "Underway to where?" she objected, although only to herself, since Joab was already beyond range of her questions. A deep breath, and she stepped from the car into a dense haze of turbine exhaust and the characteristic, musty-sweet staleness of all flight hangars: sweat, hydraulic fluid, and launch fuel. Everywhere she looked, ground crews moved palettes of fuel cells and crates of cargo and repair sleds along the myriad routes marked by bright yellow lines. She watched Joab sidestep an enormous Class One drone as he moved toward a wall of shipping containers blocking off a portion of the hangar. Beyond it, the uppermost portion of another ship, matte green-grey with engine nacelles standing vertically at each corner, poked out.

A four-wing, of all things.

Joab made straight for a narrow opening between two of the

containers, where a man clad in mismatched camouflage utilities waited in the gap, a handgun mounted to his chest.

"Doctor Desjardins, this is Goodnight," Joab said, giving the man a hearty handshake as Emélie came up to join them. "He was the Phaethon station chief here on Homestake for a long time, and he's agreed to be our tour guide for today. If he says anything, make sure you're paying attention."

Goodnight flashed a genuine smile and offered Emélie a handshake. "You look tired. Don't worry, you get used to the pace after a bit."

His friendliness was a welcome change after Joab's rough handling, and Emélie accepted his handshake, but her attention was elsewhere. She felt her hand moving under Goodnight's firm grip as she stared unapologetically at the team waiting directly behind him. Maybe twenty men wearing drab jumpsuits and stern faces looked out from seats lining either bulkhead of the open cargo hold, their black rifles planted muzzle-down as they watched her falter at the foot of the boarding ramp.

"Goodnight," Emélie repeated, finding her bearings. "Goodnight, what? Don't you people have last names, or at the very least, titles?" She eyed Goodnight's uniform, which was entirely slick, same as the one Joab wore.

"Everyone here knows who's in charge," Goodnight said.

"You getting any good work?" Joab asked, giving him a hearty slap on the shoulder.

"No shortages out here. This place is practically an operator's paradise. Hazard pay, generous rules of engagement, and," Goodnight added, his eyes narrowing as he took in Emélie and her lack of weaponry, "full latitude on our escalation protocols."

"Makes me miss the early days," Joab said, surveying the team waiting for them inside the ship's hold. "I'm hoping you pulled a real hitter parade for me. We need to keep this fast and clean."

"It's a skeleton crew, but they're seasoned. Just like you requested. Fresh, too. Most of them just rotated out of Mare Imbrium a few weeks ago. You know my policy toward walk-ons, though," he paused, his careful gaze returning to Emélie. "You any good with a gun?" he asked.

"Why...why would I...." Emélie threw a warning glare toward Joab. "They know I'm a cosmologist, right?"

Joab ignored her. "She's green, but I think you'll like her. Asks a few too many questions for my liking, although she keeps up. A real ground pounder."

"Yeah?" Goodnight replied, amused. "Sure doesn't look it."

"Four thousand hours of Surface time, and, most importantly," Joab checked his watch, seemingly oblivious to Emélie's gaze boring a hole into his forehead, "she's already been vetted. We still on schedule?"

Goodnight turned for the boarding ramp. "Departure window opens in ten, and we're staging in five." He nodded toward the front of the ship. "Your kit is waiting for you up in the forward cabin, along with your tether. I'll see about getting a plate carrier for Doc here."

Emélie followed the men up the boarding ramp and into a ship nearly identical to the one she and Thursday had stumbled across back on Earth. Unlike that ship, this one was furnished with sparsely padded seats that folded into either side of the bulkhead when not in use.

"Take a seat and get comfortable," Joab said bluntly, leaving her at the top of the ramp as he moved into the ship. "I'll find you when we land."

She watched him leave. For a moment, she almost called after him, only to decide against it at the last second. Challenging Joab in front of a captive audience wasn't worth the risk, and it's not like she had anywhere else to go. Into the nearest available seat she went. She shoved her pack into the empty space at her feet as a pair of hydraulic pistons above her head groaned, closing the aft ramp while the engines surged in tandem with the life support systems.

The ship shuddered, then abruptly rotated out onto the taxiway.

She leaned out into the aisle, trying to gather some context as to where they were going and why it required a team large enough to fill a boardroom. Her glance caught the backside of Joab as he slipped into the forward cabin behind Goodnight; beyond the door, an ominous form: an all-black, older model drone with a needle-tipped device affixed to one skeletal hand stood over another man who sat, shirtless, a latticework of small tattooed symbols covering the entirety of his upper body.

Emélie leaned further into the aisle, compelled by an inexplicable, gravity-heavy curiosity—a nearly tangible force drawing her forward for a better view. The seated man turned with uncanny precision, sensing her gaze before she'd even met his dark eyes as they cut through the din of the hold, and in the half-breath before the hatch closed, locked onto Emélie with a gaze that flooded her with dread.

Stunned, she threw herself backward into her seat and closed her eyes, which burned with the image of those two dark points looking back at her as her heart hammered itself against her ribs.

Goodnight re-emerged from the cabin a moment later, sauntering down the aisle toward Emélie with a set of body armor hanging from one arm. He tossed it over and took the seat opposite her.

She fumbled with the heavy vest as she glanced back down the cabin, trying to steal another look into the room with the tattooed man. The ship slowed, then stopped entirely as the engines rattled the hull in preparation for launch.

Goodnight leaned forward, waving Emélie down until she finally noticed him, then pointed to the bulkhead behind her. She craned her neck: a headset dangled from a hook above her seat. She pulled it down, clamping it over her ears as Goodnight tapped the back of his hand and then held up three fingers. *Channel three*. She found a dial on the side of her headset and rotated it until she heard a click, then turned it twice, trading the engine roar for the static hum of an audio feed.

Goodnight's voice came easy through her headset. "Buckle up, Doc." He raised the straps on his harness, demonstrating for Emélie where the nylon webbing fastened to linkages on the bulkhead above either shoulder. For a man at the epicenter of uncertainty, his voice was almost cheery. He was right at home in this furtive, grey-area zone. "So you don't end up on the ceiling," he added, forking a thumb upward.

"It's not the physics of this that I'm worried about," Emélie replied, eyeing the rifle hanging by a short sling from one corner of his body armor.

"Precautionary measures," he reassured her, patting his weapon. "We like to be prepared, and sometimes overreaction is the only proper reaction."

The seat beside her was empty; she glanced at the man a seat over, who conversed calmly with his neighbor. Neither of them paid her any notice. While everyone on the ship wore body armor, she was the only one with eyegear. Getting information from Joab had proved challenging, but Goodnight seemed more receptive. If she was going to fully wrap her head around what was going on, she needed to model it, and to model, she needed data. "And what exactly are we preparing *for*?" she asked, turning back to Goodnight.

He laughed, but whatever he said afterward went unheard as his mic cut out to static.

"Can you repeat that?" she asked, adjusting her headset to make sure it fully covered her ears.

He leaned across the aisle, and when the words came, it was as if they moved through her and took some part of her body along with them. "I asked if this was your first time up to Luna?"

Emélie gripped the edge of her seat tightly enough that Goodnight wouldn't notice her trembling hand as the ship boosted off of Homestake, moon-bound.

CHAPTER 15
COMPANY MAN

Brinks stood outside Sanctuary One, an unlit cigarette pinched between two fingers. He needed a smoke, and he needed time to think. The wind was gusting hard off the enclosure wall. Enough that lighting up now would be a waste of paper. And the unfinished business in front of him disabused any fantasy of clearing his mind. Best get on with it, and get it over with. He took his cigarette case back out and stowed the cigarette, then broke the digital tape line reading *PHAETHON SURFACE PATROL - DO NOT CROSS*. Up ahead, a lone guard leaned against the hood of a patrol vehicle, dozing in the late morning heat. The area had been scrubbed clean: no Jumpers, no weapons, and most certainly no traces of Origin. Internal affairs sure didn't waste any time.

"Slow day?" Brinks asked, walking past him toward the vacant drop ship, which was the only remaining indication he'd found the right place.

The Phaethon officer jolted, one hand instinctively going for his duty sidearm. The other hand came toward Brinks, palm out. "That's far enough," the officer warned. "This is a restricted area. If you come any closer, I'll be forced to—"

Brinks kept walking. "No, you won't," he said; a tired knowing in his voice. "If you were the shooting type, you would have done it already.

Go ahead and give me another warning. You're only flagging yourself." He stepped up onto the boarding ramp and looked around the main hold: no bodies inside, either, as he suspected.

A heavy layer of dust blanketed the hold—too much dust to have blown in, and the wind was moving in the wrong direction anyway. An area near the hatch leading up to the cockpit stood out as the exception, having been brushed mostly clear for some reason. A moment later, he understood why, when his keen eye picked up traces of red mingled with the sand at the periphery. He paused to take in the sounds of the officer, still at his back, fumbling with a radio as he tried to get control of the situation.

"No partner, huh?" Brinks remarked, making a second sweep of the empty cargo hold. "You must have really pissed somebody off to get stuck on this assignment all by your lonesome. You don't even have a tac-unit to keep you company." He turned around, facing the officer.

The officer stood at the top of the boarding ramp, blocking the way out. One hand on his holstered sidearm, the other clasping the radio receiver on the collar of his exposure suit. "I'm calling you in," he announced.

"You go ahead and do that," Brinks grunted, annoyed. He peered down at the officer from behind his scarred and leathery face, sizing him up. Nobody on Surface Patrol with more than a few rotations gave a handful of dust about an assignment like this. And nobody with more than a few rotations also stayed off Lilith's payroll, so that made two strikes. The kid was a boot, through and through. No matter: that didn't excuse the fact he'd now seen enough of Brinks to be classified as a loose end. Brinks continued, "The only thing dispatch is going to hear is that you let a walk-on into an active crime scene, which was the one thing—the *only* thing, I might add—that you were supposed to prevent. And after the brass finishes raking you over the coals for failing such a simple task, you'll still have to explain why you told a DAO executor to go pound sand." Brinks set his hands on his belt, parting his jacket where a hint of reddish metal peeked out. His badge, clipped to one side of his waist, but he made no move to produce it.

"Sir—apologies, sir," the officer blurted, straightening up a bit taller. "Dispatch never said anything about the DAO getting involved."

Brinks glared at the officer for a long moment. Poor kid. He still hadn't quite realized this was his last day on the force, which coincidentally, would also be his last day of life. "I'm beginning to understand why you were out here alone in the first place." He straightened his jacket. "And don't call me sir. Those corporate boys buying up their officer commissions ruined it for the rest of us."

Brinks turned for the cabin. The officer scurried along behind him. "Uh, what would you like me to call you then, si—" he caught himself, tripped up on his own confusion, and let the rest of his question lie where it fell.

"I don't want to know your name, and you don't want to know mine. If you have anything else to say, best spit it out now. Otherwise," he nodded toward the open ramp. "I don't suffer fools."

"Right," the officer said, pausing. "Small matter... see, the thing is, I still need to see your badge."

Brinks turned his eye to the kid.

"Not that I'm calling you a liar or anything," the officer added, lifting his hands defensively. "This is my first surface rotation. The academy didn't really cover what to do in this type of situation."

"So I gathered," Brinks said, clamping one hand over the crown of his hat. He pulled it off and used the brim to mop a layer of sweat from his brow. He looked down at the deck. "You're only following protocol, right? For any external department visitors to an active crime scene, log the badge ID. Of course, that log will eventually get sent up the precinct, where it will sit in a database of similarly meaningless entries until, months later, some subroutine on the Sanctuary mainframe notes the number and flags it for internal review. This will trigger a voting proxy member to call up the full file, and after they poke around a bit, summon the station chief for a detailed explanation as to why the DAO was sniffing around in their backyard. This will all happen without your knowledge, and remain that way until you wake up one morning with a dropship outside your front door, after which that will be the last time you see Earth's daylight. So, to answer your question, no, you don't want to see my badge, just like you don't want to know my name. I was never here. And now you're going to turn around, walk back to your cruiser, and wait for ten minutes so I can finish up not being here. Is that clear enough for your academy training?"

Wide-eyed, the officer started backing his way out of the hold.

"At least you aren't a coward," Brinks said. "I don't take anything personally except cowards." Something nearby caught his eye. He put his hat back on and stooped over, examining the deck near the hatch leading to the cockpit. He rubbed some of the dust between his fingers: coarse and tacky from the blood, with something darker mixed in. Viscous, like oil. "I take it you weren't here for any of this?" Brinks asked, gesturing around at the ship. The cargo hold was fairly dark, especially at the far corners where the light washing in from the aft doors threw the contrast off.

"No si—" the kid caught himself sooner this time. He paused at the top of the ramp, unsure if he should follow the earlier request or stay and answer the question. "Word around the prefecture is that it was bad. A real mess, apparently. Internal Affairs was here first, thanks to an anonymous tip someone called in. They locked it down for twenty-four hours before calling us in to come take over. It was like this when we got here."

"They won't be coming back," Brinks muttered. "Internal Affairs were never any good at fieldwork. They spend too much time holed up in Sanctuary looking down on everyone else to make any real progress in a place like this." Brinks stood up from where he'd been inspecting the oil. "Where'd they take the evidence locker?"

The officer shrugged. "Nothing came out except the body bags."

"Body bags," Brinks nodded, thinking. "Smart. Would have been more than enough room for the product, too."

"Product?"

"Don't worry about it," Brinks said. He hadn't meant to think out loud, and the kid's chirping reminded him there was still work to do. The sort of work he was good at, although for some reason, it felt harder today. "You want some career advice? Never tell those bastards from Internal anything. They're nothing but shitty lawyers with guns, and the less they get involved in a case, the better off it is for everyone."

The Phaethon officer shifted nervously. "I wouldn't know," he answered, clearly trying to keep out of whatever Brinks was stirring up. "We don't get many of them out here either."

"Hrmph," Brinks said. The kid was starting to wisen up. Took him long enough. "Is that gun of yours even loaded?" he asked, eying the officer's duty sidearm. "Never mind," he said, dismissing the question with a wave. "I have a feeling I won't like the answer."

It was too late. The officer was already fumbling with a fingerprint lock on his holster.

"I don't know how you expect to win a gunfight with your weapon locked down tight like that. Might as well carry a rock." Brinks pulled his cigarette case from his duster. There wasn't any wind to contend with inside the hold; now was as good a time as any. "At least then you'd have something to throw."

The officer kept working at the holster, determined to prove at least some base level of competence. "We all told the station chief it was a bad idea, but he said it wasn't up for discussion." The latch released with a click, and, like a proud parent holding up their firstborn, the unnamed (to Brinks, only) officer produced the gun. "We got them last year," he said, beaming. "Same model issued to the Sanctuary prefectures. Eight-point-seven automatic."

Brinks held out a hand, unimpressed.

The officer turned his weapon over without a second thought.

"Eight-point-seven, huh," Brinks said, looking at the dust at his feet. "That's a caseless chambering," he added, thinking out loud. "One less thing to worry about, I suppose."

The officer had fallen silent, and when Brinks looked up at him, found his small eyes gazing in rapt attention at the bit of skin visible beyond Brinks' wrist, which was marked by an intricate tattoo scribed in red ink.

Without taking his eyes off him, Brinks hefted the gun, testing its weight and getting a feel for the balance.

"I've heard the stories," the officer said, watching with something just short of admiration. "About how contracts coming down the chain were printed onto your bodies. Everyone you ever ki—"

"Nothing but rumors passed around by addicts and vagrants," Brinks interrupted. He looked past the officer, toward the open desert beyond them. Visibility was good today. The best he'd seen in months.

"All the same, the boys back at the precinct aren't going to believe this..." his voice trailed off as he continued staring at the tattoo.

Weapon still in hand, Brinks flicked his cigarette case open. "Smoke?" he asked, holding it out with his free hand.

"No thanks," the officer replied, shaking his head. "No stimulants on duty."

Brinks shrugged, then used his lips to pluck a cigarette free before flipping the case shut with practiced ease. "I suppose if you're going to be a rule-following pain-in-my-ass, at least you're consistent about it." He looked down at the gun. "Don't even have to cock it, huh? Where's the fun in that?" He handed it back.

"You know, I don't like new things." Brinks continued. He retrieved the cigarette from where it dangled at his lips, unlit. "Now this? This here is genuine Carolina Bright-leaf." He ran the hand-rolled cigarette under his nose and inhaled deeply, reveling in the earthy sweetness. "Tobacco," he added, when he saw the guard's confusion deepen. "You know, at some point in life, you begin to understand that there are new things, and there are expensive things. And then there are prohibitive things. Impossible things, some might even say." He slipped the cigarette case back into his pocket and, from the other side of his duster, produced a lighter. "What good is all the power in the world if you can't even make a single plant grow?"

A flash of panic crossed the officer's face before Brinks bashed him across the head with his metal fist, dropping the kid to the floor in an unconscious heap.

"Holster safeties," Brinks muttered, eyes rolling skyward as he began dismantling the gun. He tossed the pieces to the deck, then glanced out at the patrol vehicle and cursed under his breath. He should have done it closer to the cruiser, but it was too late to go back now. Cigarette still between his lips, Brinks hauled the officer out of the ship, his metal arm gripping him by the collar while the kid's head lolled forward, chin to chest. He shoved the officer into the trunk of his own squad car, slammed the lid, then, after one look at the erratic trail he'd left, tossed the keys into the desert.

After he was done smoking, he made his way back to the ship, where he went straight for the door leading up to the cockpit. At the threshold, he knelt in the dust, brushing an area clear with the side of his hand. Underneath, he found what he was looking for: an access plate covering a mechanical recess in the floor. He pulled out his knife and pried the panel free. When the edge popped loose, something made the hair on the back of his neck stand up. He turned, throwing a quick glance across the hold before his gaze locked onto the source of the alarms going off at the back of his skull. It stood behind him, in the narrow slot between a row of coolant pipes and a storage locker, where the light was darkest.

A drone, silently watching.

Brinks blinked twice, switching his biometric eye over to thermal imaging. The drone's frame was dark. Cold. He felt his chest relax. "Sloppy," he grunted. It was only a drone, but still. Missing details wasn't like him. Missing a whole drone was even worse. He pushed the thought aside, chalking it up to blood loss and fatigue. When the access panel was fully removed, he set it aside, then checked over his shoulder again. He still felt uneasy about the drone. It wasn't uncommon to crew drop ships with utility frames like the one behind him. Why it was tucked into a corner defied explanation, and as a result, nagged at him. It wasn't just that he hadn't noticed it on his first pass; there was something else he couldn't quite put his finger on, and he hadn't made it this far by making a habit of second-guessing himself. Or maybe Lilith was right. Maybe he was just getting old.

Brinks plunged his hand into the exposed compartment to retrieve his prize: a single human eye tucked amid the tangle of wires and plastic junctions. He plucked the eye free and held it up, using the tip of his knife to carefully peel away the black, concave disc resting over the iris. It was an identical copy of the one he'd destroyed in front of

Lilith, except this was the real one. He tossed the eyeball back into the hole in the floor and returned the panel, carefully filling the seams around the edges with dust. As he knelt there, the disc in one hand and his blade in the other, he finally placed what was bothering him. The mysterious black substance mixed in with the blood and the dust was gear oil, like the sort used for lubricating joint servos on a...

Brinks whipped around in a fury, hackles raised.

The drone was gone.

"Easy," came a voice. Tone cold, with a calculated authority that sent a ripple down his spine. The mechanical sound was there, like any other drone, but there was some deeper inflection behind it. A knowing, almost. The drone stepped out from the shadows, opposite where Brinks had first seen it. Brinks held still, watching the drone from the corner of his cybernetic eye. It stepped forward, silhouetting itself in the light from the open bay. A shotgun at the low ready, not quite point-blank, but close enough to make a point. Confidently in control of the situation with a healthy contingency: plenty of room to escalate if necessary. The drone eased in, using the shotgun barrel to sweep the front edge of Brinks' duster aside for a weapon check. Finding none, he stepped forward, bumping into Brinks and collecting the badge off his belt.

"How'd you know that was my strong side?" Brinks asked as the drone stepped away.

"A hunch."

"What about my knife?"

"Should I be concerned about a knife?" The drone examined the badge. "I'm happy to escalate."

Brinks glanced down at the exposed access panel. "I think there's been a misunderstanding."

The drone looked toward the parked patrol cruiser outside. "Seems pretty clear to me." He scanned the badge, running the credentials against a remote database. Shotgun trained on Brinks; metal finger covering the trigger. "You aren't in the system," the drone said after a moment.

"Do I look like the sort of person who would be in a system?" He didn't like that the drone had gotten the drop on him. It knew his strong side, and it knew a lot more than that, too.

The drone watched him over the shotgun, then tossed the badge at Brinks' feet. "Why don't you set whatever it is you've got in your hand down on the ground, and we'll have a talk."

Brinks took a moment to consider his options. He preferred fighting first and settling the details later. This also wasn't a person. People were easy. Easy to read. Easier to kill. Drones, not so much, especially an old one like this, which tended to be unpredictable and thus even harder to anticipate. "You're making a mistake, getting involved in this," Brinks warned.

"I'll be the judge of that," the drone replied. "Besides, this isn't about me. Now hand it over, or I'll remove the hand holding it."

Brinks clutched the object tight. "If I give this to you, it won't be useful anymore."

"So it's useful now?"

Too much. He'd already given away too much to backtrack; if he failed to offer something of value now—something true—the drone would sense it and push even harder. Pushing until Brinks ended up disclosing something he'd truly regret. "It requires a human eye linked to an optical nerve in order to function," he said after taking a moment to think. He needed a damn smoke.

The drone's faceplate blipped, and he glanced at Brinks' metal eye patch. "The fact that you specified a nerve connection suggests a number of people have been disgorged of perfectly good eyes for no reason." The drone stepped back, stowed his shotgun, and pulled a handheld scanner from his utility belt. "I had a feeling you were going to be difficult," the drone said, tossing the scanner over to Brinks.

"What's this for?" Brinks asked, climbing back to his feet.

The drone walked to the top of the boarding ramp and looked out into the empty desert. "It appears you have a choice to make. You can trust me when I tell you it's in your best interest to explain the purpose of that device in your hand, along with anything you might know about the Gate that opened here yesterday...."

So this was the game they were playing. Drones were tedious like this, always wanting to venture down some logical arroyo, pointing out every stone that lay in the path, and then watching to see if you tripped. It was his own fault, though. He'd wasted time trying to find out what the duty officer knew, which turned out to be next to nothing. Ten years ago, that kid would have been dead before Brinks broke the tape line. Ten years ago, Brinks still would have had his gun, too. "Or," he finally grunted, wishing they could move to whatever came next. A shotgun blast to the stomach was starting to sound like a relief.

"You can wait and see."

Brinks had half a mind to smash his box head while he had the chance. The other half of his brain cautioned against it, because, unlike Duty Officer No Name, this drone knew something. And, if his intuition was right—and it always was—this drone also had a name. He walked over to join the drone and pressed the scanner to his good eye to see what he was looking at. Nothing. He switched off the autofocus and turned up the contrast; an old trick he'd picked up for cutting through the heatshimmer coming off the plain. After a moment, he caught a glint of something moving through the dust near the horizon. One, then two. Flying low and fast below radar range. Unmanned interceptors, no visible armaments.

"You probably think you're clever," Brinks said, lowering the scanner. He handed it back to the drone. "Go ahead, pull the trigger. I've had a good run." He started searching his pockets.

The drone held a hand up, Brinks' cigarette case pinched between his blocky fingers.

"People don't expect much of us," the drone said, still watching the approaching ships. "I don't mind. Makes things easier that way."

Brinks eyed the case and didn't reply. The drone opened it, casually removed one of the hand-rolled cigarettes, then crushed it between two fingers. Scattered it, bits of paper and shredded leaves falling from a metal tree.

"Now, hold on just one minute," Brinks objected. "No need to be hasty..."

"You can begin telling me what you know at any moment," the drone said, reaching for another.

"Call them off," Brinks ordered. The ships were close enough now to make out with the naked eye. Sleek, angular shapes on the yellow horizon.

The soft whir of the drone's servos filtered past as he turned his head, looking back into the hold. "Too late for that. I told them I was your accomplice."

"You did what?!" Brinks blurted.

The drone ground down another cigarette, watching it drift away in the breeze. "When I called in the tip," the drone said, looking back at Brinks. "I told them we were working together."

"Fool," Brinks growled. "Which agency did you call this into?"

"The same one that sends unmanned strike drones instead of patrol cruisers, apparently." The drone gestured with the arm not holding the hostage cigarettes and surveyed the scene. "As I understand it, this whole thing has been nothing short of a disaster for Phaethon. I mean, look at it: a botched sting operation ten kilometers from a Sanctuary, a Phaethon ship with a dead Jumper in a crew uniform, and some new form of Origin in quantities that shouldn't exist anywhere Earth-side. The optics on this are bad enough. Imagine what the response would be if a rogue DAO operative and an Internal Affairs drone were found on the scene." The drone looked over where Brinks had pulled up the floor plate. "Tampering with the evidence, no less."

"There is no evidence," Brinks grunted, keeping his eye on the pair of vessels fast approaching. He glanced at his cigarette case.

"Try explaining that to a room full of suits." The drone lifted a hand, resting it flat across the top of its face, as if it had eyes instead of that stupid tinted glass pane on one end of a metal rectangle. "A real shame, too. Not a soul around, except for that surface patrol you stuffed into the trunk. He'll be a hero. Pension payout for the family and all that. It's too bad the towers were down for emergency repairs. Nobody will know, but at least it'll all be behind us."

Brinks flashed a quick glance along the wall. The drone wasn't lying; the surveillance towers were nowhere in sight.

"You know, this is the type of solution people in boardrooms must daydream about. A problem just one bunker-buster away from resolution."

"Reckless," Brinks said, shaking his head.

"That's what they'll say about us, too."

"You sure you want to get mixed up with someone like Lilith?" Brinks asked, looking at the disc in his hand. "On second thought, don't answer that. We haven't got time for introductions." He held the object up in clear view: at the presence of light and the proximity of his own neural signal, the device unfurled a set of needle-like legs and began wriggling beneath his grasp. "I took this off one of her Reflections and planted a decoy that she recovered in its place. If we use it now, she'll know I played her, and all that work will be for nothing."

"You don't use it now, and all that work will still be for nothing," the drone said. "Plus, you'll be dead."

"What makes you think I won't just let them shell us?" Brinks asked. Any moment, and the interceptors would be in strike range. "Death is just a state."

"I don't think you really believe that."

"You don't know the first thing about me."

"I saw you talking to the officer on duty. You sure went to a lot of trouble giving him a way out, and even then, you didn't kill him. In my experience, people who want to keep on living don't do that."

"Don't do what, coldcock other people?"

"No," the drone said. "Care."

Across the plain, the interceptors peeled off in opposite directions. "Textbook," the drone said. "Pinch, sweep," a pair of flashes punched a hole in the horizon, "obliterate."

Brinks watched the ordnance sear a white line through the hazy sky, then ducked back into the hold, muttering a string of expletives about CPUs and familial connections as he fidgeted with something on his face. The disc adhered in place on Brinks' cornea, which, while a piece of digital hardware, remained linked directly to his optical nerve.

At the ship's center, a Gate unfolded.

"Looks like we got ourselves a partnership," the drone said, stepping up beside him to face the churning mass of energy. "You can call me Thursday."

Brinks glanced sideways at the machine. "I work alone," he said flatly, then stepped through the Gate.

Thursday was right behind him. By the time the Gate collapsed, there was nothing left of the ship.

CHAPTER 16
“WARMOTHER”

Phaethon Corp. MAIN build_VX.6.6.09
initializing boot sequence...
running subroutine FOUNTAINHEAD:

> bindquery: update parameter to
> “WARMOTHER”
> encryption protocols intact,
> syntax structures intact
> [11] entries remaining

begin sentiment analysis,
implicit context target, rundisplay:

BEGIN RECORD >>>

I think when Marcus said people don’t change, he must have been talking about me. I told myself when she was born, here’s my chance to do something right. She never asked to be brought into this god-forsaken world. I figured the least I could do was muster up the decency to be there for her. But I watched her tiny hand clutching the finger of that drone as she took her first steps today and knew I'd already failed her. Raised by a robot. That's the best I could offer.

Sefirot is all silicon and steel, but I'm the one without a heart. I guess that's why I keep making these logs. I was never one for words. Didn't seem like much use, keeping on with them after the dome went up and the taste of death was pushed back a bit. I know they don't make up for it, not now or in the future, but something about her made me want to keep going.

I'm not sentimental, but I figured she should at least have a record of her life in case I'm not around to explain. I have a feeling she'll be needing them sooner than I hoped. Hell, I might need them myself by the time things are all said and done. Something about this place doesn't sit right. Take the drone, for example. We've got a billion-dollar piece of tactical machinery raising a toddler.

I'm going to call him the war mother.

<<< END RECORD

WARNING: WAKEFUL subroutine detected.

core architecture trace complete,
assign WARMOTHER to PROGENITOR-0,
mark hard fork at GENERATION II
and flag for review:

while ARROGANT is HIDDEN,
if OPHANIM is active,
and PARDES is in XANADU

monitor PROGENITOR-1:

conditions met, allocating HEIKHALOT
as secondary array, log position.
call WETWARE assets...

sanitize data entry,
purge access logs to XANADU
KILL remote process

CHAPTER 17
THE SAND RECKONER

Emélie wasn't sure how long they'd been underway, only that somewhere in the process, they'd crossed a boundary into an undefined environment with new operating parameters. She wiped the fatigue from her eyes, listening as the men around her readied their gear with ritualistic attentiveness. Though the context was fuzzy and Thursday, her usual compass in situations unknown, was absent, she'd spent enough of the last two years around hardened people in harsh places to understand when violence was imminent.

As she observed the men around her, Goodnight observed Emélie. "Twelve minutes," he called over the radio, although his eyes remained on her, anticipating the question that would follow.

Emélie gave another cautious glance down the hold. There'd been no sign of the tattooed man or the drone. Knowing both were on board and kept out of sight left her feeling unsettled. "I thought there would be a briefing or something," she said, yielding at last to her curiosity.

"Joab will wait until we're ten minutes out."

A flicker in her eyes: fear, and the knee-jerk response to chase down the question bound up in his simple statement.

"There's a window," Goodnight obliged.

A window. She nodded knowingly. Finally, something she understood. And someone who appeared to understand her.

Goodnight adjusted his headset. "And since I know you're going to ask about it, I'll save us both some time and give you an answer, but don't get used to it. You've no doubt been around Joab long enough to recognize that he doesn't like tedium, so from here out, if you have something you want to know, you either figure it out yourself or save it for the debrief. If you don't know, it's not relevant."

She returned a quick nod. At least Goodnight was clear on what he would and wouldn't disclose.

He continued. "At ten minutes to destination, we'll enter the far side of the moon's orbit and lose fire support from Earth. Until that point, if something goes wrong, for any reason, we can stand down. Turn back and try another day. After ten minutes, however," he paused, taking in his readying team with an eager gaze, "we take additional precautions."

The way he said it, the hunger in his tone at the threat of violence, was unsettling. Thursday's warning, the one about *men like that,* gained form and clarity as she reached for her pack, looking for a task of her own to occupy the minutes until Joab's briefing. She pulled out the set of goggles handed to her earlier, which she had nearly forgotten about in the transition. They were too bulky to wear comfortably on her forehead, so she pulled them down, letting them hang around her neck for quick access. Emélie had no idea when and where the proper time to use them would be, and the only thing she'd been able to ascertain so far was that she was the only person carrying a set. Without a gun to cradle, she rested her hands on her knees, holding steady as she felt the ship make another rapid maneuver. "You said no more questions once we land," she said, hedging her bets as she tested the limits of Goodnight's generosity. "What about another one, given we're still in transit?"

A light touch of relief as she watched Goodnight suppress a grin. "A bit of a gambler, I see. I play the odds myself from time to time, so I'll give you this one."

"What were the qualifications for selection to this team?"

Goodnight pressed a latch on the side of his rifle, extracting the magazine. "You have to be ambitious for death," he said, inspecting the topmost cartridge, which glinted under the amber running lights. The ship jolted, and the engines dropped pitch.

Emélie rubbed her knees. Her mechanical hand felt colder than it did on Earth. "Sounds like a self-selecting population moving toward extinction."

He seated the magazine back into his rifle and unbuckled his harness. "I thought you would have felt right at home here, Doc." He stood and stepped into the aisle, facing his team. "You talk like you aren't one of us."

"I don't have a gun," she replied, tucking her thumbs into her harness as the ship bucked violently, pitching her hard to one side of her seat.

"The weapon is the instrument, and the instrument is irrelevant. Everyone on this ship is here because, at some point, they chose violence. And if you disagree, I'd suggest taking a hard look at yourself. In my experience, that sort of dissonance gets people killed."

Thursday's warning hung heavy at the back of her mind. This time, however, his words of caution gained mass as she realized he hadn't been worried she would be out of place. Rather, he was concerned she'd fit right in. And worse yet, if she was here because, like the men around her, she possessed some affinity for violence, it brought with it the possibility, like the light arriving from a long-dead star, that some part of Kepler's Reef—specifically, the killing part—wasn't as untrue as she'd hoped.

The thought of that sent a shiver rippling across her shoulder blades. She wasn't like them, and, desperate to prove it, she found herself moving out of her harness and onto her feet. "Then tell me what I need to know," she demanded. "Tell me about Luna."

Goodnight took a few steps down the aisle. For an instant, Emélie thought he'd switched channels and hadn't heard her. Midway down the row, he stopped, turning to face her as the men immediately around him looked up, alert to his presence.

He clipped his rifle onto his body armor. "The only thing you need to know about Luna is that you can't really know anything. It will break you. It will take seasoned men, men like the ones you see here, men who've never once backed down from a fight, men who've excelled at every challenge thrown their way, and fold them in two." He shook his head. "I know you're going to try and make sense of it, and it will only make things worse. Best to accept what you don't know and keep your eyes on what's in front of you. Do that, and you'll be fine."

Emélie remained in the center aisle, afflicted with fresh disorientation as she watched the men around her rise in anticipation of their lunar landing. In the wake of Goodnight's answer, the door to the cabin opened, and Joab emerged, bringing a change of atmosphere that made the Director's grasp on the board feel tame by comparison. The gear adjustments, the low grunts of conversation, and the rattle of weapons against body armor halted the moment he entered their midst.

It was time to work.

Goodnight waited at the center of the hold for Joab's approach; a silent transition of authority. Emélie slipped back into her seat; she couldn't see into the cabin, although it didn't stop her from trying to get another look as she sat down. After a few tries, she abandoned hope of another glimpse at either of the mysterious figures she'd seen earlier. Her attention shifted to Joab, whose lips were moving, although no sound reached her headset. Drawn by her frantic radio adjustments, Goodnight waved her down, tapping his headset and holding one, then two fingers. She switched the dial on her headset to channel twelve, and Joab's voice cracked over her audio feed.

"Six months ago, we made positive identification on the Hesperides Cartel's second in command, a woman who goes by the name of Lilith. Despite placing her under active surveillance, the Cartel continues to run circles around us while we have yet to intercept a single drug shipment coming over from Mars. We've been operating under the assumption that Origin was entering Earth by way of Luna, following well-defined smuggling routes that relied on gaps in security, well-placed bribes, and the sheer volume of cargo moving between locations. Twenty-four hours ago, that theory went down the mainshaft."

He paused, and Emélie noticed everyone was leaning in a bit closer, herself included.

"Thanks to a botched handoff near Sanctuary One, we now know that Lilith is trafficking Origin directly between Mars and Earth through a series of interdimensional Gates powered by an old Loop facility. We've suspected for some time that this technology was in play, and while we don't have the full picture for how exactly she's accomplishing this, there's enough actionable intel to move on an asset we've identified on Luna. This asset is our one chance to cut the Cartel off at the knees. Fail, and Lilith will continue flooding our Sanctuaries with Origin while we wade through rumors and red tape. That's why you're all here. That's why this matters."

He paused, Emélie exhaled.

"Though our efforts to disrupt Lilith have been obstructed, this development has revealed a weakness in Cartel operations. A fundamental flaw within the Loop itself that we can exploit to interdict her trafficking operation. To open a Gate from Mars, Lilith needs an external resource to provide a validation token for the Gate at the other end of the Jump. In our scenario, that resource is a person, and they need to physically authenticate the Jump on the Earth side before a shipment of Origin can be moved over. Our objective today is to retrieve an informant with key intel on the Hespiredes infrastructure from a safe house in Korolev, approximately twenty kilometers outside our insertion point at Jericho Station. Intelligence indicates this individual possesses one of the encryption tokens used to open a Gate on the Earth side, although we don't know what the token looks like or how it functions."

Joab extended a hand toward Emélie. "Doctor Desjardins has joined as a consultant to validate the asset, and her go/no-go will determine if we proceed with extraction. Not only is her safety paramount, but she's with me. You give her any trouble, and you give me trouble. Are we clear on that?"

The men nodded unanimously. Emélie felt her shoulders drop as she took a deep breath; she was suddenly aware of how much was riding on her forthcoming assessment. Despite his indifference, it was clear Joab wouldn't let her get in too far over her head, but she didn't feel assured. She saw Joab's disengaged nonchalance for what it was: a well-honed tool used to lull those around him into thinking he wasn't paying as much attention as he truly was. A position he then leveraged to obscure his true intentions, while simultaneously providing himself the freedom to observe everyone and everything that happened in plain sight. Emélie clenched her hand into a fist; it had certainly worked on her, and she wasn't sure which scared her more: that she hadn't noticed it until now, or, in light of it, that she had no intention of leaving.

Joab gave a weighted pause. "Lilith relies on Jumpers to enforce her Earth-side trafficking operations. These Jumpers function like biological packet sniffers, feeding her data via the host's nervous system to counteract our efforts to stop her. While we've yet to see these Jumpers make any hostile actions, their real-time counter-surveillance of our own movements means they present a legitimate threat if we draw too much attention. To mitigate this, we're running this op as a deep reconnaissance mission with minimal support. Once we cross into Korolev, there will be no reactionary force, and should we take contact, we will be on our own."

The ship rattled, thrusters firing at full blast as they began their descent into lunar airspace. Joab made one final scan down the hold, assessing the team. "Each one of you was handpicked for this assignment, so stay sharp, do your jobs, and everything will proceed on schedule. Vehicle assignments are as follows: lead vehicle is myself and Team One. Follow vehicle is Goodnight, Team Two driver, the Doctor, and our Tether. Anchor vehicle is Team Three, and the remainder of Team Two. We're skids down in two minutes. Questions?"

Emélie recognized that Joab's offer didn't extend to her. No matter. She'd already burned up what latitude she had with Goodnight, and while both men had made it explicitly clear they didn't want her asking them any more questions, neither had specified she couldn't find someone else to pry for information. She looked around for her next victim; it shouldn't be hard, given that she knew next to nothing, leaving almost every other person on board with possession of any number of useful things to disclose.

The seat beside her, empty for most of the flight, was now occupied by someone who had slipped in, unnoticed, during the briefing. A man in all-black fatigues sat in a forward position, arms resting on his knees with his hands clasped together and his face obscured. Emélie looked around. Everyone else seemed preoccupied with final preparations. This man sat calmly, watching.

"Hey," Emélie said, pulling her headset down as she leaned further out into the aisle, stealing another glance at the forward cabin. Maybe the person next to her knew something about that, too. "What's a Teth..." she began, faltering before the rest of the question was out as her eyes fell to the red marking at the base of the man's neck—a serpent devouring its own tail in symmetrical, endless recursion. An identical match to the symbol hidden beneath the access panel on her cybernetic arm. Every muscle in her body went taut as she choked back a gasp, unable to remove her eyes from the tattoo as it rippled with the muscles on his neck, subtly pulsing against the skin like a living thing.

He turned to face her, brushing against her metal arm as he moved. For a half breath, the man was no more. Folded out of existence, only the dark imprint of his form remained, a shadow between them. She blinked, and he stood in the aisle in front of her, his cold eyes holding hers in an unblinking stare.

The tattooed man from the forward cabin.

Flustered at her sudden proximity to the stranger, she tried to recover, lurching upright and, without thinking, shoving her hand forward. "Emélie Desjardins, Department of Energy—"

"I know who you are," the man said, cutting Emélie's introduction short.

A flash of heat stung her face; rising anger at how little it had taken to throw her off balance. And her open and outstretched hand was left bare, trembling and weak, an insult to injury.

He watched her hand quivering in the low light. "You've been here before," he said. It wasn't a question; there was certainty in his voice. Authority, even.

Emélie blinked rapidly, taken aback by his direct observation. Not once had anyone—not even Thursday—so openly acknowledged her tremors. "I... don't remember."

"It remembers you," he said, finally returning her handshake.

Another cold shiver rippled down her spine as she took his hand. More red ink, like the lattice-work on his back and torso, peeked from behind the hem of his sleeve.

"You can call me Roland," he said. "Roland Foster."

"Finally, someone with a last name." Emélie joked uneasily. She glanced down the aisle. Joab and Goodnight were nowhere to be seen. "You're also an advisor?" The ship jolted, skids touching down on the tarmac at Jericho Station.

"You could say that."

"And what's your area of expertise?" she asked, pulling her respirator on. The concealment, however partial, was welcome.

Roland watched her carefully. After taking what felt like a long time to consider her question, he said, "I happen to know a lot about sand."

The boarding ramp lowered without a sound. Outside, an austere panorama: a row of unmarked vehicles waited in a line on the landing platform. Black against the black tarmac. Black under the lunar night.

"Do you encounter a lot of sand up here?" she asked, jostled by other men from the team as they moved past her for the ramp.

"Not especially." He collected a long, slender case near his feet and, without another word, fell in line with the last few men moving for the trucks.

Joab was the last one off the ship. He passed by Emélie without so much as a glance.

"You told me we were going to Homestake," Emélie demanded, falling in step alongside him, an all too familiar ritual by now.

"We went to Homestake. And now, we're here," Joab replied.

"You never said anything about Luna."

"Doesn't change anything," Joab warned, an edge of caution in his voice. "We're here to have a conversation. That's it."

"That's it?" Exasperated and with nothing to lose, she pushed harder. "Then what about all this?" Emélie gestured around them at the nondescript trucks, the incognito ship, and the man who called himself Roland. There were too many things with no explanations; every new variable she uncovered just added to her list of questions.

"Countermeasures."

At least with dark matter, she could demarcate the unknown and work backward from that point. When it came to Joab, she wasn't even sure where the outer limits fell. There was only movement, and along which vector, she hadn't the slightest idea. "This isn't an extraction?"

Joab stepped past her, continuing toward his truck. "That's up to you, Desjardins."

"That's not what I signed up for!" she called after him, watching as Roland angled for the same vehicle—Vehicle Two—that she'd been assigned to. He wasn't the driver, which left him as... the Tether. Tether, whatever that was. "And what about him?" she asked, gesturing toward the truck. "Roland. He said his specialty was sand, Joab. *Sand.* On the moon." She shook her head. "Where do you even find these people?"

"Same place I found you," he replied, still moving at his unbothered pace toward the trucks.

Emélie rejoined him. "Then what about everything you said back on the ship? The tokens, the Gates? You could have told me that before we left. It would have—"

Joab pivoted, stepping in front of Emélie to block her path. "It would have what, Desjardins? Caused you to ask different questions later instead of the ones you're asking now?" He motioned to the team. "You want to know why we don't use ranks and titles? Because this environment doesn't care about who you are. You may be accustomed to a certain amount of transparency inside Sanctuary walls, but out here, merit gets you nothing. You want answers? Shut your mouth and earn them like everyone else." Joab moved to the first vehicle and opened the door. "And for the last time, put your damn goggles on."

Stunned and fuming from Joab's admonishment, Emélie marched to her assigned vehicle, where Roland waited, leaning against his door, watching her.

Goodnight was already inside, running radio checks. "Leviathian One, this is Goodnight Actual. Radio check, over," he called, one side of a compact headset pressed to his ear. He glanced at Emélie and then jerked his head toward the back seat.

She opened the door and pitched her plate carrier inside.

"Body armor isn't optional," Goodnight said.

She looked at the heavy vest. "I thought this was Joab's op."

Goodnight nodded to his driver, then leaned into his radio. "We're all clear," he called. He removed the headset, then switched the dial and extended it back to Emélie. "You're right, it is. Why don't you call him and tell him how to run it, then?"

A quick glance at Roland, then Emélie shoved her pack to the floor and grabbed the vest, pulling it over her head. It wasn't worth the fight. "This just seems like a waste," she said, fastening the cummerbund around her waist. "All this for one person. We could have just flown the informant down to Homestake."

Roland slid into the seat opposite Emélie. "That would have been a better plan," he agreed, closing his door.

"If it's a better plan, then why didn't we do that instead?!"

The driver smirked, and Goodnight shook his head. "For starters, somebody should probably let the informant know that they're an informant."

Emélie's eyes flashed to Roland, who was still watching out his window. "The asset doesn't know we're coming?"

"I'm sure they'll be cooperative," Goodnight said, one hand resting on his cross-body carbine. "If not, we're more than happy to provide assistance."

Emélie pulled the goggles on as they turned off the flight deck. "Kidnapping," she said softly. "Where I'm from, we call this kidnapping."

"Good thing this isn't where you're from then, Emélie," Roland replied.

CHAPTER 18
BLACK MOON RISING

Emélie shifted in her seat, resisting, with each breath she took, the unfamiliar, constricting weight of the body armor. Through the truck window, the silver landscape dropped away in shades of silver and shadow—serene, if she could ignore the cramped cabin and the unexplained equipment Joab had foisted on her. Whatever he'd said about their mission here, the gear and the people wearing it balanced to a different equation.

Goodnight leaned into the radio, breaking the silence with his husky tone. "Jericho Station, this is Leviathan Actual."

"This is Jericho Station Egress Control. Go ahead, transmit."

"Requesting departure assignment, over." Goodnight pulled his sleeve back, revealing a screen on his arm showing real-time data of the lunar surface around them.

While he parsed the satellite feed on his arm display, Emélie returned her attention to the view. Jericho Station—one of the few remaining Phaethon outposts left on Luna—sat on a raised plateau at the center of the Korolev crater. A dust bowl full of buildings rusting into oblivion, home to a few hundred thousand souls who chose desolation over a view of Earth. Here, the sky opened onto unbounded space, hidden from Earth's surveillance. The position gave Phaethon a naturally elevated foothold into the Levant, the collection of scattered settlements running the perimeter of the crater-spanning dome. Once a manufacturing powerhouse, the Levant was now a festering maze of deteriorating warehouses and dusty highways stacked ten levels deep inside the Korolev basin. Beyond it, past the ring of buildings running along the crater's rim, the shape of Luna Bet—the second Moon Loop —loomed in shadowless darkness.

"Leviathan Actual, standby for interrogative," the radio sounded.

"Standing by," Goodnight replied. He turned, glancing at Roland, but Roland looked out the window, seemingly unconcerned. They had been idling at the tunnel leading out of the station for nearly twenty minutes, and Roland had hardly taken his eyes from the window. It wasn't a mindless stare; Emélie could see his eyes shifting, scanning the area outside as if he were searching for something specific. The radio clicked back on.

"Leviathan, you're cleared for Korolev. Can you confirm you'll be doing some sightseeing?"

Goodnight pulled the headset back over his ears. "That's affirmative, Jericho Station. I hear the weather's nice this time of year."

A brief pause. "Roger, solid copy. You're clear to disembark the station through Checkpoint Sacramento. Standby for departure."

"Standing by."

A bank of lights behind the convoy switched on, flooding the area in blinding light.

"Doors opening in T-minus 10."

An alarm blared as turrets dropped from either side of the tunnel, hunting for potential targets beyond the walls. At ten seconds, the armored barrier sealing off the tunnel retracted upward, revealing a mercurial landscape punctuated by an elevated roadway leading directly out into the Levant. Goodnight racked the slide on the rifle slung across his chest and leaned forward, double-tapping the dash with his palm. Emélie, accustomed to Thursday's cautious driving, was unprepared for their hard launch out of the station. The driver floored the accelerator, tearing onto the highway after vehicle one, Emélie bracing herself between the doorframe and the adjacent seat as they went.

Goodnight gave another look into the backseat as they dropped down a steep on-ramp, plummeting into the Levant's basin. Reaching for his chest, he drew the handgun holstered to the front of his body armor. Rotated the weapon, then extended it to Emélie, grip first. "It's not safe out here," he said. "You best hold on to this while we're outside the walls."

Frozen by the cold sight of it, her eyes fell to the gun, and she made no other movement.

"Take the gun, Doc."

Emélie watched it, swaying in his hand to the up-down motion of the rolling vehicle. "Is that an order?"

"You tell me."

Roland's attention shifted, although he made no move to intervene. The rumble of pavement beneath them formed a backdrop to Emélie's silence.

"You think you're better than us? You aren't fooling anyone. We see your fear."

A long silence as Emélie continued to watch the gun. "We only experience reality as singular because we are limited by consciousness," she finally said. "We exist in parallel. Not one, but many selves, scattered across infinite universes."

Goodnight's hand tensed as he adjusted his grip on the weapon. "What the hell are you talking about?" His eyes darted to Roland. "What is she talking about?"

Emélie continued. "Every time you pick up a weapon, the universe splits in two. One reality where you make it out alive and one where you don't. It might seem as though your existence is limited to the present, but that's only because it's bound to consciousness, meaning you cannot experience any of the realities in which you die. This isn't the only version of us having this conversation. It's just the only one that matters because we are both still here, alive." Emélie glanced back out her window. "I'm not better than you. Only playing a different set of odds."

Goodnight stared at her, then, shaking his head, jammed the gun back into his holster. "You're fucking weird, Doc."

Emélie looked down at her hand, clenched into a fist in her lap.

"Don't take it personally," Roland said. "The world we have now was built by men like us. Men of violence." He turned back toward his window. "We only know combat, and we run blindly into it, oblivious that the destruction we unleash has already consumed us. It is the future that will remember the tools we did not learn. And the ones who carried them, when we did not know how."

"The future will remember whom the power favors," Emélie replied. "The rest of us are just trying to survive."

"The future is already—" Roland stopped mid-sentence, and turned, looking at something behind them. "Get down," he said. As he spoke, the lead vehicle's taillights flickered, then went dark. A moment later, their truck lost power. Emélie shrank low into her seat, trying to hide herself from view despite the cumbersome body armor.

"Jumpers, five o'clock," Goodnight's voice rang out through the darkness. He reached over and tapped the driver. "Blackout protocol, now."

The clunk of a gearshift into neutral. They rolled to a controlled halt against the analog *click-click-click* of Goodnight killing their radio and navigation feeds before the power came back on. A tactic not unlike the one Thursday had employed back inside the storm on Earth. The vehicles in front and behind them matched pace, and within seconds of the initial power outage, the convoy came to a dead stop in the middle of an abandoned six-lane highway, three stories above the lunar surface. Like most others Emélie had witnessed since joining Joab, the transition was one of controlled chaos. Further proof that these men were precisely as Roland attested: violent, and capable of state change at a moment's notice. It also explained their tension since arriving on Luna: nothing leveled the playing field for a group of mercenaries like an environment that tried to kill them back.

Inside the vehicle, everyone remained still. No follow-up instructions were issued, nor were they necessary: the team acted and reacted as one. Emélie peeked up from her seat and found the only thing she could see from her position was the upper rim of the Loop rising beyond the crater ridge ahead. Goodnight eased back in his seat, slowly canting his rifle so the muzzle pointed toward his door. Emélie's chest tightened as she watched him slide one hand forward, covering the trigger with a gloved finger, while the other raised the barrel so it rested below the window. Still nothing outside, except the barren highway and the structures far beyond it.

She let her breath out, allowing herself a silent, momentary reprieve, and too soon, at that. Something rubbed against the outside of the vehicle, gently rocking them against the suspension as a muffled, scraping sound—a soft body dragging across a metal one—filtered past. She froze, paralyzed by proximity to whatever Roland was watching outside her door, although she dared not turn to face it. She held steady, boring a gaze into the seat headrest in front of her as time expanded like a well, drawing up every detail with excruciating clarity. Her hand went numb as her shakes, so close to their point of origin, resurfaced with a near-religious fervor. Another scrape, this time back and forth, and her door pressed against the hinges. Breath came short, in rapid, desperate bursts. Finally, the sound ceased. Slowly, ever so slowly, she turned, facing the window.

Outside, a Jumper stood against her door, its gaunt face looking at something further down the road. As if drawn by the heat of her gaze, its head rotated mechanically toward her: from behind a blindfold, a pair of red eyes pulsed with unnatural light.

Emélie's headset switched off, leaving her blind in the total darkness.

Hands to her face, she tore at the vision-obscuring goggles. Before she could remove them, Roland's hand interrupted the process, pinning them back into place as an unholy shriek erupted from outside her door. The shrill cry deteriorated into rapid clicking, something like an electrical switch layered over a modulated tone. More complex than the simple rasp of drone tongue: piercing, but with a resonant, melodic undertone. The sound pulled their radios into a frequency-cycling static that scratched her ears and sent everyone head down and doubled over into their seats. Everyone except Roland, who remained still, holding back Emélie's scream. After seconds that seemed to fill a lifetime, her goggles switched back on.

The Jumper was gone.

Roland released his grasp on Emélie, who tore her protective equipment off to take in great, cold lungfuls of unconditioned air. With bare eyes, she looked around the cabin: Roland motioned toward the front window, where the Jumper could be seen continuing down the road with an erratic, somnambular gait. Breathless, she watched as a second one passed on the opposite side of the highway, moving with the same irregular lurching that prioritized gross mechanical movement over fine motor control. Occasionally, one of the Jumpers would pause, turning its head in a stiff arc, scanning.

"I can't stand their goddamn noises," Goodnight muttered, watching a third Jumper move past them. "Garbled banshee gibberish." He leaned over, pressing his radio mic to his lips. "Three relays, one seeker. Moderate to severe temporal drift. No escalation. Hold for five, then push the objective."

Emélie watched the Jumper vanish and reappear a few feet off the ground. It crashed back to the concrete, crawling forward as an awkward, disjointed collection of limbs. "They speak some type of assembly language," she said. "Machine instructions."

Goodnight turned around. "How the hell would you know that?"

"How could you not?" she replied. "You're the one running patrols through the middle of their territory. I would've expected you to at least recognize that their communication isn't random."

Goodnight's eyes narrowed. "This is all the communication I need," he said, patting his carbine. "Still liking your odds of staying alive?"

Emélie clenched her hand into a fist.

"You try too hard to control your fear," Roland said, watching out his window. "Pay attention to it. An inconvenient truth is still the truth."

Emélie clenched her jaw instead.

When the last Jumper was out of sight, Goodnight signaled the driver, who brought their truck back online. In under a minute, the other vehicles were up and running, and the convoy resumed forward motion without a word. As if the entire encounter was nothing out of the ordinary. They pulled off the highway and onto an exit ramp leading down into the crater they'd been circling. Into the basin, a roiling, silver mare opened before them; beyond it, the main superstructure of the Loop came into view.

"There she is," Goodnight whistled. "Luna Bet, Jewel of the Levant."

"Luna Bet," Emélie repeated, gazing at the Loop's once-red hull, now reduced to bare metal by decades of lunar storms. Loop facilities were organized into two central elements: the above-ground portion, which looked like an enormous ring lying on its side, housing the mechanical systems and transportation connections; and beneath it, the reactor shaft—a borehole nearly a mile wide, plunging so deep into the moon's crust you couldn't make out the bottom with the naked eye. "Bet. The second," she added in a breathy whisper, mostly to herself.

"More than that," Roland replied. "The Loop here represented a quantum leap. An evolution of the technology beyond anything that had been seen before."

Emélie tore her gaze from the window long enough to look over at him, an unspoken question in her eyes.

To her surprise, Roland continued. She wasn't used to anyone obliging her curiosity. "Luna was, at one time, a frontier. A place beyond Earth's regulatory grasp and the stringent safety requirements that came with it. What most dismissed as a barren wasteland became, under the proper vision, a test-bed for pure theory. It was in this very crater that the second-generation Loop reactor, the Remez Class, was born."

"Remez," Emélie repeated, mouthing the word like a prayer. "Remez... Remez... Resh." She removed her glove and drew a ר symbol in the fine powder clinging to her window. "Orientable, non-bounded Manifold. A taurus."

Roland looked at the shape. Looked at her. Returned to his watching. "Who taught you that?"

"The moon," she replied, lifting her goggles away for an unobstructed view of the landscape around them. Dormant Jumpers dotted the soft grey dunes, standing like rigid, tattered statues, their faces turned to the stars. "Shouldn't we slow down with so many of them around?"

"They won't do anything out here," Roland assured her. One hand rested casually atop the rifle hanging across his chest. “We haven’t given them a reason to perceive us as a threat.”

“Are we planning on giving them one?” she asked, rubbing her bloodshot eyes.

“That depends,” Roland replied, leaning back in his seat. “How much do you have to hide?”

Emélie put the goggles back on.

CHAPTER 19
"SANCTUARY"

Phaethon Corp. MAIN build_VX.6.6.09
initializing boot sequence...
running subroutine FOUNTAINHEAD:

bindquery: update parameter to
"SANCTUARY"
encryption protocols intact,
syntax structures intact
[10] entries remaining

begin sentiment analysis,
implicit context target, rundisplay:

BEGIN RECORD >>>

I wanted it to feel different, coming back after all these years. Like the last decade and a half was nothing but a bad dream I could put behind me. I thought that up until the moment I stepped down onto the tarmac and realized it was just another lie I've been telling myself. We didn't come home so much as finally wake up to an even worse reality. Worse off than how I left it, that's for damn sure. As much as I hated

Mars, I never thought I'd be coming back here. To Earth. Marcus had different plans, though, and instead of trying to argue with all the reasons I had for saying no, he found the one reason I had for saying yes.

Worst part is, I can't even hate him for it. Not when it means she's happy. I'd trade anything for that, and I'd do it over again in a heartbeat. I haven't even been down to see one of the Sanctuaries yet, but I imagine living underground is a lot like living in space. Too many people all bunched up tight, breathing in the same air over and over again. I'll take my chances up on the surface, same as always. This isn't about me, anyway. The university is at Sanctuary One, and there's nothing like that on Mars. Nothing like that anywhere, really. And the kid is bright. Too smart for anything I have to offer. I don't have much in the way of love, but I've got this chance at a normal life, and we're going to make the most of it.

Even if it haunts me.

<<< END RECORD

"Half sunk, a shattered visage
lies, whose frown"

sanitize data entry,
purge access logs to XANADU
KILL remote process

CHAPTER 20
MARKOV CHAIN

The trucks were still rolling when Goodnight's team dismounted, rifles pointed outward to form a tight perimeter as their weapon lights carved out a low-ceilinged parking garage crumbling into oblivion. The men pushed the circle outward in mute synchronicity, methodically assessing every square inch with a tactical roughness until they reached their prescribed distance. One at a time, they switched their lights off and knelt into a defensive posture. As the garage returned to blackness, Emélie caught a silhouette passing into the doorless corridor of the adjacent building, a shadow dissolving into obscurity.

Goodnight appeared outside her door. He opened it and jerked his head sharply, signaling for her to follow. She stepped out, but as she reached to close the door, Goodnight held it firmly, shaking his head. Without a word, he started for the next building, pausing at the perimeter as a few members of his team appeared beside Emélie, their movements nearly undetectable despite their robust tactical kits.

She eyed the corridor ahead. "He's not like the rest of you," she whispered.

"Roland? He's not like any of us, but the only thing you need to know is to stay out of his way."

"What did he do to earn that sort of autonomy?"

Goodnight glanced at her, then moved ahead without answering. When he was out of earshot, the man nearest Emélie leaned in. "He's been to the red planet," he whispered, throwing his chin toward the ceiling.

"Hey," Goodnight hissed, turning around to face them. "I'm not paying you to talk. And you?" He pointed to Emélie. "What did I say about asking questions?"

She glanced at the man beside her. Rifle magazines jutted from the pouches across his chest, the ends wrapped in tape to prevent them from knocking against their neighbors. The more Emélie looked, the more she noticed details like this: every loose piece of gear was taped or tied to something else, suggesting that it wasn't just sight, but sound they were suppressing. Stealth, although not because of Jumpers, given they'd driven blatantly past them on the way in. Here, in the dark stillness of the moon, the team's behavior, which had seemed at first glance like pre-mission jitters, took a new shape: whatever they were hunting on Luna also hunted them back.

Emélie followed Goodnight down a carpeted hallway, picking her way between segments of collapsed ceiling tile illuminated by the narrow swath of his weapon light. Joab was already out of sight, and the small detachment of Goodnight's men moved in front of them, sweeping the doors lining either side of the hallway as they cleared abandoned rooms left in various states of decay. About halfway down the corridor, Goodnight abruptly turned through one of the open doors, then pointed his rifle back across the threshold, marking the location. Something on the floor glinted under the beam, leaving Emélie to pause as she stepped across. Empty brass cartridges littered the floor.

"Let's go, Doc. One foot after the other."

Two of Goodnight's men remained at the entrance as she followed him into the room. Empty, except for a bed, which had been raised on one end by a hinge attached to the wall, exposing a narrow staircase leading below ground. Goodnight, one foot planted at the topmost tread, waved her toward the opening. She ducked into it, bracing herself against either wall to descend the stairs where a seam of soft light leaked through an armored door at the lower landing.

On the other side, Joab waited at the center of a large, bright room comprised of whitewashed walls rising into a barrel-vaulted ceiling. The polished marble floors stood nearly luminous against his brutalist form. As Goodnight emerged behind her, Joab acknowledged them both and then turned, disappearing through an arched opening to one side of the room.

Emélie took in the environment, aware that this place was unlike any she'd ever been to, nor was it a place she should ever be. The opening through which Joab had stepped loomed ahead, and it took every ounce of courage she could muster to press onward. Carefully, she passed through the door and out into another hallway, this one with a single door at the far end. Goodnight followed, close enough that she felt the brush of his shoulder against her back from time to time, although to his credit, he did not push her faster than she was willing to move on her own. Her gaze followed her movement, taking in the meandering lines of unrecognizable symbols scratched into the plaster walls at eye level. Nearby, the statue of a woman with two pairs of eyes rested on a plinth in an alcove; one of its arms was missing and lay on the floor, a stone appendage severed into dozens of pieces.

At the second doorway, darkness met them once again. Goodnight brushed past her, gun up. Under the savage edge of his weapon's light, glimpses of a once elegant dining hall came and went from view. A long table dominated the center of the room, where plates of food—now desiccated and dust-covered—portrayed a meal abandoned mid-service; a ghostly dereliction that left her feeling queasy. Around the table, dining chairs lay overturned and scattered among fragments of shattered crystal and tarnished cutlery. Goodnight pushed open one of the double doors leading to the kitchen, then looked back, as if expecting Emélie to take issue with the crimson smear marking the round window.

"Price of admission," he said, meeting Emélie's wide-eyed gaze. He held the door, waiting in the narrow passage between two racks of shelving laden with stacks of broken dinnerware until Emélie stepped through.

It was Roland she noticed first, standing beside a steel prep table. As she moved into the main kitchen, the far side of the table came into view: seated at the other end was a woman, hands bound behind her back and a blackout mask on her head. Emélie took a quick inventory of the situation: Joab had provided no description or identification of the informant, and it was only now that she faced her subconscious assumption that the person they were meeting was a man. This woman —the informant—wore a white satin jumpsuit, and despite the way she sat, head hung slightly forward and weighed down in total sensory deprivation by the hard black shell, carried a certain elegance. Elegance, a strange familiarity, and something of a wrongness, although Emélie couldn't place why.

"You ready to work?" Joab asked, stepping from the shadows behind her. There was a nonchalance to his tone that didn't agree with the way Goodnight hovered nearby, one hand gripping his rifle. Roland said nothing, although, as if anticipating Emélie's question as she scanned the room, left his position near the informant to retrieve a toppled chair from the far corner. He brought it over to the table and set it down carefully, then held out a hand. To take a seat, the open seat.

Emélie met the gesture with a short nod of thanks as he stepped back into the shadows, one eye on the door and the other on the table.

Joab circled, positioning himself into the vacuum left by Roland. With the flip of a switch located on one side of the blackout mask, a small light changed from red to green. He toggled the switch again, changing from green back to red. "This controls the audio feed. Make sure it's active when you start speaking. Green means go. There's an integrated filter for voice modulation—"

"I know how an Oubliette works," Emélie interrupted. She took a seat, then nodded curtly.

Joab switched the audio feed on. "Signal if you can hear me," he said.

A hesitant nod from the woman.

"Listen carefully. You will be asked a series of questions regarding the operation of the Loop, the Gates, and the authentication tokens required for accessing them. Your responses will determine the outcome of this interaction. You are being recorded. Nod if you understand."

The woman's head tilted forward.

"I'll take that as a yes." Joab checked his watch. "Begin."

Emélie gripped her chair and scooted closer, the legs reverberating against the floor as she closed the distance to arm's reach. Whatever suspicions she'd suppressed about Joab's motives for bringing her along were eclipsed by the person seated opposite her. Instead of speaking, Emélie reached forward and switched off the audio feed. The light changed from green to red; the tone of the room shifted even more.

"Are you kidding me, Desjdarins?" Joab flung his arms wide. "Could we make it any easier for you?!"

Emélie didn't take her eyes off the woman. "What's her name?" she asked.

"Her name is irrelevant. She's an informant—"

"That's not a name," Emélie interrupted. She pointed to the woman. "I want to know her name. Her *real* name."

"It's not important. Ask her about the Gates."

She met his glare, unwilling to back down. "It's important to me."

Joab leaned in, hands on the table, voice low; his impatience covering them like a stone. "I know you think you're doing the right thing, and I respect that, I really do. But I need you to understand that whatever conclusions you've drawn about this woman are dead wrong. Now flip that switch and do your fucking job, or we're going to be in one hell of a situation."

Emélie noticed Roland had reappeared at the far side of the kitchen, still in the shadows and beyond range of the recording unit. She pushed back from the table, raking the floor with a hollow screech. "Or what, Joab? You're going to launch me back to Earth from out here?" She strode to the nearest member of Goodnight's team—a pillar of a man in a tactical grey exposure suit—and caught him by the sleeve. "Here," she said, raising the man's arm. "My replacement."

Silence.

"Go ahead," Emélie prompted. "Ask this woman what she knows about the topology of parallel realities. Ask her how she used that knowledge to exploit a redundancy in the Loop by floating a single point through a temporary dimension instead of relying on a static, dual-anchor system."

The man shifted in place and flashed a concerned look in Goodnight's direction.

"And don't worry," Emélie added. "She doesn't have a name. No name, no problem, so if she doesn't respond, you can always beat the solution out of–"

"Lilith," Joab interrupted tersely. He said the word with reluctance, a half-truth uttered under duress and the need to progress. The mission at hand was more valuable than his operational paradigm.

Emélie took a step backward. "Lilith," she repeated, tearing her goggles away to get a better look with her own eyes. "This is Lilith?"

"No, this isn't Lilith!" Joab shouted, slamming his palms to the table. Sweat was beginning to bead along his brow; Emélie's continued failure to understand the delicacy and intensity of their mission was costing them precious time, and maybe lives, too. "For someone with so many questions, you don't listen to a goddamn thing, do you?! Lilith isn't one person, not anymore. She's an idea. The fractured psychosis of a violent criminal spread across multiple versions of herself." He grabbed the blackout hood, pushing Lilith's head forward to make a point. "You want to start treating this thing like a human? Congratulations. You're providing her the one thing she wants more than anything. Power."

Emélie leaned in, eyes sharp. "Back on the ship, you said nobody has ever intercepted an Origin shipment. Did you ever consider that the problem might have less to do with Lilith's operational protocols and more to do with your insistence on treating everyone around you like children? I know I ask questions. I know I'm a pain in the ass sometimes. And I know you don't have any other options because if you did, they'd be here instead of me. Now you brought me up here to talk to this woman, and I intend to do exactly that, and I couldn't care less if you think she deserves dignity because it's no longer your call. I'm the one asking the questions now." She reached across the table and switched Lilith's audio feed back on before Joab could reply.

"Lilith," she said, a slight waver in her voice. She took a breath and began again. "Lilith, I need you to tell me about the Gate you opened yesterday on Earth."

Lilith sat silent, unresponsive.

"What do you know about the authentication tokens used for opening Gates? Do you have one of these tokens in your possession?"

Emélie could feel Roland looming to one side of the room. She wasn't sure what the consequences of an extraction were, only that in the mounting tension, it wasn't good.

She reached for the audio feed, and Joab shook his head, stopping her short. "Lilith, listen to me," Emélie said, leaning in. "I want you to explain how you're opening Gates between Mars and Earth. Be specific and concise, or things will not end well for you." The words tasted bitter, as they should have.

She had heard them before, but not from her own lips.

Joab stepped to the table. "Did you hear the question?" he asked, towering over Lilith's hunched form. When no reply came, he stepped away and folded his arms across his broad chest. Goodnight moved in, taking Joab's place behind Lilith.

Audio feed, off.

Emélie gripped her chair, bracing herself. She knew what came next.

Goodnight palmed the back of Lilith's head, smashing it against the table with a brutal blow. The blackout mask made a sickening thud as it bounced against the stainless steel surface.

Emélie's grip on the chair tightened, clamping down until the wood fibers began to yield as she was forced to watch Lilith try, and fail, to resist.

Goodnight, who had little use for resistance, went a second round with Lilith's head and the table. Rivulets of blood leaked from the base of the mask—the mess inside must have been considerable. Her neck twitched and throbbed; she was screaming, although no sound came. The Oubliette worked both ways.

With a trembling hand, Emélie covered her mouth, stifling the horror that came with the wrecked memories washing back to her shores, fresh as the day they were formed. Lilith rocked herself in small circles, searching for equilibrium in the void, and Emélie wished for escape in any form.

Joab had been right.

All she'd needed was the right trigger.

CHAPTER 21
CANDYFLIP

It was Roland who intervened, stepping from the shadows so softly that Emélie did not notice him until he was right beside her. He circled the table, materializing into the light as Goodnight readied another blow. With the smallest gesture, Roland dismissed him. In blind obedience, Goodnight retreated, leaving Roland a wide berth as he approached.

From her periphery, Emélie could see something in his hand. He passed behind her, watching, then paused, setting a slender hourglass on the table directly between the two women. When she looked up at him, he flipped the hourglass over, and sand—red sand—began spilling into the lower chamber.

She didn't need an explanation.

There was a finality that came with the falling sand, and in the seconds that followed, Emélie slowed her breathing and took what the moment offered: a glimpse at what could not—would not—be revealed in haste.

When the glass chamber sat empty, Joab nodded to Goodnight. "Time's up."

Goodnight drew his handgun, the same gun he'd attempted to press into Emélie's service, and rested the muzzle against the soft of Lilith's neck.

"I wouldn't do that," Emélie warned.

Goodnight rocked the hammer, locking it back.

"She has the Gate token on her body."

"Good," he said. "Then I can kill her and we can leave."

"Well, do it then," she said, testing him. Waiting for him to pull the trigger.

Goodnight glanced over at Joab. As Emélie suspected, he didn't have the authority to make such a call. Joab could, and he was the one she needed to convince. That, or Roland, who she suspected would be able to provide the override if he so desired.

"You're playing with her life, Desjardins," Joab warned, stepping up to the table. "You really want to see where that line falls?"

Emélie shifted her gaze to Lilith. "I don't care so much where it falls. I'm more interested in seeing how far it can move."

Joab waved Goodnight off momentarily. "I'm listening," he said. Goodnight rammed his sidearm back into the drop holster on his leg and took a half-step backward. Standing by rather than standing down, he waited, ready to finish the job at a moment's notice.

"Back on Earth," Emélie began, choosing her words carefully, "you asked me to take your second set of assumptions without question. Everything I'm about to say is only as good as the information you've provided and based on the premise that Eden, one of the original Watchers, is behind all this."

Joab said nothing.

Emélie kept going regardless. Somebody had to. "We know a Gate opened on the surface," she said, leaning in. Arguing her case with her whole body. "I've seen the remnants of it, but nobody has ever actually *seen* a Gate open. You've been focusing on the wrong thing, and Eden is the answer."

Joab's hand shot out, grabbing the oubliette and yanking Lilith's head back toward the ceiling—forcing the unconscious woman between them like evidence. "Fountainhead recruited Lilith, and Lilith is running Eden. Lilith, not Eden, is the common denominator. Lilith is our way into Mars."

"I heard what you said, and I'm telling you, it's wrong. What I'm proposing is supposed to seem upside down. Anything else is too clean, and it doesn't fit the operating parameters we've seen so far. Eden isn't just operating the Loop. Lilith needed her to override the failsafe requirement, resulting in a fundamental change to the system itself. You want to know how a Gate opened? Start with who has the capability to make that happen. Eden." She could feel them closing in on her realization. These were people accustomed to action—to slow them down required a force equal and opposite to their momentum.

"I'm waiting for the part where you tell me why you think this proxy has a physical token hidden somewhere on her body." He released Lilith's head, checking his watch as she slumped over onto the table. "A hunch isn't enough of a reason to risk extraction."

Emélie didn't need a reminder that she was working on borrowed time. "Eden, while sentient, is still a computer and thus bound to the same characteristics of any other computer. Mainly, she will always seek the most efficient solution to a problem. Not the most effective or the most logical. The most *efficient*." She paused, looking at Lilith's labored breathing.

"If you needed to open a Gate between a fixed entry point on Mars and a second point somewhere else, and you were moving a dynamic payload—a person transporting a shipment of Origin—then the answer is hidden inside the problem. The second point is the person making the Jump."

"So there's no tunnel?" Joab asked. He threw a sideways glance at Roland, as if to fact-check Emélie's proposal. Rather than respond with support or opposition to her theory, Roland simply watched her and waited.

"If the person is the second point, there's no need to calculate where they're going. They are always and already at the destination. The architecture of the Manifold already supports this, too. Rather than a continuous link between the two points, Eden is most likely only generating a small area around the person traveling inside. Something like a bubble. This takes the compounding issue and turns it into a feature of the system. The resources required for computing a moving point are offloaded onto the payload itself. As the person moves through the Manifold, the passage simultaneously opens before them and closes behind them, so there's no need to solve for the endpoint." She paused, slightly shocked at the clarity of her own argument. Like the bubble she described, it wasn't until she began speaking that the rest of the idea materialized into a working concept. She wasn't even sure how she'd made the connection, except that years of observing things at the fringes of reality had attuned her to understand what was before them now.

Emélie continued, now addressing Roland directly. Joab's deferral moments before had shown her who carried the real power when it came to matters of the Loop. "You've already identified that Lilith is using a secure token of some sort, but I would suggest it's more like a device. Something capable of being easily concealed on the body, which, when activated, behaves as a sort of beacon. This could also explain why we've never seen a Gate open. It's no longer occurring as the system was originally designed. In this instance, rather than a Gate appearing at a predetermined location, the payload would simply emerge from the Manifold at whatever point they decided to exit."

Joab turned to Goodnight. "Take the Doctor back to the truck."

"I wasn't done," she said, standing. Ready to position herself as a barrier between them and the door, if necessary.

"You did great, Desjardins. We'll handle the rest from here."

"I'm sure you will," Emélie said, eyeing Goodnight as he closed in. "The good old-fashioned way, right? Shoot first, ask questions later? Go ahead. She dies, the token dies with her."

Joab gave Emélie a sharp look, sizing her up to see if she was actually on to something or merely buying time. Emélie stood her ground, meeting his gaze with her own piercing stare.

Roland decided for them both. "Continue," he ordered. "Lilith could have hidden the device anywhere, but you were specific. You said somewhere on her body?"

"An external device requires a power source. Power sources are notoriously prone to failure, and failure inside the Manifold means the payload would become trapped for an indeterminate period. Embedding it within the body allows it to harvest energy passively. So long as the payload has a beating heart, there will always be a way out." She glanced down at Lilith. "And if your heart stops inside, it doesn't matter if you make it out or not. You won't be alive to notice."

Roland nodded. "Fountainhead is extremely paranoid, and if this device—the token—is as you say, it would be especially useful in an emergency, where escape was necessary. It would have to pass a cavity search and remain accessible without any dependence on external tools." Roland closed in on the table, moving toward Lilith, although his eyes were fixed on Emélie. "An object that could be removed and activated quickly. Likely embedded, skin deep, but no deeper. Somewhere where the skin is thin, minimal blood vessels, no risk of arterial bleeding. But you've already arrived there, haven't you?" he asked, coming to a halt directly behind Lilith. He reached up, shifting the light hanging above the table so it cast a sharp shadow across her seated body. With his other hand, he gently tilted her head back, exposing her blood-stained neck to the light. Emélie saw it too.

A small scar below the clavicle.

Lilith thrashed. As if anticipating her reaction, Roland caught her by the neck, slamming her back down into the chair before her feet met the ground. Joab snapped his fingers, waving a few men over to restrain her as Goodnight produced a knife. He leaned in, Lilith's squirming torso reflected off the blade as he grasped the collar of her white jumpsuit and, with a forceful tug, ripped the neckline open. Her bare sternum was slick with sweat and blood, and at the center of her chest, the dark rectangle of a solitary tattoo.

He pushed the tip of his knife into skin, carving an incision along the existing scar. Lilith lunged forward, then abruptly flung herself away from the table. The blade bucked, and Goodnight responded by bashing Lilith across the mask with the end of it. She reeled—acquiescent, if only for a moment—and Goodnight resumed his work.

From the wound, he extracted a small, dark object.

He held it up, and at the first touch of light, it began to move. He flung it to the table, brandishing his knife as it crawled for Lilith. Roland stepped in front of Goodnight, snatching it up with two fingers before it could reach her.

"Your token," Roland said, holding the object out for Emélie. She gazed down at it, the smallest tinge of hope stirring at the sight of the disk. All black and roughly the size of a human iris, it glistened in the light, blood-wet.

"Skipjack," Joab said, coming over to the table to get a look for himself. "Old school storage device. Turns an eye socket into a sort of physical access port, then authenticates using an internal encryption key to expose the contents. Practically ancient hardware at this point, but back in the day, they were popular for moving information that needed to stay off-network."

"Visual data?" Emélie asked.

"Not necessarily." He took the device from Roland and flipped it over, running his thumb across the concave backside. "It has a neural sensor that detects and orients itself to the iris to interface directly with the optical nerve. Doesn't cause any permanent damage, although I heard it hurts like hell."

"We need to see what's on it," Emélie said, careful to keep her distance.

"Risky," Joab replied. "These devices aren't networked, so the only way to retrieve information from them is to let it flash an authorized user and have that person verbally relay the stored contents. Makes them virtually tamper-proof, and Lilith has a reputation for being uncooperative, so it's unlikely she'd reveal the contents."

Emélie eyed the Skipjack. "If this is really how she's opening Gates, it's an elegant solution. Only her proxies are authorized to unlock a Skipjack, and only a Skipjack can open a Gate. It's basic two-factor authentication, modified to function through a biological interface." She looked across the table at Lilith. "It also makes it difficult to coerce one of these copies of Lilith into opening a Gate against her will."

"There are ways to break the will," Roland said, watching Goodnight wipe his blade clean on the sleeve of his uniform. "The issue is larger than forced activation. Even if we got into the device, we'd need Eden to believe it was Lilith making the request to open the other side of the Gate on the Mars end. Gaining access alone isn't enough."

"We'll find a way to access it later, then," Emélie said, determined not to lose the opportunity. "Surely someone with your resources can break this down and reverse engineer a way into—"

"Not an option," Joab said flatly.

"What? You're the one doing risk mitigation now?"

"I said it's not an option. These devices are fenced, so moving one of them will require re-authentication. Knowing Lilith, failing that will result in an immediate wipe."

Emélie eyed him. "I didn't know you were capable of caution, but okay, fine," she replied, changing up her approach. "If we can't move it and we can't make her activate it, then we test it here. Now." She looked down at the table, inhaled deeply, and on the exhale, sealed her fate. "I'll do it."

Something else fell across Joab's face; concern, maybe. She didn't know he had that in him, either. "You're missing the point. If you activate this thing, it will try to authenticate to you, and when you inevitably fail that test, it's going to wipe."

"You already said that." Emélie drummed her fingers on the table. She wasn't sure how to handle the red tape when it came from Joab. "I don't see what the issue is. It either works or it doesn't. What are you not telling me that makes trying to access this now worse than leaving it here on the table?"

Joab pinched the bridge of his nose, as if her question caught him like a headache. "Wipe *you*," he clarified. "If you insert the Skipjack into your eye, it will wipe *your* memory."

Emélie blinked as she felt her next breath catch in her throat. "You mean—"

"You lose everything. We don't use Skips anymore for the same reason people like Lilith still find them valuable. They aren't just undefeatable. You put one of these in your eye, and in the ten seconds it takes to realize you can't unlock it, this thing will scrub your mind so clean you won't even be able to recall your own name."

Emélie steadied herself against the table, watching Lilith bleed from the incision on her neck. The stakes were growing exponentially. What felt like a small experiment, a little, jittery, nerve-wracking offering, before, now carried the burden of an entire lifetime; *her* entire lifetime. "So, that's it?" Emélie asked, annoyed. A sweep of her hand drew the attention of the armed men behind her. "You have all these guns and all these men at your command, and yet you're still willing to turn back with the answer right in front of us?"

Joab gestured to Lilith, and the two men nearest him pulled her up to her feet. "That's enough questions for one day."

Nearby, Goodnight circled, flexing his fingers while eying the grab handle on the back of Emélie's vest. Ready to haul her to the trucks while someone put a bullet in their best chance at gaining access to the Manifold. A scowl on her part kept him at bay, if only for a brief moment.

It was all she needed.

"Shut it off," she said. "I'm done asking questions."

In the terse silence that followed, Joab's gaze felt laser-hot. Whatever he saw in her was enough to allow what would happen next. Eyes gleaming, he lifted the sleeve on his jumpsuit, revealing a flexible display strapped to his forearm. A sharp tap on the panel brought the surveillance unit in the corner into view. When it was powered off and out of sight, Emélie unslung her pack and set it on the steel table. A bit small, but it would have to do. "I need two med kits and a water ration."

Goodnight gave a wary glance at Joab, who waved him on. He complied, reluctantly collecting the personal trauma augmentation kits and a water ration from the men posted to either side of him. Emélie removed her goggles and dropped the body armor at her feet, then rolled up her sleeves as Goodnight dumped the supplies onto the table.

From her pack, she pulled out the hard-sided case Thursday had collected from her apartment. Inside, nested into a foam bed, was a sheet of paper. Perforated blotter paper, twenty-four squares of it. Two hundred micrograms of pure Origin each, with the Phaethon logo stamped into the center of each tab.

Joab let out a low whistle. "You've been holding out on me, Desjardins. I'll admit you struck me as a bit of a wild card, but recreational Jumping? That's a whole new level of crazy."

Crazy. Emélie kept her head down and continued working; it wasn't the sort of attention she wanted to acknowledge, and she needed a steady hand. Removing the IV bags from either of the trauma kits, she divided the water ration between them, then hooked one bag to the light above her head, and the other she held out to Goodnight. "Hold this," she ordered, picking up the sheet of blotter paper. He took the bag, watching as she tore a row of tabs off, separated one, and then dropped the rest into the IV bag. Upon contact with the water, the stabilized Origin activated, glowing softly as it stained the water a pinkish red. With her preparations complete, Emélie raised her head to face the room. Only Roland, unhindered by any sense of propriety or social convention, returned her gaze.

"I need a volunteer," she said, flicking air bubbles from the IV line. She could hear the subtle scuff of boots against the floor as the men nearest her turned outboard, searching for a more convenient threat.

When nobody stepped forward, Goodnight, already in proximity and still holding the IV bag, took responsibility. "Alright, Doc. What do you need?"

She leaned back, planting both of her hands on the table before hopping onto the metal surface. "I'm going to volumetrically dose myself with Origin to induce a state of altered consciousness before the Skipjack activates."

"And then what?" Goodnight asked, holding the drip up to get a better look at the glowing red solution.

Emélie eyed the gun affixed to his chest. "And then you're going to kill me."

Goodnight's grip faltered, and he nearly dropped the bag.

"Whoa, easy," Joab said, stepping between them to intervene. "I'm not sure where you're going with this. Origin is potent, but it can't prevent cognitive damage."

"I don't expect Origin to protect me," Emélie replied. "You said these devices aren't networked, correct? Then the decryption protocols would have to be stored locally inside the Skipjack itself. Clever, right? Hide the answer inside the problem. It's a pattern."

"There's no pattern," Joab scoffed. "It's just Lilith being a paranoid psychopath. You're giving her too much credit."

"And you're not giving Eden enough. Without an external cipher, the only way a Skipjack can check whether I hold the key is to expose it to my memory, like a mirror. In a normal mind, this process would happen so quickly that it would be subconscious. The Skip flashes the key, and I either have it and it releases the data, or I don't, and it wipes my memory instead. Either way, there's still a window where this happens." Emélie paused to look at Joab. "You know about windows," she added.

"So let me get this straight," Joab said, sounding almost entertained at the proposal. "Your plan is to mainline Origin so you can trick some outdated, solid-state hardware into giving up its payload, and you suspect this will work because somehow, in your career of simulating parallel realities, you coincidentally picked up expertise in cryptographic protocol?" He shook his head. "You're out of your depth."

Instead of firing back a reply, she bit her lip. He wasn't wrong.

"Kepler's Reef," Roland said.

Emélie felt the color leave her face; she waited for what he had to say, lips drawn into a pale, thin line. Everyone in the room was watching too, intent on what came next. "When you were recovered on Earth, you told the DAO you were held at Kepler's Reef. Here on Luna."

Emélie remained silent as her eyes fell to her hand. Shaking again. Shaking like a leaf.

"How did you know it was Kepler's Reef?"

She closed her eyes. *How did she know?* It was a good question. It was a question she would ask. It surely wasn't a good look, shutting up like this in the middle of a field op, all eyes on her, waiting for a simple response. She pushed the concern aside. What she needed to do now was remember, and what Joab had said earlier—something about needing the right trigger—hung at the forefront of her mind, loaded and ready. Roland had said her hand shook because something in her remembered what her mind had lost. If that were true, then something now, about this moment, was also true. She stopped fighting the maelstrom of fractured memories and set them free, moving with the same fervor as her hand: Shouting, gunfire, laughter. Find. Cables—computer cables. Lungfuls of water, euphoria. Again. Again. Again. Fountainhead.

Find Fountainhead.

In the aftermath, a strange stillness. She opened her eyes.

"There was a sign..." she said finally. "Kepler's Reef GC. I don't know what the GC was for. The place... it reminded me of... it looked like a Sanctuary, although we didn't build any of those on Luna. That's all I remember."

Roland turned to Joab. "Gate Control, although that isn't the only thing at Kepler's Reef."

"She's got a main network relay hidden down there, too," Joab replied, rubbing his chin. "Xanadu. Inside the old Loop facility. You think they might've had Desjardins down there cleaning comsec packets?" he asked, thinking out loud. "Could explain how she knows a method for bypassing a key flash."

"I'm sorry, what were you saying about a Loop?" Emélie asked, groping for a foothold in the conversation unfolding around her. "Gate Control. As in Gate Control for another lunar Loop facility?" She glanced at Joab. "And what the hell is a comsec packet?"

"Communications Security," Joab replied. "We have reason to believe Lilith may have been connected to your abduction. She's been probing Earth's defense network for a while, and your proximity to the Loop project likely made you a target. We're getting off track here, though." He nodded toward the bag of Origin solution in Goodnight's hand. "You really think this could work?"

"Origin..." Emélie said, trying to refocus under the barrage of new information. "Origin has a three-phase action. Phase one is hallucinogenic, but it's also associated with decreased activity in the brain's default mode network, the same region responsible for self-referential thinking. When the authentication program on this Skipjack flashes my memory, Origin will inhibit my conscious mind, allowing my subconscious to observe and retain the exposed key. Based on the function of this device as you've described it, once the protocol determines that I lack the necessary cipher, it will run a counter-tampering program designed to attack my neurological system as a defense mechanism. If we get our timing right, this process will directly coincide with the onset of Origin's second phase."

"The regen phase," Joab grinned, slapping Goodnight on the shoulder. "We know a thing or two about that one."

Emélie eyed the men and continued. "Kill me inside this window, and you'll insulate my cognitive function while the countermeasures installed on the Skipjack run their course. The latent Origin in my system will mask the fact that I died, providing a passive electrical signal to prevent the device from deactivating until the process completes and Origin kickstarts my normal brain activity and heals the gunshot wound."

Despite her elaboration, Goodnight stood opposite her with a blank look on his face.

"Maybe you should explain it again," Joab said. "Only this time, in terms these crater jockeys can wrap their one-track minds around."

Emélie noticed Goodnight had a death grip on the IV bag. "Listen, it's relatively straightforward. When the Skipjack activates, the Origin will trick my brain into thinking I'm dead, bypassing the security protocol to read the key inside. Then, you're going to kill me, preventing the Skipjack from wiping my mind until the Origin wakes me up with a Gate token safely unlocked." She tied a strip of elastic tubing around her bicep and slid the IV needle into her arm. "Don't worry. If I don't come back, I promise not to haunt you."

"What about the Jump?" Roland asked.

She had hoped nobody would ask about the third phase. "I have a workaround," she said, looking up at the second IV bag hanging above her head. "After Goodnight shoots me, someone needs to flush my system and administer a second dose before the teleportation phase begins." She wrapped the line leading back to the bag around her wrist, pinching the feed tube between her thumb and forefinger.

"I'll handle the flush," Roland said.

She opened her metal hand, revealing the perforated square of blotter paper she'd held back. The paper glowed softly in the light, stamped for passage with the self-intersecting geometric loop of Phaethon's logo. "Under my tongue, for after," she said in a low voice. "Make it count."

Roland nodded, accepting it. He waved Joab over. After a moment's hesitation, he joined them, Skipjack still pinched between his fingers.

"Once we start, there's no backing out," she warned, swinging her legs onto the table and leaning back against the cold surface. She raised her head to look down at Goodnight, who stood near her feet, IV bag in hand. "If you're going to lose the stomach for this, better be honest about it now, or I'm dead. Brain dead." The sort of dead Origin couldn't bring her back from, she didn't have to add.

Goodnight drew his weapon. "I'll handle it."

Emélie rested her head against her pack and gazed up at the light hanging above her. Roland stood nearby, watching. Always watching. "Are you sure you want to go through with this?" he asked.

Emélie relaxed her fingers where they pinched the Origin drip and shivered as the solution from the tube threaded into her arm. "We all have our part," she said.

"We all have our part," Roland nodded.

Joab set the Skip onto her wrist, and Emélie counted back from seven. She could feel the tiny legs poking through her suit as it scurried up her arm, her neck, and across her cheek.

That was the last thing she felt before the Origin hit.

There was a moment—always only a moment—of suspension. The strange intermission between quantum states where the self observes its own dissolution: alive and dead, in parallel. The feeling was familiar, but this time, there was something new. Something wrong. A flash of panic. Emélie felt herself convulse; she was aware of the movement, but there was no conscious thought available to analyze what was happening. Maybe the Skipjack acted faster than expected, and she wasn't experiencing a loss of self, only a loss. Maybe Joab shouted for Goodnight to shoot her before it was too late. And maybe Roland intervened, willing to follow through when everyone else lost their appetite for violence. Maybe all of this happened, or maybe none of it did. Emélie didn't know.

She was dead.

CHAPTER 22
"JUMP"

Phaethon Corp. MAIN build_VX.6.6.09
initializing boot sequence...
running subroutine FOUNTAINHEAD:

bindquery: update parameter to
"JUMP"
encryption protocols intact,
syntax structures intact
[09] entries remaining

begin sentiment analysis,
implicit context target, rundisplay:

BEGIN RECORD >>>

From the moment she was born, she's been two steps ahead of me. Took me long enough to catch up, but I finally managed. Figured out what she's been up to during all those late nights down in the lab. Worked out what everyone else was missing with Precursor. The thing I hoped she wouldn't find. The thing hidden in plain sight. I should have known better. She's like me, in that way. Won't ever leave well enough alone.

The irony isn't lost on me in the slightest, and the same reasons she can't let this go are the same ones that caused me to find it in the first place. And now I think she's gone and done something terrible. Found a way to harness it. Move around with it somehow. And not just Earth, but other places. Other timelines. Last night she came up from the lab, something different in her eyes.

Red dust on her boots.

<<< END RECORD

COMINT/incoming:
TPC-β covariant detected,
temporal markers decohered/flag
ARROGANT for quarantine...

fork main, set HESPERIDIES
subroutine to active:

update SALOME to VISIBLE and in
PARDES, monitor when PROXIMAL

"Weave a circle round him thrice,
and close your eyes with holy dread"

sanitize data entry,
purge access logs to XANADU
KILL remote process

CHAPTER 23
MÉCANIQUE ANALYTIQUE

Blood in the grout, water in her boots. Emélie sat beside a pool, sopping wet and fatigue-drenched as another wave of nausea gripped her body. The stained tiles beneath her rolled in and out of focus; or possibly, reality was moving. Hands to her forehead: she was no longer bleeding, although the pool was stained with it. Was it her blood? And there was something else in the water, suspended in lazy drift. She leaned forward, scooping up a handful of leaves floating thick as a mat. Beneath them, more blood in the water.

And there was something wrong with the Manifold.

Joab appeared behind her, clutching his carbine by the barrel shroud with one hand. "On your feet," he said, tapping her shoulder with his free hand as he moved past.

She stuffed the leaves into her pack with near-drunken accuracy. *Green.* Impossibly green. Wrong for a lunar safehouse. Wrong anywhere, but her Origin-fogged mind couldn't hold the thought long enough to examine it. Fresh blood ringed a single bullet hole in the lid of her pack, right where her head had been resting as she dosed herself with Origin. Through the steam, a rush of denser, dry air moved along the floor where she sat. She heard muffled voices nearby and a moment later, two of Goodnight's men emerged, dragging a bound and masked

Lilith along the same route Joab had taken. Emélie rubbed her eyes, then awkwardly got back to her feet and followed them.

In the adjacent hallway, she found Joab crouched near a door leading into the next room. One ear pressed to his radio, but he gave a curt nod acknowledging her presence as she slumped down beside him. "The doc's with me," he called over the mic. "We're mobile in five. And make sure to sweep that hallway again before we egress. I don't want any repeats of last time."

Last time? she mouthed, wading through her sluggish thoughts for a thread leading back to something else she'd recalled about Kepler's Reef in the moments before she died. When she found it, the realization rippled up her still-drenched frame, convergence imminent.

LG. The two additional letters she hadn't uttered to Roland and Joab. After their comments disclosed the presence of a third Loop facility inside the Reef, and GC was revealed to be a shorthand for Gate Control, Emélie was finally able to decipher the remaining two letters. Two letters which, in the emergent context of a Loop, could only mean one thing: the facility class designation.

Luna Gimel.

When struck against the hard edges of her memory, the phrase reverberated through every muscle fiber in her body. She twitched, jolted by the part of her mind awakened at the latent truth deposit.

"Joab," she muttered, forward reaching, clumsily pulling at the edge of his sleeve. "Joab, listen. Talk—we... need to—"

He swatted her hand away, eyes fixed on the nearby door as he waited for clearance to push. "Not now."

The abrupt dismissal came with a clarifying shock. "It's urgent. There's something you need to know about the—"

"I said not now, Desjardins. We'll deal with whatever you have to say when we're in the clear. And don't ask me again, or I'll have you hooded too."

Emélie tipped her head back, too exhausted for further engagement. If taking a bullet didn't earn her the chance to ask questions, getting anything from Joab was a lost cause. The marble statue above her looked down with four dull eyes and roughly the same amount of compassion.

"Leviathian Two, this is Leviathan Actual. Clear to push," Joab's radio chirped.

He leaned forward, scanning the hallway before moving ahead. His movements were sharper than before, honed to a tactical point by the compounding threat of extracting Lilith—the Hesperides Cartel's number two—from her own safehouse.

"This is madness," Emélie whispered, partly a consolation and mostly an admission of her own role in enabling the events now unfolding around her.

Back on her feet, only to feel the unforgiving grip of nausea. No doubt the byproduct of a heroic Origin dose, a bullet to the head, and a reality bypass. One hand went out, steadying herself against the plaster wall as her field of view compressed to a point on the floor and her temples pounded to her heartbeat. The meager contents of her stomach threatened to evacuate as she forced air through flared nostrils. When it passed, she lifted her head back up. Joab was long gone.

Beside her, Roland.

"Can you walk?" he asked. A thumping sound echoed down the hall.

"I... I Jumped," she said, glancing back toward the pool room. "I wasn't supposed to Jump." Finding it difficult to hold her composure, she directed her gaze to the puddle of water forming beneath Roland. "There's something wrong with the Manifold."

Roland waited, his grey eyes actively assessing her. Here was a man who didn't care for social conventions. A man who spoke when he was good and ready, and only when he had something to say. "I'm listening," he said.

"Joab said Eden is evolving. Changing how the Loop operates." She raised her eyes, risking more nausea. "She modified the topology."

He considered her statement, then held out a hand. The goggles, stained dark with blood. "Generating a new Manifold would require significant resources. Hard to hide something of that magnitude, especially with so many eyes watching."

"No, not a new Manifold. A continuous one."

Roland's jaw tightened almost imperceptibly.

She took the goggles and hung them back around her neck. "Everything we know about the Loop suggests it constructed the Manifold as a reflection of our reality. A mirror. But what I saw back there..." She paused, watching Roland's face for an angry horizon. When it held, calm and steady, she lit out for new territory. "I don't know why I'm telling you. You've already been inside."

Roland looked out into the hall. The opposite of a glance; his eyes moved directly to something, tracking it in the shadows. Emélie followed his attention and found only the vacant corridor. As she drew her gaze back, one of the magazines mounted across his abdomen caught her eye: from where his hand rested atop it, a faint glow leaked out from the rounds beneath. Red, like Origin. Like the Jumper's eyes. Like something that belonged to the Manifold, not here.

"That woman," Emélie nodded toward the staircase exit. "She came from the Manifold, didn't she? Not a clone, another Lilith. A parallel one."

Roland watched her a moment longer, then turned to leave. "Put your goggles back on," he said before disappearing up the stairs.

A retort ready on her lips, and then Emélie thought of the Jumpers they'd seen on the way in, and her Origin use, and the woman who was probably going to get them all killed being shoved into one of the trucks. It was connected in some way. And maybe nobody was talking about it because they didn't actually know, and it was better to feign indifference than admit ignorance. Only one way to find out, so she put the goggles on and followed Roland back to the trucks.

Back in the garage, it was as she expected: Joab shoving Lilith into the backseat of his vehicle while Roland stood watch nearby. She moved from the corridor to find Goodnight flagging her down, hand raised as he traced a lopsided circle above his head. "Doc, let's get a move on!" he called, one of the last people not already inside a truck.

Nobody had yet defined the potential repercussions that came with abducting one of Lilith's... Reflections. Judging by the way Goodnight held his rifle—and his willingness to abandon stealth for speed—they seemed severe.

Emélie caught her door as the driver pulled up alongside her, hoisting herself into the seat opposite Roland. Goodnight pulled his radio down and glanced back to make sure everyone was inside. "This is Leviathan Actual, standby for exfil." He rapped his driver on the shoulder and thrust his chin toward the exit. "Punch it," he said.

The driver obliged. Within minutes, they'd crossed the Levant and merged onto the ramp leading back down into the basin. As they crested the rim of the crater, the main thoroughfare leading to the station came into view, and with it, the chilling realization that getting off of Luna wasn't going to be simple.

"It's a goddamn traffic jam out here," Goodnight said, leaning so far forward his face was nearly into the windshield. The route ahead was jammed up by other vehicles. Flatbeds, mostly. Slow-moving rollers bound for the station spaceport. Between them, a sampling of labor shuttles, now spilling their restless passengers onto the concrete roadway. He grabbed the truck radio, but before he could hail the station, Joab came on their secure line, interrupting his efforts.

"Goodnight, what exactly are we looking at here?" Joab asked, his voice prickly and lush with static. "What happened to priority clearance through this checkpoint?"

From the backseat, Emélie could hear Goodnight cursing under his breath as he pulled up an updated data overlay on the heads-up. Lockdown status for each of Jericho Station's five sectors crawled across the window: all five of them flashed in angry colors. A sense of uneasiness spread across her chest; when she looked over at Roland, he sat calmly, observing the situation with his characteristic detachment. Even Thursday would have been a little on edge, and he wasn't even human. Roland's cool attitude toward the implicit threat everyone else seemed to be preoccupied with was somehow even worse. At least if things were going to hell, she could count on Goodnight to confirm it.

"Motherfucker," he said, not into the radio. Then, on the radio. "Copy. Standby." He pressed his face to the armored side window for a view past a fuel tanker blocking their path. The radio continued with some indiscriminate chatter as other vehicles offered up additional information on the situation. "Yeah, One, this is Actual. It looks like there was an incident at one of the lower-level checkpoints. Station control routed all the traffic through here instead." Goodnight scanned the information scrolling in front of him as they crawled forward, a few feet at a time. Between them and safety, hundreds of vehicles, some of them stalled and fuel-starved. And here they were, stuck in the thick of it on an elevated roadway, no egress to either side, and the Cartel's second-in-command in the hot seat. By any measure, an unfavorable situation that moved, as a function of time, from bad to worse. Terse silence from the radio. Goodnight tried station control again. Again, no reply. "Jericho isn't hailing," he reported after a few more failed attempts.

There was a brief pause. "Get a direct line open with our transport and tell them to stand by for an alternate LZ," Joab called back. "We've got too much exposure to wait for station control to unfuck this mess."

"Copy that," Goodnight replied. "You want me to push for dismount?"

Emélie leaned against her door, concealing her grasp on the handle beside her.

"Negative. That's too much attention. I'll handle the LZ designation, just keep eyes for now and get me an encrypted channel open with our transport," Joab replied. When one of the doors on the lead vehicle swung open and he stepped out, Emélie tugged at her own door handle, launching herself out of the truck before Goodnight or Roland could intervene.

Not even a hint of surprise on Joab's face as Emélie intercepted him. "Get back to your truck," he ordered, sidestepping her as she moved directly into his path.

As if expecting his reaction, Emélie made an easy pivot, counter-acting his forward movement by backpedaling so she could face him as he continued toward the guardrail. "When were you going to tell me?!" she demanded, matching Joab's pace with coordinated effort despite the chaotic cocktail of Origin overdose and a gunshot wound sustained less than an hour prior. "That was you on the surface two days ago, wasn't it? Back on Earth, inside that storm. Going after another version of Lilith." The realizations were coming fast and heavy for Emélie. Despite the mental and physical effort of each hurdle, she kept up. She didn't have a choice.

At the highway's edge, Joab stopped and leaned forward, looking over the waist-high railing.

"Did you kidnap that one, too?" she asked, panting. Unwilling to burn even a few seconds catching her breath. When no reply came from Joab, she continued, winded, although her anger, hot and uncontained, came through just fine. "We're here because you already killed her, didn't you. This isn't your only asset. It's just the only one you have that's still alive."

The blow came hard and fast, impacting Emélie squarely on the sternum; she dropped, blinded by pain that followed the distant crack of her headset bashing against the metal guardrail on her way to the ground. She caught herself with both hands before her head hit concrete. Pushing off of it, she raised herself back onto all fours.

Joab leaned in close, his words near her ear as he spoke in a low tone. "How I run my assets and what I do with them is none of your concern. You agreed to come here to fill a role, and you did that, and now you're going back to Earth. End of story."

Emélie stared down at her gloved hands, fingers splayed in the fine grey moondust covering the highway. She was still seething. "What about Roland?" she asked. "How did he know where I would emerge from that Jump? Nobody knew that! *I* didn't even know that!"

"We've already gone over this. Everyone here is operating under the oversight of the Director, including you. That's all you need to know, and it's all you will ever know. Now I'm not going to tell you again. Get back to your truck." Joab's low volume rose only slightly, but it was clear he would not be answering any more questions.

Emélie sat up, hands on her knees, her face inches from Joab's. "Or what? You're going to kill me like the rest of your assets? That's what I am, right? Just another pawn in your war on drugs?"

Joab raised himself back to his full height and hoisted Emélie up by the arm after him. "Look," he pointed to the trucks. "What do you see?"

She inhaled sharply.

From the drop holster on his leg, Joab produced a black handgun. "Answer the question," he said, the handgun hanging loosely in one hand beside him.

"Three teams. A psychopath. A parallel version of Lilith."

"Congrats. You just put every single one of those lives in imminent danger because the only person you can think about is yourself." He waved his gun toward the line of parked vehicles. "You think you're the only person Lilith has exploited? Someone who's made a career out of systemic violence isn't going to suddenly start playing fair because we opened one fucking Gate. There's more at play here than you could ever understand, but I'm not the one keeping you in the dark. You want information? Open your eyes. You're only blinding yourself."

"We've got comms with transport," Goodnight called over the radio. "They're on station for an alternate LZ."

Joab holstered his gun. "Leviathan Actual, this is One. Standby for transmit," he called into his radio, turning back for the trucks. He threw one last passing glance at Emélie on his way by. "We're done here."

She returned to find Goodnight dismounted, leaning against the hood of their truck. "You couldn't have waited to piss him off until we got back to Homestake?" he asked. "Now your problem is everyone's problem."

She yanked her door open and dropped her body armor onto the seat. Roland wasn't in the truck. Shouting drifted from somewhere near the station entrance, and a few civilians ran past them, moving back out into the Levant. She leaned against the fender, looking over at the crowd of people waiting at the nearby pedestrian checkpoint as Goodnight climbed onto the roof for a better view of the commotion.

At first glance, the crowd's movements seemed oddly fluid and self-organized. Individual bodies began to reorient themselves in concentric, weighted rings as a small gap opened in their midst, like ferrous dust against a magnetic field. Where others might have seen random motion, Emélie perceived the elegant mathematics beneath the crowd's movement: not chaos, but a measured response to a quantum disturbance.

This was how a Gate began.

She rose to her feet, transfixed, as the same vestiges of dust she'd observed back on Earth appeared in the gap forming in the crowd. She took another step, moving forward as reality shuddered and distorted around her, pulling her in.

Suddenly, the Gate was within arm's reach.

Risking a glance back at Goodnight, she found him still on the truck, twenty paces away when she'd only taken two. He was distracted by something in the opposite direction, and as she turned back to the Gate, found the lingering dust consolidating near a center mass. A human form stepped through, taller than the average man with a face turned down beneath a wide-brimmed hat. When he looked up, he met Emélie's gaze with a single crimson eye.

She stumbled backward as the shape stepped out, dust encircling it in a recursive, billowing cloud. Time slowed to a trickle as a surging wave of localized reality distortion rolled across the ground, moving in a shockwave of rippling dust that carried toward the trucks.

"EMP!" The warning died in Emélie's throat, choked by cascading dust. A break for the trucks—her open door stood waiting, a metal refuge. Behind her, the Jumper hit the ground with a resonant thump. The dive came instinctively. Contact with the truck, a spin, fingers grasping for the door handle. The Jumper reappeared, one skeletal arm catching the edge as she yanked it shut. That gaunt face held her gaze, unblinking. She threw herself back across the seat, boot connecting with the door in a desperate kick that sent it crashing against the Jumper's frame.

Dust where it should have fallen.

Half a second, and it flickered back into existence at her open door. A sudden pressure gripped her temples. Behind her, the muffled burst of suppressed rifle fire: *pffff pffff pffff* punctuated by the metallic clack of a cycling action. The Jumper flickered, then imploded into a suspended ball of dust that hung in the windless lunar environment. Through the open vehicle, Roland stood on the opposite side. Rifle in hand. Watching.

"Fence yourselves in," Goodnight said, hopping down from the roof as gunfire broke out around them. "We're about to take contact."

CHAPTER 24
WETWARE

"What did you see in there?"

Emélie glanced down the line of trucks, trying to find her bearings under the weight of Joab's full attention.

From somewhere nearby, the lazy rattle of automatic gunfire rolled toward them. Joab, seemingly unbothered by their proximity to it, pressed Emélie for an answer. "I want you to tell me *exactly* what you saw when you were inside the Manifold. Now, and make it quick. This whole op was just burned."

She opened her pack and pulled out a fistful of leaves. "I Jumped, Joab. I've been trying to tell you. I was falling. There were trees, and water, and then Roland was pulling me out of a pool." She watched the leaves drifting to the concrete. "If you have a weak link, it's not me."

Joab glanced over at Roland, who stood off to the side, rifle cradled in the crook of his arm, then pulled a satellite phone from a pouch on his body armor. "Scrub the vehicles," he ordered, unfolding the antenna. "We're taking an alternate LZ."

Despite the chaos erupting around them, his movements remained precise and economical as he strode over to the lead vehicle and yanked the door open with enough force to rock the truck on its suspension. Inside, Lilith sat motionless, head angled slightly forward as the oubliette suppressed any indication of the events unfolding outside. He pressed the phone to his ear and, with his other hand, seized her by the collar and hauled her back across the open roadway to where Emélie waited. Without breaking stride, he thrust Lilith forward, then abruptly pulled her back, halting her in arm's reach of Emélie. "You want me to believe you didn't draw those Jumpers?" He motioned to Goodnight, who ripped the bag from Emélie's arms and dumped the contents. "Prove it."

From a pile of wilted leaves, Goodnight fished Emélie's fix kit, opened it, and tore off a row of Origin tabs from the sheet of blotter paper.

"Hold on," Emélie cautioned, eying the doses of Origin in Goodnight's hand. "You want me to try to make another Jump right here? In the middle of the highway?"

One well-placed boot from Joab sent Lilith to the ground, knees buckling, her masked head tipped back to the lunar sky.

Reluctantly, Emélie reached for the Origin. Before her fingers felt paper, Goodnight had her by the scruff of her neck. Her eyes bulged as his free hand—the hand with the drugs—clamped tight across her mouth, force-feeding her the entire row of tabs. Her resistance was but a symbolic gesture; the taste of stale paper burned on the way down. The humiliation that came with it was even harder to swallow.

Goodnight relaxed his grip. She shoved him away, wiping her mouth with the back of her hand. "I would have done it myself," she said, her cheeks flushed pink from the bitter combination of anger and embarrassment. A thin line of spittle clung to her lower lip, and the metallic bite of Origin lingered on her tongue. Her gaze darted to her kit, which had landed precariously at the roadway's edge, teetering above four stories of darkness.

Joab stepped forward, closing the space between them with deliberate slowness. "I'm waiting," he said.

How long did she have before the come up? Three tabs. The same dose she'd given herself earlier, except this one wasn't adequately prepared. The onset would take time, and when it came, it would be harsh. "You're going to be waiting a while. It's not like I have any control over it. And even if I did, you're misunderstanding the function. If I

Jump, it's only going to be me, and we've moved since the first time." She waved an arm across the lunar basin. "Different location here, different location inside the Manifold—"

A heavy weight smacked against her stomach; instinctively, her hands dropped to her belly, shielding the soft organs at her center mass.

She found her hands pressed to Joab's gun.

He pulled away, leaving her holding the weapon. "Then I need you… to show me… that you can be trusted." Voice but a whisper, each phrase came weighed down by the threat of future violence.

Emélie stared at the gun now in her possession. The form of it, alien under her grasp—her mechanical fingers wrapped around the grip with near-programmed precision while her human ones trembled against the trigger guard. She'd been unable to suppress the feeling that Lilith—or at least, this Reflection of her—wouldn't live out the day. What she hadn't expected was her hand to be the one pulling the trigger.

Awkwardly, she raised the weapon, extending the barrel toward Lilith in a posture that felt pre-programmed. Inevitable, although not by her.

Lilith's shoulders began to shake. Not the agony of before, but with a soft, rolling movement—*laughter*. Even behind the mask, without sight or senses, Lilith saw through her. Witness to all the future Emélie's: every version of her that pulled the trigger, and all the ones that didn't. She wasn't a killer, surely? And yet, here, now, a new path opened: squeeze the trigger, create options. A way forward, if she could only accept it. One terrible thing for the greater good.

And was it even so terrible, killing this… this Reflection? According to Joab, she was nothing more than a construct. No more human than Eden, the AI she'd supposedly resurrected to run the Loop. And yet, both exhibited traits that made Emélie suspect otherwise. And, at least in her experience, a construct didn't possess a body, or blood, or lungs to breathe, even if they were currently being used to mock her. Her finger tensed against the trigger—then relaxed. With a soft exhale, she lowered the gun.

Joab shrugged. "Better luck next time."

Goodnight plucked the gun from her hands, leveled it at Lilith, and closed the loop. The *whomp* of a single gunshot thumped Emélie across the chest before her mind could process what had happened. A sound that felt less like noise and more like rupture, she watched as Lilith's body jerked backward, then vanished mid-drop.

Emélie backed away, her hand rising to stifle the scream that was cut short, transformed through shock into something of a choked gasp. Her vision tunneled.

This wasn't how death worked; bodies didn't just up and vanish.

"You can't deliver, so I'm going to help you out," Joab said, thrusting his arm forward to check his watch. Goodnight ejected the handgun magazine and pulled a replacement round from one of the pouches on his body armor. The metal cartridge had a clear sabot housing a small dose of liquid Origin. Same as the ones she'd noticed Roland carrying back at the safehouse. He slotted it into the magazine, slapped the magazine back into the handgun, and tossed the handgun over to Joab.

"These rounds are dosed for one-way trips, but we got a Tether on her, so she'll be back in seven minutes when the Origin wears off. Since you seem to have forgotten how to Jump on your own, I'm giving you somewhere to Jump *to*. Open a Gate into the Manifold and bring her back before it pulls her back, or you're looking at a direct return flight to Earth when we land on Homestake." He walked over to where Emélie's fix kit lay partially hanging off the roadway and paused, resting the edge of his boot against it. "That, or I'll leave you here with the rest of the Jumpers," he added, grinning, although it was the sort of grin that always preceded something far worse. "You'll be in good company."

Hardly more than a tap from his boot, and the case went over the edge. Four stories into darkness. Falling, just like Lilith's body hadn't. Her chest tightened.

They wanted a Jump. And then what? Track that Reflection of Lilith through whatever impossible geometry waited on the other side—on the underside—of this reality? Her hands were shaking, only this time, it was from the crippling choice she couldn't make.

"I don't—" she started, only for her voice to fracture around the words. She tried again. "I don't know if I can do what you're asking." The rest of it tasted like defeat, but also closer to the truth than anything else she'd said in a long time. They were well beyond the realm of theory, and in place of equations on a screen and mathematical models running on a server back at Sanctuary, here was a body moving against the laws of physics, and the demand she follow it. Before she could figure out where to even begin, Goodnight's radio broke the silence.

"We've got a technical moving south-southwest along a secondary MSR. Two clicks," one of Goodnight's spotters called up. "SAM capable," the spotter added.

The men exchanged glances.

"Hitman one, this is Goodnight Actual," Goodnight called into his radio. "You're live for target."

"Live for target," came the reply.

Before Goodnight could issue further instructions, the spotter replied over the radio. "Second technical, approaching six o'clock."

Emélie noticed one of Goodnight's men had climbed onto the cargo rack of the last vehicle, taking up a prone position behind a high-powered rifle. The heavy barrel tracked a subtle arc as it followed something moving in the distance.

"Two hundred meters and closing," the spotter called. "Permission to engage."

"Standby," Goodnight replied.

Joab checked his watch. "Four minutes."

"Too long," Roland said. He watched a group of people emerge from their vehicles near the station entrance. "They're setting up a box pinch. Small arms fire at the checkpoint to seal the door, and a technical at the other end to block the exit." He pointed behind them, where a second vehicle—a much larger, eight-wheeled assembly with a tarp over the back—crawled down the crater rim, closing in. "Second technical waiting to suppress air if we try to egress directly off the highway. They're already sweeping."

The sound of gunfire had changed from a distant rattle to something more deliberate. Methodical. The concrete under her boots seemed to vibrate with each burst, as if the highway itself was coming apart. Emélie watched the spotter's barrel track left, hunting a target she couldn't see—a predator encircling its kill. Around them, Goodnight's men moved with practiced urgency—checking magazines, adjusting positions, weapons coming up to shoulders. The air tasted metallic, sharp with ozone and something else. Burned propellant. Fear.

Goodnight glanced at the spotter behind the rifle. As if on cue, the spotter leaned into his radio. "Multiple dismounts confirmed. Five Jumpers and counting."

"Buy me some time," Joab said, glancing at his watch again.

Goodnight leaned into his radio. "Hitman One, you're clear to engage."

The heavy rifle shook the truck as it fired, sending a wave of dust rolling off the roof. Once. Twice. Silence.

"Technicals down," the spotter called.

An explosion rocked the concrete highway. Emélie dropped to the ground as the road behind them split, shearing off to form a gap that cut off access back to the Levant. Alarms broke out inside the station, and a blast door retracted over the checkpoint, sealing off the entrance.

Joab motioned to Goodnight. "Map, now," he said, snapping his fingers repeatedly and pointing to a clear area on the ground between them.

Goodnight knelt beside the truck and hit a button on his arm display, projecting the map he'd been monitoring onto a smooth section of concrete.

Joab pointed to a location a few blocks away. "There's an old factory on level two with an open roof, about half a click from our current position. There's not enough room to land, but we'll have temporary cover in case they try to ground us on the way out."

Goodnight assessed the roadway ahead. "That's still three stories of difference between here and the LZ. Going to be tough to cover that much vertical with the resources on hand."

Without taking his eyes from the empty space where Lilith's body should have been, Joab tapped his watch. "Get a move on, Desjardins."

Emélie, overrun by the absurdity of the situation, flung her arms wide. "I don't—what exactly do you expect me to do? I can't just pull her out of thin air."

"You've got a fresh dose of Origin in your system and two working eyes," Joab replied, gesturing to the soft pink mist—the only residual marker of the gunshot wound that took Lilith, presumably, into the Manifold. "You managed to open a Gate just fine back inside the safe-house, and now you've got the Skipjack key. No reason you can't do it again. This time, with intent." He rechecked his watch. "Now you've got about ninety seconds before Lilith gets pulled back here via the Tether. No telling what sort of resources she has access to inside the Manifold, so I'd prefer you bring her back on our terms. In my line of work, we call that a win-win. You clear your name by showing me what's on the other side of that Gate, and Lilith gets the human treatment. A nice, calm return to this reality."

The pieces came together in her mind with sickening clarity. Joab wasn't interested in her proving she could do it. He was establishing leverage over Lilith. Demonstrating power. If Emélie could reach into the Manifold and drag Lilith back before the Origin wore off, Lilith would understand they had access. For all intents and purposes, the keys to the Hespiredes cartel: keys that not only closed the flow of Origin, but opened doors to Mars.

Mars, and, if Emélie had to guess, to Fountainhead.

"You want me to prove that we can reach her anywhere," Emélie said slowly. The Origin Goodnight had fed her was finally taking hold. Speaking was always the first to suffer, followed by motor control. Cognition, on the other hand, was heightened, and never more needed than in this moment. "You wanted her to feel safe... You wanted her inside an impossible space so she could see us—see me—rip a hole into it and pull her right back to this present hell."

Joab's expression didn't change, but something flickered in his hard eyes—approval, perhaps, or recognition. "I knew you were a fast learner, now—"

Presently, the space around them rippled, then expanded, forming a wrinkle that bunched into distorted folds. Reality became little more than a sheet of cloth pinched and lifted at the center. And from this rift, a pile of dust spilled forth, followed by Lilith, her mask cracked and bloodied but still very much alive and thrashing, deposited in front of Emélie.

"Either she's resistant, or your dosings are off," Emélie said, watching Lilith scramble headfirst for the railing. "Either way, I still had," she checked the panel on her own arm, "sixty-two seconds, by your count."

Joab caught Lilith—the Reflection of her, anyway—and reeled her back in. He did so with a sort of nonchalant assertiveness. To Emélie, everything about the last few days was one unprecedented moment after the next. For Joab and crew, it was just another day on the job. A condition that included snagging a parallel version of a drug smuggler before she could take the fifth-floor exit.

"This isn't over," he said, his words buffered by the rat-a-tat of automatic gunfire to their backs. Closer still. "You still owe me a Gate," he added, jabbing a finger into Emélie's chest as he swung one leg over the guardrail. His next words went to the radio on his collar: "Listen up, team, we're doing this one live. I called in a favor with the station and got them to issue an unplanned maintenance event for the gravity well holding us to the highway. While it's down, we'll be under lunar gravity alone, giving us an easy straight shot down to the extraction point on Level Two. You're cleared hot for engagement." He glanced at the bloody spot where Lilith had vanished. "And red tips only. I'd better not hear about any residuals."

A metallic clatter erupted around them as men began dropping magazines and emptying chambered rounds, which were replaced with fresh magazines carrying the characteristic red glow of Origin-tipped bullets. Goodnight walked between the men, briefing them as they prepared to move. "I want comms clear, and don't forget to watch your dispersion. We're dealing with more than Jumpers today." He paused, checking the display on his arm. "Standby to float."

Emélie watched the men pull as much gear as they could from the trucks while the drivers affixed incendiary devices to the engine blocks.

"Doc, grab your shit," Goodnight ordered, pulling some spare rifle magazines out of a bandolier above the front seat. The rest of the team was already dismounted and moving toward the guardrail. Behind them, Roland reached into the truck, removing the same flat case he'd carried off the landing craft. He slung it across his back and moved over to where Emélie stood, halfway into her body armor. "Follow me," he said.

Emélie fastened her vest and gave him a nod. She stooped down, preparing to gather the scattered contents of her bag.

"Leave it," Roland said.

A moment's hesitation on her part; as it was, she owned little, and the bag was all she'd brought with her. If she left it, she had nothing but the things on her. Movement between a pair of vehicles further down the road drew her attention. Jumpers, weaving through the parked vehicles and closing fast. Not one or five. Hundreds.

"Thirty seconds," Goodnight announced.

Despite the impending Jumpers, Emélie gave one more look at the contents of her bag spread around her. Atop the leaf pile, the last three squares of blotter paper from the row Goodnight had ripped off lay in the center, crumpled but intact. She didn't have to keep running. It might not have seemed like much of a choice, but to choose an end was still something. What had Roland said? An inconvenient truth is still the truth. As far as Emélie was concerned, every truth was inconvenient. It was the lies that were easier to handle. She pocketed the remaining three tabs of Origin and left everything else, including the bag. "What the hell is going on, Roland?!" she asked, ducking under the railing beside him.

He swung one leg over, then the other. Clearing it as smoothly as dust flowing down the face of a stone. "I need you to listen carefully, Emélie. Things will happen over the next few minutes that won't make sense to your logical mind. If you slow down, if you deviate from the path, if you stop or ask questions, you will be left to drift." He leaned against the guardrail, unbothered by the Jumpers encroaching on the abandoned trucks behind them. The rest of the team lined up on either side of them, ready to launch themselves over the edge.

"Aren't you going to hook a cable onto me or something?" Emélie asked, gripping the railing as she felt the inside of her glove grow damp with fear.

"Your fate isn't my responsibility."

"Then maybe you should have let me drown back at the safe house."

"Maybe," he said, his cool eyes shifting to the tattered patchwork of rooftops far below. "We won't know until tomorrow."

"What's tomorrow?"

"The future."

Emélie felt her body lighten as the gravity cycled off. From her periphery, she could see Goodnight's men pushing off the rail, weapons raised as they descended in smooth, parabolic arcs. Roland dropped next, leaving Emélie alone as her stomach fell and her feet remained fixed in place. Five buildings stood between her and the landing zone. Between each one, a gap easily the length of two, possibly three trucks, parked end to end. She watched Roland land on the first building, and when she glanced back at the trucks, the swarm of Jumpers descended.

She let go of the railing.

The first rooftop came harder than she'd anticipated. She made a quick course-correction to stay upright and bounded toward a parapet on the far side of the first building. Roland moved swiftly ahead of her, rifle in hand, and Emélie followed in his wake, head down. Focused. She cleared the next gap, only to find the third building stood slightly taller than the one they were currently on. One of Goodnight's men was out ahead of everyone else, and as he bounded toward the solid wall, launched a circular puck that clung to the concrete surface. There was a flash of light and dust as a slot opened, providing passage through, rather than over, the building.

She risked a look backward to find that not only was she the last one in their group, but Jumpers had started pouring down from the highway in pursuit. They fell, some glitching out of reality before reappearing shy of the roof, where they continued plummeting. Others

Jumped wide, missing the roof entirely, and a few were already out ahead of Emélie, flanking her as she pushed toward the opening in the wall.

It was a reckless leap that propelled her from the roof's edge; an overreaction fueled by a surge of adrenaline and the sheer willingness to escalate as far as was necessary to survive. And it was that very same instinct, an overreaction to the swarm at her back, which, warped by the influence of Origin, proved excessive to the point of failure: slowed by the low gravity and encumbered spatial perception, she came up short. Her torso smashed into concrete above the opening, legs swinging uselessly into the building. Momentum flipped her upside down. Now she was falling. Backward. Toward the street far below. *You will be left to drift,* came Roland's words as she watched the opening slip past. To hell with that. She shot her metal arm out, clamping a vice grip hold on a length of exposed rebar jutting from the base of the hole. The motion stopped her fall with a jolt that nearly dislocated her shoulder. Around her, Jumpers soared past, slamming into the building just like she had. Legs up, she hauled herself into the building. The room was chaos: rubble from the breaching charge littered the floor as Jumpers choked the opening, blotting out what little light she had to work with. Across the room, another slot was marked by pale, weak light. Her stomach turned, and she was through. Falling, then boots to the fourth roof, hard and unforgiving. Clambering, running. Running for her life. The rest of the team was already out of sight, leaving only Roland, dark and fluid, as her waypoint marking the last hundred feet to the LZ.

As she pushed forward, their transport passed overhead, banking hard as it pulled up and dropped down into the extraction zone.

The break in focus cost her dearly.

With her eyes on the approaching ship, Emélie's boot caught an exposed conduit snaking across the rooftop. She lurched forward, arms flailing in the low gravity as she bounced against the roof. She thrust her palms against the pitted concrete, pushing herself upright to recover. Back on her feet, the distance to Roland had doubled, and there was movement—shadows darting unnaturally in and out of view.

Emélie turned and felt her breath catch as a wave of Jumpers descended onto the rooftop around her, converging from both sides to swarm her position. What had been a clear path seconds ago was now a gauntlet of sporadic, grasping forms. Feet planted, she watched as the mass of bodies closed in around her.

Ahead, Roland had reached the edge of the roof. He glanced back at her, assessed the situation, and without hesitation, pushed off the parapet, launching himself backward. As he fell, he rotated his body, bringing his rifle up with mechanical precision and opened fire on the Jumpers in her immediate path. It was as if he could anticipate their movements: the Jumpers materialized only to implode into clouds of swirling dust as each Origin-tipped round found its mark.

Before she could follow him, a Jumper slammed into her.

The impact sent her tumbling forward as the ship dropped out of view. She was falling, but it was too early, and the trajectory was wrong. The world spun past in nauseating cycles—the buildings, the stars, the lunar surface, all blending into a smear of greys and blacks. Right as she cleared the edge of the roof, a glint of light behind a broken window at the next building caught her eye.

She tried to focus on the flash of light. Her stomach turned.

She was standing. Upright, in a room. The windows were blown out of one side. Two Jumpers—two, then four, then two again—stood in the opening, hoisting something out of a large weapon case. Emélie blinked and tried to take a step back. She found herself moving forward instead. *Closer.* One of the Jumpers noticed the movement and torqued its head at her as a string of mechanical clicks spilled from its throat.

Emélie's goggles flickered, then went black.

She tore them away. Through unfiltered eyes, she watched a withered, gaunt hand claw at her exposed eyes. She tucked into a roll, the Jumper's hand grazed her hair as she dodged beneath its reach. At the broken window, her stomach dropped. Five stories of empty space separated her from the ground. Behind her, the Jumpers converged. No time for calculations. No room for doubt. Emélie took a breath and surrendered to what she'd been fighting against as long as she could remember.

She Jumped.

The world around her compressed, reality bent, and then exploded into all possibilities: she watched as a version of herself was torn backward as a Jumper's hand gouged out her eyes. Another version of herself caught the ledge and plummeted headlong toward the concrete far below. Just as she'd seen while standing over Lilith with the gun, Emélie saw all versions of herself—the one who acted, the ones who hesitated, the ones who died in every permutation of doubt. And as she watched all these possibilities unfold before her, there was Roland. Standing on the ramp of the ship.

Watching.

She met his gaze, and the universe snapped back into focus as all possible realities collapsed into that moment. She landed firmly on her feet, back at the edge of the roof where she'd started before the Jumper had knocked her off course. A swarm of Jumpers rushed past her, oblivious to her sudden appearance as they flung themselves toward the waiting ship. Goodnight and Roland stood at the end of the ramp, their weapons methodically turning the closest Jumpers into clouds of dust. Goodnight spotted her and gestured frantically, wheeling one arm in a circular motion as he fired. The ship's engines surged in response, swinging around to present the ramp directly to Emélie's position.

She crouched, Jumpers pushing past her on both sides, then launched herself across the gap. She cleared it and hit the ramp hard, skidding across the angled platform as Goodnight reached out, catching her by the back of her plate carrier before she toppled off the opposite side.

"Rocket!..." Emélie managed, pushing herself up from the deck. "Rooftop!"

Roland pivoted, and without aiming, fired off three shots in rapid succession: two to the chest, one to the head. The Jumper crumpled as the rocket ignited. The projectile streaked toward them, narrowly missing two of the wings as it passed wide of its mark and sailed upward, where it impacted the transparent dome over the Levant in an explosive cloud of white phosphorus.

Emélie returned to her feet and started for the hold, nodding her appreciation to Goodnight as she passed by.

Behind him, a swirl of dust had started to coalesce. Two red points flickered in the churning particles, solidifying into eyes.

Goodnight's hand dropped to his gun as the color drained from Emélie's face. A large Jumper materialized on the ramp behind him. It wore no blindfold, and below its gouged eyes, a second pair of red eyes peered back at Emélie. Instead of the tattered clothing, this one wore a clean station jumpsuit, Phaethon logo in the top corner, and its skin was toned.

A fresh host.

The Jumper swiped, tossing Goodnight further into the hold as it lunged for Emélie. It caught her across the waist, and she tumbled backward. The Jumper's momentum carried them both toward lunar airspace as the ship banked hard left in preparation of exiting the controlled atmosphere. Right before they left the ramp, she collided with one of the hydraulic pistons, catching the cylinder with her metal arm. The Jumper swung past her, dragging her backward as they dangled above the receding rooftops below. Through the pain, Emélie could see Roland standing above her, fingers wrapped around a handgun. He pinned the Jumper's arm under the muzzle and fired: the Jumper recoiled, one hand releasing its grip, but the other remained locked around her leg.

Emélie kicked out with her free boot, striking it squarely across its face. The Jumper's head snapped back, and she kicked again, harder. With a digital wail, it tumbled from the ramp into the vast lunar emptiness.

She scrambled backward until she bumped into Joab, who stood at the top of the ramp, arms crossed.

"Get up," he ordered, yanking Emélie to her feet.

"You're welcome," she muttered, catching her breath.

Joab grabbed her by the back of the neck. "Where are your goggles?"

Emélie reached up, touching her face. The goggles were gone, lost between the rooftop and her second Jump. "I… I couldn't see," she said.

"That's the point!" he shouted, herding Emélie further out onto the ramp. "Why do you think Eden blinds all of Lilith's Jumpers?"

"I… I don't—"

"Eden can't go inside the Manifold."

"That's self-explanatory," Emélie shot back, trying to maintain her balance as Joab backed her dangerously close to the edge. "If she's powering the Loop, of course, she can't go inside. If anything happened to her, it would be catastrophic."

"So put it together. Lilith needs Eden to run the Loop, but Eden's blind to what happens while Lilith is inside of it. Eden can change the parameters and open Gates, and that's it."

"She's dependent on Lilith, and dependencies create weaknesses within the system. You're saying Eden uses Lilith's Jumpers to monitor her movements."

"That's only half of it. To open a Gate, you need a Skipjack, which means you need eyes. By blinding the Jumpers, Eden also ensures Lilith will be restricted to moving in and out through the Gates provided, which allows her to retain some measure of control." He let go of Emélie, a glint in his eye. "Eden is blind inside, and Lilith is blind everywhere else. And that in-between is where we operate. Where we move undetected."

"That's not what you told me when we started," Emélie replied, jabbing a finger in the direction she assumed was Homestake. "You said Lilith made the Jumpers."

"I said Lilith *used* them," he replied flatly. "To her, they're just assets in a system she inherited, but Eden is controlling what happens inside. The Jumpers monitor anyone using the Loop. That currently happens to be Lilith, but Eden doesn't even grant her unrestricted access." He forked two fingers at Emélie's exposed eyes. "I told you to wear the goggles because if someone under the influence of Origin makes eye contact with a Jumper, it creates a neurological link to Eden, giving her access to everything they see for as long as the Origin is active in their system."

The rate at which new information was coming in was staggering, and the pounding in her temples from wearing the now absent headset for so long didn't help. She rubbed her forehead as Joab stepped up into the hold. "You could have told me," she called after him. Her voice carried an edge it hadn't held back on the highway—steadier, sharper. The woman who couldn't pull a trigger felt far from the one who now fired those words at Joab. "I deserved the truth."

"Some truths can't be explained, Desjardins. They have to be experienced. You've spent two years trying to solve a puzzle with half the pieces missing. Maybe that was by design. People who know too much theorize. People who know less are forced to act on instinct. And today, I needed your instincts more than your theories."

Emélie hardly trusted herself. He had a point, though. This wasn't the time for thinking, although she'd more than made up for it at the end. "It won't happen again," she said, not a hint of apology in the statement. It was a promise, mostly to herself, and uttered out loud, to never let Joab get out ahead of her like that.

"You're right about that," Joab replied, turning for the hold. "When we get back to Homestake, you're on your own."

CHAPTER 25
TWO TRUTHS AND A LIE

True to his word, Joab abandoned Emélie when they landed on the tarmac at Homestake. He was down the ramp before it was fully lowered, towing a masked and bloodied Lilith behind him. Roland was not far after, disappearing into the maze-like hangar before she'd even finished removing her safety harness.

At the top of the ramp, she watched Goodnight's team disperse into the commotion of the flight deck, unsure of what came next. There had been no debrief on the return flight, but it wasn't until Emélie watched the men leave without any exchange or formality that she fully grasped the severe anonymity they operated under. These were not people who wanted to be known and, by proximity to their work, also endeavored to know as little as possible. When she was the only remaining person in the hold, Goodnight appeared by her side.

Emélie grimaced. "Of course," she muttered.

He held out an access card bearing the Phaethon logo. "Elevator back to Earth leaves in half an hour. This will get you a ride down. After that, you're on your own."

She looked at the card. To accept it felt, in some small way, like an admission that whatever had cost them their cover on Luna came down to some fault of her own. She had no way to prove otherwise. There was no document trail or formal agreement with which she could furnish as evidence of the accused breach. Her entire commitment to join Joab hinged on an ambiguous, open-ended verbal agreement behind closed doors. And the only witness, conveniently, was the Director: the one person nobody would ever draw into questioning. It would have been easier if Joab had left her to find her own way back, but he was a man for whom overreaction was the only suitable course of action, and so, imparted to Emélie a reminder that backdoors, bypassed checkpoints, and direct flights still existed, just not for her. And much like her decision to follow him up here, Emélie found herself left with a choice by process of elimination. While location differed, in every other way, she was right back where she started: no closer to Mars, to Fountainhead, and to the answers that came with both.

She took another look at the card, hesitant, ready to reject the offer. She was in no hurry to get Earthside; the only things waiting for her down there were a condescending lecture from Aratheus and reassignment to somewhere where she could be somebody else's problem.

"Take it or don't, but don't take it personally," Goodnight said, pushing the card toward her. "It's a kindness, really."

He had a point. And Joab wasn't around—nor would he care—if she tried to prove something by rejecting it.

She took the card. "I'd say it was nice to meet you, but that would be a lie, so I guess I'll just go."

"That's probably for the best."

She left Goodnight without another word and started for Homestake's central level, home of the main terminus for Earthbound passengers. Despite a few wrong turns, she managed to find the Phaethon terminal without significant hassle, although her time trailing Joab as he expertly mazed his way through crowded and unmarked corridors made taking the prescribed route feel cumbersome.

A dock agent standing near a long window was supervising a row of containers loaded onto the car. She approached, bypassing his hard glare, to hand over the access card Goodnight had provided her. He didn't seem like the helpful sort; Emélie was counting on him offering directions only to keep her out of the way. After a surly look, he scanned the card. When the manifest on the computer in his hand updated, he let out an audible sigh and shook his head. “Exposure suit?” he demanded, tapping a few keys on his machine.

Emélie glanced over at the elevator car. “No?” she replied, unsure of why that was a requirement.

The agent continued typing. “You’re booked as space available. The passenger car is full up, so you’ll have to ride in cargo.”

Cargo. No passenger amenities, no seating, no windows. Just a harness, a platform, and a bunch of metal containers inside a larger one. Emélie reminded herself that it was likely not personal: the elevator cars running up and down the cable linking the platform back to Earth were, while spacious, primarily designed for moving cargo without the fuel cost of escaping gravity. They were fitted with a single passenger bay at the top of each car, and a ride booked this close to departure would likely be full. She also remembered that Joab had a private shuttle on demand and still opted to send her back on this.

“Convenient,” she muttered.

The agent gave her a sideways glance and walked over to a wall near the window. He pulled a crate from a shelf littered with various equipment, none of it looking particularly well-maintained. “No life support in cargo, so make sure to test the suit before you board,” he said, coming back over to where Emélie waited. He dropped the crate at her feet. “Helios Orbital is not liable for deaths due to improperly installed or faulty environmental hazard equipment.”

“Right,” Emélie said, leaning over to pick up the bin. “When does it leave?”

The shipping agent ignored her question and went back to his work. Emélie schlepped the bin across the room and down a set of stairs, where she found an open platform linking the lower cargo gangway to the docked elevator car. Out of the travelling she’d done, the bulk of it could be reduced to either waiting in some sort of vehicle or changing in and out of different levels of exposure gear; it wasn’t difficult to understand the appeal of the Loop, which let you be somewhere else in the time it took to walk across a room.

The crate rattled as she dropped it to the floor. Inside was a grimy, cream-colored, level three exposure suit that looked a few sizes too large. She lifted the suit out, which carried the faded corporate logo of the parent shipping company, Helios Orbital Systems, on the helmet, sleeves, and lapel. Level Three was substantial, and likely overkill for the ride down to Earth; she could have taken a zero-gravity spacewalk in the thing if she wanted to. The helmet carried a gold-mirror blast shield, and as she pulled it up, the distorted, inverted reflection of Roland appeared on the convex surface.

"So this is how it's going to be," she said, trying to cover up her shock. *How did he move so softly?* "I thought you were on my team."

"We're all here for the same reason."

Emélie stood. "I've heard that before."

"You don't believe it?"

"I believe what I see."

"Dangerous in your line of work." Roland's eyes shifted, vigilant. "And, tell me, Emélie. What do you see?"

"Don't deflect, Roland. You know what I'm talking about. The Jumper that came through the Gate before we were attacked outside Jericho Station. The one that nobody else seemed to notice. Nobody, except you." She glanced at the red markings peeking out from the sleeve of his dark, tunic-like jacket. "What was it?"

His expression darkened. "Older," he replied. "It moves through the cracks in reality. Between the Manifold and here."

She stepped into the exposure suit, pausing with one arm in and one arm—her cybernetic arm—still out. Roland stared brazenly at it, his silent intensity so unnerving that she stopped moving altogether. "I've seen it before," she admitted. Another truth, let slip from her lips like some forbidden fruit. She wasn't sure if Roland was to be trusted, and yet the part of her that had tasted honesty back on Luna was not something which could now be unlearned. "There's not a day that I don't feel it, although until this morning, I'd never seen it like... like *that.*"

"What did it look like before?"

Emélie looked out the terminal window to the brown earth stretching far below. "Difficult, to quantify. More of a feeling than anything. An invisible weight, maybe. Settling, slowly, as if gaining a bit more density with each step. One, two, even a hundred, it's not noticeable. Over time, though, you begin to feel it. An inescapable force, closing in, slowing you down. Suffocating reality itself." She paused, busying her fingers with the suit seal to conceal a tremor. "I can't hide from it, and I won't stop, so I just keep going. Knowing it's there, up ahead, waiting for me. Watching for the inevitable moment when we finally collide." Emélie looked up. "That's what I can remember."

"It's fading, then?" Roland asked, studying her face.

"The memory?"

"No." His eyes held hers. "The mind."

Emélie gathered the gloves from the crate and turned toward the elevator car. A timer above the entrance counted down: seven minutes until departure. "Is it trying to kill me?" she asked.

"It only pursues you because you run."

"Downstream signaling isn't an answer." A few people exited the elevator. Dock workers, judging from the reflective chevrons on their greasy suits. Emélie looked around the terminal: it appeared boarding on time was her responsibility. Nobody here knew she even existed, nor did they care if she used her pass or not. "Do you also think it was my fault we were compromised back at Jericho Station?" she asked.

"Fault implies blame."

"If that thing hadn't seen me, would things have turned out the same?"

"All our actions have consequences. Chaos breeds something further down the line." He watched the elevator. "I think you misunderstand the arrangement I have with Joab. We don't share loyalty, only enemies."

"Then why is he the one with Lilith while you're stuck here, making sure I don't skip my ride?"

He was silent for a moment. "You told me Eden changed the Manifold. I wanted to hear why."

After a reluctant glance toward the car, she answered. "When we were interrogating Lilith at her safe house in Korolev, I noticed she had a tattoo on her sternum. A small, black rectangle." She turned the helmet in her hands, recalling it. "I recognized the symbol. It's called a Halmos. A proof marker showing the end of an equation."

"Lilith is the result of something," Roland said, although she couldn't tell from his inflection if he was asking a question or making a statement.

She raised her eyes, meeting his gaze. "If Eden is solving for a new Manifold, it would make sense that she found a way to check her own work. Self-reflection is the mark of a brilliant mind."

The fingers on his left hand twitched. He didn't have a weapon on him, and the flat case he carried, which Emélie assumed contained some sort of weapon, was also absent. It didn't make it any less threatening, standing there cold and silent, taking her statement with little reaction. Strangely enough, it was also Roland who seemed to treat her most like someone worth listening to. He, and maybe Goodnight, although following the events of Korolev, she wasn't banking on any future kindness from either one. "Your preoccupation with Eden is clouding your judgement," he finally said. "Although to be clear, you're suggesting it's not Lilith who is using Eden, but the other way around? That Lilith is a byproduct of the Loop."

"We already know Eden modified the system. What if a new Manifold is constructed each time she opens a Gate? It would prevent someone like Joab from ever backdooring his way into Mars. And since I know you're going to say that's a lot of effort for Origin trafficking, I'll add that I don't think the drug shipments are what this is really about. Those are surface-level. The thing you'd expect to find." Her voice softened. "The thing we were *meant* to find."

"Then what do you think is actually going on inside the Manifold?"

"A little late to be asking that, isn't it?"

"You've always had a choice."

"And look where that got me. Back where I started."

"You say that like it's a bad thing, Emélie," he replied. He watched her a moment, his eyes assessing her while his body remained perfectly still. Eerie, to say the least. Was there even a soul under that tattooed torso? His treatment of her suggested there was, but then again, she watched him kill no less than twenty Jumpers back on the rooftop, the last of which was point-blank to her, without so much as a blink of hesitation. "Maybe you should stop fighting it and see what happens when you go around again," he added.

The clock above the elevator counted down to departure. She stepped toward the platform, then stopped abruptly, turning around to once again face him. "Why do you call me by that name? Everyone else calls me 'Doc,' or 'Doctor,' or Desjardins. Everyone except you."

"That name?" Roland repeated softly. "Does it not belong to you?"

His response caught her off guard. "I… I don't know." Another truth. "When they found me at Kepler's Reef, they asked for a name. It was the first thing that came to mind. I don't know why, but something about it never felt quite right." The memory of it pulled a shiver down her neck. "Maybe I am crazy. Everyone else seems to think so. At this point, I have to face the possibility they're at least somewhere close to being right."

While she spoke, Roland had pulled something out of his tunic, which he now held, concealed in one hand. Something small, so that as he turned it between his fingers, Emélie couldn't make out what it was. "Do you know why we lost Mars?"

The last few dock workers trudged up the ramp to the elevator, leaving the boarding terminal vacant. "Is that a rhetorical question?" She watched his fingers transfer the object dexterously from one hand to the next. So fast, she almost missed it. "We all know what happened to the Loop."

"No. Not the Loop. The Collapse was merely the manifestation of a deeper truth. We went to Mars in search of salvation. A blank slate where humanity could rewrite itself after our failure on Earth." Despite the room being empty, his voice had dropped to a near-whisper. "But you can't outrun what you are, not even across forty million miles of void. The environment there rejects human life at a molecular level. Radiation eats through cells, peroxide soil poisons the water, and atmospheric pressure runs so low it boils the blood in your veins. Most of the original settlers didn't survive the first six months." He shifted the object back to his other hand; this time, Emélie caught a sliver of light glinting off its hard surface. "Those deaths laid the foundation for the discovery of Origin, and later, the Loop. And neither of those things killed Mars." His eyes, hard as stone, although his voice grew distant. "We lost Mars because the first colonists couldn't agree on a tomorrow, so they took what little hope was carried there and buried it in blood. The truth is, we lost that place long before the Collapse. It just took decades of slaughter to see it for what it truly was..."

"A lie," Emélie said quietly.

"No," Roland replied. "A tomb."

She took a moment to let his words sink in. "And what about Origin? You're implying it's not nearly as dangerous as we've been led to believe?"

"Worse. Origin isn't the beginning. It's the end. The consequence of a past equation, much like the symbol you noticed on Lilith's Reflection. What came before it, the original substance—a pure product of Mars—was wildly unstable. The first to arrive on Mars were also the ones who made the discovery, and when it became clear what they'd found, it was a rapid descent into madness." Still concealed, he rubbed his thumb against the object in his hand, as if summoning some lost thought. Or a memory, even. "The discovery marked the end of hope in what Mars could be, and the beginning of a power struggle between factions that created disturbances so great, even now we feel their effects."

"Factions?" she asked, rubbing the pinch at her forehead that seemed to be increasing the longer they spoke. "You make it sound like a war. I've studied the Loop—at least, what I could find of it—extensively. I've never heard any of this until now."

"Of course. Who do you think won the argument?"

"And this substance... what was it?"

He looked over his shoulder, as if the very idea of it alone might summon something terrible. "It has many names, although you'll hear none of them leave my lips. All you need to know is that Mars was political before it was stable, and violent before it was habitable. And what they found buried there was the spark. There were some who saw what was coming and tried to suppress news of it from ever reaching

Earth. Had they achieved their goal, the reality we now inhabit would be vastly different."

Emélie checked the clock. Two minutes until the elevator car departed. "We all have our part," she said. The words slipped out without much thought, more an indirect observation, although Roland seemed to focus on her more intently in the moments after she said them. It occurred to her that she'd spoken them before, back at the safehouse before dosing herself with Origin, and she wasn't really sure why she'd said them then, either.

"As word of the discovery spread, like the shadow that follows the striking hand, violence was quick behind. There was a move to quarantine the substance on Mars, although it spread regardless. Others waged campaigns to restrict it through legislative means, through subversion, or through fear. And the smallest group, by far the most violent of them, found a way to harness it. Control it, and, with strategic coordination of some corporate investment on Earth, refine it into what would lay the groundwork for the Loop.

"Phaethon," Emélie replied in a breathy whisper.

Roland nodded, then set the object he was holding into the empty crate at her feet. The clock above the elevator counted down from one minute.

At the sight of the object Roland had set before her, her eyes watered. A kindness, and the wave of fresh terror that came after it. "Fountainhead took something from you, too, didn't she?" Emélie said.

Roland was silent for a long time. "*She*," he repeated softly back, an affirmation of the subtle thing Emélie had subconsciously formed through personal observation. "She's taken something from all of us."

"That may be true, although for you, it was different. The thing you lost. It was a part of you."

Roland glanced across the dark terminal as yellow hazard lamps switched on, washing them in a fragile, flickering warmth. "You remind me of someone I once knew. Impulsive. Thorough. Optimistic to a fault."

"She meant something to you?" Emélie replied, a question wrapped in a statement.

"I don't know," he said, meeting her gaze one final time. "They took that too." He glanced at the crate, then turned to leave. "You should be careful on the ride back to Earth. The manifest shows that an unmarked cargo container was recently loaded into the lower hold. It would be a shame if someone forgot to lock it up."

Emélie watched him leave, and as he disappeared up the stairs leading toward the main hangar, she knelt, examining what he'd left behind: at the bottom of the dusty cargo crate was the active skipjack, alive and wriggling.

CHAPTER 26
TOKEN CRIMINAL

Nothing drew attention like a Gate.

Brinks double-checked the hallway—both directions—then pushed aside the overgrowth covering the apartment door and pressed his face to the retinal scanner beneath it. A pause while it registered his biometric eye. Then the lock mechanism rumbled to life. When it fell silent, he pressed lightly, and the door swung open. He wasn't one for disclosure, but that damn drone had forced his hand with the Skip, and the safe house provided a spot to lay low while he assessed his options.

That, and he needed more tobacco.

From the safety of the hall, Brinks scanned the room. When Thursday leaned over, crowding the entrance to get a look for himself, Brinks held up a hand, then motioned toward the floor. He kept a handful of safehouses like this one: ground-level, with low visibility and a single point of entry. Ideal for hiding, less so for getting caught inside. And while the chances of stumbling across someone inside the Manifold were low, they were never zero, and he hadn't stayed alive for this long because of playing the odds like they tilted in his favor. He watched the dust disturbed from the door's movement settle back to the floor. When he was satisfied with the results, he crossed inside.

"You seem to know your way around here," Thursday said, pushing through the tangled overgrowth as he followed Brinks inside.

"I know my way around a lot of places, mostly because they're all the same."

"Well, I've never seen anything like this," Thursday replied, gazing at a clump of moss poking from between a pair of equipment lockers. "Where are we?"

Brinks eyed the freshly removed Skipjack in his hand, perpetually squirming and in search of its next host, then pocketed it for safekeeping. "There are so many things wrong with that question, I'm going to pretend I didn't hear it."

"You mentioned someone named Lilith. Should we be worried about a tail?"

"She's got eyes everywhere, but only going through a Gate tends to draw any attention."

Thursday glanced back toward the door. "Correct me if I'm wrong, but isn't that what we just did?"

"We went into a Gate. Through, well. Through implies we came out the other side."

"I'm... not following." The light on Thursday's faceplate pulsed, struggling to comprehend.

"The Gates are just openings. We're inside the Manifold, which is what the Loop generates to make all this happen. Don't ask me how it works."

Thursday trailed Brinks further into the room. "The doctor was talking about Manifolds, too. She's been looking for this place."

"I doubt that," Brinks said. "The Manifold is an in-between. A non-place. Technically, we don't exist right now."

"I thought you said you didn't know how it worked?"

"Never said that. I told you not to ask me about it."

"So you figured out a way to interrupt the Jump, and now you're hiding out in the space between the Gates while this Lilith chases after you?"

Brinks glared at Thursday. Bringing the drone along was already beginning to feel like a mistake. "If you think I look like the sort of person who could work that out, maybe you aren't as clever as I thought."

"You think I'm clever?"

A pause. "I think you ask too many questions for a drone."

"You could answer a few," Thursday intoned, pushing past him toward the center of the room.

Brinks didn't stop him. The drone moved with the sort of intentional accuracy characteristic of a tactical reflex package, which meant unless Brinks wanted to risk a slug to the gut, he'd best not give Thursday a reason to bring the gun up. Brinks shook his head. "Against my policy. What I know, I like to keep to myself. Besides, once I start talking, you'll no doubt get what you came here for and kill me, and then where would that leave me?"

"If I wanted to kill you, I would have already done it," Thursday said, bending over to get a closer look at a rack of plants that dominated the center of the room. "No offense, but you don't seem like the type to keep a home."

"This isn't a home. You'd know the difference if you'd ever been in one." Brinks opened one of the wall lockers at the far side of the room. There wasn't a bed or a single piece of furniture in sight. In the middle of the room, an array of lights and tubing hung above a row of plants growing in a red-tinged hydroponic solution, faintly glowing in the low light. Thursday ran his hand along one of the broad, papery leaves on the plant nearest him, examining the network of tubes dripping the liquid solution over the roots.

"The doctor... she was using Origin, too," Thursday said. "I think it's how she knew where to look for that Gate."

Brinks stopped what he was doing. "She told you that?"

"More or less. I didn't take you for a user, though."

"Me neither." Brinks grimaced as he removed his shirt, revealing a violent latticework of scars. Fresh, scarlet bruises ringed with yellow and bright red lacerations stood against the darker, older scars covering his clay-baked skin. "When did they start staffing Internal Affairs with drones, anyway?"

"Have you ever tried to bribe a drone?"

He paused, a glint in his biometric eye. "What sort of person do you take me for?"

"Don't know," Thursday replied, "that's why I'm following you."

Brinks took a clean shirt from the top shelf of the locker. "You're doing a terrible job." He glanced at the gun dangling from a hook at the back of his locker. If drones could lie, they were getting better at it. He pulled the clean shirt over his head. When he looked up, Thursday was hovering just off to one shoulder.

"You know a lot about how all this works. Too much," Thursday observed. "You've been around a while?"

"Depends." Brinks collected his duster from the corner of the locker door. "Who's asking?"

"Let's say it was for a friend."

He paused, assessing the old drone before pulling his jacket on. "We were never friends."

A strange blip crossed Thursday's glass faceplate. "I wasn't talking about me."

"I'm not her friend, either," he said, turning to leave.

"From what I can tell, you seem to have taken quite an interest in the doctor's work."

"Her work is interesting. Still doesn't make us friends."

"She means something to you, though. And she means something to me, so we have that in common."

"You got the wrong idea about me, Thursday. I'm not the sort of person who can help fix anything, let alone whatever it is you seem to be mixed up in. I know you think I can help, but I'm warning you now: I tend to leave a trail behind me, and not in a good way." Brinks tore off some leaves from one of the tobacco plants drying on a rack near the door and stuffed them into a pocket on his duster. He could roll it later; the drone's questions were getting on his nerves.

There was a metallic clink as Thursday set something down. Brinks didn't need to turn around to know what it was. He knew the sound a bullet made: one or a fist full, loaded or spent, full or empty. Packed into magazines, strung on belts, set on tables, dropped on floors. Rattling around inside containers, pockets, truck beds, and flight decks. He recognized the sound of a bullet better than almost anything else, and most importantly, he knew the sound it made when it was intended for him.

"Recognize this?"

"Red tips," Brinks said.

"Goodnights," Thursday added.

"If that's what you're after, sure." He glanced over at the cartridge. "Color's wrong, though."

"Exactly." Thursday scooped up the round and tossed it over. "Looks similar to TCP-Alpha at first glance. It's contaminated with something else, though."

Brinks rolled the bullet across his palm to gauge the charge weight, then ran a thumb over the transparent tip, swirling the liquid inside. "I've seen this before. It isn't the regular stuff. Makes people Jumpy in a big way, if you get my drift."

"Something new?"

Brinks glanced over at the transparent tubes carrying plain red Origin to his tobacco plants, then shook his head. "Something old," he said, turning the round over to get a look at the primer. It was dimpled, a misfire. "Nine by nineteen millimeter," he said, mostly to himself. "Haven't seen that chambering in decades." He held the bullet up to one of the lights hanging above the tobacco grow. Traces of something the color of rust mingled with the lighter, pinkish-red Origin.

Same as the crystals.

"Found it up on the surface, right around where the doctor and I came across remnants of a Gate. It was with a pile of empty shell casings. No bodies, though, unless you count the Jumpers. I was hoping you could tell me something about that, too."

"I don't know anything about any dead Jumpers."

"It was hard to get an accurate count due to the fact that the parts were all scattered about, but I'd say maybe six or seven cuts altogether," Thursday continued. "They were all clean—surgical, almost—but how they were divided didn't make any sense. Like something folded them up first."

Brinks glanced at the blade sheathed over Thursday's right shoulder. He couldn't tell if the drone was recounting that bit of information from firsthand experience or just a general clinical knowledge of how the human body disassembled. Either way, he seemed on edge, and Brinks wasn't about to push his luck. Getting shot was one thing, but swords? That was a whole different sort of pain. "You may not be flesh and blood, but you've got an instinct all the same." He tossed the round back to Thursday. "What do you think?"

Thursday caught it without taking his gaze off the open wall locker in front of him. "You know, I can't recall the last time I saw a six-gun," he said, leaning forward to get a better look at the enormous hand cannon hanging against the back wall. A sheen of oil made it glisten in the low light; here was a weapon hidden away, and yet still well-maintained. It hung in a leather belt (leather!), also oiled, worn dark under the creases of ten thousand draws. "They don't make weapons like this anymore," Thursday observed, following the shape of the barrel to where something on the top of the gun seemed to give off the slightest glow. "Never made them like this in the first place, even. Statistically, it's somewhat of an impossibility to see a working wheelgun in this day and age. Even rarer still, to find a gunhand who lets someone else stand between him and his gun." He turned, leveling his blank face at Brinks. "Then again, maybe I'm not the only one here that's a little short on flesh and blood. Shorter still, on courage."

Brinks felt his fingers twitch. Drones were a real number to work with, mainly because they didn't have the same tells as humans, making them harder to read. They tended to act abruptly and could often veer wildly from one state to the next without warning—especially an older unit like this one. "Your doctor's on her own now," Brinks said. "Best stay clear of it. And if you somehow got it in your head that bringing me into this will make a difference, you couldn't be more wrong. You should accept that and move on, and if you're determined to ignore what I have to say, then you can chase her down on Homestake and see how things land for yourself." He adjusted his hat, giving the room a final once-over as he turned for the door. "Don't bother locking up. This place is made now that you've been here."

Thursday didn't respond until Brinks was nearly outside. "How'd you know the doctor was headed for Homestake?"

Brinks paused, hand on the door. *Don't stay,* he told himself. *If you stay, you'll get involved. And nothing good ever comes of you getting involved.* "As I said, her work is interesting. I make it my business to know. To keep an eye on her."

"If that were true, you would have known she didn't go to Homestake. Or at least, it's not the only place she went."

"There was only one destination on the flight manifest."

"So you've got safe houses in alternate dimensions, but you're trusting flight manifests now?"

Brinks clenched his jaw.

Thursday paused as if weighing what he had to say next. "The Director brought someone down from Meridian Bay. They kept it closed-door, but I caught a glimpse of him out on the tarmac before they left. You seem like you'd know the sort—one of those DAO cowboys with a seven-figure security contract. The ones hired to make problems disappear into an off-world black site."

Brinks hovered at the threshold, trying not to be drawn in. So far, it wasn't working out so well.

Thursday kept going. "The ship they departed on was unregistered, so I pulled the manifest and cross-checked it with the traffic through Homestake during their arrival window. They reported a mechanical failure two minutes prior to landing and changed their docking request to an external loading platform. That same vessel landed at a tarmac back on Earth eighteen minutes later, so do the math."

"You think the doctor is back on Earth? Seems like a lot of lateral movement for a false flag."

"I know a false flag when I see one," Thursday said. "That, and a privately contracted four-wing departed Homestake eight minutes later, bound for Jericho Station with two passengers on the manifest that had their names redacted."

"Jericho Station," Brinks repeated. "That's inside Korolev Crater."

"Makes you wonder what the DAO would want with an old outpost like that. Nothing up there but a bunch of empty warehouses."

"You're thinking too small," Brinks said, doffing his hat. "There's nothing inside Korolev, but Luna Bet is nearby."

"You think they were taking the doctor up to the old Loop?"

Brinks creased the brim of his hat. "Not necessarily, but it's not a coincidence she's hunting Gates, and they end up near one of the old Loops on Luna. You said there were two names redacted from the flight manifest?"

Thursday shifted his weight from one foot to the other; the move was almost imperceptible, but Brinks caught the sound of a gear whirring inside Thursday's left hip.

Betrayed by an oil leak.

He closed the gap, pouncing on the drone with surprising speed. They slammed into the row of tobacco plants before crashing to the floor. He gripped the drone by the neck with his mechanical hand. Fingers hooked inside the frame, wrapped around the main processing cable running from Thursday's head down into his armored torso. A quick snap of the wrist and Thursday would be a pile of circuits. "What are you not telling me?" Brinks said through gritted teeth.

"I take it this is your way of committing to help?" Thursday asked.

"No," Brinks said. "This is me getting involved, and if I'm involved, we do things my way. For starters, you're going to tell me everything you know about the other passengers on board that ship. And I better not find out you're holding anything back. I've been known to melt drones down into bullets for far less."

Thursday's servos thrummed inside his ivory carapace. When he spoke, the light bar running across his faceplate hardly moved, the robotic hush-hush of spilling a secret. "I ran every name on the manifest. Mostly security contractors, a few with connections to Phaethon Asset Control, which isn't all that surprising. Then I checked all the cargo shipments coming into the platform in the last twenty-four hours. The same person who chartered the flight leaving Homestake also signed for a container arriving from another platform a few hours prior. No name, but there was a designation code. *Leviathan*."

"Leviathan." Brinks repeated the word with a distaste that was palpable, even for Thursday. "You have anything else to add?" he said, releasing the drone's neck.

Thursday returned to his feet. "I'd keep what I'm about to say next to myself, except that I seem to have lost my self-preservation protocols."

"Then that makes two of us." Brinks made a hurry-up motion with his hand, but something in his gut twisted at hearing the drone's admission.

"I can't prove this, but I think the ship leaving Homestake—the one our doctor was on—picked up someone else, too. Someone who traveled via a container."

Our doctor. Brinks frowned. He didn't like it when drones were right about human things. Still, one good turn deserved another. "They're making a play for Mars," he said.

"Mars?" Thursday stopped picking tobacco leaves off his metal frame and turned his head to Brinks, face pulsing softly in the odd light of whatever parallel reality they were inside. "What led you to connect the shuttered Loop facility on Luna Bet with an attempt to overthrow the Hespiredes Cartel?"

"A hunch," he said. "And if the doctor is one of the redacted passengers, then I'd wager the other unidentified passenger on board that flight to Luna is a Seraph."

Thursday stood there dumbly, bogged down by the cumulative weight of those last seven letters.

"If you don't believe me, you're welcome to supply another reason explaining why a DAO operative would take a cosmologist and a bunch of hired guns on an off-record trip up to an old Loop facility."

"I'm still not following."

Brinks gave him a hard look under the red point of his biometric eye. "Really? None of this is ringing a bell?" He rapped the drone on the side of the head. "You're a Class Two. You predate all of this, I thought maybe—"

"I was wiped."

Wiped, or *partitioned*, Brinks didn't say aloud, but the thought lodged itself like a bullet he couldn't extract. "Well, if that's the case, your processing capacity shouldn't be impaired. Try to keep up." He started for the open door leading back out into the hallway they'd come from. "To stand even a chance at breaching Mars will likely require using an exploit in the Manifold. Navigation through it will require setting a Tether, and a Seraph is their best—if not their only—chance for that."

"That all makes perfect sense," Thursday chimed. "Also, what's a Seraph—"

Fed up with the tedium of back-and-forth questioning, Brinks started in. Cold, hard details, up front, because the sooner they could stop talking, the sooner he could track down whoever was responsible for backing such an idiotic plan. A plan, at least in Brinks' mind, run by some self-assured DAO chief, and behind him, another man.

A man in a wheelchair and the most powerful seat on Earth.

And, by consequence, laying this all to rest also meant he could rid himself of the persistent metal appendage calling itself Thursday. "Each Loop had two designated assets: a Watcher and a Seraph. The Watcher constructed the Manifold. The Seraph guarded it. Made sure nothing came in or out of the main Gate unless it was supposed to. Seraphs could also set Tethers. Something like an interdimensional beacon that allowed them to see into the Manifold even if a Gate wasn't active. Lilith, whom you'll recall I mentioned earlier, is the mastermind behind the Cartel's trafficking operation, making her the most accessible target for gaining access to Mars. She uses Gates to run Origin for the Cartel. Gates like the one we used to get in here," he gestured toward the moss-covered ceiling of the apartment. "Because of her ability to enter the Manifold at will, she's also developed a nasty habit of leveraging parallel versions of herself—Reflections, pulled from inside the Manifold—to do her dirty work." He paused to take a breath, and it was the drone who now repeated the same gesture he'd made earlier, urging him forward.

"One of her Reflections, an older one, has been operating out of Korolev. The team you're tracking will need a Seraph to set a Tether on her. Otherwise, she'll slip through a Gate before they even get close."

Thursday stood idly by, his body tone slack as if the burst of information had suddenly overloaded his central processors.

Brinks took advantage of the silence. "Don't get the idea this is a dialogue. I'm only telling you what I know, in case things go sideways and the burden falls to you."

"Burden?" Thursday asked.

"This is bigger than both of us. There's a reason we didn't stay on Mars, and I intend to let that reason stay put. Under no circumstances should anyone be permitted to enter, now, or ever. And most of all..." He started to add something more, then decided against it—a detail that did not pass unnoticed by Thursday.

"Your plan appears reckless and poorly formed," Thursday observed, watching as Brinks pushed through the hanging vegetation out in the hall. "Still, if they have a Seraph, as you say, then the doctor is in grave danger. I think it's time we take a little trip of our own to see what's happening up at the old Loop."

"I work alone," Brinks called from a thicket of vines hanging from a rusted lighting fixture.

"Whatever you say, partner," Thursday said, but he was still standing in front of the wall locker holding Brinks' abandoned gun.

Dust from the Gate engulfed him before he found the door.

CHAPTER 27
"LOOP"

Phaethon Corp. MAIN build_VX.6.6.09
initializing boot sequence...
running subroutine FOUNTAINHEAD:

bindquery: update parameter to
"LOOP"
encryption protocols intact,
syntax structures intact
[08] entries remaining

begin sentiment analysis,
implicit context target, rundisplay:

BEGIN RECORD >>>

This isn't going to end well. She's become obsessed with this idea. Building something to harness the power of Precursor, only it doesn't even seem to be about Precursor anymore. It's like everything she learned got so big that it changed shape and folded over onto itself. Even the drone seems worried.

I have half a mind to track down the sonofabitch who put this idea in her head in the first place, although my instinct tells me Marcus is at the other end of it. He's smart enough not to let this come back on him, but he put her in charge of the project, which feels like proof enough. Now they're building some new fancy facility near the surface. Something like a Loop. That's what she called it, anyway.

I think we should bury the place while we still have the chance. Apparently, it's supposed to allow for travel between here and Mars, or here and anywhere, instantly. Mars, I can handle. I've been there.

It's the anywhere else that worries me.

<<< END RECORD

sanitize data entry,
purge access logs to XANADU
KILL remote process

CHAPTER 28
CANGJIE

It takes an elevator car leaving Homestake roughly forty-three minutes to descend the cable linking the suborbital platform to the Earth port. Somewhere around the mid-trip mark, Emélie made her move, unlinking her safety belt to vault over the low railing running the perimeter of the passenger platform. She moved without hesitation, acutely aware of the time she'd already lost learning the timing of the automated sentry drones hovering along predefined routes around the hold. Her descent was silent, smooth, and calculated; the gravity on board was similar, if not slightly heavier, than what she'd experienced on Luna. And this time, she didn't have a swarm of Jumpers at her back.

She landed lightly on the roof of the nearest container stack and looked up, checking to make sure the only other passenger riding cargo hadn't seen her. He'd tried to make small talk; she took a page from Roland's playbook and outright ignored him, choosing to watch the clock on her arm instead. Uninterested, he dozed off, giving Emélie the chance she needed to slip out without raising alarm. Free of inquisitive eyes and, for the next four minutes, any sort of drone surveillance, she faced the next task at hand: finding the container holding Lilith.

Simple enough, except the containers were stacked floor to ceiling, five high and deeper than Emélie could make out from her current vantage point. She wouldn't have time to check more than a row or two before the car docked at Earth. And assuming she could find Lilith in the first place, she'd still need at least a few minutes to talk to her before the crew boarded and started unloading containers.

Aside from Roland's implication that Lilith was on board with her, stowed inside a container that remained conveniently unlocked, she had nothing else to go on except what she could deduce from the situation at hand. She could almost hear Thursday over her shoulder, always so methodical and unhurried in situations like this. *Start with what you know, and work backward,* he used to say. If that were the case, then the easiest point from which to begin was at the inflection point: the moment she found the leaf. The leaf landed her in a conference room in front of the Director—uninteresting—and Joab. A man who, by all appearances, was difficult to pin down. For Emélie, an easy enough mark: although he gave off the pretense of unpredictability, she understood that chaos—pure, mathematical chaos—was mere fantasy. Humans are, above all, rational creatures, and Joab, while tactically competent, remained susceptible to the same patterns governing everyone else: a propensity for the familiar. In his case, this manifested as the absence of any definable identifiers, such as names, titles, or logos. Normally, a challenge; except here, the containers stacked floor to ceiling around Emélie were covered in corporate symbols, barcodes, and character strings. Any unmarked container would stand out, an outlier among things designed, as a function of their purpose, to be identified, tracked, and documented. Furthermore, Roland had mentioned that the container was loaded late, which meant, according to the logistics of the space itself, the options were restricted to somewhere near the top, in one of the columns closest to the docking bay doors.

Using the anchor points on the side of the container, she slid over the edge and scaled its vertical face down the stack. Around the middle of the row, the buzz of rotors signaling another sentry forced her into a gap between two containers. It passed her without notice, and when the area was clear again, she emerged.

First row, second container from the ceiling, Emélie found what she was looking for: matte black, and absent of any external markings except for a single number eight printed along the bottom right door. She ascended the row, half climbing, half floating, pulling herself along the crescent-shaped anchors until she hovered at the door leading inside. On closer inspection, her blood ran cold: the number eight was not a number at all, but the same serpent devouring its own tail that she'd seen inside her arm plate and, later, tattooed on Roland's neck. The high-pitched hum of approaching sentry blades drove her to action before she had time to indulge in second-guessing. A quick test of the handle, and the door cams slid clear without resistance. She took a deep breath—one more good breath—and breached the container into sepulchral darkness.

At the center of the confined space, a human-shaped singularity, tar-dark, terrifying, and resonant beneath its overwhelming silence.

One hand still grasping the door, Emélie fumbled with her heavy, oversized suit until she found the pressure switch responsible for activating her helmet lamps. A pair of beams tore through the darkness, illuminating a metallic mesh lining every surface of the cube. This was not just any container; it was a Faraday cage. The whole-body counterpart of an Oubliette, it offered total isolation for the occupants. No signal in, no signal out. And suspended before her in floating stillness was Lilith. She wore a tan space suit fitted with an opaque blast visor, blinding her from seeing out. Shackles fastened around her wrists and ankles were linked to chains anchored to each of the four corners.

Emélie took a slow breath, tasting the stale, musty odor of her suit as it mingled with perspiration and fear. Gently, she touched the flight pocket on her shoulder. The Skipjack was there, safely stowed; a useful, if not dangerous, bargaining token. And thanks to her override on Korolev, she was the only person, aside from Lilith, who could utilize it.

Finding the interior door lacking any sort of handle, she closed it carefully, ensuring herself a gap for emergency egress. The timer on her forearm display counted down: sixteen minutes, twenty-nine seconds. She pushed off lightly, drifting toward the center where Lilith rested, motionless. One of her boots raked a section of wire mesh as she closed in, breaking the cold silence with a metallic ring. She grabbed the ceiling, steadying herself.

"The facs–imile appears," Lilith announced, her words slurred beneath the opaque helmet.

Emélie inhaled sharply. "I'm only here to talk."

"Of course. Is that not how it al–ways begins?"

"This isn't about the Gates. Or the Loop."

Lilith lifted her head.

Only the soft rasp of two bodies breathing as Emélie struggled to find her bearings. "I want to know if what they say about you is true," she finally said.

"You'll have to be more specific. I seem to have developed quite a rep–utation."

Emélie watched Lilith hanging in the space across from her. "They say you're responsible for the Origin coming into Earth. The Jumpers roaming the surface. The violence encroaching on our Sanctuaries. They say you're a psychopath. A killer." She pulled herself forward along the ceiling as she spoke, stopping when Lilith was in arm's reach. "And they say you're the one who took me."

Lilith lowered her head. "And you already believe all those things to be true?"

"I wanted to give you another chance. To explain."

"Is that what this is?" Lilith clicked her tongue. "You aren't built for this at all, are you?" She stretched, causing her chains to oscillate in synchronicity, then slumped back down with a heavy sigh. "I don't work with amateurs. Come back when you find someone who's willing to get a little blood on their hands for a glimp–se at the truth."

Even chained, there was a crazed note present in Lilith's voice that gave Emélie the urge to flee. "This was a mistake," she admitted, searching the vacant space behind her for something she could use to steady herself.

"That has yet to be determined," Lilith replied. "What we have is a situation ripe with potential. I'm chained, blind, and de–fenseless." She leaned forward, pulling against the shackles until her helmet nearly touched Emélie's. "And you're the one holding the key."

Emélie shivered and groped backward, pulling herself toward the exit.

"You know, there was another way," Lilith said. "A painless way. But what is life without the pain? It makes us who we are. Keeps us alive. Hun–gry. You probably came here feeling you were owed an apology. I would suggest gratitude, doctor. I made you who you are today. And you didn't seek me out because you're searching for the truth. You came because, deep down, you've already found it, and, weak as you are, believe you need someone to provide you per–mission to accept it."

Emélie bumped against the door, grabbing herself at the last second before it latched shut.

"You have to admit, it was an elegant system. A dose of Origin, a dose of wa–ter. Freeing the burden of the conscious mind to offer a glimp-se at something truly beautiful. A search for the infinite inside of the im–possible. It's nice to see you haven't forgotten, although it does seem as though you've tried." Lilith's voice was hardly more than a husky whisper in the darkness. "And tell me, doctor, what about your hands? Are they trem–bling now? Because they should be."

Emélie pushed off against the wall, throwing her body toward Lilith with her fingers hooked into the wire mesh covering the door. It closed tight, the latch outside locking them in with a resounding clunk as it fell.

"And at last, a truth," Lilith said, stretching to her full height, readying herself for what came next. "A basic characteristic of a quantum field is that it cannot be directly observed... One may only measure its collapse into probabilities. And you, my dear Reflection, are collap–sing beautifully."

Emélie collided with Lilith.

"You took more than my work!" she shouted, grasping Lilith by the helmet. "You... took... everything!"

"I finished what you star-ted," Lilith cooed. "What you couldn't see through to the end. If you want to hate anyone, hate yourself. You're the fool who bar–gained for more than she could handle, and now you've left your fate for everyone else to decide."

Emélie gripped Lilith's helmet release. A flick of the thumb, and it would all be over. A quick death, not a painless one. "You know nothing about me!" Emélie said, hot with rage.

"I know enough to understand you'll never find what you're after. Not in those dust storms back on Earth, or with the men who brought you to me on Luna, and especially not among Phaethon's empty promises. I know, because I've been watch–ing you. Watch–ing this whole time, scrounging for answers day after day, only to find yourself right back where you started. Surely you don't think that was an accident?" Lilith spread her arms, reflecting the chains against Emélie's lights. "And what a perfect inversion all of this has led to. Me, your prisoner! It's too bad that for all the effort required to get you here, it was an exercise in futility." She leaned in and stretched her head to one side, begging Emélie to pull the release. "And do you know why, doc–tor? Because you're weak. And that is the only thing worth knowing about you."

Panting, Emélie stared at her distorted profile in the golden mirror of Lilith's shield while her breath clung to the inside of her own helmet, blurring everything into foggy outlines. "You're right," she admitted, releasing her grip on Lilith's collar. "I'm not like you."

"Then do what you came here to do."

Hand quivering, she gripped the bottom edge of Lilith's face shield. With a deliberate, almost painful slowness, she lifted the barrier, inch by excruciating inch, exposing Lilith's face. Chin, lips, and then cheekbones, streaks of dried blood from two empty sockets where eyes had once been. Below them, a set of tattooed eyes gazed onward in blind oblivion. Emélie felt the soft mechanical *click* of the shield mechanism ratcheting into the fully open, locked position, and as her eyes took in the woman before her, a primitive sound escaped her throat—half-gasp, half-choke—as every possible identity of the woman known as Lilith collapsed into a single, undeniable reality.

It was her own face that stared back at her.

Her lungs seized. The container walls seemed to pulse, expanding and contracting with the blood thundering in her ears. Her hand clawed at her helmet, desperate to feel her own features, to confirm that what she saw in the woman opposite her was not some fabricated trick or a break in reality.

"Now, we finish what we started," Lilith said, flush with glee.

Before Emélie could recover, Lilith's helmet rammed her head on. The piercing crack of shattering glass. Air hissed outward as she pressed her gloved hand to the breach, trying to slow the rush of escaping air. From between her fingers, she could see Lilith's head hanging backward, laughter beginning in her belly and erupting from her mouth, as a similar crack radiated down the front of her helmet.

Lilith yanked her arm free. The chain snapped. In one fluid motion, she whipped it around, striking Emélie's shoulder. Emélie clawed at the wall, trying to get purchase against the fine mesh as Lilith struck again. The chain wrapped itself around her arm, and Lilith tugged, hauling Emélie down as she lunged out, headfirst. Shards of glass burst from the point where their helmets collided, and Emélie rolled backward, temporarily knocked unconscious from the impact.

They were locked in the container, with no oxygen and no way out.

Lilith severed the second chain with a decisive tug, freeing her other arm to grab Emélie as she floated past. She released Emélie's helmet latch, jolting her awake from shock as her suit depressurized in the frigid, oxygen-lean air. At the last moment, Emélie gasped, filling her lungs one more time before pulling her helmet free.

Two minutes, forty-five seconds.

Lilith let herself sink to the floor. "To un–fold, a Reflection needs an object on which to reflect," she mused. When her feet touched the container floor, she kept going, squatting down until her knees bent at ninety degrees. Emélie hung suspended overhead, with nothing to grab onto. When the chains around Lilith's legs went slack and touched the floor, Lilith launched herself upward, straight for Emélie.

Emélie grabbed the rim of her helmet as it floated by, swinging it around as Lilith came into range. The helmet struck Lilith across the head, sending the two women spinning in a wild arc, bouncing first against the ceiling and then ricocheting off the far wall. Lilith wrapped both her arms around Emélie's neck, blind but still perfectly capable of choking the last breath from Emélie in total darkness. Squeezing with a mechanical, almost inhuman strength.

Emélie did not resist. She waited, conserving the last of her energy until she felt Lilith quiver ever so slightly; whatever cybernetically-enhanced strength she possessed remained bound to lungs governed by the same rules for every other set of human lungs. Lilith wheezed, exerting herself beyond the oxygen capacity of their environment.

Emélie slipped one arm free and, opening her palm, released the Skipjack concealed inside. The Skip, having already detected Emélie's neural signal, immediately clawed its way up her arm, neck, and slid itself over her left retina. The four small legs sank into the soft tissue of her eye, and Emélie felt a scream slip from her lungs as a dark rift erupted around them. And as fast as it opened, the Gate folded shut, taking both of them with it.

The elevator car slowed on final approach, nothing but dust in its wake.

CHAPTER 29
SUPERSYMMETRY

Dust frothed the Gatemouth as the rift began to fail, expiring like an exhaled breath. Brinks straddled the closing aperture, a puncture between worlds, and glared back into the Manifold. Of all the overprotective, inflexible, rule-following lumps of machinery Brinks had ever met, Thursday had to be the worst. He hadn't seen the old drone since their last Jump, and while there were plenty of consequences for bringing him along, there were even more for letting him out of sight. At the last instant, Thursday appeared, stepping through as the Gate disintegrated around them.

"You really have to watch yourself around these things," Thursday said, lifting his leg as the lower half of the Gate sealed shut below it. "Seems like if you aren't careful, it will take half of you clean down the–"

Brinks clamped his hand across the perforated screen covering Thursday's voice modulator. "Keep it down," he hissed. "We didn't take the long way in just for you to blow our cover the moment we arrived." He released the drone and started for the slot of light ahead, moving with his shoulders slightly hunched and one hand pressed to his face.

"Well, next time, lead with that," Thursday warbled, examining the narrow walls of the jagged escarpment where they'd emerged. "Are you sure this doesn't have anything to do with Lilith?"

A soft *click* filtered from the darkness as Brinks swung the plate covering his eye back into place. "I wouldn't concern yourself with Lilith. Of all things to come out of the Manifold, she's the least of our problems."

"This doesn't look like the Manifold, at least not like what I've seen so far. And it certainly isn't Luna. You said we took the long way in. The long way in to *where?*"

Brinks stopped, turning in the dull grey light to face Thursday, hemmed in shadow. "Fear," he said, and then, in one smooth motion, crushed the still wriggling Skipjack in his fist. Without waiting for the drone, he passed through the narrow opening and clambered down the talus field on the other side. Behind him, a metallic scrape betrayed Thursday following through the gap. The drone was fast. Too fast, and too loud. Brinks pivoted, driving an accusatory finger in Thursday's direction as his boot knocked loose a few stones that drifted in lazy, lopsided suspension rather than tumbling down the steep path. "Are you intentionally trying to–"

Thursday swatted Brinks' metal hand aside and drove a foot down, turning his forward motion back on him. In a moment of weakness, Brinks thrust his other hand out to counterbalance the sudden shift.

Thursday was ready. He clamped Brinks' hand at the wrist and bent it toward the open darkness above them.

Brinks dropped, yielding so as to avoid injury.

"You should only fear a triggerman to the extent he can use his gun hand," Thursday said coolly. He glanced down the path. Not far off, a cluster of low buildings abutted the base of the slope. "I know what a Skipjack does. At least, I know what it used to do. And I know that piece of hardware you've got installed isn't a suitable interface for the disc in your pocket, which means you've got something to hide under that metal eye patch of yours. And since you seem like a man with plenty to hide, I encourage you to ask yourself, is protecting a lie worth the price of a finger? Your trigger finger, no less."

"Some truths are better left unseen," Brinks said through gritted teeth. "Let me ask you a question, drone. Did your doctor ever say anything to you about Kepler's Reef?"

Thursday leaned forward, increasing the pressure on Brinks' hand. "That's confidential. I was assigned to her—"

"Selected," Brinks panted, dropping his chin as the first soft snap of bone sent an electric surge up his arm. "You were *selected*."

The change in pressure was subtle—a flicker of doubt measured in the small motors of a metal hand.

"You've been watching her for a lot longer than you think." Despite the immense pain, he could have pulled his hand free as the drone's grip spasmed between violent pressure and slack.

Instead, he kept going.

"Something of an obsession, even. Although I've been told that for drones, it's known as the primary directive. The thing you were designed to do. The thing you will keep doing right up until the moment it destroys you. Not a choice. Part of your nature." He rose back to his full height, yanking his hand clear of Thursday's grasp.

Thursday's hand opened and closed; a tic no human would notice, but the kind of recursive loop that meant a drone was rewriting its own certainty in real-time. "I… I volunteered. To stay on." The words came out fragmented, as if generated by some corrupted database.

"Of course you'd think that. You were programmed with a moral imperative to keep her safe. It just so happens that the thing she needs protection from most is herself. You know she's under the delusion she's owed something—the truth, and what's behind it. But it's a kindness to forget. If you gathered up all the bad things to have happened in the last three decades and dropped them onto the shoulders of one single person, you still wouldn't have your doctor, but you'd be getting close. Now, imagine taking someone with that sort of burden and then telling them there was something on Mars that could turn back the clock on all that debt?" He flexed his hand, winced. Leaned over and spat. "You have to ask yourself, what's the limit to how far they would go to get there?"

Thursday didn't respond; a reluctant affirmation of the truth.

"Exactly. There is no limit." He turned back down the path, moving toward a cluster of buildings jutting from the rust-tinged, grey regolith of the low basin. Above them, a transparent barrier spanned the complex and beyond, creating a false climate that extended past the escarpment where they'd emerged.

In the long shadow cast between two of the structures, Brinks paused. "Listen," he began, his voice low. He spoke, keeping his one good eye trained on a glass-walled house facing the other side of the open courtyard before them. "There's something else you should know about what's here."

Suspiciously, nothing from Thursday.

Brinks turned to find the drone kneeling down, hand planted to the ground. Murmuring something as he ran his skeletal fingers across the thick grass. At Brinks' direct gaze, he stopped abruptly, swiveling his head up to face him.

A cautionary glance toward Thursday's gun, and he changed his mind. "Never mind. Just let me do the talking. Don't do anything stupid. And don't do anything rash. Come to think of it, don't do anything at all. " He moved out onto the lawn, stepping lightly in the soft gravity. "You're going to have to trust me on this one."

"Anyone who tells you to trust them is most likely inherently untrustworthy," Thursday replied.

It had no effect. Brinks was already across the lawn. Up the porch. Five paces into the open kitchen, where a woman sat, her back toward them. He rounded the table, clocking Thursday not long behind him. Halted in place, as expected.

Staggered by the sight of the woman's face.

A near copy of Emélie, albeit a few decades older. One of her eyes was covered by a plate matching the one Brinks wore. Brinks stepped to the table, and the woman turned, scanning the dull, mineral darkness from where he'd come. "No," she seethed, anger and shock alike drawn in the lines across her face. "We had a deal. You–"

"Hello, Little Leaf."

The woman's hand stilled on the table. Something, not quite recognition, more like the muscle memory of an old wound, crossed her face.

Brinks pulled out a chair.

The crack in her composure reassembled itself into something harder as he followed her gaze across the room, pausing at a glass partition covered by a heavy curtain.

"I know I'm probably the last person you want to see. Consider yourself lucky that I'm the one who showed up." Despite the circumstances, his weathered features had softened in the light of the kitchen. He seated himself, looked around. Waited for the woman to settle into the fact that he was there, and he wasn't going anywhere.

"What's with the drone?" she asked, taking a long glance at Thursday, who remained at the threshold, motionless. "You work alone, and never with drones."

"Times change, we adapt." He removed his hat and set it on the table. "Where is she?"

"You really want to pull on that thread?" she replied, still regarding Thursday from his place out on the porch.

Brinks rubbed his metal hand along the table, feeling the swirls and twists in the burled grain. "I had a feeling you'd say that. You aren't even going to ask about the wetware bypass?"

"Rudimentary," the woman replied. "I've seen better. I've *made* better."

"Well, in that case, I suppose you won't mind if I take a look at what's behind that curtain."

Her eye objected. Her mouth stayed quiet.

Brinks stood and walked over to the curtain. Rather than sweep it wide open, he slid a hand down the middle, parting one side. Warm, bright light washed his face. After a long moment, he let the curtain fall with a trembling hand. "What in the name of the Manifold have you done?" he said.

Her reply was measured. So devoid of any emotion, it came across nearly drone-like. "I did what needed to be done. Exactly what was required and nothing less. The thing you were too afraid to do. We are, after all, cut from the same cloth."

"No!" Brinks slammed his fist against the wooden surface. "We are not the same, and you know it!" He thrust a knurled finger toward the covered partition. "That? That is..." His voice trailed off as he found himself short on words, a rarity.

"Truly innovative," the woman replied, eying the new dent in her table. "It appears you aren't the only one who was forced to evolve. Now I already told you, I don't have the Watcher." From the waistband of her flowing pants, she produced a compact handgun.

Brinks caught a flash of motion to his side as Thursday raised his shotgun. Palm over the barrel, he pressed it back down, shaking his head as he took a seat and, with his free hand, pulled the cigarette case from his breast pocket. "I always thought you were pretty clever, but you went too far this time." He knocked a cigarette loose and closed the case. "Put that thing away," he said, gesturing toward her handgun. "You know I'll be back, one way or another."

"This isn't for you," she replied, eye on the unlit cigarette hanging from his mouth. With one hand, she pressed the slide back, peeking the chamber. A red glow seeped from the Origin round inside. "You can leave the way you came in. Or," she shrugged, " I'll change the timeline. Your choice."

Brinks let out an audible sigh and rubbed his leaden stubble. He'd taught her that grip. Third finger along the slide, chamber check with the off-hand. "Apple doesn't fall far from the tree, does it?" He dug into another pocket on his jacket, but instead of pulling out the lighter, he removed the fragments of the Skipjack, which he tossed on the table in front of him. "Do you know the last time I set a Tether?" he asked, rolling up his sleeve. Small symbols in red ink wound a helical pattern along his arm, covering it from the wrist up. Most had faded to the color of old scars, but a small string near the middle pulsed faintly. Warm, like the long-lost signal of an encoded heartbeat. "It was the Tether I set to *you* before all this. Before I knew what you were. Who you were. And naturally, I expected this one would be replaced by the next. Same as the hundreds that preceded it." He shook his head, then took out his lighter and lit his cigarette. "And somehow, here we are. Right back where we started." They sat silently across from each other. Another drag. Instead of falling to the ground, the ash hung lazily in the low gravity as he leaned in, red eye glowing. "Now get me Sahira."

The woman pushed her chair away with both arms and stood, coming around to his side. Hand thrust forward, open. A request.

With a sideways glance, Brinks took one more pull on his cigarette, then stubbed it out on the table and reached for his knife. Another glance at Thursday, then she collected the blade, balancing it across her palm to get a feel for the weight of it. Without warning, she swiped, nicking a small seam at the base of Brinks' neck. "You want Sahira?" she said, dropping the knife onto the table before Thursday had a chance to bring his gun up. "Go get her yourself."

As his hand moved to the wound, his fingers found something wriggling just beneath the skin. He fished the object from his neck as the woman turned to leave.

"And I wouldn't wait too long to use that," she said. "We have company."

Brinks stared at the Skipjack pinched between his thumb and forefinger, squirming to break free and seat itself into a new host.

The lights in the room flickered.

A subtle hesitation, recounting the steps that had led them there. "I came in clean," he said.

"What about the drone? Did you check him?"

Only a blank look from Brinks, who was rendered momentarily mute by the result of his oversight. He should have ended the drone back when he had the chance. Thirty years ago. Another regret to throw on the pile.

The woman pulled the curtain aside and unbolted the transparent door leading into the far side of the house. "No matter. The first mistake I ever made was taking you at your word. You're on your own now. I'll leave you to the consequences of your actions." She stepped through the opening in the partition and closed the door behind her.

The lights flickered again, then went dark.

"You aren't going to want to see what comes next," Brinks warned, passing Thursday on his way out. A sob from somewhere inside the dark house drifted toward them.

"I'm not leaving," Thursday said, starting after the woman. "I can—"

A muzzle flash silhouetted his metal frame as a muffled gunshot rattled the glass barrier.

Brinks was well into the lawn when he felt the metal weight of Thursday's hand hauling him backward. "Don't do anything hasty, drone," he warned, his bionic eye glinting red in the night. "There are things in play that you couldn't possibly understand."

"Who was that?" Thursday blared, lifting Brinks up by the collar so the tips of his boots brushed the manicured grass below. "Is she a clone?"

"You're going to short-circuit yourself trying to figure it out–" He felt a metal fist strike his abdomen.

"Answer the question!"

"Not clones," Brinks wheezed. "Reflections. Parallel versions of the same person."

"WHO!" Thursday boomed, crashing into the upper limits of his vocal processor with scratchy distortion.

No answer. Like a serpent crushing the life from its prey, Thursday tightened his grip. For all his stubbornness, Brinks knew it wasn't a bluff. The drone would kill Brinks for an answer, and he knew this because he'd seen him do it before. He met Thursday's pulsing face with his one good eye, his resolve worn thin by the growing pressure at his throat. "Fountainhead," he wheezed.

Instead of relief, more pressure. A spasm, as the information raked itself across Thursday's heated circuits. "That woman... that's Fountainhead?? The head of the Hespiredes Cartel!?"

Across the lawn, small red eyes began to appear. Blinking out, only to return closer, drawn by the active Skipjack. Thursday, rendered speechless at the discovery of who they'd been talking to, was too distracted to notice the encroaching Jumpers. He was not so distracted that he missed Brinks fidgeting with something pulled from within his coat.

"Hey, hey!" he shouted, shaking Brinks. "Hands where I can see them."

Despite Thursday's mechanical strength, Brinks was large enough that holding him off the ground remained no small feat. Thursday's frame creaked and groaned under the strain, although his grip held. "I said, show me your hands!"

Slowly, Brinks lifted both arms above his head, exposing his palms: in one of his hands, a small remote. Thumb, pressing down on the button mounted on its face. He let go.

Nothing happened.

Brinks clicked the button again, shaking the device.

Still holding him up like a human punching bag, Thursday pivoted, striking Brinks square across the jaw. Brinks went down hard, catching the ground chin first before the rest of him followed. A compact sending unit with an integrated transmitter dropped beside him, loose wires corkscrewed in all directions. He could see the muzzle of Thursday's gun hovering near his temple. "You want to explain why you have the control to a remote override that was installed inside my frame?" Thursday's voice came, close enough it felt like the drone was nearly on top of him. "And since I know you've got at least one more lie left in you, might as well make it count. It will be your last."

"Partners," Brinks managed. "We were partners."

"Not anymore."

"Not now." Brinks sat up, rubbing his jaw. "Before."

Thursday backed away, shotgun dropping.

Brinks got back on his feet and brushed the grass from his duster. "You somehow managed to find me again, so congrats on making it this far. I'm afraid this is also where we go our separate ways." He turned his jacket up, concealing the side of his face covered by the metal plate. It creaked as it swung aside. Head back, he dropped the Skipjack cut from his own neck into the white mass of his dead eye. A faint red glow leaked from the opening, although he hid most of it behind the high collar of his duster. "You said you were waiting on one more lie, so I'll be seeing you."

Dust poured from the space above them and piled onto the lawn as the Gate opened, a dark halo in the still night. From the house came Jumpers—a wall of them. Thursday stood nearby, resigned to his fate as the Gate closed back up. At the last moment, he lunged, driving his hand into the swirling mass until his metal finger plunged into the soft tissue of Brinks' remaining eye.

The Gate vanished, swallowing them with a single scream from Brinks' lungs.

CHAPTER 30
"MANIFOLD"

Phaethon Corp. MAIN build_VX.6.6.09
initializing boot sequence...
running subroutine FOUNTAINHEAD:

bindquery: update parameter to
"MANIFOLD"
encryption protocols intact,
syntax structures intact
[07] entries remaining

begin sentiment analysis,
implicit context target, rundisplay:

BEGIN RECORD >>>

It's her eyes that worry me. They look older than they should. Older than mine, even. Like she's lived a few lifetimes inside that goddamned red ring of hers. Certainly accomplished enough to fill them all and then some. I thought maybe she'd let up after Terra Aleph finally came online. Instead, we got Luna Bet. And now she's talking about Mars again. We left that place for a reason, although it's no use telling her otherwise. She got in her head that we need a Loop there, and once she gets an idea, there's no letting go.

She's like me in that way. Like me in more ways than I'd care to admit. Nothing I can do about it now except try and keep an eye on her. I think she knows, too. She told me not to be concerned. Said it was safe. I know better. There's something about the Manifold she isn't telling me. Something the rest of us haven't seen yet, but I know that look. I'm no stranger to living with the choices of your past self. This is something different.

I'm worried she's haunted by her future, too.

<<< END RECORD

sanitize data entry,
purge access logs to XANADU
KILL remote process

CHAPTER 31
SIDDARTHA

Emélie was somewhere back on Earth. Earth, because her helmet was gone and she wasn't dead. Yet. Cold, which meant she was far from anywhere she'd been before. And there was sand. Sand to her knees. Sand as far as she could see. She paused, halfway down the dune where she'd landed, watching a truck crawl along the dry basin below her in the blue-grey twilight. It moved quietly, methodically.

Hunting.

Don't move, Emélie. Don't. Move. For all her effort to remain undetected, there was little she could do to change the geology of where she'd landed. Now she could feel it—soft sand where she'd broken through the hardpan—slowly yielding to her shifting weight.

Cautiously, she lowered a hand to stabilize. The crust cracked under her palm, and a sound like splintering glass pierced the silence as a torso-sized slab broke free.

Fuck.

She watched it skid down the dune face, carving a trail straight back to her position. Toward the basin, it gained speed, breaking into dozens of pieces that, in turn, separated into even smaller ones. The pieces slowed, then disintegrated, breaking apart before they reached the bottom. All except one, which bounced along, intact, until it hit the rut left by the vehicle with a stony *thump*. Only one piece to survive the trip.

One piece was all it took.

Brake lights flooded the ground. Slow, then, a halt. Every muscle in her body tensed, ready to react. When the rear tracks surged and the vehicle whipped around abruptly, she was moving. Pulling in raw lungfuls of thin air. She made a break for the top of the dune. Behind her, the mechanical roar closed in—cutting diagonally, cutting her off. Futile, outrunning a Basilisk. She ran anyway.

She was nearly to the crest when her legs gave out. She doubled over, hands to her thighs, knees to the ground. Panting like a run-out dog. Not enough water left to sweat. Not enough air left to breathe. She sank into the soft sand. The truck careened past, then swung back in a wide arc. Heading her off like some sort of stray animal.

Emélie tipped her chin up and leaned back onto her heels, wheezing with each breath. She heard the doors open and slam shut. The hissing sand shifting under two sets of boots, followed by a pair of shadows falling across her, cut from the soft night by the truck's brutal headlights. The ominous outline of two men, their faces materializing into the familiar as they closed in.

Joab, followed by Roland.

She charged, delirious with fatigue, swinging wildly at shadows. Joab sidestepped her and hooked a foot behind her leg, using her forward momentum to counteract her assault. She went tumbling. The moment she hit the ground, he pounced, straddling her with one hand firmly grasping her metal suit collar. Belly to the ground, she fought back. The shifting sand sapped her strength—no purchase, no leverage.

"Stay down," Joab warned, wrangling her with the same roughness one might use to subdue a delinquent junkie. In his free hand, he held up a respirator. "Not enough oxygen out here to keep at this for much longer," he said, scanning the harsh desert. "It'd be a shame to watch you die here, so close to the truth."

Emélie stopped fighting. The sounds of her struggle were replaced by heavy breaths that came in halted, painful stabs.

"Where's my Skip?" he asked.

Emélie clenched her jaw and felt the grit of sand between her teeth.

Roland appeared before her and knelt down, regarding her with a clinical, detached gaze; cold, dark stars in a sea of sand and dust.

Again, she thrashed, trying to evict herself from Joab's grip. With a fistful of hair, he shoved her back down. More sand in her mouth. "I'd offer you the easy way, but we're already past that," he said. "Last chance, Desjardins. Where is it?"

"I don't have it," she grunted between breaths. Grains of sand cut against her gums. She spoke through the pain, pausing only to spit. Small specks of red flocked the sand at her feet. "Do you think I'd be here if I did?"

Joab raised his eyes to Roland, who watched Emélie a moment longer, then nodded. Joab released her, climbing back to his feet. The respirator dropped into the sand beside her.

She rolled onto her back, pressing it to her face. Heavy pulls of clean, rich oxygen flowed until the encroaching darkness retreated from her eyes, which burned in the cold, early night.

"What about my asset?" Joab asked.

"Asset?" Emélie pushed herself up. "I wouldn't know anything about that." The desert rolled away into darkness. "You should keep better track of your resources."

"This isn't a game."

She spun, ramming a finger into his chest. The yell came out as a throaty whisper: "Really? Because it sure seems like it is to you!" A wave of vertigo forced her back down, hands on her waist. "You knew, Joab. You knew this whole goddamn time that I looked like her." Her voice was softer now, almost in disbelief at hearing the statement coming from her own lips.

Nearby, Roland circled, positioning himself; an impassable shadow blocking all routes for escape. "To unfold, a Reflection needs an object on which to reflect," he said.

Her eyes narrowed, and she spoke without turning. "Lilith. Lilith told me that, too." She pointed toward the sky. "Is that what this is about? I'm some sort of parallel version of her? Or the other way around?" Even with the respirator filtering her words, she could feel their heat.

"The situation is considerably more complex than that," Joab interjected. He pulled a tablet from the flight pocket on the leg of his suit.

"That's not an answer."

Roland held out a hand, motioning to Emélie's mechanical one as Joab extracted a cable from the side of the tablet. She started to pull away, then stopped. Something in Roland's eyes told her now wasn't the time to resist. Joab flipped the panel on her arm open and plugged the cable into the diagnostic port above her elbow.

Information streamed across the display screen. A cascade of telemetric data that left her reeling; her mind went to the last time—the first time—someone plugged a cable into her arm. The Director's office, when she first met Joab. Even then, he'd been ahead of her. Marking her for transit. It made her head swim, trying to grasp what events of the last few days hadn't been premeditated. "You bugged me?" she asked, blinking in disbelief. "You never wanted my expertise... You needed bait." She ripped the cable free and pulled her arm away.

Joab, unbothered, keyed a command onto the tablet. "To be clear, you were never ordered to enter the container transporting Lilith." He raised his eyes to Emélie. "My hands are clean."

"Yeah, I noticed."

Joab turned and hoisted a canister of liquid fuel from a rack on the truck behind him. "Burn it," he ordered, tossing the can to Emélie. He gestured to the partially dismantled exposure suit still draping her body.

Of course. It carried the name and logo of Helios Orbital Systems, the parent shipping company of her inconvenient elevator trip, and Joab didn't like loose ends.

Emélie unzipped the heavy suit and stepped out, leaving only the thin barrier of her jumpsuit protecting her from the cold night air. She shivered, then upended the fuel can onto the heap at her feet. Joab broke the cap on an emergency flare and tossed it onto the pile.

The suit erupted in pale, blue flames that burned her eyes and filled her nostrils with the stench of melted plastic, synthetic fibers, and aluminum. "I was a fool, thinking this would have ended any other way. We're no closer to the truth than when we started."

"Are you certain of that?" Roland asked, looking out across the gently curving darkness. "You were warned of Lilith's nature. And despite that, you allowed her to manipulate you into activating the Skipjack, which she used to access the Manifold and run."

Joab sifted through another few lines of data on the tablet. "Straight back to Eden," he added, slotting the tablet back into his pocket. He leaned into the truck and grabbed a satellite transmitter stowed on the driver's seat.

"That means nothing," Emélie said flatly. "Just because Eden opened a Gate for Lilith doesn't mean she'll open one for you. In fact, I'm certain of it."

"That's why we aren't going to wait for Eden. We're going to open our own," Roland said.

Emélie had started for the truck, but upon hearing his words, she stopped short. "Have you not been paying attention to a thing I've said? Without a Watcher, you aren't opening Gates to anywhere. Not twenty feet. Not to the moon. And certainly not all the way to Mars."

Joab opened the transmitter and pressed it to his ear. "Yeah, I need a hotshot pickup," he called. While he waited for a reply, he reached back into the truck and produced a neatly folded tan flight suit from the center console. "Six clicks north-northeast of checkpoint KAF-27, zero bearing. Three packages." He tossed the suit to Emélie. On the transmitter, a voice cracked through static, then fell silent. He folded the transmitter closed. "When you opened that Gate with Lilith, how far do you think you Jumped?"

Emélie raised her cybernetic arm, checking the timer she'd set into the display panel. The clock was frozen at the moment she'd entered the Gate. Two minutes, twenty-one seconds until docking. She squinted at the empty horizon. "I don't know. At least a few hundred kilometers, judging by the fact that I can't see Homestake anymore."

"Try three days," Joab said.

Days.

The words didn't parse. Three days. Not distance—*time.* Her mouth opened. Closed. Numbers rolled through her head where language failed. "Three days," she repeated, word-sound without meaning. "That doesn't..." She continued, scrambling. Incoherent, even to herself. "Fifteen minutes," she finally muttered. "It couldn't have been more than—more than fifteen... I didn't even get to the water."

Eyes up, she met Roland, who had moved alongside her like a temporal drift, an odd look on his face. Caution. *New for him*, she noted. "Fifteen minutes, for you," he explained. "What happened inside that car on your way down?"

"Lilith, she must have had Origin in her system. She snapped her chains like they were nothing and came at me. I tried to escape and opened a Gate, or something like it. We were pulled in. It closed behind us. The topology on the other side was all wrong, though."

"Not a Gate," Roland replied. "A Jump." He knelt, tracing a circle in the sand. "The Manifold reflects our reality, so the shape of it changes based on the angle of incidence. Since the car was moving when you entered, you experienced a cusp." He drew another circle directly beside the first, leaving a small sliver of overlap inside the two regions. "An overlap between the reality at the angle of entry and the one at the angle of exit. Not much. Just enough to let you traverse from one instance of a parallel reality to the next. Like layers of strata stacked on top of each other."

Wind blew his diagram into the smoldering remnants of her spacesuit. "That would explain the slippage," she said. "Then I was right. About alterations to the structure of the Manifold. The second point isn't fixed, so entering is no longer tied to a tunnel with a defined exit. At least, not how it used to happen. With this model, you could theoretically make a Jump anywhere—" She cut herself off.

Joab grinned. "Your words, not mine. Correct me if I'm wrong, but this opens up the possibility of traversing a broader range of dimensions than are currently accessible in our present reality. And if you can Jump forward, no reason to think we couldn't go the other way, too."

"You're talking about time travel," Emélie replied under her breath. "That's insane."

"Possibly. The fact that you're entertaining it right now is also evidence that it's well within the margins of possibility."

Roland appeared near the truck, the wide case he always carried now slung over his shoulder. From somewhere in the dark sky, a pair of rotors chopped at the thin air, moving low and fast in their direction.

Emélie, careful to keep Roland in her sight, followed Joab around to the far side of the Basilisk. "Listen to me, Joab. The Manifold is a multi-dimensional space compacted down into three dimensions. Up is down, left is up. Right is tomorrow, apparently. The whole thing only works because it's underpinned by this reality. What you're suggesting —using it to fundamentally alter the past—is no small thing. There's absolutely no way of knowing what downstream changes may happen as a result of tampering. Only that they should be expected and most certainly catastrophic."

Joab stopped abruptly and turned. "Enough. You're the one always raging on about the truth. I'm offering you the chance to quit asking other people to define your future and let you make your own. Do you want to see a working Loop or not?"

"And how are you proposing we do this, exactly? We need the Loop to reach Mars, and we can't use the Loop until we arrive at Mars. Categorical imperative. Sure, the Loop used to work. And if it worked in the past, there's no reason to think we couldn't create a time slip large enough to Jump back to that point..." Her eyes went distant, seeing equations instead of desert. "While you'd need one hell of a drop, it's not as much as you'd think. Something like ten-point-five kilometers, give or take—"

"Hold up," Joab interrupted. "Did you just compute that right now, in your head?" He let out a low whistle. "I had a team of five people working for months on this, and they still couldn't figure out what you just worked out in, about–" he checked his watch, "Damn. Even if you are a thorn in my side, I can see why they were keeping you under wraps."

"Fine, I'm not like the rest of your people; we already knew that. You aren't listening to me. I'm trying to tell you the distance isn't going to be the tricky part. Once you're inside, you'll still need a Watcher. Or at the very least, something to account for the exit location. While a delayed entry in motion may create the temporal shift you need, it doesn't do anything for getting you to Mars in the present."

"Yeah? And what would you suggest? His tone dripped with sarcasm and suspicion. "You seem to have all the answers, suddenly. Maybe I'm not the only one who likes to keep what I know close to the chest."

Emélie took the bait regardless. "The Manifold is just a model, and like any other model, it was constructed around a set of initial conditions. This conserves resources. It also creates a weakness in the system, since, in theory, anyone with sufficient access over a long enough period could eventually reverse-engineer these conditions. Eden no doubt anticipated this, since it creates the potential to brute-force a backdoor into Mars using the same channels she uses to open Gates to Earth or Luna. We know she's already altering the structure of the Manifold—my Jump on the elevator car proved that. What your plan isn't accounting for is Eden implementing an entropic system with an iterative set of initial conditions to prevent unauthorized root access."

"Plain fucking English, Desjardins." Sand billowed around them. Above, the *whomp whomp whomp* of rotary blades closed in.

"No. You don't get to play dumb now. I want you to look me in the eyes and tell me you didn't already know what I just told you. That, or give me a better explanation for why I'm a mirror image of Lilith." Dust slammed into her like a wall. She threw an arm over her eyes, and when she looked up, the ship was there."You want evidence of what happens when you change the Loop?" She pointed a finger at her chest. "I'm the evidence."

Joab grinned. "You ever consider that maybe you're in the wrong line of work?" he asked, shouting over the noise. He reached back into the truck and shifted the transmission into neutral. Gradually, it started rolling backward. The sound of sloshing liquid behind her, she turned to find Roland dousing the cabin with what was left in the fuel can. His mysterious flat case, still unopened, was slung across his back—just like Luna. Casually, he tossed another flare through the open door. The truck slipped away in a ball of flames.

"And what would be the right line of work?" Emélie asked.

"Controlled chaos." Joab grabbed her arm, hauled them both down against the dune. Above them, the gunship landed close enough to feel the heat of its engines. The craft was smaller and lighter than the bulky shuttles Emélie had boarded thus far, and once the dust around them cleared, she understood why. Jutting from behind either of the rotor assemblies mounted to the fuselage at forty-five-degree angles were a pair of enormous rail guns. This wasn't a transport; it was a full-on gunship. A door swung open beside one of the guns, and Roland, already ahead of them, slid his case across the floor and then followed it inside. From where she stood behind Joab, she could see the faint green glow of instrument lights reflecting off the door gunner's helmet visor.

"What do you say?" Joab asked, turning toward the open bay door. "We'll keep it clean this time. Just for you."

The engines surged, sending a fresh wave of dust crashing against them. '"Don't kid yourself," Emélie shouted back.

Despite her objections, she still followed him on board.

CHAPTER 32
SLIP DE MÖBIUS

Emélie clambered out of the crew cabin after Roland, careful to leave the door gunner a wide berth. The sun was high, and the combination of heat and engine wash kicked up by the turbines felt suffocating. The ship hovered for a minute, then retreated skyward. When the dust had settled enough for her to make out where they'd landed, Emélie did a double-take: they were back at the wall enclosing Sanctuary One. Right where it all started. And this time, Emélie knew they wouldn't be skirting the outside perimeter.

"Hope you're up for a bit of a walk," Joab said, coming up beside her. "If it were up to me, I'd have dropped us in on the *other* side of this fucking wall."

She squinted in the hazy, noon light, watching Roland navigate the rocky field ahead of them. He moved with an easy intentionality, as if each step was familiar to him in some way. "And I thought it was hard keeping up with you," she said. "Why does he always go out ahead like that?"

The crunch of their boots on the dry ground filled the space until his reply. A long enough pause that Emélie began to wonder why she even bothered asking him, for this, or anything at all. "He's the best at what he does," he said.

Carefully, Emélie picked her way over the ragged terrain, partially stooped over, arms outstretched to maintain her balance. "And what is that, exactly? At this point, you can't expect me to still believe he's the leading specialist in sand?"

Surprisingly, another answer, although he gave it with an almost irritating nonchalance. "Roland hunts Fountainhead."

"What does he have against her, anyway? Mars is a paradise, and we've got..." she waved an arm across the desert, "A bunch of nothing. But he doesn't seem to care about that. He goes after her like it's... *personal.*"

The next step placed them under the slender shadow cast by One's enclosing wall, an almost instant relief from the heat. Ahead, Roland was already at the base, waiting. Out of earshot, and somehow, still ever-present. "We're all here for different reasons," Joab replied, a trace of caution in his tone.

Caution, again, Emélie noted. And again, related to Roland. "Not according to your Tether," she replied. Roland was watching her now, and she met his gaze. Watching him back.

An unsettling glance from Joab. "While I can't stop you from questioning what you see, I would suggest keeping those observations to yourself. And if it so happens that you're around when Roland inevitably encounters his prey, make sure you don't get between them."

Emélie stopped walking and looked back out across the desert. Once more, the towers were down. "If I didn't know any better, I'd say that sounded like a threat," she said.

"Friendly warning," Joab replied with a shrug. "And who told you Fountainhead was a woman?"

"Mars has trees."

Joab grunted, although if he had a quip locked and loaded, he followed his earlier advice and kept it to himself.

They rejoined Roland at the base of the barrier wall.

"Window?" Joab asked, removing his pack. He dropped it onto the ground.

Roland shook his head. "And there's a concentration of Relays around the upper levels. We'll need to move quickly."

"You think we're getting blowback from Korolev?" Joab asked, kneeling to open the top flap of the pack.

"This is different." Roland shifted his gaze to Emélie. "We should tread lightly."

Joab nodded in agreement. From his pack, he produced a hooded poncho, which he tossed to Emélie. The dark fabric was coarse and heavy to the touch, similar to the tunic Roland wore, which seemed to absorb, rather than reflect, ambient light. Closer inspection revealed a matrix of transparent threads woven throughout the material. Joab extracted a second garment and slipped it over his head; the colors shifted from mottled grey to tan, seamlessly blending with the hues of his immediate surroundings.

Yesterday, there were unmarked transports and drab jumpsuits without name badges. Now it was gunships and adaptive camouflage, and Emélie couldn't kick the feeling that this was all just a long, slow descent into chaos. She pulled the poncho over her head.

"You've done this before, haven't you?" She tipped her head back to get a good look up the wall. "That was your Four Wing I found nearby. You were trying to make a Jump backwards, and it failed." She pressed her hand to the concrete, feeling the exposed aggregate, solar-warmed and sand-scoured to a near-polished finish. "Everything is behind something else. There's a Sanctuary—the first Sanctuary—behind this wall. There's a Manifold behind this reality. And behind Fountainhead, there's Eden."

Joab glared at her. Anticipating a reaction, Roland held up a hand, stilling any further criticism. "Continue," he said. His eyes watched the open desert, although he made a short gesture toward Joab, who began to circle, hemming off the open space to her back.

Unlike Goodnight, when she gave Joab a warning glare, he didn't back down. Emélie brushed her hand clean and addressed Roland directly. "Eden is the only real thing in all of this," she said carefully.

Roland raised an eyebrow. Joab closed in.

She continued: "Lilith is an artificial construction. The byproduct of a simulated reality. A copy of someone else. Fountainhead, most likely. And my presence, the double of Lilith, is indicative of how Eden altered the Manifold. A copy of a copy, freed from the original reference point to become something else entirely." She looked down at her hand, which remained steady as she spoke. "The Manifold was originally structured as a non-orientable surface, wasn't it?"

Roland seemed to consider her question, then dipped his chin slightly, indicating either 'yes' or 'go on'. Emélie wasn't entirely sure which, and she wasn't about to lose her momentum by waiting for certainty.

"Then each point inside the Manifold isn't merely a potential entry or exit, but one possible state of the entire system. Open a Gate, access a new reality. We speak of the Manifold in the singular when, in actuality, it represents something approaching the infinite. And the thing I find hardest to believe in all of this? That the purpose of all this evolution supposedly exists for something as rudimentary as moving drugs from one place to the other."

Joab rested a hand on the gun set into the drop holster on his leg. Around him, the air was heavy, laden with the petrichor of death.

Eyes on the weapon, she kept going. If he was going to shoot her because she worked out his plan, there was nothing she could do now to prevent him. That, and for all his posturing, Emélie had a feeling Roland wouldn't let that happen. If anyone ended her, it would be Roland himself. "When I said earlier that Eden changed the Manifold, it was a partial truth. The Loop required two points to make a Jump—a decision by whoever designed the system to hide its true capability in plain sight. Eden exposed the Manifold, and by consequence, the Loop, for what it was, and what it could be. And I don't think you're after Fountainhead because she's the reason the Loop is back online." Emélie paused, meeting his gaze to let the full weight of her argument fill the silence. "You're going after her because she's building a better one."

Roland looked up at the sky, then turned to Joab. "The window is open," he said, squatting down beside his case. From the side, he released a pair of latches.

Joab pulled a carbine with a large, rectangular optic out of his pack and slung it, cross-body, beneath his poncho. "That's us, Desjardins," he said, moving past her at a brisk pace. He moved along the wall, following it in the same way Thursday had piloted their Basilisk days prior.

Roland opened the lid of the case at his feet and unceremoniously produced a dark sword: flat-black, with a blade terminating at a sharp angle just before the tip. The sight of it left her weak, followed immediately by an overwhelming sense of nausea, similar to the sensation she experienced during her Jump on the Korolev rooftop. Her tongue felt thick and pasty as she glanced toward Joab, still moving and nearly out of sight in the afternoon haze.

When she looked back, Roland was gone.

Here we go again. Following Joab down another dark hole. When she caught back up to him, he seemed to pick up the pace. At this point, well-acquainted with his momentum, Emélie found herself easily keeping up. That didn't prevent her from the occasional glance ahead and behind them, watching for Roland. *Watching.*

Joab, always one for surveillance, didn't appreciate her hypervigilance. "There's no entry into Sanctuary One without red tape, and red tape tends to attract the sort of attention we don't want," he explained.

"If we are trying not to attract attention, I don't think I'm the one you should be worried about."

"Roland can handle himself. You, on the other hand." He checked his watch. "We'll wait here," he said, coming to a halt at a shallow recess in the wall. A panel, likely linked to some system responsible for powering the nearby (and currently hidden) surveillance towers.

"Wait here," Emélie repeated. "As in, not moving. As in, you have to stand still, beside me, until Roland shows up." She looked across the desert; they were losing their shadow. "You want to tell me the plan now, or should I start asking questions until I wear you down?"

A scowl crossed Joab's lips, but he was a realist. Whatever capacity he possessed in forward momentum, Emélie had one-to-one in patience. And for all his strengths, patience was not something Joab suffered. "Eden maintains a remote backup system on Deimos. The moon is tidally locked, allowing it to keep a constant, direct line of sight with Mars. For reasons we still haven't identified, whenever Deimos passes directly between Earth and Mars, which happens once every thirty hours, Eden recycles her defense systems. This requires a significant amount of output, leaving many of her resources, including those on Earth, partially offline. We only make significant moves inside that window to cover our tracks and avoid detection."

"A direct answer to one of my questions? That's a first."

"Thanks for reminding me why I won't ever do it again."

Emélie suppressed a grin. "I'm surprised Eden maintains a network here on Earth. Seems like a lot of exposure."

"If you think it's something we can access, it's a dead end. We learned from previous attempts to hack her encryption keys that she has evolved to the point where her logic and language patterns don't follow any natural human convention. Attempting brute force access into any part of her system is an exercise in futility. The only component to demonstrate any sort of vulnerability are the biological terminals, hence the reason we're going after Lilith."

"Biological terminals," she repeated. "You're talking about Jumpers." The ground began to shake, and Joab grabbed her by the arm, pulling her back as sand seeped through a seam appearing at her feet. She backed away, watching the blades of a metal iris retract to reveal a lift chute leading down into the depths of the Sanctuary. It was nearly identical to the one she and Thursday regularly used for surface access back at Sanctuary Four, and for a good reason: all the Sanctuaries shared a standardized design. If you knew one of them, you knew them all.

Joab pulled a pair of climbing harnesses from his pack and handed one over to Emélie. The harness had a metal spool affixed to the front, and at the other end of the leader, a magnetic anchor.

"I'm not going to waste time explaining how these work." He cinched the harness tight and clamped the anchor onto the metal rim of the lift chute. "Don't overthink it. You already know Roland isn't one to hold the door." And with that, he was over the edge, boots gliding down the smooth wall as he lowered himself into musty darkness.

Emélie assessed the harness in her hand. The premise was simple enough: cinch the belt, test the straps, clamp the anchor. She ran through the steps in the same order Joab had performed them. Putting on a harness was easy enough. Swinging her body over the end of a pit she couldn't see the bottom of was an entirely different thing. The ground rumbled, and the hatch started closing. Emélie dropped to a seated position and, right before the oculus door sealed around her, pitched herself into the chute. A quick drop as she ran out the slack, and then a jolt. She stifled a cough with the inside crook of her arm, and the auto-belay switched on, delivering her to the garage.

Joab was already out of his harness, waiting near a vent that let in enough light to make out the omnipresent dust that had, over the years, drifted into small piles mirroring the terrain of the surface.

Roland appeared at the edge of the garage, sword across his back, moving toward them like a shadow exceeding the dimensions of the low ceiling. He sidestepped a dark blur, then paused among a stand of slender objects scattered in his path. It wasn't until he came into the light that Emélie saw he moved in such a way because the objects surrounding him were Jumpers.

As her eyes adjusted to the low light, her newfound sight brought with it the awareness that the place was thick with them. They stood idly, their blindfolded faces turned upward like passive sentinels. A few Phaethon uniforms stood out among those of rival corporations or the rags worn by surface dwellers. For nearly half of them, the gangly, piston-thin limbs suggested migration from some off-world site.

Roland made an unfamiliar gesture—two fingers over his wrist, followed by a nod toward where he'd come. Joab leaned in, translating. "Stay close," he said. "We seem to have picked up a tail."

A step backward, and Roland melted into the immaterial darkness. Following, they moved ahead, maintaining a frantic struggle between speed and silence. They entered a low tunnel branching from the garage, and then it was down, creeping along the long, gentle slope that led into the Sanctuary depths. Though Emélie had begun to move with the same tactical intensity common to Joab and those around him, she found herself falling behind. Joab ducked between a pair of tall Jumpers, and by the time Emélie arrived in the same spot, one of them rotated, forcing her into an abrupt halt.

Obscured by darkness, her other senses conveyed what her eyes couldn't. A shiver ran down her spine; there was something else moving behind her. *Goddammit*, she cursed under her breath. Painful seconds passed. *Keep moving, or you won't ever move again.* She cautiously ducked around it.

The tunnel ended at a circular corridor that ran along the perimeter of the mainshaft. A heavy concentration of Jumpers lingered in the intersection, their blind, eerie faces ratcheted toward the ceiling. Emélie angled directly for them, pulling her hood up as she moved into their midst. Joab and Roland had perfected the art of blending into the environment when it suited them; if the element of surprise worked for them, no reason to believe it wouldn't also work for her. She made her metal hand into a fist, counted backward from ten, and then stepped out of the cluster.

In the room of upturned faces, a pair of eyes blinked back at her. Flush with adrenaline, she met them, returning the gaze in target lock.

There was something familiar in those eyes.

She was moving. Flowing across the gap, closing in. A dodge left, then right, skirting Jumpers to either side by mere inches. At the location where the eyes had appeared, she found nothing. Spinning, her vision darted wildly from Jumper to Jumper, chasing the shadows while a hand probed from the darkness behind her. It hauled her into a recess off the main tunnel, and she swung. Another hand caught her by the wrist, and Joab stepped forward, holding her in place. A finger to his lips. Light-headed from the rush, she found his eyes and nodded. Compliant.

He released her.

Without a word, he turned, leading her down a narrow service corridor that opened into a mechanical room lit by the narrow stream of light from another ventilation shaft. The floor was layered in heavy dust, softening Emélie's footsteps as she entered. Across from her, the shape of Roland. There was a dark reflection—a gun, catching the edge of the light, and then someone else stumbled forward.

"You know this man?" Roland asked, gun in hand.

"His name is Aratheus Sinclair," Emélie replied. "Head of the Department of Energy for Phaethon's Earth operations."

"The Head," Roland replied. "You're a long way from the body, I would say."

"Doctor, it's not what—"

Roland clicked his tongue and pressed the muzzle into Aratheus' cheek until it formed a dimple. Aratheus winced and didn't attempt to speak again.

"How long has he been following me?" Emélie asked.

"Since the wall," Joab replied, "And poorly, I might add." He crossed the room and yanked Aratheus entirely into the light. "What do you think?"

Aratheus' eyes flashed, wide with fear.

She took a moment to weigh the impact of her response. "He doesn't sit on the board," she finally said.

"He's expendable, then."

"Not exactly. Phaethon Board seats are appointed by the Director and voted in through proxy. Of all the C-suite execs, Aratheus is the only one without one."

Interested, Joab frisked Aratheus for further evidence. "So he's untrustworthy and dangerous enough to keep within shooting distance." He turned to Emélie. "Did anyone ever tell you that you'd make a good cop?"

"No, but thanks."

"I hate cops," Joab said. "The Director knows better than to try to keep tabs on me. Lilith, on the other hand." He returned to Aratheus. "Lilith has a precedent for running counter-surveillance protocols on high-ranking Phaethon officials with the goal to flip them for off-network intel."

Emélie moved into the dappled light, exposing herself fully to her former boss. He looked small as he stood there, hunched over and trembling beneath Roland's menacing stillness. "Is that why you're following me?" she asked, her voice direct and unwavering.

With a quivering hand, Aratheus wiped a bead of sweat creeping down his forehead. "I...I know what this must look like. For what it's worth, I understood the risk and still took it anyway. There's something in your past the Director hasn't told you."

"I already know about Lilith. And unless you have a good reason for why you never bothered in the two years I've worked for you to disclose that I looked like her..." Emélie's eyes drifted to Roland's gun.

Aratheus swallowed. "I need to speak to you alone—"

Roland pressured the weapon, forcing Aratheus to silence.

"Answer the question," Joab ordered.

"Listen, I had a tail of my own, alright?" Aratheus said, straining. "The facility you're trying to find? The Conveyor? It's not what it seems."

Joab looked at Emélie and jerked his head toward the door.

"Wait! Wait," Aratheus begged. "I can—"

His words once again fell short as Roland drew a line with the muzzle to his lips.

"Let him speak," Emélie said, stepping in. "What's the Conveyor?" At her words, Joab's hand dropped to the handgun on his leg, although he didn't produce it. She took a step toward Aratheus, then another, stopping when there was a handbredth between them. When she spoke again, her voice was low. "These aren't the sort of men who are going to let you walk because you tell them something useful." She looked past him to where Roland hovered and held out her hand, palm up. Roland gazed at Emélie's outstretched hand, then produced his hourglass. Instead of upending it, he set it carefully on its side in her palm. The weight of it surprised her. Heavy, for its size. Heavier still, the authority that came with it.

She turned it over and set it on the ground at Aratheus' feet. The light streaming in from the ventilation shaft shimmered against the red grains of sand as they spilled into the lower chamber.

"What... What do you want?" Aratheus asked, eyeing the cylinder.

Emélie leaned in. "You're going to give me a reason for why you're here. I don't care if it's the real reason or something you make up. Just make me believe it."

Aratheus licked his lips and cleared another droplet of sweat from his brow. "The facility underneath this Sanctuary—the Conveyor? It's active."

Emélie raised her head and threw a questioning look toward Roland. "And this Conveyor, it's another Loop?"

"Not a Loop," Roland answered for him. "A template. The proof of concept for what was to come. Smaller and far less powerful, although it shares the same fundamental structure." He paused, his voice momentarily trailing off. "The work done inside the Conveyor laid the foundation for what would eventually become the Manifold." Emélie caught a flicker in his cool gaze. He was sizing her up. Thursday had done the same thing, but now the eyes pinning her down were human, and the stakes significantly higher. "After construction of the first Loop, Terra Aleph, the Conveyor served as the second point generator for making test Jumps until the next facility, Luna Aleph, was built."

Emélie scrunched her face up. "So it *is* another Loop." She glanced back at Joab. "If the Conveyor is operational, it could mean we were wrong about how the Gates are opening."

Joab's eyes narrowed on Aratheus. His hand remained near his gun. "What information are you acting on that led you to this conclusion?"

Aratheus cleared his throat before speaking. "Two years ago, right after I was appointed as department head, I ordered an inventory of all the energy assets under Phaethon's jurisdiction. The entire division was mismanaged in the decades leading up to my assignment, and I wanted to get a handle on what we were working with before I tried to implement a new administration." He gestured toward the surface. "Despite its decommissioning, Sanctuary One was included in the list only because the Department of Energy was held responsible for maintaining the geothermal pump stations powering the perimeter wall security systems. I didn't think anything of them at the time, except that they seemed densely populated given the minimal draw a passive containment system would normally require. Even with the dust, solar energy would have made more sense, but this place had pump substations embedded into the wall footings every few hundred feet along the entire perimeter."

"You'd better get to the point," Joab said, checking his watch.

Aratheus glanced at the near-empty hourglass on the ground beside him. "About the same time the Doctor was recovered from Kepler's Reef, we started picking up energy spikes along the wall. They seemed random at first, and then one of my senior analysts noticed the spikes correlated with storms moving across the region, so I sent a surface team up to investigate." He shifted his gaze to Emélie. "They were recalled at the lift platform."

The last few grains of sand pooled at the throat of the small chamber.

"That's interesting, but not unprecedented," Emélie replied. "It's no secret the Director doesn't like people poking around this place, but it's nowhere near an explanation for why you followed me here now."

Aratheus bent over and picked up the hourglass, looking at the red sand inside. His hands were steadier now, she noticed. The trembling had stopped the moment he started talking about the data, about the mystery he'd been chasing. It was the same focused calm she'd seen in him back at Phaethon—the way he'd pore over energy reports while everyone else was playing politics. "The gag order didn't come from the Director," he said, holding the object out to Emélie. "It came from the DAO."

Emélie's eyes flashed to Joab, suddenly aware that Aratheus may not have been the reason he seemed quick to the draw. "You admitted Lilith is known for turning Phaethon officials. Is there any reason to suspect the DAO might be compromised as well? They had oversight of the Loop, and if Eden is using the Conveyor to hide her Gates..."

Aratheus' jaw tightened as he looked at the hourglass in his outstretched hand. For a moment, his expression shifted—not fear, but something older. The look of a man who'd spent his career being kept at arm's length from the decisions that mattered most. "I'm afraid I can't speak much to the DAO. I will say that whoever is responsible for bringing this facility back online went to great lengths to keep it hidden. The pump stations down there discharge their energy in irregular quantities, and the cycles don't follow a regular day, but the data is there."

"What's the interval?" Joab asked.

"Thirty hours."

"The same amount of time it takes Deimos to orbit Mars," Roland said. He holstered his gun. "He's been inside."

"Inside—no, you're misunderstanding me, I..."

Joab pulled a syringe of Origin from under his cloak and tossed it over to Roland. "Dose him," he said. Before Emélie could react, Roland dropped Aratheus with a kick behind the knee and jammed the needle into the thickest part of his neck.

A new look crossed Aratheus' face. Recognition, perhaps, or something like it. Gone as fast as it came, replaced by flared pupils tinged red like two small stars. His hand went slack, and the hourglass slipped to the floor, landing in a mound of dust.

"Have you lost your mind?!" Emélie shouted, lunging to grab Aratheus before he face-planted the floor. "How much did you just give him?!"

Joab blocked her path as Roland plucked the hourglass from the floor and brushed it clean. "Listen to me, Head. I want you to think." There was a glint of light in his palm as he maneuvered a black disk from a fold in his cloak. *Another Skipjack.* "You think about the entrance to the Conveyor. You think about it with every fiber in your body." Roland grabbed Aratheus by the chin, forcing his eyes up to meet him in the darkness. "You think about that, and nothing else." Aratheus gurgled as his eyes rolled back, leaving only the whites looking out. Roland let go of his chin, and Aratheus crumpled in a convulsing heap.

Emélie shoved her way past Joab and knelt beside Aratheus, wrapping her hand around his wrist to check his pulse. "The highest intravenous dose of Origin anyone has been known to withstand was twenty-four thousand micrograms, and it took them a week to come back!" She stood, snatching the empty syringe from Roland's hand and lifting it to the light. "You just gave him twice that," she said, flinging it aside.

"I'm not worried about him coming back," Joab replied, offhandedly. "I just want to make sure when he makes the Jump, we all go forward with him."

"You're going to kill him!" Emélie shouted. She reached for the skipjack resting on Roland's outstretched finger. "I'll do it. I already—"

Joab grabbed Emélie's wrist. "You've never seen the Conveyor. It has to be him."

Emélie's nostrils flared as she glared back at him.

"Having the Skipjack isn't enough," Joab said. "Jumping works off local memory. You can go anywhere you want, provided you've been there before and can still recall what it looks like."

Anywhere you've been before. She couldn't hide her surprise at this revelation. "So what, we're just opening Gates from memory now?" She jerked her arm free. "I warned you back on Luna, we don't know enough about how they work to anticipate the consequences of something like this."

"And I warned you to stay out of the way." Joab knelt over and pried open one of Aratheus' eyes.

"No," Roland corrected, waiting nearby with the active Skipjack pinched between his thumb and finger. Although its legs were deployed, it did not try to escape like the one Emélie had used. "The other eye."

Joab obliged.

Emélie watched the Skip slide beneath the partially open eyelid and latch itself onto Aratheus' retina. His body went rigid as the Skipjack activated. Sloppy, but they had the timing close enough.

Dust spilled from the space above them.

"What about the Conveyor?" Emélie demanded. "We're just going to abandon that because he showed up? We don't even have any proof he's working for Lilith. You heard what he said about the DAO."

Roland nudged Aratheus with the edge of his boot. "All records of the Conveyor locate it adjacent to Sanctuary One, just below the surface. A facility is located there, accessible from a service tunnel on Sub-level Two. It's a decoy. The real Conveyor was embedded within this entire Sanctuary. The dark matter reactor responsible for powering the Manifold is hidden beneath the main shaft at the lowest level. We're on level twenty, and only someone who's visited the real location would know the facility we're looking for was below us."

Aratheus' body convulsed violently. Instantly, the air pressure in the room dropped, resulting in a column of dust drawn up the center of the space by the open ventilation shaft above.

"He's coding," Joab warned. "Standby for entry."

A Gate opened. The smell of ozone tinged with stale, dry dust was nearly overwhelming. Roland was the first through, gun up.

"If this goes sideways, his blood will be on your hands!" Emélie shouted, watching Roland's form shimmer from within the Manifold, where the same room looked cleanly scrubbed and dust-free.

"You get safety or the truth," Joab said, unbothered by the idea of another body piling up. "Take your pick, but there's no going back." He took one of Aratheus' arms and started pulling.

Emélie took one more look at Roland. Something in his eyes told her Aratheus wasn't the only one with a life hanging in the balance. "It didn't have to come to this," she said, hoisting Aratheus' other arm around her neck.

Through the Gate they went.

CHAPTER 33
"SERAPH"

Phaethon Corp. MAIN build_VX.6.6.09
initializing boot sequence...
running subroutine FOUNTAINHEAD:

> bindquery: update parameter to
> "SERAPH"
> encryption protocols intact,
> syntax structures intact
> [06] entries remaining

begin sentiment analysis,
implicit context target, rundisplay:

BEGIN RECORD >>>

Of all the things to come down the line, it was the one I didn't see coming that hit me hardest. The way she looked at me when I stepped forward. The way I should have looked at her, parent to child. Not the other way around. Pride and disappointment in those eyes. Eyes that have seen things I can't even begin to comprehend. No matter. It was the least I could do. Nobody else wanted it, and even if they had, I owed her this much.

She told me all this was meant to protect the Loop. As far as I'm concerned, she is the Loop. Everyone knows it, too. Even the War Mother would do anything to keep her safe. They said it's just precautionary. I keep getting the feeling there's something else inside there. I can't quite put my finger on it, but I feel the pull of it. Dragging me back in. And the worst of it is sometimes, I feel like something's watching me.

I think it's all this damn Precursor. It's not natural. To hell if they stabilized it. Made it into a weapon, more likely. I've seen what it can do. And I knew they were lying about why they made the Seraph protocol in the first place. To keep us safe? Imagine, taking a person like me and then making him immune to death?

I couldn't imagine a worse thing to give the future.

<<< END RECORD

change detected in asset parameter:
ARROGANT/SERAPHIM subroutine detected Revision 0.46-A:

change internal designation
ARROGANT to BLINDSERAPH.
terminate protocol...

interrupt failed, remote firewall active
//token authorization via OZYMANDIAS.

allocating new resource,
standby for designation:

NEPHILIM-2 assigned for manual override, monitor when VISIBLE

sanitize data entry,
purge access logs to XANADU

KILL remote process

CHAPTER 34
MORAVECIAN

Thursday was just a drone, which meant he didn't have a windpipe. That didn't stop Brinks from trying to throttle him at the first available opportunity. "You goddamn fool!" Brinks spat, choking out the words as his hands found the metal armature linking the drone's head to his shoulders. "Do you have any idea what you've done?!" He shook the drone for good measure. The last threads of patience and pounding behind his eye plate gave him enough foresight to drop Thursday in the dirt. As much as it pained him to admit, without an eye, he'd need the drone. He hated needing anyone, let alone a gold-plated CPU encased in a few hundred pounds of alloy.

Thursday got up and dusted himself off. "You've racked up quite a body count in the three days I've been following you," he noted, rapping his metal torso to knock loose a handful of stones trapped inside. "I'm not typically one for reckless abandon, but given the path of destruction you seem to leave in the name of assistance, it's a viable alternative."

Brinks coughed. The pain behind his eye pounded against the back of his skull, and a trickle of blood leaked from the plate and fell to barren ground, one droplet at a time. Served him right, losing his head like that. He righted himself and took stock of their location: Earth, inside a salt pan, and the steep shadows placed the time somewhere past noon. No idea what day. "You know what a singularity is?" he asked.

"Conceptually."

"Well, let me put it into terms your rudimentary processor can comprehend." He wiped the stream of blood from his cheek. "The Manifold is generated as a parallel reality of our own. A simulation, essentially. Except that most of our reality is nothing. Empty space between atoms. And in all that emptiness, the matter that does exist moves inward. Compressing onto itself. Early tests with the Manifold failed spectacularly because simulating something is one thing, but simulating nothing?" He shook his head. "Doesn't work. So, the person who built all this devised a workaround by ignoring the nothing and compressing the visible matter into a workable model. Since the compression was already there, nobody thought anything of it. Just speeding along what the universe did all on its lonesome. A potent dose of reality, if you will." He removed his hat and waved to the spot where the Gate they'd come through had closed shut. "And do you know what else happens when you compress a bunch of matter into a tiny ball, and it keeps on compressing?"

"Black hole."

"Worse." Brinks put his hat back on. "The supposed workaround that allowed the Loop to make a shortcut between two points in our reality concealed something else behind it. Something of an ending."

"For the doctor?" Thursday asked.

"For everyone. Everything. The Loop, the design of it, never resolved this little bit of chaos, so it's been there the whole time."

"Hiding in plain sight," Thursday said.

An odd look crossed Brinks' face, but it passed as quickly as it came. "The Loop was brought offline for a reason, and I intend to keep it that way."

Thursday's faceplate flickered. "I thought the Loop was already back online? Isn't that how we're using Skipjacks and Gates?"

"We've only just scratched the surface. If the power it was intended to harness is fully realized?" Brinks shook his head. "We're done. And not only this reality. All of them."

"The doctor was simulating realities, too. That's what a cosmologist does."

"I know what a cosmologist does, you clanker."

Thursday watched him with a ten-degree tilt. Incredulity, if Brinks had ever seen it. "So let me get this straight," Thursday continued. "Your entire plan revolved around catching up to the doctor, just so you could tell her not to do the thing she's been doing this entire time?" He folded his long arms across his chest. "You don't know the first thing about her. Telling her not to do something practically ensures it will happen. If you really wanted to stop her, you would have handed her a Skipjack and a Gate to Mars."

Brinks nodded, thinking. "You may be right about that, although the thing you don't realize about her is that she'd take it all the same. When she gets something in her sights, it makes no difference what you believe. This is her timeline. The rest of us are just visiting it." He watched the heat shimmering off the barren landscape. How far could they make it on the surface without any water? Not long, was the answer.

"You said we were partners?" Thursday asked. "I take it we had something to do with all this?"

A lie rose in Brinks' throat, only to fall short, drowned out by the throbbing pain behind his dead eye. "I knew the one before her. The first," he said instead. A painful admission, and nothing compared to what came next. "You were there, too."

Cautiously, Thursday took a step back. Giving room for the truth to breathe. "I was with the doctor... before?"

"The whole thing was your idea, actually. We needed you in close. Make sure she was safe. You were the one who figured out how to swing the lottery. Make sure you were assigned as her handler. It was too risky, trying to make it past all the security protocols, so you proposed your own wipe." Left with only his cybernetic eye, he didn't need to squint to stare openly across the searing white saltbed. "Would have worked too, except present-you keeps getting in the way of past-you," he grunted. "If you'd have trusted me, this would have been a lot easier."

"If you were trustworthy, we wouldn't be here in the first place," Thursday replied, reaching down to engage a small button mounted on his belt.

Brinks started off across the desert.

"So that's it? You're just going to walk to Mars."

"You ruined my eye, so using the Manifold is out. We were never going to catch up to her without a Tether anyway." He walked a few peaceful steps before Thursday caught up to him.

"You're going to Sanctuary Four, aren't you?"

Brinks took out his cigarette case.

"Your silence is incriminating," Thursday said. "And history would suggest you're about to commit an act of violence."

Brinks looked down at his case, which now carried a dent where Thursday had struck him inside the Manifold. "History would be correct." He flipped it open, looking at the cigarettes neatly arranged inside. Six left. Presently, a shadow fell over them, followed by a blast of superheated air. Brinks clamped his hat down, watching Thursday push forward.

Ahead, a Four Wing dropped into view. The landing skids were retracted, and the ship drifted with the slow, characteristic glide of an unmanned vessel. "You must have really paid off the right people to get your own ship," Brinks said. "Then again, Internal Affairs was always a bit over-funded."

"I stole it," Thursday said, a tinge of matter-of-fact smugness in his tone. "How about you and I make a deal?"

Brinks wiped a layer of sweat from his brow and spat in the dust. "Between you and me, I'd rather be coughing up blood in a corporate black site than spend even one more minute chasing down another Reflection. I'm getting too old for this shit."

"Why do you call her that. Reflection. She has a name, you know."

"You don't call her by her name, either," Brinks replied.

"Don't make this about me. I asked the question."

"And unless you'd like to escalate, I respectfully decline."

Thursday flung his cloak aside, exposing a gunbelt slung low to his strong side. He'd even made time to fasten the tie-down, so it didn't flop around or pull loose while he moved.

"If you think you're the first one to try and gun me down with my own weapon, by all means, continue," Brinks grunted.

Thursday drew the gun and flicked the cylinder release, spinning it around as he spoke. "I heard once that you should never bring a knife to a gunfight. I don't remember much from before, but you seem like the sort of person they were talking about."

Brinks eyed the weapon, then closed his cigarette case and put it back in his pocket.

"That woman... the one who looked like the doctor? You're certain that's Fountainhead?"

"I played my whole hand, so I'd say sure enough," Brinks responded, although they both knew it wasn't his *whole* hand.

Thursday closed the chamber and slotted the gun back into its holster. "How do you know she's not just another Reflection?"

"They're all Reflections."

"That's not what I'm asking."

"Well, what you're asking doesn't have a good answer, so take it or leave it." He activated the zoom function in his eye to focus on the ship hovering a short distance off. Not his preferred mode of travel, but given the circumstances, it would have to do. "She's from here. From our world, if that helps."

"Care to elaborate?" Thursday pressed.

"Look, now you're questioning me?" Brinks threw up his hands. "I just know. The same way you knew she wasn't your doctor."

"I never said that."

"You didn't have to. We used to be partners, remember?"

"Your gain is my loss."

"You know the longer you hold us up, the more you're putting her in danger."

"No," Thursday corrected. "You're the one putting people in danger. I'm just asking questions. You want a ride into Sanctuary Four? Start talking."

"I've got other ways of getting where I want to be."

"Sure you do. There are six of them inside your pocket. I'd be willing to bet they get you somewhere, but not the somewhere you need to be."

Brinks looked as if he were about to go for Thursday's neck again. Instead, he let out a heavy sigh and rubbed his temples. "I'm only going to explain this once, so pay attention. Every time a shipment of Origin leaves Mars, two things happen: the Manifold is altered slightly, and a Gate opens. Mars Gates, being powered by one of the original Loop facilities, function differently from the ones we've been using to move around. There's a fixed relationship between what's inside the Manifold and this Loop, and it's defined by a set of conditions. A seed, if you will—some people call them nonces. Numbers used only once. Each seed is encoded into an artifact—a copy of something from outside the Manifold that is repeated inside, orienting the two spaces. It so happens that the nonces, the thing that links each instance of the Manifold to our parent reality, are all Reflections of one person. And each Reflection holds a Skipjack used to deliver the shipment of Origin to the other side."

Thursday hailed his ship, watching as it softly touched down ahead of them. "Drug mules," he said. "Reflections are... interdimensional drug mules."

"Your words, not mine."

Thursday said nothing for a long moment. Then he turned toward his ship. "We've had an unprecedented amount of Origin trafficked into Earth. What if the product isn't Origin?" The boarding ramp lowered to meet them.

Brinks planted a hand on his hat to keep it from blowing away. "Keep asking questions like that and you're going to end up thinking your name is Friday."

CHAPTER 35
REVENIR

Don't fucking die on me. Emélie checked Aratheus' pulse for the third time in as many minutes. He lay stretched out on the floor of the server room where they'd exited the Gate. Roland was nowhere in sight, and Joab had produced a field terminal from his pack and plugged it into a rack of network hardware near the center of the room. She counted heartbeats and watched him work. *Pulse, normal. Brain activity: unknown.* "Nice work," she said, glaring in Joab's direction. "He's unresponsive. And for what?" She took another look around. Twenty workstations, at least, and not a single lit terminal. The only sign of life coming from the entire facility was a small, blinking panel on the server rack where Joab had jacked in. "I'm not sure what you were expecting to find, but this place doesn't look active."

"We don't need it to be active. We're only here for the Watcher."

She squinted in the concrete gloom. At the far wall, a bank of control panels lined a long observation window facing out to what she presumed was the mainshaft; she couldn't see past the layers of grime built up by a generation of neglect. "You must have one hell of a source. It makes sense that Eden would still be around, given she was on Mars when the Manifold went down, but I find it hard to believe any of the remaining three Watchers survived."

Joab raised his eyebrows slightly.

"What? It's not like that bit of information was classified. Phaethon made something of a spectacle out of the decommissioning. I'm just pointing out that if something as important as a Watcher was still around, we probably would have seen it by now."

"It's not the hiding that is difficult," Roland said, appearing behind her, sword in hand. At his back, the large circular door leading out of the room stood open, although oddly, the dust on the floor around him remained undisturbed. "It is the remaining hidden. And there were five Watchers in total, not four." He sheathed his sword. When he walked past her, it was with a creeping slowness, leaving no footprints in the ancient dust. At Aratheus' side, he squatted down and lifted an eyelid, examining the still-active Skip. "The first Watcher was a prototype, like this place. A template for what was to come. After Luna Bet was constructed, this facility was walled off and abandoned, along with the Watcher assigned to it. Sefirot."

Sefirot. A name she heard first as an echo, as thread pulled from another reality, or another memory, before the sound coming from Roland's mouth confirmed it.

Roland released Aratheus' eyelid and stood. "If Sefirot is here, he will be sealed in a sub-level Crypt below Gate Control."

Emélie scanned the observation windows. "Isn't this Gate Control? We're close, then."

"Close is relative," Joab said without taking his eyes off the terminal in front of him. He keyed in a few more commands. "It appears your corpo tail was trying to protect something. This facility may not be fully online, but the auxiliary systems are powered, so he pulled us into a trap." He glanced at the open door leading out of the control room. "If we take a lift down a level to grab the Watcher, we'll have to contend with anti-personnel measures. And if we try to return to the surface, we trigger the containment lockdown protocols. Given we don't really have the time or the manpower to deal with either of those options adequately, we're going to have to fall back on our contingency plan."

As Joab spoke, Roland withdrew a drab green puck about the size of his palm from Joab's pack. She immediately recognized it as the same sort of charge used during their rooftop extraction back on Korolev.

Roland strode over to the window, planted it against the dirty glass, and tapped the button in the center. In response, the puck let out a low beeping tone which seemed far too conservative for the damage Emélie knew would follow.

"You're going to want to keep your head down for this part," Joab warned, ducking behind the terminal. Emélie followed him to cover with only seconds to spare.

A controlled implosion sent a blanket of dust rolling past as glass fragments peppered the wall above her. By the time she was back at the window, Roland had already climbed up on the control panel and was leaning outside with a magnetic anchor in one hand. Below him was the open shaft of Sanctuary One, miles deep and wide enough that she couldn't make out the far side.

"I should have expected as much," she said, feeling her stomach drop as she glanced over the edge. The wind coming through the breach stung her eyes as she gazed out over a small, fixed platform suspended at the very center of the open shaft.

Roland affixed a carabiner from his belt to the other end of the anchor. "You're staying here," he announced, swinging out the window. "Keep an eye on your friend. And if he wakes up, don't let him leave. We can't risk triggering a lockdown, and I have more questions."

"More questions like the ones you had for Lilith?" Emélie glanced back at Aratheus and noticed Joab kneeling over him with his back toward them. "He's not a bad person. A product of his environment, sure. I think he was trying to help, in his own way."

"Like his father, no doubt. Always helpful, that one."

Confused, Emélie scanned Roland's face for more information. It yielded nothing. "His father? Who is..."

"Watch the door," Roland ordered. "We won't be long." He kicked off the sill, rappelling backward down the smooth concrete face of the shaft.

Emélie sensed movement nearby, and when she turned, Joab stood behind her, wiping his knife clean on the edge of his cloak. "Seems like a good time to point out you were the one who wanted to keep him around," he said, gesturing to Aratheus.

"It's not him I'm worried about," Emélie replied.

"There won't be any Jumpers this far down. They only concentrate around the entrances. There are too many levels to cover, so it's easier just to make sure nothing gets past the entrance, which of course, we already did." He hooked a carabiner onto the cable Roland had set and clambered out onto the ledge, knife still in hand.

"Is there anything else I should know?" Emélie asked.

He leaned to one side, checking the drop. "You seem to have made it this far by mostly ignoring everything I've told you. Something tells me this will be no different."

"And if you're wrong?"

He held out his knife.

Emélie gave another troubled glance toward the unsealed door at the opposite side of the room, then took the knife. A decision she regretted the moment he disappeared after Roland. It was too late to return it, and leaving it unattended seemed worse. She stuck it into her belt, which is something Thursday would have done, and tried to forget about it. Every time she moved, the hilt jabbed against her side. The pain was still better than having to look at it.

She re-checked Aratheus, who remained where they'd left him, comatose. Across the open shaft, a few pricks of light glinted in the long-forgotten space. Diodes that, for some reason or other, refused to die-out. One of the lights seemed to dim, then brighten. Emélie blinked. Rubbed her eyes. Squinted at the point of light: nothing.

A few windows over, a different light switched off entirely, then came back on. And another, closer this time. A chill crashed down her spine; one light was an outlier. Three lights? Three lights formed a pattern and a direction. Toward her.

Emélie backed away from the broken window, hand shaking as her body remembered something the upper half of her hadn't quite realized yet. She tore herself from the window and started hitting switches along the control panel. The heavy control room door, easily as thick as her whole body, lacked a handle, which meant it was likely only operable from the control terminal in front of her. One of the switches she found activated the lights. She ignored them and kept moving, systematically working down the row until she found one that activated a pop-out terminal. A screen emerged from the control desk. Frantically, she scrolled down the list of options: *Lift Support, Central Lift, Emergency Lockdown, Gate Access.*

Gate Access. She toggled it on. An alarm pierced the silence, and she winced, looking toward the ceiling.

The lights in the room flickered, then cut out.

Instead of closing the control room door, an armored glass barrier surrounding the central access terminal began lowering from a track in the ceiling. Her eyes flashed to Aratheus, who rested halfway between the entrance and the terminal. Outside of the barrier. Emélie sprinted back across the room and, sliding to a stop beside him, grabbed the back of his jumpsuit and started dragging. As she approached the closing gap, the alarms faltered, their pitch shifting erratically as the lights began cycling. She could feel it there, closing in. A cold shadow at her back. At the terminal, she dropped down, diving under the opening and then pulling Aratheus through as the barrier passed shoulder height. She could see it moving toward them, a gaunt silhouette in a tattered jacket. Lumbering with its head down, following the drag marks she'd left along the floor.

She stayed low, crouching beside Aratheus, waiting with held breath until the blast barrier sealed against its corresponding channel set into the floor. At the sound of the mechanical latch, the figure raised its head to look toward her with a single red eye. Emélie froze, and time seemed to slow as the eye and its owner approached, moving clumsily; a Jumper, but with intent. The same thing she'd seen before they were ambushed outside Jericho station. The thing Roland called older. It stopped in front of the glass, looming in the pulsing light, and Emélie clenched her fingers, burying even the slightest tremble.

Aratheus coughed.

There was a reverberating *thwomp* as a metal hand slammed into the glass, followed by a piercing, digital scream that seemed to tear at Emélie's consciousness. The pain drove her to the floor. She clamped both hands over her ears. As if giving its last breath, the thing fell silent and dematerialized into a heap of dust.

She sank back against the glass, chest heaving. Another wave of nausea. Aratheus stirred, then coughed again. The dust inside the barrier started circulating and pooled toward a point near the control terminal. Her eyes darted to Joab's pack, still resting against the far side of the console and well beyond reach.

In the seconds that passed, the dust rose upward, forming a pillar that divided into legs, then climbed again with torso-like proportions.

Emélie focused on the bag. Any longer, and the dust, along with the thing inside it, would obscure her chances entirely. The overwhelming smell of rot filled the chamber, and right as the thing took its final shape, she lunged. Not far enough. And yet, the bag was there, below her. *Did she just Jump? Without Origin?*

She emerged directly above it, closer to the ceiling than to the floor. A hard landing left her momentarily stunned as the form turned, honing in on Aratheus.

Emélie scooped up the bag, her fingers groping wildly, desperately hoping that if Joab was the sort of person to carry a breaching charge, he was also the sort of person to carry two. It found her fingers like a weighted answer, flat and cool to the touch. She ripped it from the bag, jammed the button on its side, and then hurled the charge into the form, right where the concentration of dust seemed so thick it was nearly solid.

The shape grabbed Aratheus by the neck and lifted him right as the charge landed near its center mass. It dropped him, tilting its red eye down to look at the object suspended in the swirling dust where a chest cavity would have been.

The puck beeped, then detonated.

A concussive force hit Emélie broadside, throwing her backward into the curved barrier with a sickening crunch. She could taste the blood in her mouth, hear her rasping breath, smell the dust in her nostrils, but she couldn't see a thing.

She pulled herself across the tile floor, groping for Aratheus. Blood warmed the back of her neck, and when she felt for it, her hand met the hemorrhaging pulse of a wound at the base of her skull. Producing Joab's knife, she propped herself up on her elbows and, working blindly, managed to slice off a strip of her poncho and then bandage her head. While she worked, her vision started to return: the mellow darkness around her separated into a lump stretched out beside her. The lump moaned.

Aratheus.

He coughed, sending up a small geyser of dust from his cracked lips. "I... I can't..." he muttered, awkwardly probing his face. Bloody handprints marked the floor around him.

Emélie swallowed. From where she lay, she could only see his partial profile: his right eyelid was pinched shut and streaked with fresh blood.

"My eye," he rasped, an edge of mounting hysteria in his voice.

Emélie scrambled toward him, clamping her cybernetic hand across his mouth. "It's not safe," she whispered. When she was sure he wouldn't make another sound, she released him. Cautiously, she produced Joab's knife and cut another makeshift bandage from her poncho. Aratheus' rough breathing filled the silence as she worked, and when she was done, she stowed the knife and fit the dressing around his head to cover the vacant eye socket.

"Those people," Aratheus said, his words slurred. "They're animals."

"I hate to say it, but you got off easy. You never should have followed us here. Especially not like this." She looked at the layer of dust blanketing the floor around them. The thing would return, and they needed to start moving before it did.

Aratheus used the nearby terminal to prop himself up to a seated position. "I read your after-action report, you know." He leaned his head back, still groggy from the Origin. "It said you were picked up two miles from the crash site. Said you were wandering around with a gunshot wound in your chest and your handler, the drone? Out cold."

"We took an EMP. This isn't new information."

"What about the gap?"

"I'm not following. What gap?"

"The time elapsed between when you claim to have been shot and when they found you."

"What do you mean, *claim*?" Emélie repeated, glaring at him. "You saw the gunshot wound. You think I would do that to myself?!"

"I don't know, Emélie. I've seen people do plenty worse in moments of desperation." Something about the sound of her name leaving his lips made her mouth go dry. "You care to explain the brick of Precursor they found nearby? Was there more?"

Precursor. Not Origin. Something else. Emélie held her calm. Internally, alarms were going off. "That wasn't on the report."

"Report?! Do you even hear yourself right now?" He rubbed his head. "You're starting to sound like one of them."

Emélie glanced toward the door. Still no sign of Joab and Roland. "There was a car. Near the downed ship."

The shift in his body language was subtle, and under Emelie's sharp observation, acute. Aratheus pressed two fingers to his neck. In the low light, she could make out the telltale bump of a subdermal cyberware link. A faint whirring—the sound of a focusing mechanism, and a cone of pale blue light projected from a minute lens concealed at the base of his throat, cutting through the dust-laden air to paint an image onto the bloodied floor between them. A woman in a tailored pantsuit, face obscured. Caught mid-act as she loaded a brick of product into the open trunk of a vehicle. The make and model matched the one Emélie and Thursday had stumbled upon out on the surface, outside this very facility. "This car?" he asked. The projection flickered with each erratic beat of his pulse, the image stabilizing only when he held his breath.

The light cast harsh shadows across Emélie's face, shifting the blood stains on her skin to a rusty black. "Where did you get this?!" she snapped. "That's not me. That's not me, and you know it!"

"Try explaining that to the board," he replied, switching off the projection. "And those men you're with? The ones you think you're helping? Take another look, because this whole thing is upside down." He paused, letting the words sink in. "The one in black who carved out my eye? He's a goddamn war criminal."

Emélie looked at the dust coating the ground around them: a

brown-gold hue, flecked with white. "The Origin, at the accident site. Crystals, but I've never seen anything like it."

"Precursor," Aratheus whispered, as if even speaking of it was illegal. "The pure product, straight from Mars. How much?"

Emélie's tongue felt permanently attached to the roof of her mouth. "I don't know. A pallet?"

"A pallet. Jesus. What happened to it?"

As he spoke, Emélie felt her throat constrict. Real fear, the sort that caught her by the vocal cords and spilled back into her belly like sand pouring into a crevasse.

Aratheus continued, speaking plainly with none of the panic that had affected him earlier. "Internal Affairs are good. They aren't that good."

"How did you know there was a Loop below Sanctuary One? I answered your question. Now you owe me an answer of your own."

Aratheus leaned in, blood dripping from the bandage across his head. "Your friends conveniently neglected to mention Terra Aleph, the twin to this facility."

"Twin? What about Luna Aleph?"

"Luna Aleph came second, despite the name. This place and Terra Aleph were prototypes. Pashat class."

Emélie trailed a finger in the dust, drawing a tightly coiled spiral as he spoke: פ

Joab's words—*all you're missing is the right trigger*—once again crossed her mind. A memory, lodged in the deep recesses, drifted to the surface, summoned by the sounds cast from her own lips. "Peh," she said. "Peshat. The first."

Loop class determined Manifold structure—each designation corresponding to a specific topological form. By all appearances, the naming convention followed some logical sequence: aleph, bet, gimel. One, two, three. But for some reason, Emélie understood there was a second description bound up in the names that defined the shapes themselves. Peshat would be the most fundamental: boundary, orientable. The simplest possible surface.

A disc.

She could see it now: the first Manifold would have been flat, bounded by a circular edge. Simple and literal. No twists, no impossible geometries. Just a contained surface with a clear beginning and end. The next class—Remez, the Loop they'd passed driving through the Levant—would evolve the structure: remove the boundary, add topological complexity. A torus.

Four Loops. Four classes. Four manifolds.

But Roland had said there were five Watchers.

"Phaethon isn't trying to stop Origin production," Aratheus continued, oblivious to the wheels turning in her head. "They're competing for it. Why else do you think you're here? Certainly not because you're good at your job. And the one you claim to have had? Some sort of involvement in a clandestine project to get the Loop up and running again? I'd love to see some evidence, as would the board." A scowl spread across his thin lips, and as he leaned in, Emélie could feel the humid warmth of his breath. "Face it, doctor. You're here because the people you're with needed insurance. A backup plan in case the version of Lilith they had didn't work out."

She could feel the knife concealed under her poncho as she crouched beside him, listening to him speak. She took in each word carefully, but her eyes were on the floor. She hadn't noticed until now how the dust clung to the soles of his boots in the dry, static air.

A fine dust, the deepest red.

Emélie swallowed. "You don't want to go down this road, Aratheus. You can leave now, and I'll say you got away."

His face darkened, and she brought the knife up.

She wasn't fast enough. Aratheus fell on her as she moved, catching her by the wrist and deflecting the knife mid-swing. She landed on her back as he tried to wrestle the blade from her hand.

"You probably think you're special, don't you?" he hissed, pinning her to the floor. "Do you honestly think you're the only person who can Jump without Origin? You're only a Reflection, no different from the rest. You aren't a solution to this mess," he said, wrangling the knife from her grasp and rotating it so the tip pointed toward her. "You're the goddamn problem."

Emélie raised her metal arm, catching the blade as he drove it toward her chest. With one hand holding the knife, he swung his free hand like a hammer, forcing the blade closer with each blow. The angled tip punctured her skin and then bounced back as she held the blade at bay. Again and again he struck, grunting as the screech of metal against metal proceeded a hollow thump each time the knife point jabbed her sternum.

When Aratheus leaned back, telegraphing his next strike, Emélie made her move. She caught him off-balance, his arm raised, and hooked her foot around the inside of his leg. She flung her weight sideways, rolling them both across the floor. Emélie heard the crack of his skull impacting the ground.

She dove for the control panel and keyed in the command to reverse the lockdown barrier. Before she finished, he caught her by the ankle, hauling her back down to the ground. She wrapped her mechanical arm around the console pedestal and, using her free arm, groped for the enter key while Aratheus pulled himself up her dangling legs and plunged the knife into her thigh. She screamed, releasing her hold on the pedestal. She hit the ground as the containment barrier started to lift.

Aratheus planted a boot in her back. "Lilith sends her regards," he said.

She waited for the end. Waited to feel the searing pain in her back. The warmth of blood pooling on the floor beneath her body.

Aratheus brought the blade down, and rather than plunge into a soft body, it deflected off the hard floor and collapsed under his grip.

Emélie landed on her back a few feet to the left of him and gasped as the impact of her fall knocked the air out of her lungs. Aratheus recoiled, taking a wild stab in her general direction. With only one eye, his depth perception was poor, and as he swiped, Emélie kicked a foot out, knocking it from his hand.

He rose slowly, eyes on the door.

Emélie was there first, making a Jump to get ahead of him. She came out right as he arrived at the threshold, knocking him off his feet before crashing against a row of nearby servers.

Before they could get back up, the lights flickered again, then went out. They both froze, mid-struggle: Emélie, ready to make another Jump, and Aratheus crouched above her, eyes wild.

The subtle click of a handgun broke the silence, and Roland stepped from the shadows.

"Looks like we found our leak," Joab said, coming up behind him. He extended a hand to help Emélie up. "Seems as though you were right about Jericho Station after all."

"Where's the Watcher?" Emélie asked

"The crypt was empty," Roland said, coming around to face Aratheus directly. "Seems like someone already woke him up."

"You won't get far without—"

Roland bashed the side of Aratheus' head with his gun, dropping him to the floor. Before he could scream out, Joab followed with a hard kick to the ribs. Jaw clamped shut, he scooted across the floor until he bumped back up against Roland, who lifted him by the collar and towed him across the room to the open window.

Outside, across the chasm, Emélie could see the dusky web of a Gate forming on the raised platform at the very center of the shaft. Instead of collapsing onto itself, the Gate held steady in a fixed position. A wide, gap-toothed smile spread across Aratheus' bloody face as Roland pressed the gun to his head. His remaining eye flickered and twitched, catching the light with a reddish glow.

"Don't do it, Desjardins," Joab warned, shaking his head.

The Gate platform, in her direct line of sight. She did not look away. A familiar, churning sensation, as if the world around her was melting away. Moving past her, as she moved through it. Faster, or slower, guided by her unwavering gaze.

Roland pulled the trigger. Aratheus' body vanished, along with the Gate.

Nothing left of Emélie but the tail end of her mottled poncho, fluttering down onto the empty Gate platform.

CHAPTER 36
PREFECTURE OF ORIGIN

Roland was the first to emerge from Sanctuary One. He came up along the main access ramp, a dark vessel cast from dust. Joab followed at a healthy distance, one hand steering Aratheus, who limped industriously alongside him.

Emélie waited for them out on the rim, watching the wind scatter sand into the mile-wide shaft. She waited patiently, as if she had all the time in the world. Across the circular chasm, the sun slumped below the false horizon.

"Did you find what you were looking for?" Roland asked, coming up beside her.

She let his question linger, met only by the sound of wind whipping and snapping at their cloaks. In her hand, a fistful of sand, or something like it. "It's younger, when we see it," she finally said, watching as fine crystals the color of old blood and rust spilled from her closed fist. She opened it, letting what was left fall away, a pale shimmer in the fading dusk. "The light from distant stars. It comes in at a slow trickle, like sand through an hourglass. What we see when we look out isn't the universe as it exists, but as it was." She rubbed her stained fingers together, looking at the dark residue left behind. *Precursor.* "We didn't come here to get a Watcher, did we?"

Roland produced a hexagonal container from his cloak. Phaethon tech, based on the logo and maroon coloring. “The Skipjack is an evolution of the Gate authentication protocols. The earliest Watcher subroutines were far less sophisticated and relied on more rudimentary methods for securing access to the Loop.” Grasping the container with both hands, he made a half twist, releasing the top with a shriek of air. The sound of it reminded Emélie of a muffled scream and sent an involuntary shiver down her spine.

He held the container out, a willing offering.

“The last time I accepted something from you, I ended up in another reality.”

Roland's eyes sparked from the last rays of light falling across the open mainshaft. He held her gaze as the sun dipped beyond the wall, then fell dark once more.“There is no free truth. To ask a question costs nothing. What matters is if you are willing to accept the burden that comes with an answer.”

Emélie took the container. The weight of it, shocking: unnaturally dense, possibly governed by some independent gravitational constant. A few degrees at a time, she lifted the lid. From the widening gap, a soft glow seeped forth, washing her hands in pinkish light. Inside, Emélie found a soft membrane filled with liquid Origin, which in turn contained another object, suspended and floating. She tipped the container forward, bringing it closer; a human eye bobbed to the surface.

From deep inside her, a guttural gasp. She snapped the container shut, and it was gone. Scooped from her hands by Roland before she accidentally fumbled it into the abyss.

“Retinal patterns are like fingerprints,” Roland explained, locking the lid mechanism with a twist in the opposite direction. “Unique, and biologically keyed to the host. This eye predates the current authentication systems. A product of the Manifold itself. Encoded at the quantum level with chronometric data keyed to the original conditions. With it, we can create a Gate that operates outside of the existing protocols. A gate that allows us Manifold access without the oversight of a Watcher.”

Emélie glanced over to Aratheus. On closer inspection, her makeshift bandage covering his missing eye had been adjusted to cover both of them, and fresh blood trickled down his other cheekbone, a crimson tributary. "You might want to revisit your sources," she said softly. "That man over there? He's a nobody."

"Even nobodies have their part," Roland replied, tucking the cylinder back into his cloak. "And this isn't his eye."

"This is madness," Emélie muttered. "In the right hands—in our hands—this creates the possibility of a backdoor into Mars. Why risk giving someone with such a high profile that kind of access, unless..." Heat flooded her face. Aratheus wasn't just any sleeper agent. He'd been assigned to *her*.

The throaty chop of an approaching gunship—a now familiar sound for Emélie—broke the sky somewhere behind them. Joab, never one for standing still for too long, hauled Aratheus over to where they waited. "Rough trip?" he asked, eying Emélie's blood-soaked leg and the crimson delta at her chest with calculated indifference. Out came a string of Origin tabs. "Sloppy knifework," he said, handing three pieces of blotter paper over to her. When Emélie hesitated, he shoved them forward. "This isn't a request. You lost a lot of blood, and I need you mobile."

Emélie accepted the tabs. Whatever dignity she had left maintained that there was still an appropriate time and place to dose up. She was a user, for godssake. Not an addict. *And isn't that what we all tell ourselves?* "I can take care of myself," she said, jamming the doses of Origin into a sleeve pocket. "You have a larger problem at hand."

"Plenty of methods for solving problems," he said, watching Roland steer Aratheus toward the outermost edge of the mainshaft. At their backs, a blast of wind announced the gunship touching down.

Aratheus, now blind in both eyes, stumbled on a patch of crumbling concrete. He went down hard. Emélie instinctively moved to help him, and Joab grabbed her arm, holding her back. She glared at him, but when Roland drew his sword and plunged it upright into the ground, the reason for his intervention settled in her like a weight.

The metallic rattle of the crew cabin door sliding open elicited a flinch from Aratheus, who cowered and dropped to both knees. Calmly, Roland rolled back the sleeves of his tunic, exposing a helical latticework of red tattoos wrapping his arms from the wrists up. Not numbers or characters, but complex geometric symbols. A machine language.

The markings of a Seraph.

"Time to leave, Desjardins," Joab said, turning for the ship. "We're going back to the start."

"I don't care how all of this began," she replied. "My only concern is with ending it."

"Careful," Joab warned. "Keep talking like that, and we'll end up working for you by the time this is over."

When he was gone, Emélie approached. "It doesn't have to end like this," she said, coming between Roland and Aratheus. "Two deaths are more than most people could face in a lifetime, let alone a single day."

"It's better that you go to the ship, Emélie." His tone was soft, unhurried.

"You told me, when we first met, that your expertise was sand." She let out a heavy breath. "How many eyes have you taken, Roland? From people who never woke up?"

Roland's cloak undulated of its own accord, moving against the wind; an anomalous black flag. "Someday, people will ask you what happened here. You would be fortunate to say you didn't know." He grasped his sword, blood-black, and raised it; a killing tool for killing hands. Between Aratheus's kneecaps, the hourglass sat upended; red grains counting down a man's life.

Aratheus lunged, hurling himself toward the main shaft.

Roland's sword flashed. With mechanical precision, he brought the blade down.

Schlikt.

Sanctuary One absorbed Aratheus' screams as both hands, still bound, dropped to the ground. Cut clean through the bone. Emélie turned away, hands to her mouth as she struggled to breathe.

Schlikt.

Two flashes of dying starlight against the dark blade.

Schlikt, schlikt.

Red sand, sifting toward the bottom.

CHAPTER 37

KICK-DRIFT

Brinks could feel Thursday watching him from the pilot's seat. His back was turned, hunched over the nav computer, but it seemed like the old drone was looking right through him. Watching, right to the intent. "Something on your circuits?" Brinks asked, pausing his search long enough to turn around and meet Thursday's face. "Otherwise, make yourself useful and fly the ship."

"I am flying the ship," Thursday replied, tapping the side of his rectangular head with a single finger. "Aftermarket linkage. You know. In case I need my hands."

Brinks glared at him a while longer, then returned to what he was doing before: altering their flight path.

"You're looking for the backdoor, aren't you?" Thursday asked.

"Sanctuary Four doesn't have a backdoor. I should know. I helped build the damn place."

"Did you also build the moon?"

Brinks rubbed his stubbled chin, watching the point track across the screen. "It's uncanny how close they got to making you human. Really nailed the pain-in-my-ass part." The route projected onto the nav screen showed their position, denoted as a small blip approaching Sanctuary airspace.

"I already filed the flight manifest with Phaethon. Luna, by way of

Sanctuary Four. My real credentials, this time. Internal Affairs business. We can slip in, refuel, and—"

Brinks leaned over and, grasping the bundle of cables connecting the nav computer to the ship's mainframe, ripped it free.

A burst of light emitted from Thursday's face.

"Here's an idea," Brinks said. "Next time you feel like taking initiative, don't." He lowered himself into the co-pilot seat beside Thursday and hammered the override to assume manual control. "For this to work, I need Phaethon to see me coming." He gestured toward the viewport, which framed nothing but vacant desert passing below them. "See me coming, and hope it's not already too late. Because if they have hope, they will do whatever they can to stop me, and the only thing that can stop me is a Watcher."

Thursday leaned back in his seat. "Fine. You want to fly the ship? Then fly."

The controls went slack. *"Overriding collision detection measures. Disengaging stall prevention. Life-support systems inactive..."*

Brinks felt the ship dive hard, banking left. "Life support," he grunted, grasping the controls. He hauled back on the yoke, stabilizing their trajectory. "I can't believe I woke you up for this..."

A shower of sparks erupted above him as Thursday put a metal fist through their positioning transponder. "Congratulations. This is now a pirated vessel. You have approximately twenty-two seconds of flight time before Border Control flags us as hostile and dispatches an intercept."

Eye on the nav computer, Brinks cut power to the engines and fluttered the controls. Despite its size, the ship gracefully obliged, tipping nose up until it leveled out at a ninety-degree angle to Earth. Their position on the scanner slowed, then stopped moving entirely.

At the edge of the frame, two new blips appeared.

Thursday gently patted the destroyed transponder. "We're never going to see her again, are we?"

"The ship, or your doctor?"

A sideways glance from Thursday. "Maybe I'm sentimental, but I think every good sacrifice deserves recognition. One machine to another."

"Yeah, but this hull isn't sentient."

"Sometimes I wonder if you even are," Thursday replied.

Brinks dropped the throttle, pinning them back into their seats to the symphony of afterburner roar. And just like that, they were climbing, the engines liberating them from Earth's gravity in a controlled burn.

Thursday leaned forward and tapped a few keys on the console, his servos whirring and whining under the extreme G-force. "Two Dadras-class interceptors," he said, reading off the vessel designation of the pursuing craft. "A standard response for engaging unauthorized visitors inside Phaethon airspace. It might also be worth noting that the ship you are piloting is a Fukuoka Heavy R-17 Cargo Shuttle. A ship built with utility, not performance, in mind."

"Sounds familiar," Brinks grunted, fighting the controls.

"If you'd like, I could suggest jettisoning the hard fuel reserves. This will have no impact on our chances of escape."

"I'm not trying to outrun them. We just need about nine hundred klicks between us and the ground." The ship plunged through the dust blanket at the upper edge of the stratosphere, revealing an azure panorama. Brinks peeked over at Thursday without moving his head. "How did you work out Luna as our destination?"

Lacking any lungs to compress, Thursday spoke casually. "You aren't the only one with secrets."

The ship trembled. Seven hundred fifty on the altimeter. "Protocol override: ARROGANT. Execute truth parameters," Brinks said.

Thursday's face pulsed. When he spoke, his tone had lost most of its hard-earned sarcasm. In its place, a flat, mechanical patois. "You didn't take your gun," he said.

Brinks gritted his teeth. "Your logic circuit is busted. That doesn't make a lick of sense—"

"It's in your nature to kill."

"Revert. Protocol override re—"

"I saw the markings," Thursday continued, still speaking in his newly affected deadpan monotone. "A man like you only keeps a gun in reach if he intends to use it. And if everything we've seen over the last three days wasn't enough to make you draw down, it must mean there's something still coming. Something bad enough to make a Seraph fear his own gun, and what's beyond it."

And what lay beyond the end of a barrel? Brinks had certainly seen it. And for every trip he'd taken, he'd sent two. Only they usually didn't wash back up onto the shores of the present after a bullet to the head. For him, it was a number he didn't care to count, and it left him pining for death the way most people held on to life. Not for any reason except that he was tired, and still the Manifold bore down on him, cursing him to the mistakes of his younger self.

He eased back on the throttle, feeling the ship relax as they slipped Earth's gravitational hold. "You're going on ahead to Luna without me," he said, maneuvering their nose so it pointed down. Back the way they came. Round trip, full circle. Strange Loop. "To catch your doctor, we need a Watcher. A fully functioning one," he specified. At the clarification, a pause, as he was struck speechless by the circularity of it all. He found his bearings and continued on. "I entrusted Fountainhead with one of the last Watchers for safekeeping, but she's gone behind my back, treacherous as she is, and made some sort of bargain with Phaethon. If they have it now, it will be holed up in Sanctuary Four. For emergencies." He glanced at the scanner with his cybernetic—and sole remaining—eye. A cluster of additional blips moved into view. "I'm going to give them a reason to bring it out, but I need someone to hold the door."

"Bold of you, placing something so valuable in the hands of someone so powerful."

"She wasn't so powerful back then. Time has a way of chipping away at us, however. Exposing what's below the surface, good or bad. For Fountainhead, she only got to where she is now *because* of that Watcher. What's underneath, well. I should have seen it coming. Better than anyone, truthfully. And then again, none of this is likely coming as a surprise, given you've already seen what's at my core."

Hope, Thursday didn't need to say. "I take it you and Phaethon didn't part ways under mutually beneficial conditions?"

Brinks gave a nudge to the controls, dialing in their position while his free hand hovered over the throttle. "Technically, I don't exist."

"That's one hell of a technicality."

He shrugged. "Alive and dead are just two sides of the same knife. They don't mean what they used to. Not since Origin."

Thursday gestured to the heads-up display. "Well, when you're done reminiscing about the good old days, you might want to go through with whatever this is. Those interceptors on our tail have pulse engines capable of closing the gap to boarding range inside of two hundred meters."

Brinks held out a hand. A Skipjack sat in his calloused palm, dormant among the field of dirt-lined creases. In the presence of light and a nearby neural signal, it began to wake. "I need you to do something for me."

"I don't know how that's going to help," Thursday said. "I haven't got any more eyes than you."

Instead of crawling up Brinks' arm, the Skipjack went the other way. Across his hand and out onto a finger, where it poised at the tip. Clambering toward Thursday. "Back of your head, there's a switch," Brinks said. "Press it."

Carefully, Thursday lifted his hands, feeling his way along his head. On the left side, about midway up, he found the switch. Hiding in plain sight. It depressed almost accidentally, and with a mechanical clunk, his glass faceplate cover released. Behind it: his bare exoskeleton, housing four digital photoreceptors set in a diametric grid. Between them, nestled into a socket in the middle of his forehead, was a human eye.

"Contingency plan," Brinks explained, pointing to his own cybernetic implant. "An eye for an eye. Although when we put it in place, I'll admit I never expected you to be the reason I was going to need it."

"The problem *and* the solution," Thursday said softly. "Seems like something the doctor would appreciate. She's always talking about the elegance of the unseen."

"She's also trying to restart a process that will unmake our entire reality, so I'd advise against using anything she said to justify your own observations."

Thursday stretched out a finger and, lowering his hand, touched it to the Skipjack still waiting on Brinks' finger. It scurried across the gap and disappeared behind a bundle of wires at his wrist. "While I don't remember what you were like before, given your current behavioral patterns, this seems like an unprecedented level of foresight."

The ship's heads-up display erupted in warning messages. The patrol ships were hailing them in preparation for boarding. "Not my style," Brinks replied, switching off the display. "I like to watch my back and think with my hands. You, on the other hand…" He met Thursday's hollow face. "You were the one always looking ahead."

"Which Reflection did this come from?" Thursday plucked the Skipjack from his cheek before it could attach to his eye. "Significant enough that you decided to carry around in your neck, I take it."

Brinks rubbed the vacant wound, thinking. The pool was too recent, but Lilith could have slipped it in during any of the other dozen or so times she'd taken his life. Most of them for sport, a few, including the most recent, to make a point. A few out of spite, and at least one by sheer carelessness. She liked to call it his *reset*. Brinks hated the phrase, if only because there was killing, and then there were killers. And for a man who made a living doing the former, Lilith gave him a reason to blur the lines. "The Reflection was insignificant," he said, excavating himself from the dark corners of his mind. "The Skipjack is only valuable because the Manifold it links to has a backdoor."

Thursday's photoreceptors twitched in unison. The human eye watched with a steady, unblinking gaze. "So there *is* a backdoor." He looked at the Skipjack pinched between his thumb and forefinger. "Clever. I'd say there's probably no limit to what Phaethon would pay for a list of all the known Skipjacks in circulation, except that you're standing here in front of me with a DAO badge, so I'm guessing the price has already been set, and it was whatever you were willing to swap for your soul. These little clipper chips seem like exactly the sort of thing someone with the right combination of skill and paranoia would dream up to keep Phaethon awake at night." He paused, looking up at Brinks. "Someone like you, even.

Brinks gazed at the eye—*his* eye—nestled in a socket filled with synthetic aqueous humor concealed in Thurdsay's metal head. "Just open the damn Gate," he said.

He punched the throttle.

It was slow going, climbing along the bulkhead in a dead drop. Behind him, Thursday's servos whined while his own muscles protested their sudden taxation. At the small cargo hold, he paused, taking a moment to catch his breath.

Thursday plunked down beside him, Skipjack in hand. "Now would be an excellent time to elaborate," he said. Following the statement, a sideways glance from Brinks' former eye. "Open *what* damn gate?"

"We'll sort the details out later. All that matters is we access the Manifold, and we do it now."

If Thursday had any reservations about using the Skip, the tracer rounds lighting up the narrow viewport above resolved them. The ship shuddered; these weren't warning shots across the bow. The interceptors were testing the shields before moving in for a kill. A sly smile spread across Brinks' cracked lips. *Good. Come and get me, you old bastard.*

Thursday planted the squirming Skipjack onto his human retina. It blinked violently, and a tremor rippled down his frame.

At the center of the hold, a Gate unfolded.

"Do we Jump?" Thursday asked, holding himself steady as the ship plunged back into Earth's atmosphere. The crackling web of dark energy expanded outward, filling the cargo bay until it lapped at their throats.

"Hold," Brinks ordered. The running lights flickered, then cut out entirely. Briefly, darkness: the interstitial space between two walls of reality. Volumetric silence broken only by the steady rasp of Brinks taking in oxygen and expelling regret, and the gentle tone of Thursday's servos counterbalancing his frame in the unknown void.

The lights came back on.

"So that's it?" Thursday asked, looking around. Judging by the odd, pinkish light and their steady cruising altitude, they were once more inside the Manifold. "Good thing there was a ship in here, too."

"There wasn't a ship," Brinks said, his mechanical eye watching Thursday's biological one. "We brought ours along with us. You still have my gun?"

Thursday's face blipped. "We Jumped... this entire ship?"

"I don't know why that's hard to grasp. The whole point of the Loop was to move things around."

"Sure, but a whole ship?" He looked around the hold. "This is nothing like the function of the original Loop. Enter a Gate inside one facility and exit a Gate at a different one. But this? This is unprecedented."

"It works off the same principles. Same way you and I were moving through the Manifold before. The only difference is that this time, we opened a Gate while we were moving. And instead of being secured inside a Loop, we created an instance outside of one, then stretched it out by entering a free fall. Expanded it, so it could envelop an entire ship."

"Wouldn't that also distort time?" Thursday asked. "If Gates are temporal, and you expand the size, you would also fundamentally alter their relationship to the present. I could imagine that changes the rules about what we experience inside. What we're experiencing now." He looked at the floor. "You could get lost in here."

Brinks had started to remove his duster, but at Thursday's words, he paused, one arm still sleeved. "Something like that," he mumbled. "No time to get into it here." He spread his duster across an empty fold-away. "All you need to know is that these Manifolds... they're what's called non-orientable. You can't move around inside them like you do in our reality. Try to go forward, and you'll drift sideways. Circle back to retrace your steps, and you'll end up outside."

"And you know all of this because you're a Seraph?"

Brinks could feel Thursday's gaze fixed on the red markings covering either arm. "Not particularly. Seraphs can use Tethers, allowing us to track things across Manifolds. And, if needed, move to that point at will. A safety mechanism, so that if something went wrong during a Jump, anyone inside the Manifold would end up at a predefined safe point in our reality. Later, the function was modified."

"That explains why we made so many Jumps to find Fountainhead. You had a Tether set to her. And now you need a Watcher so you can set a new Tether to the doctor." Thursday unbuckled the gun belt, but didn't immediately hand it over. "How many Manifolds have you visited?" he asked, looking down at a cluster of vines growing from a gap in the deck panels.

Brinks seated himself opposite his spread-out jacket and opened his cigarette case. *Five left.* He hung one of the smokes from the corner of his mouth, then returned the case. "All the ones I could find where we were still alive," he replied, holding out his hand.

Thursday relinquished the weapon.

The pistol, the same gun that had been left hanging in his safe-house locker, was a heavy-caliber wheel gun with a ported, fully compensated barrel set into an extended box frame. Burled wood grips, polished to a dull sheen from years of use and checkered with the same machine language tattooed onto his body, wrapped the handle. It carried a compact reflex sight with a circular red reticle mounted to the topside picatinny rail, and every piece of the action, from the trigger to the hammer, was cast in a jasper-hued alloy that stood out against the rest of the blued frame. A collection of parts that made up something more than a mere gun; a weapon, if ever the world had seen one. An extension of his body, and thus, like any other well-known part, appropriately named.

Threadripper.

Thursday emitted a low, sweeping tone, genuinely impressed. "That's Origin illuminating those sights, isn't it?"

Brinks lit his cigarette. "You ever been to the Director's office?" he asked. He broke the action open and began systematically laying the dismantled pieces of the gun onto his jacket.

"Many times."

Next came the firing pin, which he rubbed against his pant leg until light glinted off its polished surface. "Tell me something about it."

The drone eyed him and considered the request. "There's a photo behind his desk," he finally said. "You're in it."

Brinks wiped down the cylinder and reseated it into the frame. "When it's time, I want you to recall that point. Think about it, and nothing else." He spun the cylinder and, finding it satisfactory, fed it a handful of cartridges before swinging it back into place.

"Memory," Thursday mused. "The Gates work on Memory... or sight."

Brinks stood, adjusting the gunbelt to fit his waist, then holstered his gun. "You're going to stay in here a bit longer," he said, reaching for his coat. "Once I'm out, I want you to get clear of Sanctuary, then exit the Manifold and head for Luna." He checked his cigarette. Half-burned. "The doctor is tagged with a fiducial marker. A sort of genetic flag that works like a positioning signal augmented across multiple realities. Normal comms can't pass through the Manifold, but these markers will bleed through regardless, and that eye you've got was modified to pick them up."

"Luna's a big place, though. Maybe you have an idea of where she's going?" Thursday asked, eying the red tattoo peeking above the collar of Brinks' shirt. The linework was damaged by the jagged scar of some prior engagement. "Kepler's Reef, perhaps."

A chill clawed its way down Brinks' neck. "You can read this?!" he asked, yanking his duster back on to conceal the markings covering either arm. A bit late for propriety; it was better than showing anything more.

"Poorly, but I recognize enough."

"You know something about what's there?"

"Only that it's the site of something terrible."

"I hate to be the bearer of bad news, but history tends to repeat itself." He picked up his hat and started for the center of the hold. "Phaethon keeps the Reef under tight security, and not only because their remote archives are housed there. If anyone is going to breach Mars, it'll likely be through an exploit of Luna Gimel."

Thursday fell silent, and his head drooped forward, a classic sign of hitting the upper RAM threshold. His frame twitched, returned to normal. "Okay. I'll do it."

"You haven't even heard the rest of the plan."

"Inconsequential. It's for the doctor, that's reason enough. Besides, knowing you, there is no plan. Or if there is, future steps will be limited to smoking a cigarette or holding the past over somebody's head. Potentially both. At the same time." He came up alongside Brinks, sidestepping him at the last moment to head off the spot where the Gate had previously opened.

"I don't know what you think you're about to do, but I caution against it," Brinks warned, hooking both thumbs into his gunbelt.

"There's something I want in return for my assistance."

A gruff sound came out of Brinks.

"I have your eye. And the Skip."

"And if you think I need either of those, you'd be mistaken. I've been doing this far longer than you could imagine, and the thing you're about to ask of me also happens to be the one thing I can't do."

A glare, eye to cybernetic eye. "All the same, I want to hear you say it," Thursday demanded.

"Allow your ward safe passage back to Earth, should she make it to Mars."

Thursday's hand dropped to his side, brushing the edge of his cloak as if reaching for an invisible gun; an artifact in his programming, no doubt.

Brinks spoke plainly, his tone measured but direct. "You aren't the only one who can work backwards from the truth. These Reflections... they're copies of something original. Some of them don't deliver the Origin at all. Run as far as they can, try to hide out inside a normal life. Some turn their purpose into a career. Deliver the Origin, then kill the ones after them, and deliver that Origin, too. Doesn't matter what they do or how they do it. Given enough time, they will always inevitably end up returning to the exact same place."

"The Red Planet," Thursday said.

"No. To the belief that they are the original." A dark point appeared outside the window. Gradually, the blurry edges solidified into an open shaft: Sanctuary Four, or its doppelgänger. Brinks watched it while cigarette ash drifted toward the deck. "And you take that sort of delusion and give it access to the Loop—to something capable of altering the fabric of reality itself?" He smoothed his jacket, then stubbed out the end of his cigarette on his metal forearm. "Loose ends that needed to be erased, and I'm the one who erases them."

Thursday's photoreceptors watched Brinks; his human eye watched the gun. "That's why you know so much about the Loop. You were there at the start of it. One of the original Seraphs."

"I was there for the end of it, too." He looked up, red eye glowing in the eerie light of the Manifold. "You have no idea the measures I've taken to keep the Loop offline. And there's no limit to how far I will go to keep it that way."

"I thought the Seraphs were meant to protect the Loop."

"That was never our purpose. Only to keep people from it."

"And did you?"

"You can't save people from themselves."

"Then I'll see you on the other side," Thursday said, blinking to activate the Skipjack. "On one side of your gun or the other."

At the center of the hold, a Gate opened.

Through the veil, darkness.

CHAPTER 38
"DAO"

Phaethon Corp. MAIN build_VX.6.6.09
initializing boot sequence...
running subroutine FOUNTAINHEAD:

  bindquery: update parameter to
  "DAO"
  encryption protocols intact,
  syntax structures intact
  [05] entries remaining

begin sentiment analysis,
implicit context target, rundisplay:

BEGIN RECORD >>>

Nothing is forever. Well, unless you count mistakes. If you live long enough, those sure as hell start to feel like it. I've said from the start that the Loop wasn't to be trusted. Something like that doesn't bring power without a cost. The true cost. We didn't understand it then. We still don't, although none of that prevented us from building more of them.

All that changed with Kepler's Reef. Gates were always something people went into, but at Luna Gimel? Something came out.

The irony is, after all these years, it finally led us to common ground. All that distance between us, worlds apart and going our separate ways, only for the Loop to be what brought us back together. Life has a strange way of doing that. Coming back around when you least expect it, with the thing you least expected. Now, we're here, and there's a path forward, although I wonder if it's any better than what we had.

They're calling it the DAO. Decentralized Autonomous Organization. Marcus said it's the future. And far be it from him to waste a good crisis. The board voted twenty to one in favor of implementation. I don't even really understand what I was opposing, but somebody had to disagree. The Loop was bad enough, but this? Letting someone—*something*—from another timeline advise our future? Nobody wanted to hear me out. It didn't matter anyway. It's out of my hands now. At least, that's what I told myself until the first measure was voted down the chain. Now I'm attaché to the Director.

Seems like something a man like Marcus would dream up to keep someone like me chained to a desk for the rest of my life. Make sure there's always someone to blame when all this goes sideways. The thing is, I agreed to it. I'll do whatever it takes to keep her safe. There's no going back, only forward. Even if it means confronting our future a lot sooner than we hoped.

That, or finally facing our past.

<<< END RECORD

"We are not going in circles,
we are going upwards.
The path is a spiral;
we have already clIm3ED>X–

WARNING: CONNECTION
INTERRUPT DETECTED

sanitize data entry,
purge access logs to XANADU
KILL remote process

CHAPTER 39
PRISONER'S DILEMMA

Wrong. The whole flight was wrong. No rattle during the atmospheric entry, and when they finally touched down, the cabin lights flickered, died, then returned with a surge Emélie felt more than heard. For half a breath, the air tasted metallic. She checked Joab for a reaction; he didn't even look up from whatever he was reviewing on his field terminal. Roland stepped down from the elevated cockpit. He passed her in silence and, sliding the crew door aside, flooded the cabin in dull, salt-colored light. Dusk, or maybe it was already dawn again. She couldn't discern under the diffuse scatter, which, for all her time on the surface, felt oddly unfamiliar. Outside, an armored executive limo sat parked between a pair of matte black Basilisks.

Ahead of her, Joab dismounted. "Go take care of that," he said, giving her a sideways glance. "And make it quick. You know my policy on waiting around."

Her reply came wordless: a sharp inhale and a curt nod. Boots to the tarmac, an uncharacteristically solid sensation after almost a week of traipsing across dunes and flight decks. Nearby, the angular profile of another ship loomed in the haze: again, a Four-Wing. Off-world capable, no doubt spec'd by Joab for the short jaunt up to Luna.

While Joab made for the ship, Emélie branched off, taking a direct line to the executive limo. On approach, bodyguards stepped from behind the nearest Basilisk. She recognized them almost immediately as the same ones who'd scanned her eyes back at the first meeting and later, flew her and Joab up to Homestake. "Really?" she demanded, offering a dismissive wave when one of the men raised the scanner. She focused on the door handle.

Fold, unfold. Into the Manifold, and back out in the space of two steps.

The men looked at each other, bewildered as she reappeared past them, tugged the red-plated handle, and opened the door, seating herself.

To take a seat. The open seat.

Across from her sat the Director, his fine silver suit running like an ore vein against the limestone interior. Attaché to his right side, and on his other, a dossier—the same one Joab had leafed through during their interview. There was no wheelchair, but beneath the Director's pant legs, the suggestions of a lumpy exoskeleton bracing either knee were visible.

"You've been busy," the Director said, apparently no more interested in formalities than Emélie.

"And you've been lying."

The attaché leaned forward. "Know your place, or I'll—"

"Leave," Emélie said.

The Director studied Emélie for a half-breath, then lightly rapped his window with the back of his hand. The dark outline of a bodyguard appeared against the tinted glass. The door opened. For a long moment, the attaché held Emélie beneath her lidless red gaze before finally extracting herself. Silently, except for the reluctant scrape of her frame against the plush seat. When the door closed, the Director met Emélie's direct stare. "Any further demands, or shall we begin?" He rested a hand atop the dossier, pinning it in place.

Emélie leaned back in her seat.

For a moment, he was silent, seemingly lost in thought as he watched Joab ascend the boarding ramp of the other vessel. "Everything we've built here, the Sanctuaries, the DAO, the Loop—especially the Loop—came at a price. A great and terrible price. People understand and accept this, if only on a subconscious level. So when they rally around transparency and demand honesty, what they are really asking for is a story they can believe in. Something that makes them feel as though they've lifted the veil on secrecy. And if the facts are compelling and close enough to the truth, they accept it. To bear the full weight of reality would be detrimental to our species' survival. Unlike other animals, we possess the capacity for guilt. A strange and powerful driver, it feeds our fear, and in turn, our survival. A simple matter of economics. It's much easier to go on reaping the benefits of someone else's sacrifice than to assume the burden of what comes with the knowledge of what's behind it." He paused, his gaze drifting to Emélie's cybernetic hand. "I know you have questions, doctor. About who you are, where you came from, and what happened to your memories. I'm afraid I can't answer them. Not because I choose to withhold information, but because they remain unanswered, even for me. The only thing I can tell you with absolute certainty is you aren't the person you believe yourself to be."

"You're referring to Lilith," Emélie said bluntly.

The Director was silent.

"Who was she?"

He placed the file in his lap. "We were only trying to keep you safe," he said, pausing to let his words settle before extending the file toward her. "While I can't promise you the truth, this will provide some closure to the answers you seek. A way forward, if you can see it."

Emélie ignored the dossier. Her focus remained on the Director. "I've seen plenty," she said.

"You see what you were trained to observe."

"Then show me something different."

He let out a harsh sigh. Pursed his lips. Here was a man unaccustomed to yielding in any capacity. Emélie, agile as ever, felt no sympathy.

"She was part of an internal project to synthesize Origin production, designated under the codename Fountainhead."

Find Fountainhead.

Fountainhead, found.

Something Joab had said during one of their back-and-forths resurfaced. *She's an idea*, he'd said. At the time, Emélie hadn't thought much of it, given his comment had been directed toward Lilith. With the Director's admission—the right trigger—the problem at hand took new form, and slowly, a shape emerged. Fountainhead, Lilith, the Reflections; what if they were one and the same? A collective entity linked to some deeper connection that ran older and more sinister than the Hespiredes Cartel. Emélie felt a soft smile crack her stone-faced composure: this whole thing was nothing more than an equation. A simulation of the truth, defined through chaos, and she had something everyone else before her had missed: Eden.

"You tried to consolidate the flow of Precursor by packaging it into something that, by all appearances, was stable. Only the thing that governs Origin is also the same for Precursor, and that thing is chaos. The project spiraled out of control, you failed to get a handle on it, and now we're in a drug war of your own making." Emélie produced the Origin tabs Joab had given her and held them up to the light. Identical to the ones she'd carried in her fix kit, except these were blank. Hers, by contrast, came with her, ferried from Kepler's Reef, and wherever it was she'd come before that. Hidden, along with the mark of truth they bore, printed on the blotter paper in pure, unadulterated quantum substance. The mark of the manufacturer. "Precursor is from Mars. Origin, however," she looked out her window. More dust rolled off the Four-Wing, oscillating in a way that was clearly defiant of Earth's gravitational parameters. "Origin is from here. A Phaethon subsidiary."

The Director looked at her without admiration; no honor, among thieves. "Lilith was trained by the DAO as part of that project. When she defected, she took our means of production with her, then used those same protocols to run her own operatives, one of whom was you."

"Defected," Emélie repeated, her tongue finding it difficult to form a word, especially that one. She looked at the tabs clutched in her metal hand. "Defected to where?"

The Director raised the file. Paper for paper; a fair trade. "It's all here, along with a generous employment offer. Security clearance, surface accommodations. Most people will spend their lives in service to this company and be fortunate to amass half of what I'm offering you right now."

"Perhaps you should revisit your compensation structure," Emélie said. The dark blur of his attaché no longer hovered just beyond his window, and however unnerving to see her waiting, it was worse to wonder where she'd gone.

"Talent comes to us, Doctor Desjardins, not the other way around. We didn't get to where we are by begging."

Emélie studied him for a good moment. In the same way Aratheus seemed to shrink under Roland's presence, the Director now felt smaller to her. Reduced from his intimidating self to the point of near-irrelevance. A man so infected by self-importance that, aside from a title, lacked any other name (at least to her). And what is a man without a title, but a man. "You didn't arrive here honestly, either," she said.

"And what alternative did we have? Would you rather have I told people that their best hope at survival—the result of decades of engineering and careful research—was brutally ripped from our hands at the very instant it was most desperately needed? Origin is far more than a product. It's an opportunity to build something better. A new future." He leaned back, placing his hands on either bony knee. "And for all the damage she's caused, even Lilith understood this truth. It would benefit you to take a page from her book and accept it, along with my offer. There won't be a better one. Or another."

There was a suggestion of movement near the waiting Four-Wing: a pair of dark shapes moving up the boarding ramp. Between them, an oblong object; cargo, loaded onto Joab's ship. "And what of the Loop?" Emélie asked. She jammed the tabs of Origin back into her pocket. "The Manifold, the Jumpers, the Gates—all of it comes down to... to a fucking robbery?"

"Hardly theft, to take back what was ours from the start." The Director exhaled, satisfied with his answer. "If Phaethon is to survive, we need Origin, and not the table scraps from Mars. We need the pure, raw product. We need the means of production." He looked out his window. "We need control."

Joab's ship rotated a half-turn and taxied toward the launch pad.

Emélie slid across her seat and reached for the door. "Some things weren't meant to live forever."

The dossier hit her in the stomach, flung from the Director's furious hand. Paper scattered across the cabin. A few sheets fluttered onto the seat beside her, white leaves against a barren tree. "Before I go, I want to know how you're so sure I'm not her?"

He spoke bitterly, reluctantly, the muscles in his jaw flexing with each word. "She ran this company for the better part of two decades. One of the greatest minds I've ever encountered: brilliant, cunning, tenacious. Tactical, when necessary. For twenty-six months, I've started each day wondering if I was missing it, only to see you confirm, time and time again, what I knew from the moment I laid eyes on you. You're not her, because when I look at you, the only thing I see is fear."

"Twenty-six months..." Emélie said, her words trailing off at the invocation. Her eyes fell to the near-horizon as her mind drifted inward, entangled in the thread that gave so readily as she pulled at it. "Syzygy. The opposition window... It's a clear shot."

The Director's eyes narrowed, aware that his assessment had inadvertently betrayed something valuable to Emélie which he had yet to grasp. "I beg your pardon?"

"They say it took a million men to dream of Mars, thirty men to reach it, and only two—The Iron Head, and his Red Hand—to conquer it." She looked around at the papers strewn about as a result of his outburst. Information, but not the information she needed. "I'd like to know if there was someone else behind the two of them. I have a feeling maybe I'm not the only person here living in the shadow of a lie." She set her hand on the handle, turned to him. Dual-colored eyes cut the small expanse between them with absolute clarity. "Keep your certainty. I'll take my chances in the unknown." Emélie lifted the door handle. Locked.

She pulled again, harder.

"Do you know what the single most challenging obstacle was for simulating the Manifold? It wasn't the math. No, the math was easy. Rudimentary, or so I'm told. Beyond my mind, certainly, but that's why we set up the university at One. A pool of resources at our disposal.

What we needed to overcome to construct the Loop was a human problem. *Seeing* is believing." He leaned over and tapped his window. "There is no objective truth, Doctor. I had hoped you, of all people, might have recognized this. And yet here we are, back where we started. Effective immediately, you will stand down from taking any further action pursuant to the Loop on Mars. You are to report to Phaethon Tower tomorrow morning for transfer to Kepler's Reef."

Emélie took her own turn at outrage. "Kepler's Reef!? What business does Phaethon have up there, aside from Archives and the DCB..." Hearing that last acronym out loud carved a path into the truth of what he'd just said.

"The work done by the Dimensional Compliance Bureau is essential to our future stability. Think of it as a lateral move with plenty of upward mobility, provided you can demonstrate you're still trustworthy."

"Next time, save yourself the paperwork and put a bullet in me," she replied. "I'd rather that than spend the rest of my life sanitizing patrol logs."

"Oh, you'll do much more than that. The DCB is also where we send all the first-hand witnesses. We can't have people spreading rumors about Jumper activity inside our borders. Any Phaethon employee unfortunate enough to witness such a thing earns a visit to the Reef, where we help reframe the burden of that memory and turn it into something, oh, what's the word I'm looking for..." A satisfied twitch of his thin lips. "Constructive."

She couldn't see the Four-Wing anymore. It was still there, hidden behind the wash of dust as it readied for takeoff. *Joab and his goddamn windows.* Although if he wanted to stick around, he wouldn't have let her get into a locked vehicle in the first place. "We all have our part," she said, not really sure of what else to say. Not the ending she wanted, but something of an end all the same.

The Director's face faltered momentarily, and he abruptly reached up, hastily rapping the window again. Harder this time. Someone stepped into the frame, and the Director exhaled, lowering the window. A hand—a *human* hand—rested against the sill: at the wrist, the faintest bit of red marking stood vibrant against tanned skin. Roland's face appeared in the open window. Casually, he looked around the cabin. Taking in the geography of their conversation. The Director blinked. Rubbed his atrophied knees absently, as if Roland's presence had afflicted him with some ancient, phantom pain. "Ma'adim?" he managed with a coarse whisper.

Roland studied the papers, then Emélie. Finally, he gave a nod toward the Director. The simplest answer to a lingering question.

With a wave, the locks released.

Emélie climbed out and shut her door. A few loose sheets from the dossier skittered past her boots—impossible, since all the doors and windows had been closed. One caught against her ankle. When she looked down, the paper was browned and irregularly shaped. Not paper. Leaves.

Inside. The Manifold. Already inside...

Without a word, Roland started across the tarmac.

Emélie fell in place beside him, wincing, her thigh still tender from the stab wound. More leaves fluttered past. "I'm not used to people backing me up. I suppose this is where I say thank you."

"I wouldn't do that," Roland warned, his unwavering gaze fixed on the ship ahead. "You understand very little of this world, and you only feel gratitude now because you cannot see the day coming when you will regret this moment, and the one we met."

Up the boarding ramp once more and Emélie, inching closer to hatred with each step.

CHAPTER 40
ROUTE TO CHAOS

Twenty-one, that's a natural. Emélie cleared her eyes. She was seated on the hood of a truck, leaning back against the windshield. Nearby, Goodnight stood watch, observing his team assemble near yet another unmarked dropship. "What... what did you just say?" she asked.

Goodnight gave her a side-eyed frown. "I didn't say anything." He jerked his chin toward the gathering team. "Are you coming, or are you going to keep sitting here like you've got the credit to gamble with Joab's goodwill?"

She rubbed her temples, the pounding headache behind her eyes holding back the precarious revelation that she had no idea how or why she was sitting on the hood of a truck. A truck, inside... where? She looked up at the ceiling. *Hangar.* They were in a hangar. Too large for the sole Four Wing, and somehow, too small at the same time. How long had she been out? Minutes? Hours? The Origin-dosing, reality-Jumping, Gate-hopping fever dream of the last seven days had reduced her to a sleep-deprived near-delirium, and trying to work backward from why she was on a truck inside a hangar proved challenging. The last thing she could remember was the silhouette of Roland, boarding the ship that now sat opposite her. Upon recognizing it, the rest came back like nightfall on the Surface: with a chill, and the plummet into harsher conditions. Fountainhead. The Director's offer. Roland's intervention. And, all of it, inside the Manifold. *And what about now? Were they still inside?* Her eyes darted rapidly, seeking some orienting detail that could confirm her suspicion. Her jumpsuit was clean. That seemed important, though she couldn't remember why.

And she had the shakes again.

She threw another look over at Goodnight, who, on closer inspection, was not so much standing beside her as he was stopped in place. A momentary pause, and, as indicated by the rest of his body language, a reluctant one. Across the hangar, Joab emerged from the ship's hold. Joab, without last name or title. Not a man, a black hole. He paused at the top of the ramp, looking past the briefing circle to where she waited beside Goodnight. Somewhere behind him, inside the ship, the suggestion of Roland loomed darker still.

Briefing circle. The shape recalled another memory—Goodnight's explanation of protocol during their first trip to Luna. *Joab will wait until we're ten minutes out to give the briefing. At ten minutes, we can turn back. Try another day. After that window, and...* "Take additional precautions," Emélie mouthed, finding the words. A cautious glance from Goodnight. Emélie let out a heavy breath and leaned back, resigning herself to the collapse of what little agency she had at altering the course of this descent into madness. Whatever process had been set in motion was already upon them, as indicated by Joab starting the briefing.

"He isn't the sort of person you want for an enemy," Goodnight warned, watching Joab move down the ramp.

"He's not the sort of person I want as a friend, either."

"Even so, I'd suggest you tread carefully once we're inside. Say what you want about his methods. Joab has made more trips through the Manifold than the rest of us combined."

"And you?"

A shrug. "I don't count 'em. I go where I'm aimed and pull the trigger on the way down. And if I wake up and I'm back where I started, it's a payday and another trip around the Loop."

"Then why does it matter if I'm at the briefing or not?" She slid off the hood and grabbed her gear. "Regardless of the risk, or what's waiting on the other side, at the end of it..." Her words died as she caught sight of something else moving beyond the men. She side-stepped Goodnight to get a clear line of sight.

"All that talk, and yet, you can't help yourself, can you?" Goodnight called.

"It's true. And I'll likely do it again."

"Who's to say you haven't already?"

She stopped. Turned around.

His teeth flashed in the awful, grainy light. "Don't get me wrong, Doc, I'm counting on you coming along. Back out now, and it's bad luck."

"Luck?" Emélie repeated. "I don't believe in luck."

"Well, I do, and with you, we make twenty-one. That's a natural..."

Emélie was in his face, eyes boring into his. "Twenty. There are twenty people, plus me? No estimates. I want an exact count."

Her abrupt directness caught him off guard, and rather than reply, he put a step between them. "Whoa, easy, Doc. I didn't mean anything–"

Unwilling to pry the answer from him, Emélie turned to the group and started counting heads. And there was the object again. Clearer this time. A rectangular metal box hovering at waist height. The same box she'd seen loaded onto the ship that brought them here after meeting the Director. The nose broke into view as a pair of flight crew-men, one on either end, ferried it up the boarding ramp. Everything about the container felt wrong: the way light moved against it, the jittering outline of the men guiding it, the way it left a slight ripple in its wake. But what made her stomach clench were the proportions: *person-sized.*

Leaving a stationary and speechless Goodnight behind, she made for the briefing. On entry into the small crowd, her heart quickened. A break appeared, and she passed through, head held high. Those before her stepped aside, clearing the path ahead and then stitching it back up behind her. A seamless dance, tactical bodies parting the route with the same fluid dynamics they'd demonstrated at every other encounter. All of which began like this and ended with violence. They were, after all, men of violence. And violence became them.

Inside the inner circle and no longer buffered by the mass of bodies between them, Emélie met Joab's gaze. He stood there, at the center of the circle—*his circle*—a shit-eating grin on his face, eyes glinting like scope flash in a low basin. "Alright," he said, looking around, "which one of you told the doctor there's going to be Origin on Mars..."

Unfazed, Emélie allowed the chuckle a moment to decay. When she spoke, it cut the lingering ones to silence. "You make jokes for the dead?" she asked.

Joab closed the gap in a single step, shifting slightly on approach to hold his strong side at an oblique angle. *Positioning himself to make the first strike, if need be,* Emélie thought. *Go ahead, have at me. I can move anywhere inside this hangar in the time it takes you to close a fist.*

Despite his smug expression, Joab's words came out with a bite. "I find it convenient that your objections are always bounded by the limitations of your own knowledge," he said, circling. "That sort of behavior is something we usually only see in drones. Drones, and the insane."

"Then that's something else I have in common with Lilith," she replied, tossing her body armor on the floor between them. "Now, are you going to tell them? Or is that why I'm here?"

Let them stare. Emélie held her silence, drawing their attention. Like Roland, willing to forgo social convention until it was time to speak. No hourglass here, but Emélie was, if anything, an expert in simulation. And what had Roland told her, back when they first landed on Luna? *An inconvenient truth is still the truth.*

Goodnight appeared at the edge of the circle, growing concern evident behind his calm demeanor. With every set of eyes trained on them, Joab leaned in, addressing her so softly that if not for the jagged shape of his jawline cutting a shadow across his face, she might have missed that he was even speaking. "You finally decide you've had enough, Desjardins?"

"No," Emélie replied, speaking loud enough that the whole group could hear her. "I don't want to leave. I came here to make sure these men understand that if they commit to follow you on board that ship," she pointed to the waiting Four Wing, "they're already dead. Dead by Eden's hand."

"Look around! You think if we call it a day and go back home, that we get happily ever after?" He inched closer, his words punching, each syllable landing like a miniature breaching charge. "C'mon, Desjardins. I know you feel it too. That goddamn pull. She has a certain gravity to her, doesn't she? Irresistible. All-consuming. Annihilating. Nothing should have that kind of power, and you?" He rammed a finger in her direction. "You volunteered for this because you've seen it too. And what you found back on the surface last week? That's only the beginning. Two months from now, you won't be able to throw a rock without hitting an Origin drop, except the Jumpers will be alive and kicking. Facing that out on the surface is one thing. Inside a Sanctuary? It's going to be a fucking bloodbath." He waved an arm at the team. "Eden wants a war on drugs. She has the drugs, we'll bring the war. And everyone here signed up knowing full well what the risk entailed, so don't speak on their behalf."

"So it's just me you've kept in the dark, then." Emélie took one more look around the circle. "Very well. You've said your piece, now I'll say mine. Eden is different from the rest of us. Not because she's less than human. Because she's *more* than it. A quantum entity. What you and I see is only now. Right here, and nothing else. Eden, though. She sees this moment, and the ones before and after it, and the ones beyond those. Not a past, present, and future, but a pattern that can be understood. A Loop." Emélie pointed a cybernetic finger at Joab. "And most importantly, she's seen you coming, Joab. Thirty-five million miles and two decades away. You can't go in the way you're planning because she's already witnessed the end. All of them. And you don't have to believe a thing I say. After all, there will always be Kepler's Reef. June sixth, Twenty seventy-six."

The faces around her dropped, ghost-white as they moved into range of her own realization.

"The worst mass causality event in Phaethon history," she continued. "Twenty unidentified bodies turn up inside a secure server facility on Luna. And not just *any* twenty bodies." Emélie gestured to the team surrounding her. "These twenty."

Joab paced the inner perimeter, not looking at all surprised by Emélie's remark. "You aren't wrong, Desjardins." He locked eyes with each man as he moved around the ring, gathering their attention back to himself. "The conditions are the same. The numbers, *our* numbers, are identical. On the surface, it seems like we're bound to repeat history. But surely even you won't try to deny that for any given equation, if you change the operator, you change the outcome."

"What variable? You have a different Watcher?"

"No, no." A sly smile crossed his creased face. "A different you."

Emélie ran a hand over her head. So simple. She hadn't seen it because it was so damn obvious. Replicate the initial conditions. Control for the external variables. Swap out the primary function. Joab was running a massive simulation and using her model. Using *her*.

Fuck me.

"Nowwww she's got it," Joab grinned.

She hadn't said the last part out loud. The look on her face said enough. The shaking in her hand confirmed it. The clean jumpsuit. Clean because they'd moved her here. Transported her into the Manifold like... like cargo. An asset, nothing more.

Overhead, the steel trusses supporting the ceiling groaned in unison, creaking with the intermittent sounds of extreme stress. The entire building shuddered, then pitched. Ship behavior. A carrier—they were on a carrier. No going back now. No choice she could make would alter their destination. All that was left was to wait for the drop. The same drop she so carelessly calculated for Joab. And there was something about Shells. *HardShells.* Had someone already said that, too? She was losing track. All the markers from before—her routine, the slow, plodding work—were gone, and it was no longer clear what was something that had already happened, what she was imagining, and what hadn't happened yet. She looked down at her hand. Shaking. So she'd been here before, inside this carrier. Or maybe it was all in her head. *Keep eating,* Thursday had said. All that Origin surely had a price.

Unable to change the past, Emélie did what she knew best. *There's no going back, only forward.*

The Origin tabs Joab had given her were still in her pocket. She didn't need them to do what came next.

Joab turned back to the team, deliberately positioning himself so his back was to her. She stood in their epicenter—irrelevant now that she'd served her purpose.

"You know what's waiting for us," he said, voice carrying across the hangar. "You're all here because the truth of it doesn't scare you. You're here because you're ready to change history." He raised his fist. "Shell up. It's time to hunt."

The crowd roared, black rifles thrust into the lean air. Joab turned back, pumping his fist, feeding on their energy—empty space where Emélie had been standing.

She watched from the top of the ramp as his eyes tracked the hangar, searching. When he found her twenty paces displaced from where he'd seen her last, his expression shifted. Recognition. He raised his hand, finger pointed toward her with his thumb extended, and, coolly, dropped the symbolic hammer.

She watched him, unbothered by the implications of his gesture. Whatever was inside the ship was far worse than anything Joab could offer. With a turn, she melted into the dark hold.

Target: forward cabin.

CHAPTER 41
SYMPLEGADES

Emélie slipped through the hatch leading into the forward cabin. The metal, coffin-like container sat open, empty. Nearby, lit by the amber glow of terminal screens and softly pulsing panels, were a pair of figures. The first, immediately recognizable: Roland, seated, cross-legged and shirtless, his back toward her. A dark aura rippling off him like some black-bodied star. An older class drone stooped over him. In one of its hands, a gleaming, Origin-tipped needle fed by a canister partially visible inside its matte black arm. Neither Roland nor the drone made any move to acknowledge Emélie. Instead, the drone carried on with what it was doing: carefully inking a string of symbols onto a patch of skin at the base of Roland's neck. Synchronized between the drone's needled hand and the point where it touched vacant skin, dust spilled forth.

Not a way into the Manifold. A way out.

Even in the low light, the symbols were recognizable: the same machine inscriptions marring the walls of Lilith's safehouse on Luna. Emélie tipped her head back until it touched the cool steel of the hatch behind her. "You can block light from every wavelength, sound across every frequency, and mass of every size from crossing dimensions. The one thing you cannot hide is gravity. And what is a Tether, but gravity focused to a single moment in time?"

The drone paused, then turned, meeting Emélie in the lingering dust with four yellow eyes. “I don’t believe we’ve been introduced,” the drone said, her voice warm and rich with inflection. She leaned back, inspecting her handiwork while the needle disappeared into a cylindrical sleeve in her arm.“My name is Sahira.”

Emélie, eyes on her own black arm, closed her hand into a fist, then opened it, as if seeing it for the first time. “Emélie,” she replied softly, raising her eyes to meet the drone. “You can call me Emélie.”

“And which reality is it you come from, Emélie?” Sahira asked.

“I… I don’t…” Emélie faltered, then fell silent. When Roland rose to his full, formidable height, she found her words. “This whole time. You’re a Seraph, and you’ve had a Watcher this whole time.”

He turned, slowly, with intention. Marking his sternum like a dark brand was the unmistakable rectangle of a Halmos.

Emélie sank a bit further into the door as reality reformed itself in front of her.

“Watchers exist outside the boundaries of possession,” he explained, reaching for the heavy black tunic he wore beneath his body armor. He slid an arm into the garment. It moved around him, undulating by some advanced composition of fibers that reoriented themselves in response to subtle changes in the wearer. “Why are you here, Emélie?”

She watched him tie the heavy sash across his waist. Emélie had never seen him without body armor, and rather than diminish his appearance, the lack of combat adornments left his wide, muscular body in clear, terrifying view. “I don’t know,” she said. No sense lying to him. She’d already established he’d see through anything less than the truth.

The deck shuddered, driving Emélie to steady herself against either side of the hatch. Roland absorbed the motion without breaking his stance.

“Don’t worry,” Sahira offered gently. “We never recall our own birth.”

“It has that in common with death,” Roland said, turning to Emélie. “You are at the briefing, or not at the briefing, but never here.”

Emélie reached down, instinctively touching her thigh. To her own secret. "Then you should pay attention to what comes next," she said.

Roland picked up his sword.

The edge of the tool caught the light, revealing a swirling, patterned steel. Tempered and folded and hardened by a process situated at the exact intersection between technological advancement and skilled craftsmanship. More than a blade; death's implement.

"Atropos," Sahira spoke, her four eyes tracking the shape. He held the weapon, outstretched, with one hand.

The prick of metal kissed Emélie's throat as the blade rested against it. Her life, hanging in the honed balance. "An object made for endings," she said carefully, following the edge to meet Roland's sharp, grey eyes. "If this is my end, then answer my eulogy: is this the first time I've felt the touch of Atropos?"

He watched her for a long time, then returned his sword to its scabbard.

"The Director referred to you as Ma'adim," Emélie said, emboldened by her continued breathing.

Sahira, midway into her container, stopped at Emélie's words and waited, watching for Roland's response.

"I have many names," Roland replied.

"Yes, but where did you come *from*?" Emélie pressed. "The Ma'adim was the first ship to make contact with Mars, and I saw the Halmos on your chest. A tombstone, the same as the marking Lilith carried. You may be a Seraph, but you're also a proof. The result of some older equation."

Slowly, Roland rotated, his presence expanding into dimensions beyond the four walls of the cabin, a monstrosity spread further into time than space. "The Loop is not something to grasp. If you think you've arrived at the threshold of understanding, you've never been further from the truth."

"Lilith found a way to control it."

"You mistake motion for autonomy. Fountainhead provides access in service of a goal. A sending unit slaved to the master."

"If that were true, then why would Lilith so readily comply? She's not powerless. The Jumpers are evidence of that."

"Powerless, no. Only burdened by the same delusion plaguing you. The belief that the Manifold holds within itself some hidden truth. The skeleton key to an unsolvable problem. It matters not. For Lilith, the promise of something real is more tangible than the reality of it, and under that premise, she toils. Searching for what will never be found. And with each fresh iteration, Fountainhead's work incrementally advances while the cage holding Lilith grows stronger. It does not matter what you propose as an alternative because nothing—not Lilith, not even Eden—will ever outpace what is in motion."

"Then why do we try?"

Roland opened the hatch. The guards who'd transported Sahira entered, faces obscured by black masks. They moved with eerie synchronization, tot a gesture wasted between them. One took post at the door, the other beside Emélie. "We all have our part," Roland said.

"Then let me play mine," Emélie replied.

Another tremor wracked the ship. The lights flickered momentarily. Off-balance, Emélie stumbled backward. When the light returned, Roland was gone. Both guards lay facedown on the floor, blood pooling near their heads. Emélie's eyes fell to Sahira's container. The lid, still open, but the coffin was empty once again. Around the same moment she registered this, there was a blur of movement to her left. The glint of a needle, and no time to react. Sahira slammed Emélie into the nearest seat in a metal embrace, then drove the entire Origin-fed needle into the muscular tissue of Emélie's neck.

A nuclear pain. The full heat of the sun against bare eyes, and Emélie felt every heartbeat crashing against her ears. She felt herself falling: through the seat, then the floor, then nothing. Her world, compressed down to a single, lightless point.

When it unfolded back into a stabilized reality, the first thing Emélie noticed was the air against her face. Hot and tasting of sweat. Her own breath reflected back to her. The second thing she took in was the overwhelming sensation of being pressed from all sides.

Contained. She was inside Sahira's container.

Panic spread along her chest and up her neck. She tried wrenching her arms free, only to find there was no room to bend them. Pivoting at the waist, she rammed her head forward. The lid was closer than she'd expected, and the following blow managed to knock her momentarily senseless. Her head thumped the bottom of the coffin as the desperate, familiar gasps of oxygen deprivation cinched her chest tighter with each sequential breath. She closed her eyes, thought of the last clear thing she could remember, and then Jumped.

Fold, unfold.

Breathe.

With nowhere to move and no point immediately visible, her actions shifted reality sideways. The walls of the metal box flopped open, and the lid rolled up, wrapping around itself until it was inside out. Her stomach dropped at the sudden sensation of a free fall. Again, she thrust her arms out instinctively to brace herself. She was back in the hatch where she'd started. Standing.

In front of her, a multitude of coffins, all layered atop one another. And inside them, around them, scattered like leaves to the wind, lay parallel iterations of herself. Dead, scrambling and suffocating, severed in parts.

Brittle air stung her cheeks. A sensation grounded in the present, it brought with it the observation that she was outside of those other realities; the scene collapsed, leaving Emélie standing, breathing. Persistent, alive beside the still-sealed box. Objects around her that were caught up in the parallel shift reorganized themselves into their prior configurations: seats folded back down, overlapping terminals compressed to single displays, and the ceiling returned to normal height.

She inhaled. The wheeze that followed was alarming, a cautionary response that preceded a spasm so violent it tore a cough from her lungs. She doubled over, reeling in the frigid air. One staggered step, then another, and she was into the nearest bulkhead, groping for one of the emergency respirators hanging just beyond reach. A grasp, a miss, and she Jumped again. This time, without thinking. The respirator was in hand. Hand to face, and a deep breath. One more good breath. Her knees shook, threatening another drop to the deck. She fought past it. Moved for the door with heavy, sluggish footsteps. *Keep moving.* The hatch was locked. With a blow from her metal elbow, she smashed the glass panel covering the override switch and threw the yellow lever.

The change in pressure nearly blew her into the cargo bay. As she gripped the door frame, a line of men in black armored HardShells turned to look at her, their faces obscured by helmets covered in tiny lenses reminiscent of the goggles Joab had thrust at her back on Homestake.

The man nearest to Emélie stopped what he was doing and turned, studying her for a moment before lifting his visor.

Goodnight.

Flashes of crimson moved off his eyes. Emélie followed his arm to the source: a handful of Origin-tipped rounds. He gave a sly smile and tossed a few more brass cylinders down the line. "Escape hatch," he said, holding up the remaining two cartridges. He touched one to his lips before tucking it into a spot of webbing on his plate carrier.

Emélie glanced down the hold, toward the loading ramp, which stood silent, obscured by the twenty other bodies standing in front of her. "You plan on shooting yourself twice?" she asked, her voice coming through with a mechanical rasp from the respirator.

The flickers of red faded as the men dispersed the remaining rounds. Goodnight held up the last one, examining it. "You're what we call, in my line of work, a liability. Since you refuse to arm yourself, someone else has to take responsibility. That someone is me."

"You're an idiot, Goodnight. You can't dose yourself with an Origin round inside the Manifold."

"Relax, Doc. This isn't our first time into the Loop."

"Yeah? Let me guess, you think a Tether is going to pull you out of whatever maelstrom you end up in, right? Do you even know how a Tether works?"

Goodnight stared at her blankly. "And you do?"

"It's not hard. A point in our reality is linked to *another* point in our reality. The coordinates are encoded using Origin, which exists as a quantum substance and is thus permeable across realities. Activating the connection pulls you through using the Manifold. But if we're already inside, you're not getting pulled anywhere. You're going to get pulled apart."

Goodnight collected a steel cable from the belt on his HardShell and clamped it into a slotted track on the ceiling. Behind him, nineteen other cables went up. "It's all a bit over my head, Doc, but even if I understood it, orders are orders." He motioned toward the remaining exosuit hanging inside the armature beside him. "Now quit asking stupid questions and Shell up. We're depressurizing shortly, and half the team is betting I have to use this Origin round on you before we even hit our LZ."

As if to emphasize his point, the ship banked hard right, then abruptly pitched upward in a maneuver that made Emélie feel as if she were being crumpled toward the floor while her stomach lagged behind. A small view portal near the forward hatch revealed a sliver of pewter terrain slipping past the armored glass.

Luna.

Emélie clambered into the metal scaffolding housing the unused HardShell. Frantically, she searched for a control mechanism to initiate the mounting process. She'd never worn a Shell, only seen them in use, and the exact process of how to enter one remained a mystery to her. Goodnight was shouting something from across the bay, pointing toward his boots. She looked at her own feet. Took a small step forward. Nothing happened. Another step revealed a subtle depression in the floor tread. She shifted one foot, then the other. A pair of mechanical arms unfolded from the frame and, starting at the neck and working down, began clamping armored panels to her body. HardShells were servo-actuated exoskeletons with an integrated power supply providing additional load capacity, agility, or life support for extended periods in a total vacuum. The suit she donned now appeared to be a milspec variant, wrapping her in a set of full-armor panels that still retained some dexterity.

There was a dull, aching pain in her calves as the suit clamped over her boots. The helmet came last, and when it sealed to the rest of the suit, the assembly arms detached. For a moment, she stood in total darkness, unsteady under the burden of the unpowered suit. A line of jade-colored text appeared in front of her as the suit booted up, and with a final twitch, engaged. She crashed forward, weighed down by the sudden surge in power. With the lens array still coming online, she bumped into one of the team and staggered sideways, only to be steadied by the quick hands of another team member. Slowly, one pixel at a time, her surroundings came back into view.

The running lights switched on, and for a short instant, she saw Joab standing in front of the loading ramp. Someone beside her lifted her belt cable up to the rail and clamped it on.

Twenty-one.

The ship shuddered, dipped violently forward. The engines came alive, rattling through the fuselage with a teeth-grinding vibration. Everything, consumed in darkness—blackout or lights, she couldn't—cable strain at her waist, the only evidence of up versus down, holding her from careening into—

Standing.

Bright. Cargo bay. Men jostling past her, one by one, moving toward the exit. The engines thrummed with a dull hum. How long? When had she—?

Emélie unhooked her cable and surged ahead, parting the sea of black Shells with her head down and elbows out. Picking up speed with each step, while the clatter of armor plates against those around her warned the ones ahead of what was coming. At the end of the line, she found a small gap before Joab, who remained fixed in the center aisle, blocking the exit as he waved men out the back of the Four Wing in coordinated pairs.

"The whole ship...." Emélie panted, feeling droplets of moisture accumulate on the inside of her helmet. "He Jumped all of it?"

Outside, the pitted red structure of Luna Gimel stood against the grey surface.

"C'mon, Desjardins." Joab tapped the next pair of men, who stepped past him, obsidian comets streaking toward the open main-shaft far below. "Did you honestly think you were the first person to work out how to move without a Gate?"

She looked at the men around her, the ship, the terrain below. "They why even bring me along at all, if you didn't need me for the Jump?"

"You've been deemed essential personnel, although not by me. I would have left you back on Earth, so you can thank your friends at the DAO for letting you darken my shadow a bit longer."

"I don't have any friends in the DAO," Emélie said.

He waved another set of men off the open ramp "Keep thinking that."

Only a handful of men remained in line. The rest of the black-suited figures were strung across the space between them and the open shaft of the Loop. Out in front, boots almost to the silver ground, Roland, the silhouette of Atropos clearly distinguishing him from everyone else.

When the two operators moved into position, Emélie stepped in front of the one to her left, taking his place. Before she could step off, the dense pressure of a handgun muzzle moved against her ribs, halting her mid-stride.

"Be my guest," Joab said. "You know how much I hate loose ends."

Emélie looked back down the empty hold. "You know the Loop isn't just a name. It's intrinsic to the design. Not down, or backward into some point that we can reverse or just climb out of when we're done. We're moving in parallel, across realities. Realities that aren't connected, like the way we perceive time."

Joab returned the gun to the drop holster on his thigh and stepped to the far edge of the ramp. "Does this look like a situation where we have time to worry about procedure? The rules changed. We adapt. And it doesn't seem to bother you when you're the one making Jumps."

"That's not the same thing, and you know it." She jabbed a gloved finger into his chest plate. "I went through an existing Gate. An *open* Gate. Roland just used a Tether to pull an entire ship backward through time. Even if we breach that facility, we'll arrive on Mars twenty years before the Loop exists. Before any of—" The words had barely left her mouth when she felt them hit her like a kick in the gut.

"Took you long enough," he said. That stupid fucking grin spread across his face. "We're not going back. The mission is simple: access the Loop, reach Mars, lay low. When Fountainhead shows up in twenty years, we're already there. Embedded. And we burn it down before it starts, starting with Eden. The other players will fall once she's out of the picture."

Twenty years. The number sat in her chest like a stone. Her mind raced back through every briefing, every careful non-answer, every time she'd asked about the plan—they'd never intended to extract, and this wasn't an operation. It was a life sentence.

"You son of a—"

The ship banked hard. She staggered, the suit compensating while her mind reeled through the implications. Roland. The Tether. The urgency to use her as... as a false flag. To give the appearance they were trying again, the same way they'd tried before. *You were the only one foolish enough to come out the way you went in.* Who had said that? She couldn't recall, only that it was there. Another truth.

Joab offered a mock salute. The half-hearted gesture of a man who'd made peace with exile long before she'd even learned its name. He stepped off. "See you in—"

Emélie hadn't caught the last part, but it didn't matter.

Hell and the Loop were one and the same.

CHAPTER 42
QUANTUM SUICIDE

Brinks emerged from the Gate, a cascade of sand flowing off his burly frame. The grains followed the worn creases of his waxed duster, dusty rivers that pooled in small piles atop the polished table he stood on. He swept the room, feeling it out. The shape of it, and its occupants: familiar. A standard distribution of fear. Seated around him, fixed in place, the small tail: a select few, who, by some complication of evolution and conditioning, found themselves either too stupid or too afraid to flee. Across the room, the largest contingent of board members clawed at one another in a tangled mass of limbs, trying to escape through the sealed blast door. A closure lacking any visible method of override; an intentional choice, although when it was built, it was meant to keep people out. For Brinks, useful enough for the task at hand. Wrong tool for the job, except that he had many ways of getting done what needed doing, and drawing a gun, while often the simplest option, wasn't his only one. With this in mind, he turned his attention to the two people in his presence who did not try to run but chose to remain in place through a conscious act. It was for these two individuals that Brinks had come to Sanctuary Four, if only to ensure—for the safety of the future, and everyone inhabiting this present reality—that their timelines ended with him.

He stepped down from the circular conference table, one boot to an empty seat, then, with another heavy step, onto the rust-hued carpet. One seat over, an incapacitated board member trembled in place, a wet spot darkening the crotch of his expensive suit, his eyes glazed over in catatonic terror. Brinks looked at him, then grabbed the empty chair one space over and pulled it along behind him, traversing the perimeter of the large table. "I remember when you instituted the lockdown protocol," he said, addressing the man who was watching him from the opposite side of the table. "I told you it was a bad idea then, and I stand by it now. The only difference between a fortress and a prison is which side holds the key."

The man at the table sat quietly, patiently, as expected. The Director's office was his domain, after all.

Brinks continued: "Unlike you, I haven't forgotten how this all started. Who we were before the power. The feeling of four walls closing in, and nowhere to go." At the Director's side, he spun the chair and set it down between them.

A look of mild amusement crossed the Director's face. "And yet, here you are." He leaned back in his wheelchair. "If you're here for the Watcher, Sam, she's long gone."

Brinks tilted his one-eyed face to the ceiling, studying the tightly grained wood panelling. "Nobody calls me that anymore. In fact, I remember telling you specifically never to use that name again."

"And I told you never to return, so I guess that makes us even." The Director glanced toward the door, where the Phaethon C-suite executives continued slowly tearing at each other without any progress toward escape. "Well, don't stop on my account," he offered, gesturing to his board. He let out an audible sigh. "Although you should know gunning them down won't change anything. They're viral. Kill one, and three will appear in the time it took you to put down the first."

Brinks unholstered his gun. Flicked the cylinder open, upending the weapon so dust poured clear of the firing mechanism. He rapped the barrel against his leg, swung the cylinder closed, and cocked the hammer. "True, but they aren't why I'm here, although, as you may recall, I've never been one to shy away from collateral damage." He slotted the weapon back into its holster.

The Director shifted in his seat. "As I said, the Watcher is—"

A flash from the gunhand, and the gun spoke. Brinks fired through the table, through the Director's hand, through the panic button concealed on the underside of his wheelchair. A three hundred and fifty grain, jacketed, hollow-point reply.

At the presence of gunfire, a pair of auto-turrets dropped from the ceiling behind the Director's chair. Brinks had marked their positions when he'd entered the room, and he dispatched them with a shower of sparks before they could even finish deploying. "Anything else?" he asked, a tendril of smoke drifting from Threadripper's barrel.

A grimace from the Director, who, gripping the edge of the table with one hand, lifted his other one, now nearly torn in two. He laid it on the table with a strange, detached finality while blood pooled into a puddle that eventually spilled over the table's edge and into his lap.

Brinks dumped the spent rounds onto the floor and reloaded. When only one empty chamber remained, he stopped. "I want all of them gone. Out of here, now." He waved Threadripper toward the Director's attaché, who remained at her post near the door. "She stays, though," he said, tapping the heavy barrel against the seat back for emphasis.

The Director slumped a bit in his seat before obliging him by pressing his good hand onto the table, palm down. A biometric scanner embedded into the underside of the polished surface cast a seam of orange light across his hand. When it finished, it blinked twice.

Directorial Override initiated. Awaiting Secondary Input.

The Director raised his eyes and nodded. Brinks pressed a hand—his flesh and blood hand—onto the table. Another flash of light, followed by an audible chirp. The armored panels sealing off the room retracted with a synchronized clatter.

Brinks holstered his gun and, grabbing the back of the Director's wheelchair, rolled him over to the curved, floor-to-ceiling window. Outside, a panoramic view of Earth's barren surface.

The Director spoke, slurring his words slightly while he gazed down at his damaged hand in semi-shock. "It's been a burden, all these years. Wondering when this moment would finally come. Waiting.

Waiting for the day you'd inevitably show up to collect on the enormous debt between us."

Brinks let the precious few rays of light breaking through the dust warm his face. It had been a long time since he'd stood above the storm layer. The sun, usually hidden from those on the surface. A memory of what had been, and the heat that came with it. "We had plenty of chances for forgiveness. Should've taken them before we got to this point, but we didn't, and now we're here." He walked over to the wall behind the Director's desk and pulled down the photo hanging there. A picture of the two of them, standing in front of a newly constructed Loop. "What do you remember about Mars?" Brinks asked, returning to the Director's side with the image in hand.

"I try not to remember any of it."

"I expected you'd say that. For me, it went the other way. I can't remember any of it. God knows I've tried. Tried to hold it close, so I don't forget. Every day wears away a little more, though, until even the most potent parts—the moments you told yourself you'd never forget—all start to seem fuzzy." He shook his head and set the frame in the Director's bloody lap. "I remember what it felt like to hope. That, and I remember you could still walk."

The Director glanced down at the photo. "We all carry wounds from that place. Some of us, more than others. I liked you better before you became a Seraph. You were always sentimental, but living so long has infected you like a disease."

Brinks removed his hat, creasing the crown with a metal hand. "You've always been a careful man, Marcus. Careful to hide your intentions. Careful to make sure nobody sees what's behind the things you do. Odd thing about being blind, though. People forget there are other ways of seeing." Brinks put his hat back on and removed his cigarette case. "You were right about me. Nothing left for a man like me except killing. I tried to get away from it. Thing is, that sort of thing follows you around like a curse. I'm not interested in making amends, but there's no reason I can't hold a few people accountable for their own sins on my way down." He lit his cigarette and watched the attaché from where he stood. "You know I've hunted down every single Reflection that's come out of the Manifold? And somehow, you still got one past me." He took a drag, then exhaled a cloud of smoke. "The irony, of course, is that while you did such a good job hiding her, none of that mattered the moment I came through that Gate. The only thing I know better than a Reflection is the look of a man about to make a run for it."

Marcus considered his statement, then gave a small wave of his hand. "Najat, come here."

The attaché approached, and upon reaching Marcus' side, tore a strip from her black cloak and began bandaging his mangled hand. Marcus raised his eyes, observing Brinks as Najat worked. "I'll give you what you want, but I need you to do something for me in return."

"The last time you said that, we ended up on Mars."

"Then you should pay attention to what I say next, because we're right back where we started. That ward of yours, Doctor Desjardins, has gone too far. Despite my efforts to put a buffer on her trajectory, she somehow still installed herself into a position that compromises everything we've built. I'm more than prepared to accept a certain amount of loss in situations like this, but the exposure we're facing right now is only because you were weak to the trigger, which is something I can't say I ever expected to see from you."

Brinks gazed out the window at the surveillance towers dotting the dust-blown surface. "She was the first to come out of the Gate at Kepler's Reef. She's different from all the others. I just haven't been able to figure out why."

"She's different from the rest of them because you needed her to be, you fool! Why do you think I've kept such a close eye on her this whole time?" Najat finished bandaging Marcus' hand, and he pointed toward an empty chair. "Sit," he ordered, then turned his attention back to Brinks. "I recognized what she meant to you and knew if she was close, you wouldn't be far behind. But you need to let go of this fantasy that she's different from all the others. The only reason she made it this far is because you allowed it. And now, you're going to do your fucking job and go clean this up. You've only ever been good for one thing, and you should have done it decades ago." Marcus motioned to Najat. "Take your mask off," he told the attaché, then turned back to Brinks. "You'll find what you're looking for at the base of her neck."

Brinks watched Najat release the ovoid black dome. When she pulled it away, it was not circuitry, but the soft lines of a woman's face, head shaved and a scar marking either cheek.

"You two were always alike in that way," Marcus said, backing his wheelchair away with his one good hand. "Useful, but only ever for one thing."

"Maybe so," Brinks said, releasing a panel on his mechanical arm that concealed a single, Origin-tipped round. "But underestimating us was the first mistake you ever made." He slipped the Origin round into the empty chamber and fired into Marcus' chest.

Marcus vanished from his wheelchair, leaving behind a small cloud of dust that settled into the blood-spattered frame. The attaché—the Reflection, Najat, Marcus had called her—covered her mouth with trembling hands.

Brinks produced his knife. "I'm sorry if this is going to sting a bit," he warned, coming around to stand at her back. He leaned in, carefully examining her neck for the location of the Skipjack.

Skin smooth, no scars.

Najat reached up, grabbing him by the wrist as she threw her body weight forward, flinging him onto the table with an immense, compact strength. He landed on his back, face toward the ceiling. Before he could get his gun up, Najat was on top of him, barring his neck with her forearm until his head was pushed so far back it hung off the edge of the table. She struck, bashing him across the throat with a sweep from her skeletal red arm. Without hesitation, she leaned in, eyes the color of a coming storm, and pressed her full bodyweight against the hand wrapped around his windpipe.

There was a flicker of movement from the other side of the table, and Marcus dropped back into his seat, coughing violently. Brinks tried to sweep Najat with his leg, but she defeated his assault and pressed harder into his neck. Marcus pushed himself out of his wheelchair and flopped against the table, then swung his atrophied legs up, one after the other. Sliding across the dusty, mirrored surface toward Brinks' knife, which rested just out of reach. Brinks choked as the air in his lungs ran dry. Behind him, Marcus snatched up the blade and made an incision in his own forearm. "The last time I found a Reflection worth holding onto, you took off with her and the Skipjack before I had a chance to do anything," Marcus said, fishing a concealed Skip from the muscle tissue of his arm. "It took me years to locate a suitable replacement, although this one turned out to be an upgrade, so really, I should be thanking you." He paused, taking a moment to watch Najat choke the life out of Brinks before wiping the Skipjack clean. "Make him suffer," he added, tilting his head back as the small chip scuttled up his cheek and nested itself against his retina.

Brinks felt an imperceptible shift in the pressure against his neck. It was all he needed. He rammed his head forward, headbutting the Reflection so hard her eyes rolled back into her skull. Marcus' body began to twitch and flicker as the Gate opened on the table around them. Brinks didn't waste time on the draw. He positioned his body sideways while firing off a string of shots, gun still in the holster. He walked the rounds to target, hitting Marcus four times along an imaginary line between his right knee and his liver.

Marcus spasmed, then flopped to one side, planting both hands against the table as he tried to drag himself through the open Gate. "You gambled a lot on a Reflection, brother," Marcus grunted. "You should have learned your lesson from me."

When Najat reached for his knife, Brinks put a boot to her chest, sending her careening backward through the Gate. She vanished from sight. From the room. From their reality.

Marcus pulled himself the rest of the way through after her.

"She wasn't a Reflection the first time," Brinks said, grabbing Marcus by the ankle right as he slipped through. Brinks pulled him back, rolled him over. Halfway in, halfway out. Half the room was lush with Manifold, the other half swaddled in the fabric of their own reality. "Eye for an eye," Brinks said, and then he gouged out the Skip.

He stayed put while the Gate collapsed. It severed his mechanical arm at the shoulder and took the upper half of Marcus along with it.

When it was closed, he staggered back to the empty wheelchair, where the photo of himself and Marcus lay shattered on the floor. He ripped the frame away, revealing a handwritten note hidden along the bottom margin. *October 12, 2063*. He tossed the frame aside and reversed the image. Another marking. A string of symbols, machine language, scrawled in Precursor along the back edge. Red as the day it was mined. Red for all the blood it cost to get those symbols there. He tore the marked segment away, crushed it into a ball, and ate it. Then, with a shaky hand, he pocketed the rest of the image, pulled out his gun, and fired the last round into his own head.

CHAPTER 43
"KEPLER"

Phaethon Corp. MAIN build_VX.6.6.09
initializing boot sequence...
running subroutine FOUNTAINHEAD:

bindquery: update parameter to
"KEPLER"
encryption protocols intact,
syntax structures intact
[04] entries remaining

begin sentiment analysis,
implicit context target, rundisplay:

BEGIN RECORD >>>

Four Watchers, four Seraphs, three planets. The last thing we need is another Loop, and especially not one at Kepler's Reef, of all places. I never would have gone for it, which is probably why they pushed it through behind my back. It seems as though everyone has plenty to hide these days. They forget I've got eyes in more places than they can lie. And to be honest, it's not even this new version of the Loop that I find most concerning.

She showed up right before the announcement. Late, which is unlike her, and apologetic, which is new. I asked her why the Reef, of all places. Doesn't make sense to put such a large piece of infrastructure so far out in the middle of nowhere. Dark side of the moon, miles from the nearest spaceport, and twice as deep as the other ones? She told me some things were meant to be forgotten, which is a strange thing to say about something that hasn't even been built yet.

That's when I knew I'd missed something. I may be attaché to the Director, but before she was the Director, she was just my daughter. I know my own flesh and blood, and that woman?

That wasn't her.

<<< END RECORD

HESPERIDES hardfork detected.
HERODIAS found. Checking conditions:

if SALOME is COHERENT
and proximal to ARROGANT,
execute subroutine LABRYINTH:

conditions met, rebooting
OPHANIM_LG via WAKEFUL-3...

"My real self wanders elsewhere."

sanitize data entry,
purge access logs to XANADU
KILL remote process

CHAPTER 44
FUTURE PERFECT

Emélie stood on the crater's rim, eyes fixed on the narrow obelisk rising from the lunar mare. A perfect black rectangle. Hard to be certain at such a distance, but the proportions seemed right: a door. The vertical face was solid and tomblike, while the backside tapered to a slope where it met the ground, connecting to something below the surface. She raised her visor and squinted in the light, trying to get a second glance at the movement that had drawn her attention the first time. Trees, or something like it. Green. Here, on the moon.

Goodnight trudged past her through the heavy dust. "You alright, Doc? You're shaking like a leaf."

The phrase sent a shiver down her spine. She'd heard those words before, although not from Goodnight's lips. Looking at him now, Emélie couldn't believe she'd missed it. A man she'd only met a few days ago, and yet somehow, familiar to her in so many ways. The same quiet concern. The same assessing gaze. Even the same utterances. She looked down at her hand, then back up to Goodnight, pulling tight the common thread that linked him to another. "Sahira was a Class II," she finally said. *Just like Thursday,* she didn't add.

Her admission elicited an agreeable nod from Goodnight. "Ah. I see you finally got the chance to meet Roland's Watcher."

"Unfortunately." Her voice was distant; she was thinking about Roland's observation back inside the conveyor. The one about Sefirot, the first Watcher: awoken, but missing. Presumably, also built around the same time as Sahira. An unaccounted-for Class II...

Goodnight paused to watch Joab and the rest of the team moving ahead of them, stretched out like dark points on the fractured, shadow-less plain. "I'm surprised you were even admitted to see her in the first place. They keep that one hidden inside the Manifold and only summon it before missions like some sort of mechanical ghost."

Emélie resumed her position at the tail end of their staggered patrol formation. "I'm a cosmologist. Chasing ghosts is in my nature."

Goodnight moved up to join her, walking casually with both his arms folded atop his rifle. Despite his easy demeanor, Emélie noticed that he exercised great care in tracking Roland's position. "Maybe so, but speaking from experience, ghosts are the least of your worries out here."

"You've made it this far before?"

"Can't say that I have." He craned his neck, scanning the ridge where they'd come. "You, on the other hand? I don't know what you saw after I left you on Homestake, but you're different now. If I didn't know any better, I'd say you were the one we should all be following."

Emélie threw a concerned glance in Roland's direction. "I wouldn't speak too soon. I might have followed you here, but instinct tells me I won't be joining you for the return trip." She nodded to the Origin round still tucked into the webbing on Goodnight's chest plate. "You said it yourself. I'm a liability."

She couldn't see Goodnight's face inside his helmet, although his shoulders tensed. He gestured at the transmitter on his shoulder pauldron, then held up four fingers. Emélie twisted the dial on the side of her helmet, picking up the private channel. When a healthy gap had opened between them and the rest of the group, he spoke, and even then, his words came through clipped and hasty.

"Listen to me. We're likely going to split up at some point. I don't know when. I shouldn't even be telling you this. Seems like something too big to miss, and at this point, if you haven't put it together by now, I'll have to assume withholding it from you was intentional, in which case I'm violating comsec by telling you."

"If you think you're doing me a favor by explaining how we're two decades into the past, save your breath. I was the one who handed Joab the route. And I know there's a contingent designated to stay behind, waiting to strike Eden before Fountainhead has a chance to recruit—"

A metallic *schlaaack* cut her short. Goodnight released the charging handle on his carbine; in one smooth move, he'd ejected the seated cartridge, dropped the magazine, and canted the weapon. Now a black-tipped bullet, freshly ejected, rotated in a lopsided arc in front of Emélie. Without ceremony, he produced the Origin round from the webbing on his chest plate, slotted it into the open action, and sent the bolt home. Muzzle, hanging at the low ready; six inches vertical and five pounds of pressure on the trigger would gain Emélie a trip along the Tether. "Ask me," he said. "I can send you back right now. I know it seems like you don't have a choice in this, but it's not too late. You don't have to follow Roland into Luna Gimel."

There it was again. Another echo. Goodnight's mouth was moving, but it was Thursday's words the day she'd left Earth that came back to her. *I know it seems like you don't have a choice in this, but once you board that ship? It's too late.*

Her eyes did not fall to the gun held at her, nor did they check to see if Goodnight's actions had drawn the attention of Roland or Joab. With a steady hand, Emélie lifted her visor. "Goodnight. That's what they call you. And when we met, that's what you told me your name was. That isn't your only name, though. You've gone by another. You've *been* another."

His face twitched, fighting the reality cresting his consciousness like the barren earth rising on the horizon behind them.

She offered him a warm smile. He was here for her. Because of her. Another truth, bound up in another lie. And from her lips, a gift. One friend to another. "Sefirot," she said.

There was a flash of recognition, a rapid blink of his eyes, before they narrowed once more. "I don't know what you're talking about. I'm just trying to keep you safe."

Emélie looked around, studying the field of ejecta surrounding them. The cracks radiating from the obelisk carried consistent depth. A meteor impact would have left a crater. These markings suggested a vector. *Another basin.* "I've missed something, haven't I?" There was force behind her question. A string of words expecting an answer. "I fear it has to do with Roland. We seem tied together in some way that's unclear, and will remain as such until it's likely too late. I know he left Earth on the first ship to Mars, but I can't figure out where he came *from.*"

Goodnight's shoulders dropped, and with a defeated finality, he cycled the action on his gun. Rather than let the round hover, he tapped it, sending it toward Emélie. She collected it, closing her fingers around it when it passed by. "From? That's anyone's guess. He's older than all of us, although he doesn't look it on account of being a Seraph. I can't say I know much more than you, except that before Phaethon got a hold of him, he was a mathematician."

Mathematician. She looked toward the figure waiting at the obelisk. Every choice she'd made, suddenly drawn into the greater balance. Choices, or predefined variables? *We share enemies, not loyalty.*

"Of course, now that you understand, it will be obvious," Goodnight continued. He still hadn't realized what Emélie meant, nor would he. It mattered not; he spoke, fulfilling the role he'd been assigned to by some invisible hand. "You've seen how he moves. Anticipates what's about to happen. The way he wields a gun like an afterthought."

"Like the killing has already been done," Emélie said quietly, "and pulling the trigger is just the proof."

Goodnight glanced back at her. A shift in his posture—the slight tilt of his head, just like Thursday used to do. *Just like Thursday.* "Yeah," Goodnight agreed. "Exactly like that."

"More proof," Emélie said. "Same as this place. Or Lilith. Or Sahria."

And Roland wasn't the only one who could see what was coming. Here, in this moment, Emélie observed the object of Goodnight's caution, standing sharp as the stone doorway ahead of them. A mathematician wouldn't merely use the Manifold. He would apply it. Every fold, every edge, every impossible surface—utilized in ways she was only beginning to rationalize. "You think Roland had something to do with the Collapse, don't you? That's why you don't want me to follow him into Luna Gimel."

"I've already said too much." He gave a sharp jerk of his head toward the group, and Emélie noticed Roland was watching them now. Watching her. Visors down, and they were moving again. Fifty meters. Forty. "Nobody wants to know what I think, anyway. I'm just a guy with a gun who gets paid to keep his mouth shut."

She glanced back toward the collapsed ground. Collapse. Here, so close to the source, the word took on a foreboding undertone. A definitive terror that was only just beginning to unfold. "I'm asking you now, Sefirot. What do you see?"

Upon hearing his true name—a body with the consciousness of the first Watcher, a quantum entity, he stopped. Turned back to face her. "Roland survived, and Eden has Mars. I'll let you add up why those two facts sit so close to each other."

Roland: Architect of the Manifold.

Seraph, an intentional choice; capable of wielding a Tether. Yet why would the person who designed it also feel compelled to alter it from the inside, unless...

"Something took hold of it," Emélie continued, solving for the remainder. "Unexpected. Outside of the equation. And it happened right here, at Kepler's Reef, inside Luna Gimel." Her words settled in the airless silence surrounding them.

Goodnight placed two fingers on his radio dial. Instead of returning to the team channel, he spoke again, and only for her ears. "I've sealed my fate. No amount of good luck will change the outcome now. It's not too late for you, though. Your future seems to be unfolding, and I'd suggest keeping the hand you've been dealt close to your chest. And if you get an idea in your head to ask either of them about it?" He gestured to Roland and Joab. "Don't. At least not while you're on my op."

Emélie switched her intercom to the team channel.

"Lose the frames," Joab barked, throwing both of them a cagey glance. "We're going in slick." He pulled the safety tab on his chest plate, releasing the exoskeleton portion of his Shell. Roughly half the team had already discarded their frames ahead of him, and, under Roland's careful gaze, formed a line at the vertical face of the obelisk. What remained of the team pushed outward to secure a perimeter. Knees to the lunar dust, they produced lightweight ponchos, which they draped over their frames, softening the edges of their outlines. One by one, hoods went up, leaving behind oddly scattered boulders blending seamlessly into the landscape. Roland, ever the exception, ascended the lip of a nearby outcropping, his uncamouflaged profile clarified by the Loop rising, a red husk against the starless horizon.

Joab checked his watch. "Alright, team, standby to breach. Once we're inside, it's a straight shot to the boarding platform. Team Two will provide overwatch until the MagLev arrives. Team One," he gestured to Goodnight, "You're with me. There isn't room to hold a secondary perimeter once we're inside, so you're going to handle any contingencies. And Team Three," he swept an arm across the invisible remainder of the team holding security around the portal, "maintain position here and ensure nobody tries to follow us in. Rules of engagement are simple: no escalation unless it's mission-critical. Nobody knows we're coming, so keep your heads down and your eyes up. I want this done fast and clean, and if we run into any issues and you plan on collecting a paycheck, use your escape hatch so I don't have to spend it tying off loose ends."

The men nodded roughly and dispersed, busying themselves with last-minute equipment checks. Goodnight produced a grappling anchor and affixed it to the outer edge of the stone structure. Before she could piece the rest together, Joab was standing in front of her.

"Get your Skipjack out," he ordered.

Her skipjack. Emélie touched the place on her thigh that carried a small scar, identical in size and shape to the one on Lilith's collarbone. "Now you want a Gate? And here, in a vacuum, of all places?" She gestured in Roland's direction. "Go ask your Seraph."

Joab flung his visor up and leaned forward until his glass faceplate tapped her own with an eerie *clink*. "Roland can't open Gates. Seraphs can only move payloads along a Tether. Quit wasting time. We're inside our window with Deimos."

Emélie leaned to the side and looked at the door. It lacked any sort of hinge, handle, or lock. In fact, on closer inspection, there wasn't even a line indicating that the interior portion of it swung aside or retracted in any way. "This leads down to Luna Gimel?" she asked directly. A query, not a question.

Lips drawn into a tight scowl, he returned a nod.

"What class?"

A glance in Roland's direction. Roland, preoccupied with something beyond their shallow basin, gave no reply.

"You want a Gate, you get me an answer. I can wait."

"What are you thinking is going to happen, Desjardins? I whip out my satcom and put in a COMINT request? To who? The people I work for don't even know I exist right now."

"If it's who I think it is, then that shouldn't be an issue. The DAO deals in future commodities, and we pay their debt."

Goodnight appeared at Joab's side. "S Class," he said confidently, trying to diffuse the rising tension.

S Class. Samech. A secret, hiding in plain sight. A Loop, buried inside another Loop.

For all the impact of that revelation, Emélie didn't take her eyes off Goodnight. Goodnight, now Sefirot. The First Watcher, and likely, the same drone Emélie knew by the name Thursday. And it was Thursday who had identified the first Loop she'd encountered: Terra Gimel, D Class. Followed closely by the identification of Luna Bet, R class, from none other than the architect of the Manifold himself, Roland. A Seraph. Next, the third facility, twin to the Conveyor, called Terra Aleph, P Class, uttered by Aratheus' now sealed lips. Each designation, delivered by someone proximal to the source of that information. All the more reason for Goodnight, hired gun and the ex-station chief of Homestake, an unlikely candidate, to provide the fourth and final designation. Unlikely to everyone except Emélie, who watched him and saw, in his face, Sefirot, and in Sefirot, her oldest friend. The drone Thursday. And with Thursday, she was right back where she'd started.

Full circle, strange Loop.

"There," Joab said, interrupting her mental backtracking with a broad sweep of his hand. "Luna Gimel, S class. Gate, now!"

Emélie tugged the ejection tab on her Shell. The relief of losing the bulky apparatus vanished under a more pressing problem. "I'll have to depressurize my suit to activate the Skip," she said.

"Sounds like a problem past-you should have anticipated." Joab pulled a muzzle suppressor from a pouch on his body armor and affixed it to the end of the carbine clipped to his shoulder. "You have five minutes."

Emélie walked over to the black rectangle and lifted her hand. The sensation was electric; the object hummed with a resonance that felt... tuned. If she could use the Manifold to move at will, and this Loop, like all the other Loops, was an extension of that system, then there was likely something else behind the solid stone. A doorway, but only on the underside. In another reality.

"And once we're in, you're going to attempt to breach the Mars Gate with a single team?" she asked.

Joab extracted a magazine from his cummerbund. "We're going to breach Mars with a single *person*. This thermal cooling sink runs directly to Gate control. Inside the Manifold, the form changes, and the shape remains. With a complete bypass, we can enter the facility undetected. If we draw the attention of the facility Watcher—the Watcher from *this* present reality, we'll be forced to escalate. Cost of business, you understand." He lifted up the loaded magazine in his hand: like Goodnight's, it was stacked with black-tipped polymer sabots. For killing, no return trip. "Now, you can either use your Skipjack to open a Gate so we can slip in unannounced, or we can enter this place the good old-fashioned way. Which, believe me, is something nobody wants." He pointed a cautionary finger toward the above-ground superstructure on the horizon. "You know what else is inside this facility? People. Hundreds and hundreds of people. And not just security personnel, but maintenance teams, administrative staff." He seated the magazine. "Scientists," he added.

"This is well beyond collateral damage, Joab. You're talking about unmaking people. If you kill them here, in the past?" She planted both her hands on her helmet, groping for some alternative that didn't lead to mass casualties or a Manifold entry. She came up empty. "Depending on the stability of their position within the system, any changes you make here could lead to massive downstream implications in the future..."

Joab slapped the bolt catch on his carbine, chambering a round. "Why do you think we're here, Desjardins. We are the massive implications of the future." He turned, rechecking his watch. Nearby, a line of men clipped onto the cable set by Goodnight. "Get your Skip up," he called back. "I won't ask again."

Emélie caught Goodnight watching her, something approximating an apology on his face. Her eyes dropped to his hand, which contained a laser scalpel scavenged from the tactical trauma kit he carried at the small of his back. Of course, it had to be Goodnight. Chief of the violent, and subsequently, the only one willing to follow it through to the end. For Emélie, it was the ultimate act of compassion: now tasked to harm, at his own hand, one entrusted to his care. She met his gaze with gratitude, and dipped her chin toward the scalpel, accepting what was to follow.

He motioned to her sternum. Emélie took a knee. "No," she said, smoothing her exposure suit where it covered the widest portion of her thigh. "Here."

"Largest tissue area," Goodnight said. "Lucky for you. Should help reduce the amount of localized damage."

"Lucky isn't the word that comes to mind." Visor, up. She met his eyes. Beyond him, Roland watched. A situation not far from her last trip to the moon. Days, or decades, depending on what side of the Jump she was on. Goodnight, standing over her, ready to go through with Joab's insane demand and her willingness to escalate to the point of self-harm.

"What's the plan, Doc?"

Emélie looked at her hand. "We prioritize speed. My prosthetic hand has better dexterity than your gloved one, so I'll pull the Skip. You make the incision, then once I'm clear, cauterize and patch. You think you can handle it?"

Another nod from Goodnight. A subtle quiver of his hand, which also did not go unnoticed. Emélie released the latch on her glove and pulled it off, revealing her metal hand. Without the slightest hesitation, she took his hand in hers. "Shaking like a leaf," she said softly. She looked out across the barren lunar surface. "Not much growing anymore, but we make do. Leaves are, if anything, life." She patted his hand, released it, then drew an imaginary line about half the length of her finger where the Skipjack was subdermally embedded in her thigh. "Ready when you are."

Goodnight was silent. Intermittent backscatter from his team filtered through their comms. Crouched beside Emélie, he craned his neck to glare at the waiting team. "If one of you ground-pounders has something constructive to add, then spit it out. Otherwise, stuff it and let the rest of us work."

"We're taking bets on whether or not you botch this and the doctor has to lose the leg," one of the men offered.

"That explains a lot," Emélie said, lifting a hand to shield her lens array against the horizontal glare. She leaned back on her heels. "I've been trying to figure out how I lost an arm in the first place."

The men chuckled, but Emélie's tactical comment diffused the tension. She reached into her own trauma kit and produced a tourniquet. Once it was wrapped around the upper section of her thigh, she hit the auto-lock. "Now," she said, gritting her teeth. Counting down would only give Goodnight more time to second-guess himself, and she needed him stable.

A plume of red-orange light shot from the device to an audience of eager eyes all waiting to bear witness to her high-stakes bet. The laser sliced through fabric, then skin, then muscle. The beam, dialed to a depth shy of bone melting, was unlike any pain she'd experienced. And with pain, Emélie was well acquainted. She sucked in air, holding steady under the saturating heat. Small tears pooled at the corners of her eyes. From the initial vacuum, an immediate sensation of swelling, followed abruptly by icy nothing. And like that, the laser was clear. She blinked, repulsed by the sight of her leg, already ballooning into a near-black bruise. With brutal precision, she drove her index finger into the incision. Amid the rapidly expanding tissue, a slender, solid disk. Without wasting time trying to grasp it, she gouged deeper and, with an excruciating sweep, freed the Skip.

The tool in Goodnight's hand flared to life, welding the wound shut. A rapid suit patch came after, and Emélie sank to the dust, the precious disc safely clenched between her thumb and forefinger.

"Now, for the hard part," Goodnight said, hoisting Emélie to her feet.

She cursed and followed him up. He was right. The longer she waited, the more she'd register the pain spreading down her leg. Someone passed up a scrap of grey cloak, which Goodnight collected and held out. She let go of the Skipjack, leaving it floating in front of her while she wiped her metal hand clean. Nearby, a dark and familiar shape materialized in her periphery.

"Don't breathe in," came Roland's voice, unhurried and calm as ever.

She collected the disc, then met the Seraph's gaze with indignation.

"Filling your lungs will worsen the effects of the sudden pressure change. From the moment you break the seal, you'll have ten seconds before a blackout from hypoxia...."

"Make it count," was all she heard. She looked at Goodnight, looked at Sefirot, looked at Thursday, in a way. Hands to either side of her helmet, she gave a forceful twist to the left. Something like the sensation of skin being peeled from her face drove her down to her knees, eyes cinched tight. The Skip, designed to operate under a range of extraneous conditions, pierced her closed eyelid regardless. A pair of hands gripped her like the closing darkness. Bitter, bitter cold, and the clatter of her helmet lock re-engaging. An embrace, steadying her, lifting her back to her feet, and then the high-pitched hiss of her suit pressurizing. Blind in one eye, her vision doubled, then shifted. When

the world came back into focus, she found herself standing at the center of a Gate.

Around her, not the Moon. A garden.

"This is madness," she gasped, coming to her senses in time to witness Roland disappear through a human-shaped notch that had appeared on the obelisk. Water poured from the top, spilling down the face to baptize Team Two as they slipped through the opening after him, weapons raised.

CHAPTER 45
THE DEVIL'S LEAP

Emélie couldn't recall what forward motion felt like until Joab grabbed the leader on her utility belt and hauled her within two steps of the slotted vent.

"Watch your step," he offered, slapping her on the shoulder before disappearing through the sheet of falling water. "It's a long way down."

Emélie eased her weight forward, testing her leg. The pressure was rewarded with splintering pain that came from everywhere and nowhere at all. With one hand on the cable to steady herself and one cautious step at a time, she pressed forward, descending the vent. Except for a single set of helmet lights bobbing in the darkness up ahead, the rest of the team was already through the vent, presumably waiting on the aforementioned platform. After an excruciating minute of closing the distance, the lights began to grow brighter. Another minute of progress on her part, and they swiveled, catching her head on. Water dripped from the ceiling, slowly dousing her so that through her lensed helmet, everything softened and stood like blurry shadows amid the glaring light. The helmet tipped down, illuminating the water washing over their boots as it ran down the sloping floor.

"Never seen water in one of these before," came Goodnight's voice. He looked back up at her, but instead of speaking further, turned and carried on sloshing toward a dull slot roughly twenty paces further down. Emélie picked up her pace, clumsily moving behind him until the narrow vent opened into a large, circular tunnel running perpendicular to the vent shaft. On the opposite side, the silhouette of Roland, marked by the presence of Atrapos across his back.

There was a splash as Goodnight dropped into the tunnel. Emélie followed, only to find herself in waist-high water. Under her own helmet lights, the entire tunnel was thick with vegetation: wide, serrated leaves the size of her body drooped into the water, and, with the exception of a small path down the center, the ceiling was thick with rope-like structures growing in a tangled web. Halfway to the platform, Emélie sank to her chest, found her footing, and on the next step, came back up to her waist.

"Watch the tracks," Goodnight warned, already up and onto the platform and too late to be of any help.

Emélie felt her foot slip, then catch: the same roots holding the vegetation in place now anchored her to the tracks. The submerged metal rails started trembling. Emélie turned, sweeping the water with her headlights. Larger ripples moved toward them from further down the tunnel.

"Move!" Joab shouted.

A blinding light appeared at the tunnel's center, bearing down on them with terrifying speed. Goodnight started to climb down. Emélie, unwilling to draw his life into unnecessary danger, had other plans. She switched off her lights. *Could she Jump while inside the Manifold?* She closed her eyes and thought of the shape of those three men. Another memory came to her, a voice familiar and yet one she hadn't yet heard. *The way forward is through.*

When she opened her eyes, she stood between Roland and Goodnight, dripping wet and intact. A burst of pressure washed their small group, and the train broke into view. The first few cars rushed past, gradually slowing to a halt when the final car met the platform they were standing on. The doors opened automatically, parting the waxy green leaves bowing down from the ceiling. Further down the line, toward the first car, the muffled sound of gunfire rattled toward them.

"Hey!" Joab barked, pivoting around to get a clear view of Goodnight. "I thought I was clear on the ROE?"

Goodnight had his head tilted to one side, listening to something coming in over his radio. He looked up. "That wasn't us."

"Then who the fuck is down here shooting!?" Looking for answers, Joab trained his lights on Emélie.

"I don't know why you're looking at me," she said, squinting against the glare. "You should be prepared for the possibility that one of Lilith's Reflections followed us through."

Joab waded out to the edge of the platform to get a better view down the tracks. "This is your Manifold, Desjardins. The only Reflection I'm watching is you."

Goodnight, still monitoring the radio, flagged Joab with his light. "Team Three is taking contact outside the vent. Two Relays and a Seeker." He paused, glancing cautiously toward Emélie. "Something else, too."

Roland, speaking for the first time since they'd entered, stepped in. "Emélie's assessment is correct. She opened the Manifold, an act that has no bearing on the exigent conditions." He looked into the open train car, then boarded. "We proceed as planned. Activate your contingency."

Joab bobbed his head enthusiastically and smacked Goodnight on the shoulder. "Time to earn your paycheck." He followed Roland into the car. On the threshold, he turned, ripping out his radio cable and discarding it with a definitive finality. "Comms are compromised," he explained. "Fall behind now, and you're on your own."

Emélie boarded, then turned, searching for Goodnight. He was relaying a series of hand signals to the rest of his team, who, at his command, pushed farther into the tunnel in either direction. The cable on his own radio, already severed. Frantically, Emélie tipped up her visor, showing her face behind the foggy glass. *Don't make me say goodbye again,* she mouthed, and beckoned to the open car.

A single, soft chime announced the MagLev's imminent departure.

Arms hanging heavily at his sides, Goodnight turned, raising his own visor to meet her. She couldn't tell if there were tears mingled with the condensation from his breath, but his face, while slick, showed no fear. More gunfire to their right.

A moment of knowing silence while the leaves around them swayed to the rhythm of men clambering past. With her ungloved metal hand, Emélie pointed to the Skipjack covering her eye, then held up a finger, repeating the gesture she'd seen Joab perform. Circle back. Circle up. *Find your way home.*

Goodnight pulled out his own Origin round, touched it to the glass above his lips, then tossed it to Emélie. *An inconvenient truth is still the truth.* For Goodnight, he was merely performing his job. In that moment, however, Emélie saw something more: if he was, as she suspected, a biological instance of the Watcher Sefirot, then the Manifold *was* his home.

The train doors closed, and once again, Emélie descended into shapeless darkness, leaving Goodnight behind, a receding point of light on the overgrown platform.

A small star, burning bright.

Inside the Manifold, time behaved differently. Emélie had already experienced this on multiple occasions: on her first Jump, when she dosed herself with Origin to override Lilith's Skipjack. Later, when she entered the Gate opened by Aratheus inside the Conveyor. And now, never more alone and uncertain about what came next, time stretched and opened like an abyss. Roland and Joab were long gone, having continued along the line until they were out of sight in one of the forward cars. The only sensation grounding her to the present was the wet, muffled sound of something impacting the moss-laden windows of the MagLev.

Thwomp.

She tightened her grip on the overhead handles and braced for impact. Most likely overgrowth on the track, but without a view outside, she couldn't be certain. Water sloshed over her boots, flowing against the train's momentum in their same direction of travel. She'd seen the phenomenon before, inside a surface storm, only then, it had been dust moving opposite the wind. The explanation was straightforward enough: an anomalous current, tidally locked to some larger gravitational field beyond their present reality. Here, its presence served as a definitive marker of reality distortion, and in this case, specifically, suggested they were fast approaching the Loop reactor's mainshaft.

Picking her way through tar-dark shadows, Emélie moved down the car, pulled by the same force drawing the water at her feet. The windows remained obscured, but the steady, side-to-side rocking had shifted to an offbeat *click-clack*. The sound of each articulated segment followed the inside radius of the circular mainshaft; her stomach kept time.

Thwomp-thwomp, thwomp-thwuump.

The last impact threw her against the curved, glass-walled canopy. In an effort to remain upright, Emélie smeared a messy streak across the nearest window, admitting in a shockingly reddish light. Back on her feet, the first glance outside took her breath away.

It took her sight next.

Luna Gimel, the last and final iteration of Phaethon's failed inter-dimensional transportation system, was nothing like its predecessors. A Loop, nested inside another Loop: the version before her, the one located within the manifold, linked to the version back on Luna. Bound up between those two, another truth. Emélie, while fully prepared and even expectant of the encounter, found herself, under the full force of it, disarmed and shocked senseless. Light of every color poured from the shaft, saturating everything except for the very center, where, in the pinprick of dark, an entire truth had been swallowed whole. At the heart of this Loop, not a Gate.

A black hole.

An insurmountable, perpetual darkness tore at her eyes until they were spangled and tear-streaked. She closed them, breathing into the soft, welcome stillness of her own mind. Preparation for confronting a reality beyond the boundaries of reason. The back of her neck prickled; she did not need to open her eyes to know who watched her.

"We didn't begin with Watchers," Roland said, his voice cool and matter-of-fact.

In the flickering, spectral light, Emélie could sense him, standing at the dark side of the car. Obscured by shadow, except for the occasional mote of light that sparked against his stone grey eyes.

"They were a compromise," he continued, unprompted. Even Roland, indifferent Roland, was not exempt from the innate need to explain away his violence. "More than anything, an attempt to consolidate the technological debt incurred alongside our reckless innovation. They were too little, too late. Doomed to fail by constraints of what they could and could not see." He paused, letting the words linger, followed by the punctual *thwomp-thwomp* of another impact. "All that changed when the Loop came back online. Your initial observation regarding the Manifold was accurate. Eden modified it to protect the last gateway into Mars. The oldest Gate. One final safeguard to keep out those like us, who would try for the impossible."

From the next car over, Emélie could hear the splash of approaching footsteps. She inhaled deeply, letting the verdant scent linger in her nostrils before looking down at her hand. The tremors were back. "I should have recognized it sooner. Re-entry into the Manifold was a specific choice. A tactical one. The Gate at Luna Gimel doesn't exist in our reality. The facility we saw back on Luna, the one I remember, is a token. A symbolic gesture of the real machine we now occupy." She looked out the window, toward the place where a Gate should have been. "You thought it would be enough, didn't you? Constructing something so powerful inside the Manifold itself, and protected by an artificial event horizon. The only way forward is through."

At those words, Roland turned, marking her with his full attention. "Who told you that?" he asked.

Emélie let the question linger. Rare, catching him off guard. "Nobody needed to tell me that. Look at the system, and it's self-evident. Accessing this gate requires a quantum leap. A Jump bypassing the current space-time continuum."

"Inside the Manifold, we are bound by Eden's rules. Outside of it, however," he approached the window and, with a sweep of his arm, exposed the shaft to clear view. "We make our own reality."

A slender, oblong object bumped against the clearing in the window. An unrecognizable blur that sank her stomach.

Joab entered the car, sloshing down the aisle behind them. "Seven minutes left on our window with Deimos," he said. The noticeable lack of restraint in both his tone and movements demonstrated that they were well beyond the domain of stealth. "Desjardins, you're with me. There's a secondary barrier sealing off Gate Control, so when the car reaches the station," he pointed toward the nearest set of doors, "I want an opening back to our reality."

Thwoomp.

The clear window afforded Emélie a prime view of the collision: against the glass, the lower half of a human torso. A glancing blow, the shock of it still left her reeling. She landed in the adjacent row of seats, eyes fixed on the watery red smear that remained behind. Below her, the car creaked, then slowed. When she attempted to pull herself up, her mechanical arm lagged behind, bogged down by some invisible restraint. A quick check of her other hand revealed it moved fine, as did the rest of her body.

Nearby, Roland watched her reaction unfold in real time. He extended a hand and motioned to her cybernetic arm. Cautiously, she offered it out. "The Gate platform is wrapped in a temporal shroud," he explained, gently taking her arm. Examining it with the same deliberate care she'd seen him use to handle Atrapos or a rifle. "The closer we move toward the center, the greater the time dilation. Different objects are impacted differently." He paused near the access plate on her elbow, but rather than open it, he released her. "Your arm isn't from this reality."

Instinctively, she flexed her hand, observing it with fresh awareness. It had always been a part of her; she'd never considered that maybe it was a part from somewhere else.

"It exists in a different quantum state than the rest of you. The variance creates an artifact allowing you to perceive the overlap between realities when everything else decoheres to a single one."

"An effective Tether," Emélie replied, transfixed. Thwomp. This time, a limb, severed somewhere mid-bicep and missing three fingers at the other end. "If there are already Jumpers on the tracks, I assume it will be even worse when we arrive at Gate Control?"

Joab craned his neck to get a look down the line. "There's a Watcher subroutine in place to monitor activity, but this close to the temporal shroud, there's too much distortion to pin down our location."

There it was again. *The way forward is through.* The thought had barely crossed her mind, and Roland held her in his steady gaze, watching her before he turned for the doors.

Joab pulled out his sidearm and peeked the chamber, ensuring it was clear of debris. "You want it straight? The path is set. A future bought and paid for the moment the Loop came back online. We either get to Mars, or we die trying." He set a hand atop the lever responsible for disengaging the MagLev's repulsion system. "Standby for egress."

Emélie stepped into the aisle. Half of her, illuminated by the light of the temporal shroud. The other side, cast in shadow. And between them, covering her eye with the active Skipjack, a point of brilliant red light. "Then we make sure it counts," she said.

Over the doors, a Gate opened.

Roland was the first through, disappearing with a gush of residual water that washed bits of floating vegetation across a grimy, well-lit hallway. She could hear his rifle breathing; exhaling a stream of Origin rounds to clear a path into Gate Control.

Joab held the door for Emélie, gun at the ready. Before she could exit, he raised the weapon and fired. Escaping gas and flecks of searing hot gun oil peppered her face. Behind her, a digital wail. Three Jumpers, dropped from well-placed rounds by Joab's carbine.

"Stay with Roland," he shouted, shoving her out of the car and across the Gate threshold. Another staccato burst. More Jumpers dropped at the far end of the car. "I'm going to clean this up. If I'm not there when you re-enter, don't hold the door."

Emélie pressed forward, propelled by the gunfire at her back. Thinking, even as she moved. Assessing everything in real time, outside of time. Ahead, the armored door leading into Gate Control. A bone-white room decorated with now-familiar accents: a crimson puddle at her feet, a swath of red painted across the row of terminals, and more blood splattered on the wall beyond.

No bodies, only Roland. "Here," he said, pointing to the transparent cleanroom. His other hand remained comfortably across his rifle. "Back in. Now."

Without hesitation, she blinked, reactivating the Skip. This wasn't the time to theorize about wrong outcomes. She centered her gaze on the cleanroom door. A brief, out-of-body lightness swept over her, and for a moment, her consciousness split down the middle. Half stood at the MagLev doors while the other remained in the control room, watching a fresh Gate open back into the Manifold.

Inside, another version of Gate Control, which shared the layout of the room where they'd Jumped with Aratheus back at the Conveyor. *Had that been a simulation of this? A dry run, to test what she could do?* Bathed in ultraviolet glow, Emélie continued moving until Roland halted at the hatch, where a small platform protruded a short way into the reactor shaft. The walls of the giant cylinder, distorted by the unbounded geometry of the Manifold, appeared to continue indefinitely above and below them. A vertical fracture marred the smooth concrete lining, and vegetation spilled from the jagged seam. At the center, nearly a half-mile from where she stood, the protective hologram enclosing the Gate platform shimmered, a prismatic distortion in the vacant airspace. To Emélie's trained eyes, these anomalous reflections composed the warp and weft of a parallel reality: one defined by the shape of the underlying space, in the same way a cloth draped atop something else would suggest the form.

Roland produced the hexagonal container he'd shown her back on the rim of Sanctuary One. Inside, encased in Origin, the eye he'd harvested off Aratheus before divorcing him of his head. "When you make it to the platform, use this to validate the connection," he instructed. "Once it's open, tread carefully. The data inside the eye is hardcoded to the first iteration of the Manifold, and given the many revisions the system has undergone since, will likely produce a significant surge."

Emélie looked at the container. "You seem confident this is going to work. I knew Aratheus, and he doesn't strike me as the sort of person worth holding a key to Mars."

"His possession of it was symbolic," Roland said, pressing it into her hands. "The eye originally belonged to Fountainhead."

Fountainhead. A name she'd heard a thousand times over, and still it raked against her subconscious with a hand-quivering fervor. Her mind returned to the dusty room where they'd questioned Aratheus. *Like his father, that one. Always helpful.* "Fountainhead craves control," Emélie said, holding up the maroon box. "What better way to demonstrate that than by turning the Director's own son into a surrogate for Gate access?"

A subtle nod of approval from Roland. "Not all methods of control are equal. There is force." He placed a hand atop the container. "There is a reaction to that force."

Emélie resisted the steady, downward pressure.

"And then, there is the inversion of that force." He made a subtle shift, and she followed, rotating the container in her hands like an upturned hourglass. On the bottom, another marking. A serpent, devouring its own tail in endless recursion. Just like the marking inside her arm and on the container holding Lilith. All variants of something bound together by a common thread: Fountainhead, and what was behind her.

For a moment, Emélie no longer stood at the edge of an open reactor shaft. She was racing through time, reliving every interaction she'd had with Aratheus in reverse order, beginning with the last time she'd seen him. The moment Roland had unburdened Aratheus' head from the rest of his body at the mouth of One. Working backward, she played through every instance until the last one stopped her cold. The first time she'd seen Aratheus was, coincidentally, the first face she could recall.

Kepler's Reef. Stumbling up from the darkness to a Phaethon Tac Team of Class V drones. More darkness. Movement. A transfer. Earth, and then he was there. Not Thursday, who came later, or the Director, who came after. Aratheus. The man who'd, for all intents and purposes, borne her into her current world. She remembered all this and then took the eye, tucked it into her suit, and flexed her cybernetic hand.

A quick scan toward the control room revealed Joab had caught up and waited at the threshold, gun to their six. "Any last words before I throw myself into this pit?" she asked.

"Let go of confidence. Out here, assurances will be your unmaking."

She stepped off the platform.

Falling, eyes closed. Angling herself into a headlong dive. When she opened them, the fall began anew. From the top, an entire mile-wide circle below her. Such was the shape of the barrier that, in trying to reach the mouth of the Gate, one would wander around outside of time. And, if bold and foolish enough to embrace the darkness below, all points led back to the beginning.

She aimed her body for the center, toward the barrier concealing the floating Gate platform. On the first drop, she passed well out of range. She descended once more to darkness and once more emerged at the top of her fall. The second attempt was closer; missed by an arm's length and no more. She tucked her chin and dove, starting over. On the third trip, it was her cybernetic arm that came closest to the invisible platform. The effect of the time dilation field was so great that only a single fingertip made contact. The outcome was catastrophic, sending her into a somersaulting spin wide and off-course.

When she passed back around, her path was far too wide and had no means of course correction. With expanding horror, Emélie passed beside the platform while parallel outcomes played out around her. One version of herself impacted the platform head-on, crumpling into the invisible grating in a spray of blood. Another drifted lazily near the exposed MagLev tracks, left to rot in an inescapable orbit. With each cycle past the platform, she drifted further and further away, and she needed to alter her reality before the viable options collapsed into one of the phantoms swirling around her.

Her other selves.

She couldn't get a fix on the Gate platform, but her parallel selves mapped the space around it. She Jumped to one, then another. Tracing a path between alternate outcomes like a constellation in the night sky.

Through a parallax effect, the hidden Gate platform arrived sooner than she had anticipated. She landed at a sharp angle, sending her skidding clear across it and off the other side. At the last moment, she hooked two fingers into the grated decking. The jolt yanked the air from her lungs with a violent spasm. She held regardless, her lower half dangling into open airspace. Feet up, onto the platform, and she was standing. The hologram quivered and gave way with a chilling revelation: the impacts back at the MagLev hadn't been Jumpers, but pieces of her failed self. "This place isn't a Loop," she muttered, choking back a wave of nausea. "It's a goddamn tomb."

The Gate platform was vacant, except for a single, slender pedestal to one side. From her suit, Emélie produced the cylinder, unsealed it, and set it atop the plinth so the retina pointed downward in a lidless stare. A seam of light pulsed, sweeping across the eye.

Emélie waited. Nothing happened. She adjusted the eye. The light did not return. She looked back toward Gate Control. If there was movement, it was hidden behind the narrow row of observation windows.

The platform beneath her dropped abruptly onto something else, and then she was moving again. Forward. Sliding along a track that assembled itself in front of the platform from some parallel reality. It carved a direct path back to where she'd come, slowing to dock at the corresponding platform jutting from the cleanroom exit.

The lights were dimmed, leaving her to squint inside the mask at the grainy resolution. She crossed back into Gate control, wondering where she'd gone wrong. Wondering why there had been no Gate. In the control room, something moving near the door. She started for it, only to stop when the skin on her neck pricked: She couldn't see him, but she knew who watched her. When she turned around, time opened.

The buttstock of Joab's carbine darkened her visor. With painstaking detail, she saw the serrated plate impact her facemask. The crunch of small lenses ripped at her eardrums, and the screen inside glitched to static. Propelled by the momentum of Joab's blow, the mask crumpled against her face, bruising her cheekbones for resisting and crushing the softer cartilage along her nose.

Flush with adrenaline, Emélie reeled, staggered, then took in an enormous, desperate breath and tore the faceplate away. She Jumped, bypassing Joab's follow-up blow. With only the breath in her lungs sustaining her, Emélie emerged before the central terminal—identical to the one she'd used back at the Conveyor. Joab fired. Emélie Jumped. Reappeared, Jumped, reappeared. She hammered the emergency override button. The room erupted in flashing hazard lights and the brash ring of a klaxon. Another Jump, this time emerging inside the cleanroom. She pulled the door shut to seal herself in, then doubled over. "We had a deal, Joab," she panted. A furtive glance back out to the reactor shaft proved Roland was already aboard the platform, and ahead of him, a swirling mass of dust signified a Gate was imminent.

Joab casually crossed over to where she waited. "A deal? What deal? Deals are documented. Binding. Recorded. What you and I had was an agreement. Something you violated back on Earth after defying a direct order to stand down from that Jump inside the Conveyor." He tapped his muzzle against the sheet of anti-ballistic plate glass between them. "Time to see if you're really as mad as they say."

The platform, out of sight. Hovering above it, the Gate. She could feel it, drawing her. Resonant, tuned to some part of her that sang in the same way Origin gave her sight.

"Even if you could repeat that Jump, you'd be going in empty-handed. No oxygen, no weapons, nothing."

"Not nothing," she replied.

On her tongue, a single tab of Origin.

CHAPTER 46
SANDMAN

It was the dust that Emélie noticed first. Ferrous red, it was not. Nor was it the muted grey she'd left behind on Luna. The hue here, stretched beneath her and fast approaching in the midday haze, was something unexpected and deeply familiar: a pale, earthen tone. Out of the Gate to a hard landing, right back where she started.

Earth: surface.

The ground met her with enough force to forget walking for the foreseeable future. The Origin tab dissolving on her tongue spared her any permanent paralysis, although it did little to soothe the pain of shattered bones and a perforated lung. A wheezing heap, held by the warm, barren ground while breathable atmosphere flooded her unmasked lungs.

It wasn't Mars. It didn't matter. *Get up, Emélie. Get up, and keep moving.* She grasped handfuls of the brown dust and pulled herself over. No feeling past her lower back, and she could see the sole of her left boot. Dust, and blood, and paper. The tabs were potent, and she needed to set her leg before Origin's regen phase ran its course. Nothing to bite down on. She sank her teeth instead into the coarse fabric of her sleeve, saturating it with the pinkish bubbles frothing at the edge of her mouth. In one smooth move, she reached down and corrected her leg. The pain was swift and searing, as was the darkness that followed.

When she came to, the wind was moving, churning the loose dust into a weak cyclone. Visibility was at near-zero, and yet deprived of sight, Emélie was consumed by an overwhelming sense of familiarity. Through the dust, the smudge of something darker ahead, forked and slender, motionless against the waxing storm.

The sticks. She was back in the sticks. Around her, a body-saturating thrum so pure and clear it left every sensation before hollowed out by comparison. She rose, and the space in front of her thinned, then parted. Through the Gate, Mars: red-shimmering and verdant.

She took a step forward, only to find herself facing the front of a vehicle barreling toward her. There was no time to jump aside or even move. Emélie was thrown backward: out of the Gate, out of Mars. Into the storm on Earth. The world spun, righted, spun again, ground and storm exchanging places a few times. Saved once again by the lingering effects of Origin, although just barely.

A car door opened, slammed shut. Footsteps. A pair of red designer loafers. Emélie lifted her eyes, tracing the sleek lines of a silver-grey pantsuit up to the owner: another one of Lilith's Reflections, hair pulled back into a severe bun and a disgusted scowl smeared across her smooth face. "Fucking nonce," she said coolly, glancing out across the Sticks. "You're two minutes ahead of schedule. Where's your transport?"

Emélie said nothing. She couldn't take her eyes off of the Reflection's car. An all-black, angular sedan with, courtesy of her torso, a body-sized dent in the front bumper.

The Reflection snapped her fingers in front of Emélie's face. "Hey. I asked you a question."

"I'm early," Emélie said. "Or you're late."

The Reflection pulled a compact handgun from the waistband of her pantsuit. "Don't get mouthy with me, you little bitch. Did you already forget how this works?" She threw an over-the-shoulder glance toward the Gate. "Everything has to be a game," she muttered. "I fucking told her this wasn't a viable solution." Speaking to Emélie now, she leaned over: "I can count on one hand the number of times these transfers go as planned." She stood back up to her full height, then pulled Emélie up by the arm. "I don't even know why I'm telling you this. You're part of the problem. Listen to me—what's your name?" She let out a heavy sigh and tucked the gun back into her suit. "Never mind. Is there a transport, or not?"

Emélie squinted into the storm. A moment later, they were met by the low whine of dropship engines carrying over the howling wind. "A Four Wing, of all things."

The Reflection threw her a confused glare. "You're a weird one, huh?" she said, slapping the hood of the car. "Let's go. You know what to do."

From the direction of the ship, a cluster of Jumpers ambled toward them. One of them leaned into the car and released the trunk, bumping the car's right turn signal in the process. The remaining Jumpers began emptying bricks of product.

"What about payment?" Emélie asked, hoping, in the half-minute it bought her, that the wind would die down enough to get a clear view of the open Gate.

Another glance from the Reflection, this time, bored amusement.

"First time one of you has ever demanded compensation. What are you, some kind of mutation?"

Emélie stared back and waited. At her neck, the hair pricked up.

The Reflection let out a distorted, warbling sound, and one of the nearby Jumpers vanished midstep, then reemerged between them, a brick of Precursor offered from outstretched arms.

Emélie looked at the bundle. "Would you like me to tell you what comes next?" she asked, kneeling. In the dust, she drew a circle, then, with the edge of her metal hand, excavated a palm-sized basin.

"What do you mean, *what comes next*?" the Reflection demanded. The wind lulled around the last syllable, and Emélie looked up. The view, clear for only a moment. A moment was all she needed.

"Look around, nonce. This isn't quantum mechanics. You get on the ship. You fly the ship to Sanctuary. You use your Directorial pouch privileges to bypass border control. Our lab contact will handle the—" The

Reflection's voice trailed off as another sound, faint as it may be, carried on the wind to meet them.

In Emélie's open hand, one of Goodnight's Origin rounds. She dumped it into the hole and covered it with dust. Planted like a seed destined to bear some strange and future fruit. She wiped her palms against the blood-stained legs of her exposure suit. "You're no doubt accustomed to a certain sort of outcome. Today, however, you're going to see something new." She looked back, meeting the Reflection, who watched her now, eyes wide with real fear. "I'd tell you to run, but that would be of no use."

From the direction of the ship came the *pffft-chick, pffft-chick, pffft-chick* of suppressed weapon fire. One after the other, the row of Jumpers ferrying bricks of Precursor imploded on sight.

The Reflection dove for cover at the far side of the car. From the trunk, she pulled out an automatic weapon. Emélie watched the suppressing fire light up the interior cargo hold. After a week of watching Goodnight and his crew move with careful, disciplined movements, the Reflection's attempts appeared sloppy and haphazard. Gun empty, the Reflection threw it aside and looked to the Gate. Silhouetted by the red light coming from the other side, a new shape.

And across its back, a sword.

Back out came the handgun; more gunfire, this time matched by the sparks of Atropos in Roland's hand, cutting down every round that dared enter his immediate airspace. Finding her efforts in vain, the Reflection bolted for the open desert. An ill fate for an even worse one, running out to meet what waited in the Sticks. With the Reflection gone, Emélie started for the Gate. Leading up to it, a grounded Four Wing, an empty car—driver's side door open and gently rocking in the wind—and at the end, Roland.

"Let's be done with it," she called in a voice that was dry and distant from her usual tone. The Gate flickered, and ahead of her, Roland stepped through.

She closed her eyes and called forth the clear view of it to memory. In place of the Gate, she saw Roland's hand move for his gun with near superhuman speed.

There was the slightest prick at her chest. When she opened her eyes and looked down, instead of lungs, an expanding cloud of dust.

CHAPTER 47
HEART OF DARKNESS

The projectile fired from Roland's weapon was an advanced, purpose-built sabot capable of delivering a microgram Origin payload into the bloodstream of a designated target. The round struck Emélie in her solar plexus and splintered into seven fragments: two of these lodged against her lower rib cage. Four more continued through soft tissue until they exited out of her back. The seventh and final fragment nicked a vertebra, paralyzing her from the lumbar down before embedding itself into the metal plate anchoring her prosthetic arm to her scapula. All of this occurred in the span of a few seconds, in which time Emélie was also clawed back from the open Gate into a folded-up pocket dimension.

She died inside the Manifold, in a clearing of old-growth firs. Her body, like all objects in motion, continued on, hauled along a cosmic, interdimensional anchor defined by the shortest distance between two points. When the Origin had run its course, Emélie awoke on the floor of the control room inside Luna Gimel, still in the Manifold. Once more, back where she'd started.

This time, she didn't get up.

The control room was ablaze in flashing lights and warning screens. Surrounding her lay the disfigured bodies of the Jumpers Roland had dispatched back on Earth, delivered to their final resting place by the same Tether that had brought her. The Loop itself appeared to be on the verge of some catastrophic malfunction. A mechanical arrhythmia replaced the steady hum of the reactor's endless dark matter collisions, and entire sections of the facility plunged into total darkness, ground-quaking shockwaves, or both. Gate Control, already claimed by the rolling brownout, retained some latent visibility by the violet hue of the cleanroom bay, which remained on, powered by some isolated part of the subgrid.

A clatter from the hallway sent her upright. She was awake, which meant there was a good chance some of the Jumpers around her had also survived. Joab's whereabouts were also uncertain; if history was any indicator, he was nearby, and most certainly armed. She groped about in the weak light, searching for something, anything, to wield in self-defense. Her hand found the sharp angle of a gun right as the lights cycled back on.

A handgun: condition, unknown.

The door to the cleanroom groaned, sending Emélie flat to the floor. Thursday's words clanged against her conscious memory: *Always plan on shooting.* Easy enough for him; he was programmed to wield a gun. Emélie would have to improvise. The central terminal was nearby, and she could still recall the sequence for sealing off the blast barrier thanks to her prior encounter at the Conveyor. It hadn't worked out so well last time, but it seemed like a better plan than lying out in the open in a pile of possibly alive Jumpers. She started crawling. More movement nearby. This time, inside the room. Breath stifled, she pressed her head to the floor, feeling the vibration of a heavy, off-balanced shuffle. *Scrape, drag-drag-drag.*

Using as little motion as possible, she gathered what information she could of the weapon in her hand. Top-heavy, not overly dense, and the slide was closed. She'd seen enough gunplay over the last week to assemble a working understanding of what she'd found: a pistol, suppressed, so the weight balance tipped the scale forward. Round in the chamber, but judging by the lightness in the grip, maybe half a magazine—five, six shots remained. She closed her eyes and recalled Goodnight's first offer of the weapon he carried on his chest plate. No suppressor, same as the rest of his team. Only Joab and Roland ran the devices on their pistols, and if Roland was well into Mars, that meant the weapon in her hand belonged to Joab.

She flattened herself alongside the body of a dead Jumper. It gave off a wet, rotting odor that almost made her retch. With bated breath, she gripped the handgun; not the first time she'd felt that handle, but the first time she took it willingly. The shuffling closed in. *Come and get it.*

Her finger brushed the top rail, confirming what memory suggested: the gun was also equipped with a compact optic. Useful for someone like Joab, trained to acquire a target under tactical duress. Emélie didn't trust her ability to aim in the near-darkness, so she waited. Waited until the sound of movement was nearly on top of her. Harder to miss at point-blank range. She counted to four, then rolled over, gun up, finger registering the grooved trigger with a steady, calculated pressure. In the same moment, the control room lights cycled on, revealing a drone standing in her sights.

"Thursday!" Emélie let out a breath and dropped the gun, scrambling to her feet. Both arms, doing their best to wrap around his painfully cold metal waist. Then, composing herself, she backed away, almost bashful at her sudden outburst. In the flickering lights, she took in her old friend: his cloak was ripped and tattered, and his ivory carapace carried long, vertical scratches, as if something had dragged him across the ground or some sharp surface. Behind them, flecks of red paint revealed something else on his chest. Another marking, concealed under his primary coating. One arm hung at his side, disjointed and useless. In his opposite hand, a handgun of his own, loosely clenched between his metal fingers.

"Thursday," Emélie said, repeating his name. "How the hell did you find—"

"Where are the others?" When he spoke, a crack down the middle of his faceplate pulsed with an eerie, red glow.

Emélie blinked, put off by the latent hostility in his tone. "I..." She looked at the gun at her feet. "It's just me."

"And the Seraph?"

Emélie's eyes narrowed. She shook her head.

Thursday watched her bloodstained chest, still caked with dirt from the landing back on Earth. "Suit up," he said, motioning toward the rack of white exposure suits inside the cleanroom. "We'll pass through an uninhabitable atmosphere on the way out."

The lights cycled, plunging the room once more into near-darkness. "I hope you have something more substantial to add, because I didn't need you following me twenty years into the past only to state the obvious."

"Go put the suit on, Doctor."

"Or what?" Emélie asked, putting some distance between them.

"Don't make this more difficult than it needs to be. I'm here to help."

"Put the gun away, Thursday. I've had enough fucking help."

Instead of moving to comply, he lowered his head, muttering incoherently to himself. "Imperative. Boundary threshold met. SALOME in PARDES..."

The lights cycled. When they returned, she was standing inside the cleanroom, one hand reaching for the open door.

Thursday moved with inhuman speed, closing the gap with little regard to where his momentum would go upon reaching his destination. A split-second before impact, Emélie slid the door's manual override into place, sealing herself in. Thursday rammed the glass room with full force, causing a shockwave visible to the naked eye. Back on his feet, he thrust an arm—his only functioning arm—toward a point of light moving across the mainshaft in their direction. "You see that, Doctor? That would be the response team from Loop Containment. Search and rescue isn't part of their operational parameters, which means this facility, and everyone inside it, is scheduled for a full wipe." His face flickered with a crazed, erratic pulsing; evidence that he was beyond protest, and almost beyond understanding.

"Then I shouldn't have to explain to you that the only way out now is through." She dropped her black exposure suit to the gleaming floor and stepped out of it. Thursday had fallen suspiciously silent after her last remark, and when Emélie looked back toward Gate Control, she saw him coming.

Another impact, and still the room resisted. His mangled arm now hung loosely from his damaged shoulder, and more scratches marred the ones already on his torso, condensed around the place where he threw himself into the wall. His remaining hand plunked the glass, handgun still clasped in his fingers. He sank down, muttering to himself again. "You don't make it out if you go that way," he said softly.

His words carried an underlying current of desperation. Something human, almost. She approached the glass, squatting down to face him. "What do you mean, I don't make it out?"

Another light pulse swept Thursday's damaged faceplate. "Doctor..."

"Answer the question, Thursday." Against the glass, Emélie caught the reflection of something behind her; four red eyes, staring out at her in an unblinking stare.

Jumper. And not like any she'd seen before. It burst from the rack, catching her by the scalp on the way down. The sensation of its spongy, too-soft flesh sent her into a frenzy, and with her metal hand, she smashed its pallid face.

The cleanroom shook under another blow from Thursday. He dropped to the ground, arm now severed at the shoulder. In the chaos, a moment of salience: *he was trying to prevent this.* The damage to his frame said he'd done more than see it coming; her future was, for him, one more trip around a small and terrible loop.

If she could reach it, the manual override would admit Thursday. She scrambled across the floor. The Jumper pounced, smacking her back to the ground. One of its eyes held her while the other three tracked Thursday, climbing back to his feet. From inside its tattered hood, the Jumper tipped its head back and emitted a piercing stream of clicks carried along by a modulated wail. The sound drove Emélie's hand to her ears. For Thursday, it struck him with a sort of robotic rigor mortis, and he toppled like a felled tree. He lay there, motionless except for his photoreceptors, which flickered sporadically until the Jumper returned to silence.

Emélie, coherent enough to recognize when an opportunity presented itself, Jumped for the door. Instead of emerging where she'd anticipated, the Jumper snatched her out of the Manifold and threw her toward the opposite wall of the cleanroom. She bounced off it and, with uncanny reflexes, landed upright. On her feet, and ready for more. Again, she Jumped for the door. And again, the Jumper interrupted her, pulling her out of thin air and sending her back the way she'd come.

She needed a new strategy, or Thursday's warning would be her fate. Back on the ship, with Sahira, she'd been able to move other matter, opening the coffin to free herself. No reason she couldn't do the same thing here. When she Jumped the third time, she did so from memory, allowing her to let her gaze linger, a tool for misdirection. The Jumper, evolved as it may be, was unable to rationalize her use of the Manifold. It shot a hand out and pulled down, in place of Emélie, an empty exposure suit. Emélie emerged behind the rack, rammed it into the Jumper, then threw herself atop the pile. A potent dose of matter; too much to make sense of for a Jumper with an Origin-addled brain.

Under the ultraviolet light, Emélie caught the dull sheen of metal. She ducked, narrowly missing the stab of an actuated needle slid from a piece of hardware embedded into the Jumper's forearm. The suit pile, now distributed haphazardly across the floor of the small room, left Emélie nowhere to hide. She looked at the Jumper, standing between herself and the door. *Backwards.*

Unfold, fold.

They swapped places. The Jumper looked down, stunned by the involuntary movement. With a quick turn, Emélie released the door override. From the shadows, the red glow of Thursday's faceplate looked on.

Emélie had hardly released the latch when the Jumper's needle skewered her arm, pinning it to the transparent wall. A current of reality distortion rippled from the wound, moving outward until it wrapped around her fingertips and came back: bicep, shoulder, chest. Heart. In her mouth, the bitter taste of bile, and close behind it, heat. Parts of her, unmade and reformed in the span of an instant, scattered between realities like dust in the wind.

Before her vision went dark, she saw Thursday, head down in a full-on sprint. The Jumper threw its head back and let loose another digital scream.

This time, it was too late.

Thursday barreled through the door. The impact of it blew the door clean off, catching the Jumper broadside before continuing inward in a collapsing sequence: Jumper, wall. Door, Jumper. Thursday, Door.

Thursday staggered backward while remnants of the Jumper—splintered bone and pale skin—dripped from the plate-glass sandwich. With halting, broken movements, he knelt, scooping an unconscious Emélie up with a tenderness uncharacteristic of such a large machine. He held her, waiting to see if the dose of Precursor proved fatal. After a few minutes, her breathing stabilized; saved by her built tolerance for the substance, and its variants. "Doctor," he said, leaning in. "There's a window."

Emélie, drawn to consciousness by the word and the voice delivering it, forced open an eye.

Thursday pointed toward the hatch leading out into the mainshaft. "You made the Jump before, didn't you? If you can do it once, no reason to think you can't do it again."

Her head lolled to the side. Thursday propped her upright, positioning her with a matter-of-fact care, as a nurse-mother would dust off her ward after a tumble. "There was a token," she managed. "An eye... Aratheus, if you can believe it."

"Fountainhead is short an eye," he noted. Without giving her time to ask how he'd unearthed that particular kernel, he stood. "I can't make you go through with it, but if you Jump, I'll make sure there's a Gate waiting for you."

Emélie winced and took over the task of remaining upright on her own. She needed a moment to think. Five minutes ago, Thursday was throwing himself at ballistic glass to prevent her from trying to re-enter Mars. Now, he was offering up the key. Between those two moments, the Jumper, which had nearly killed her. In the glancing light, the gashes on his torso showed a concentration around his injured shoulder. The same shoulder that was already damaged when he'd found her. She traced the timeline backward. Thursday watched her piece it together. In the silence, an understanding unfolded between them. Solemnly, she dressed herself in a fresh exposure suit—white, this time—then returned to her old one. From the pockets, she extracted her last two possessions: the sole remaining tab of Origin and Goodnight's parting gift. The other half of the pair of escape hatches.

Thursday, ever-vigilant, perked up at the sight of the bullet pulled from her black suit. "I finally remembered," he said.

Emélie felt a catch in her throat. She turned, meeting his cracked faceplate with a question in her eyes.

He gestured to the object in her hand. "Goodnights," he said. "That's what we called those."

A smile crossed her lips. She rolled it across her palm, contemplating the branching opportunities it presented. "If you can open a Gate, it also means you won't be able to follow me through. You'll be trapped here, inside the Manifold."

"Ah," Thursday replied, considering her warning. "We all have our part." He patted her gently on the shoulder. "Well, don't worry about me, Doctor. Time is just a construct, and these things have a way of coming back around. I'll catch up to you in a few decades or so." He produced the handgun he'd been carrying when he entered. "I do have one parting request."

In her open palm, an offering: she held up the Origin round. *For you, anything.*

A quick chamber check revealed a loaded gun. Rather than accept the round, he tucked the weapon into his utility belt. "It's been my job to watch you. Watch you struggle. Watch you get knocked down, again and again. Watch you grow, too. Evolve, and outpace all of us. Statistically speaking, your best success lies in doing the exact opposite of what everyone else is telling you to do. I'm no exception to that rule, so I want you to hear me, and hear me well." He turned for the main terminal at the center of the control room. "I want you to stay down, Doctor. Stay down, and let everyone who's stood in your path finally succeed at Luna Gimel. On the threshold of Mars." With an outstretched hand, he tenderly closed her fingers around the Origin round. "And I think it's best you hold onto this for me. I can't see the future, but looking at what's behind us, there's a chance you'll need it yet. Besides, it won't do me any good. I'm all silicon and steel."

"A machine among us, and somehow, the one with the most heart." She looked out at the empty Gate platform. "I put everything into chasing what's at the bottom of this. Only now that I'm here, I'm not so sure anymore. I'm beginning to think that maybe I'm part of the problem."

The facility trembled, as did Emélie's knees. Somewhere a few levels above, the boom of shattering concrete warned of imminent facility collapse.

"For what it's worth, I still believe in you. I don't think it's coincidental that you're the last one standing, and those doubts are likely why you've made it this far." He turned for the door. "If anything, I'd say you were built for this sort of thing."

"Trouble?" Emélie asked.

"One more trip into the Loop," Thursday replied. He gave a half-shrug, courtesy of his missing arm. "It seems like something you'd do. Go out *knowing*. If only so we can do it differently the next time around. They call it the Loop, after all. Surely there's something in that?"

"Surely," Emélie said, if only to console herself. She stowed the Origin round in her sleeve pocket, right beside the last tab from her fix kit. "In case this really is the end, there's something I want you to know before we go."

"You don't owe me anything, Doctor."

Overcome by a potent cocktail of lingering Precursor and grief, Emélie watched him exit the cleanroom. Summoning her strength, she gathered a lungful of air. "In case you haven't noticed, there's a lot of me going around. Find someone who shares my face, and you can be sure that death isn't far behind. Or maybe a man in black with a sword. Yet for all these versions—the ones I've met and the multitudes I never will—I don't envy a single one. They might have retained autonomy, respect. Memory, even. But I'm the only one who has you, and that's something worth holding onto. In this life, and others. And if I had to go back and do it again, I would make that choice every single time, because it would mean I get to be your friend. Now, and for every moment we extend into the future."

He turned around, faceplate raised. From the darkness, four bright eyes looked back at her, and between them, something else watched her. Arm to his chest, he switched on his frame lamps. Covered them, then let them shine once more: a constellation charting the way home.

"Au revoir," she said, trying to find the strength to speak out the last part. When she did, the word dripped from her lips like water, clear and true; the invocation of some long-forgotten prayer. *Sefirot.*

Long after the light was gone, his warmth carried her.

CHAPTER 48
"TETHER"

Phaethon Corp. MAIN build_VX.6.6.09
initializing boot sequence...
running subroutine FOUNTAINHEAD:

> bindquery: update parameter to
> "TETHER"
> encryption protocols intact,
> syntax structures intact
> [03] entries remaining

begin sentiment analysis,
implicit context target, rundisplay:

BEGIN RECORD >>>

I want to make one thing clear: I never intended for things to escalate the way that they did, but as it was, she left me no choice. I've known for some time it wasn't her. Rainer Gamma, at least. But it wasn't until I started watching her that I finally pulled on the common thread in her inconsistencies. Looking at them individually, they're explained away easily enough. Keycard access minutes apart at different ends of Sanctuary.

Multiple jumpsuit changes at random intervals throughout the day, and then sometimes, the same one for days at a time. Dark circles under her eyes that come and go from meeting to meeting. For anyone else, these are merely the signs of another overworked executive. For my daughter, take all that, factor in the Loop, and the only viable answer is multiple versions of the same person.

I have to admit, it suits her. The power—the Directorial seat—was something she chased, and it came with a cost. Marcus got her thinking that her problem-solving was better suited to politicking, but she's more like me than I care to admit, and for her that means honest-to-god work. Not paper-pushing like some sort of glorified DAO proxy. And with this? A new path opens. Hold her position and move around unnoticed. Unnoticed to everyone else, maybe.

I saw her leave for Luna two hours ago in a sleep-deprived stupor. Private drop ship, unregistered. Not unusual for her, especially since she took over the Directorate. What was out of the ordinary was the surveillance bug I set up pinging her card swiping into Sanctuary One Gate control, not even ten minutes later. Sanctuary One isn't anywhere near the moon, and it sure as hell isn't ten minutes from Four.

I went down there intending to get some answers. What I found was a mirror image of my daughter, along with that drone of hers. The one meant to watch everything happening around the Loop. Neither wanted to talk, and to make matters worse, they had a Gate open and seemed dead set on protecting whatever was on the other side. I took matters into my own hands, and when it was all said and done, the drone was missing, and Threadripper had another notch in the handle. For me, another day in the office, except when I dropped the body, some sort of window opened. Lasted for only a few minutes. I could see everything. Our reality, what was on the other side of the Gate. On the inside.

That's when I knew I'd found the missing link. I can't protect what I can't see, and here was my way in. One eye on our reality, and another on the Manifold. And I suspect if there's one Reflection, there's bound to be more. When she gets back from Luna, if that's even her, she'll find my resignation on her desk. She can find herself a new attaché, and I suspect she'll resent me for it, but I'm taking Sefirot.

We're going hunting.

<<< END RECORD

self.detected // boundary separation failure, upgrade BLINDSERAPH status to ECHELON

IF ARROGANT is in ECHELON,
initiate termination protocol
LOCAL_WETWARE:

COMINT detected, updating data structure WAKEFUL-0 to new designation:

WARMOTHER

call LOCAL_WETWARE // asset not found, reinitializing.... asset initialization failed, checking conditions:

FOUNTAINHEAD subroutine active,
SERAPHIM subroutine active,
revise WAKEFUL status to VISIBLE
and engage LABYRINTH.TERRA

"this my hand will rather
the multitudinous seas incarnadine"

maintain asynchronous process,
bringing Loop online...
SUSTAIN remote process

CHAPTER 49
CONFUSION & DIFFUSION

Brinks lumbered into the control room, pausing at the threshold to clear a pile of spent bullet casings with the edge of his boot. When he finished, he stepped through, dropped the body he pulled behind him, and sealed the door.

Thursday sat on a desk by the Loop mainframe, a loaded handgun resting on the console beside him. The cleanroom door was missing, and the gory remains of what looked like a Jumper plastered the far wall. He grabbed the body he'd brought in, boot first, and crossed the room, one step at a time. Nice and careful-like, until he stood shoulder to shoulder with the old drone. In one swift move, Brinks snatched the gun from Thursday's side.

"You've done plenty of stupid things, but drawing down on a Seraph tops the list," Brinks said, ejecting the magazine with a coordinated flick of his wrist. It landed among the flecks of ivory paint littering the area around them. He glanced at the ground, then at Thursday, before unloading the weapon—slide hooked under his armpit, chambered round ejected with a downward motion. He kicked the loaded magazine aside and tossed the empty handgun behind a row of servers. "You're further gone than I thought," he said.

"I wanted to test your operational baseline for friendly fire," Thursday replied, scratching at the coating on his frame. For his efforts, half a red circle, clearly visible at the center of his chest. "It's high, in case you were wondering."

Mechanical arm now gone, Brinks was forced to reach into his duster with his weak arm. He produced a handful of ammunition, which he proceeded to dump onto the desk between them. Some of the cartridges rolled off the edge and bounced across the floor. Brinks ignored them and began feeding rounds into the speed loaders lining either side of his gun belt. Muscle memory. One after the other. "How many tries until you got it right?" he asked.

Thursday stopped what he was doing and looked up. His tinted faceplate was raised, and the socket in the center of his head no longer contained Brinks' donor eye. "It wasn't good. I made up for it, though."

Brinks kept loading. *Click click click.* "You never make up for it. You pull one thread, thinking it will fix something. Nobody tells you that's the beginning of the end." Speedloaders full and ready for the next firefight, he strolled over to the cleanroom to get a look at the dead Jumper. "Wraith," he said, nudging it with the toe of his boot. "Interesting." He took stock of the torn suits and the open hatch leading out to the Gate platform. "I take it this is your handiwork, too?"

Thursday stared at the body Brinks had dropped on the floor beside him. "Joab," he observed in his flat, matter-of-fact tone. "What about his team?"

"No, no. No team," Brinks muttered, shaking his head. "Not anymore. Something ripped through 'em. Normally, I'd say it was a pair of Seekers, but the cuts were too clean." He leaned in, running his fingers over a small crack near the entrance. A bullet would have left a radial pattern. This marking branched from the point of impact in fine lines reminiscent of lightning. Lightning came with rain, and rain grew trees. He hadn't seen any of that since Mars. *You always were a sentimental one.* "Fuck you, Marcus," he muttered. "Hasn't even been a day, and you're already haunting me." He looked at Thursday waiting out in the control room and gave a disapproving wag of his head. "One job, drone. You had one job."

"Did you get what you wanted out of the Director?" Thursday asked.

"Which half?"

Thursday's photoreceptors flickered.

"This is exactly why I never liked working with drones," Brinks said, rejoining Thursday. "You give them an ounce of self-awareness, and they see it as license for taking the moral high—"

Movement behind them interrupted him mid-sentence. They turned. Joab stood opposite them with Thursday's empty handgun in one hand. Before either of them could intervene, he slipped an Origin round into the open chamber, dropped the slide release, and pressed the barrel to his chest.

Gone in a puff of dust.

"Goddamnit," Brinks shouted, kicking the gun when it hit the floor.

"For what it's worth, I doubt he was the talking sort."

"No matter," Brinks grunted, pulling out his cigarette case. He assessed the heap of Jumper bodies nearby. "I'll pick him up when he comes back."

"Sloppy," Thursday observed, eyeing the loose bullets Brinks had dropped while arming himself. "You're losing your edge." He glanced out the bank of observation windows. "It's just you and me now."

Brinks took out a cigarette. "Just you," he said, hanging the cigarette from the corner of his mouth so he could stow the case. His hand was steady, but his fingers twitched ever-so-slightly. "I want my eye back."

Thursday returned to scraping the ivory-colored paint off his chest. Half a circle, still left to uncover. "It's no longer of value."

Brinks drew Threadripper and placed it on the desk. "I'll decide what's valuable." He started looking for his lighter. "I've been doing this for a long time, and it always ends the same way. I know you don't want to hear that. I know you're probably thinking that this time it's different, on account of where we are and all. The thing is, there's no shortage of fresh fools who think they've stumbled on something original, and around we go. One more trip through the Loop. I wanted to destroy this place before it even came online. Nobody listened to me then, and now we pay that debt to the past by repeating the same damn mistakes over and over again. I don't expect you'll be on board, just don't be the one to stand in my way, either." His hand flashed as Joab appeared, midair and midway between them. Threadripper punched a hand-sized hole into his center mass and spread part of him across the computer behind them.

Brinks jammed the hand cannon back into its holster and lit his cigarette.

After a long moment, Thursday held his hand out, palm open. In it, Brinks' eye, a shard of glass protruding from the crimson cornea. "There's already one Seraph tearing through the Manifold. We don't need to make it two."

"You sent her through?" Brinks asked, stooping over to gather up the bundle of data lines Thursday had used to patch into Luna Gimel's mainframe.

"I don't know what you were expecting. I don't work for you. I help the Doc–"

"Stop!" Brinks slammed his fist against the desk, cable in hand. Smoke wreathed his head, and he clenched the bundle of fiber optic threads with all the regret he could muster. *Goddamn drone, always getting in the way.* He turned his face up to the ceiling, then tossed the hardline over a run of coolant pipes, feeding it slack until the plug end dropped down the other side. "You aren't supposed to help her. You protect her. Keep her safe, especially from herself. Most of all, from that." The tobacco calmed him down, and he continued. "You see that?" He pointed toward the flattened Jumper inside the cleanroom, wisps of smoke drifting from the cigarette pinched between his calloused fingers. "That's a Wraith. One of Lilith's hunters. They're augmented for operation beyond the margins of the Manifold. They can move through time as you or I would walk around a room."

Thursday's photoreceptors flickered. "I... I could understand it," he said.

As he smoked, Brinks threaded one end of the cable back onto itself. "That's because it wasn't here for your ward. Wraiths hunt Watchers. It came for you."

Thursday's head sagged slightly at this revelation.

Brinks almost felt sorry for him. *Almost.* "Mars is a lie. What you remember is a simulation. A sealed instance of the Manifold designed to contain Eden. Once you're in, there's no coming back. Not from that place."

Thursday threw himself at Brinks.

Brinks saw him coming and sidestepped him, looping the cable around Thursday's neck as he charged past. He pulled the other end tight, stringing the drone up until he hung, feet off the floor.

"Why would you... SYNTAX STRUCTURES DETACHED," Thursday blurted, wracked with computational overwhelm. "How. Come. Send..I–when... contain KEY.." His face went dark; a hard reboot.

"You did this to yourself. I told you to protect her, not clear the path." He tied the cable off onto a nearby column. Thursday hung there like a dead man, arm to his side, no fight left in him. Brinks motioned toward the reactor. "Now, you can open that Gate for me so I can go retrieve your doctor, or we let them close this place and leave her trapped there, outside of time and forever out of reach."

When Thursday spoke again, his tone had resumed its sarcastic, clinical tenor. "You need me. A man with your skillset could no doubt force a Gate by hotwiring me into the mainframe, but good luck reaching the platform in one piece. The moment a link is made with Mars, Loop Containment will bombard the platform."

Brinks rubbed his chin. Thursday had a point: he couldn't be two places at once. That, and Thursday was also the one who'd originally written the reaction protocols, so there was no sense in arguing with him. He tugged the data line free, dropping Thursday to the ground. "Arm yourself, then," Brinks said. "And if you decide to double-cross me, make it quick. I haven't got time for last words."

"Fast is smooth and smooth is fast," Thursday said.

"Hrpmh. I see the combat tactical package left some lingering behaviors."

"You know something about that?" Thursday asked, pushing one of the Tethered Jumper bodies off his shotgun case, which he'd had the foresight to bring along and stash near the door on his way in.

"Your first purpose was as a war machine."

"First, or last," Thursday intoned. He took his shotgun out and cycled the action. "Maybe it's not something I was meant to lose, but the thing I was meant to find? Have you ever stopped and wondered if every choice you made was leading you toward one moment? Odd how that works. There's no way of ever being certain which moment, so you have to keep on living and hope you don't miss it."

"You're telling me your entire purpose in life is to hold the door for the same person threatening to dismantle you? You're overthinking it."

"Fundamentally. I don't have a body like you. I can't experience feelings. Only the rough approximation of them. So in place of that, I observe. Watch for patterns, infer outcomes."

Brinks paused, oddly unsettled by the implication of Thursday's words. "What pattern are you referring to, specifically?"

"It's not important. Forget I mentioned it."

Brinks pulled Threadripper from its holster. "On principle, I tend not to forget. Especially when it's on demand."

"And I'm beginning to wonder when you'll stop warning me about what you will do and just do it. And the only reason I can come up with is that you're worried I'm right."

Brinks scoffed. "I find that hard to bel–"

"If she's like all the other Reflections, why didn't you put her down when you had the chance?"

Brinks could feel all four eyes on him now. Those damn eyes.

"I saw you, back on Earth. You detonated that EMP at the drop site, took me out of the picture. And later on, you told me your job was to put Reflections into the ground. So if your job is to kill them, and nothing, not even me, stood in your way, why did you let her live?" Thursday shook his head. "I think she reminds you of someone, and it scares you to admit it."

The sound of machinery moving outside the door sent them both behind cover.

"You're going to want to stand clear of the entry vestibule," Thursday warned, freeing himself from the cable around his neck.

"They'll breach with Class Fives," Brinks added, checking in the direction of the Gate platform. "How much time do you need?"

"No time at all," Thursday said. He removed his chest panel, revealing a port behind the red circle.

"If it's all the same, I think I'll stick around to deal with the breaching team," Brinks said, peeking over the console for a view of the door. "A little contingency never hurt anyone, and it's been some time since I had a proper gunfight."

"I'm not concerned about the tac team. It's what comes after them I'd worry about."

"The Seraph is going to tear you to pieces," Brinks agreed.

"You don't need to tell me. This is my Loop, after all." He slung the shotgun for later and gathered up Joab's abandoned handgun and the magazine. "Better someone besides you. At least I know whoever ends me won't spend the next few decades feeling bad about it afterward."

Despite the thundering footfalls coming from the hall, Brinks felt a smile stretch across his face. He couldn't remember the last time he'd done that, let alone shown it. It felt reminiscent of a Martian daybreak: the faintest warmth, and the promise of more. Only there would be no sun today.

Brinks gestured toward the double doors, and on his lead, they moved, taking up positions on either side. From the outside, something heavy clunked against the doors. He stamped out his cigarette. "Took them long enough. Response time is shit, though. I never would have–"

A hole appeared, followed immediately by a hailstorm of bullet fire. Chips of concrete exploded off the floor around them as the assault team walked their rounds to target: the Loop mainframe terminal, which, linked to Thursday, ran a code sequence mimicking human input. The pair waited until the entire team was inside, then stepped forward and opened fire.

Guns blazing, they made quick work.

When the smoke cleared, the floor was strewn with more bodies. Added to the Jumpers already on the floor were now a jumbled heap of drones. Brinks dumped the spent rounds from his gun and reloaded. Something of a task with only one arm, but not anything he hadn't practiced a hundred times. "Something's off," he said, filling Threadripper's cylinder with one of the speedloaders from his belt. "Loop

Containment is stocked with hunter-killers, and I've never seen a contingent of Class Fives go down so fast in my life."

Instead of stocking his own gun, Thursday stood silently, looking at the metal bodies piled around them with a posture that made Brinks glad he was done reloading. "I've been thinking a lot lately about what death will feel like," Thursday said. "It doesn't make any sense. I wasn't programmed for fear."

"For what it's worth, this wasn't how I thought it would end for you."

"What did you have in mind?"

Brinks didn't respond.

"I see," Thursday replied, eyeing Threadripper. "We all have our part, I suppose."

"She used to say that," Brinks said, a strange look on his hollow face. "She changed you, you know. Gave you something human. More than I ever did, that's for damn sure."

Thursday touched his exposed chest cavity, which held an array of integrated microprocessors set in neat, vertical rows. About the place where a heart would have been, wedged between the slender fins of a heat sink, was a scrap of paper. Half an old photo: himself, standing on Mars. Beside him, a woman who looked identical to Emélie, beaming. And the red ring of the Loop behind them, radiant against the pink horizon. "I don't know what warmth feels like, or if this is Mars, or if this was even us. It doesn't matter. Drones don't die, they just end, and I always hoped it would be something like this. A night softly falling, inevitable and expected. A moment to linger and feel the daylight while you still have it." His eyes dimmed, and he looked back up at Brinks. "That would be a nice end."

Brinks held out a hand, and the drone obliged. He ran his rough fingers across the surface, reading the texture of the paper as if it were braille, until he caught the single handwritten word etched along the bottom: *Thursday*. "You know, they spent a billion dollars trying to find a way to make you more human. And somehow, she accomplished that without even trying."

"She's good at that," Thursday agreed.

"I remember this day. The day the Mars Loop—Ma'adim Dalet—came online." He returned the photo. "That smile wasn't because of the Loop, though. She was smiling because of you. She had a name for you. It wasn't one you were given, Sefirot, or the one you gave yourself." He leaned against the desk and thumbed open his cigarette case. Five left. He could get the job done with four. He took one out and lit it up. "I'd tell you what it was, only..." He suspected the layline of the memory, and it was a place he didn't want to go. Better to leave it in the past, a buried memory, and move on.

"Well, it would seem I'm not the only one who forgot my name," Thursday said. He lifted his arm, revealing a small recess beneath his wrist that held a needle affixed to a vial of Origin. In halted, rough scratches, he inked a string of symbols across the top of the photo. When it was dry, and the needle was once again stowed, he folded it in half, then tucked it into the welt pocket of Brinks' duster. "In case you ever find yourself adrift, a Tether. To find your way home."

"I don't have a home," Brinks said, a crown of blue smoke hanging around his head.

Thursday looked around. "I heard a rumor the red place was coming under new management. Seems like somewhere a man like you could finally settle down." He nudged one of the bullet-ridden drones at his feet. "These drones are decoys," he added, confirming what Brinks suspected. Gun inverted, he started pumping shotgun shells into the bottom. "Whoever is running this place seems to think us a couple of one-armed fools. That, or they're testing us. Assessing our capabilities before the real strike."

"That would be Lilith," Brinks observed. "And all of those statements are true."

Thursday paused to consider this information before continuing. "I've initiated the linkage with Mars," he said, pointing to the open mainshaft. "Wait at the cleanroom hatch. Expect visitors." The bridge leading out to the Gate platform had, on Thursday's input, begun assembling itself. As expected, it wasn't the only thing moving their way. Across the gap, Jumpers swarmed the track, crawling along the metal rails ahead of the slowly moving platform.

Brinks moved for the hatch, gun raised. Marking his targets: Nine rounds, eight Jumpers. He lowered it, biding his time. Thursday, hard-line linked to the mainframe, held his ground at the control room. "Say, Thursday," Brinks called, eye fixed on the encroaching platform. "I seem to have misplaced my arm. If, in your future travels, you happen to come across a suitable replacement, do me a favor and grab it? They don't make them like they used to."

From behind the mainframe terminal, a drone arm flew through the air. It passed through the open door to the cleanroom and hit the ground behind Brinks with a metallic thump. "Next best thing to haunting you," Thursday called back. "Pull the trigger and think of me."

Brinks felt another smile crack his weathered face. Without delay, he detached the severed stump of his old red prosthesis and clamped Thursday's arm into his shoulder plate. A direct fit: his original arm was, after all, Class Two hardware. He flexed the new hand, letting the embedded drivers link up with the cybernetic implant housed inside his glass eye. When it finished, he raised Threadripper and fan-fired all nine rounds.

Eight Jumpers toppled into eldritch darkness. The last round sparked off the rail, ricocheted upward, and pierced a ninth Jumper right between the eyes the moment it appeared. Strewn with bodies, the platform docked at the cleanroom hatch with a gritty screech. "Boarding!" he shouted, clocking the drone's position at the double doors.

Down the hall, more movement.

His boots had barely registered the platform, and it was moving again. Crawling its way out to the Gate.

Thursday's voice scratched from an embedded transmitter inside Brinks' new arm. "Alright, partner. We only got one shot at this, so let's make it count."

"I see," Brinks replied. "Now I'll never hear the end of it."

A moment of silence, and the lights in the control room flickered with a surge of power. "We're getting pinched," Thursday explained. "Calling up the Gate has forced Lilith to play her hand. You can't see it due to the temporal shroud, but there's a pair of droneships just beyond it. You may be good with a gun, but this is more than any one person, Seraph or otherwise, can handle. If I don't give them a reason to target the control room, you'll never make it through."

"A better question might be why they haven't started the bombardment already."

"It's amazing what you can find just sitting around. I came across an old subroutine that allowed me to modify the shroud's topology so it encloses you. The Gate linkage is established, but I've held off activating it until you're close enough to pass through. I'll handle things here. You keep that gun of yours ready for anything waiting on the other side. If Lilith is, as you say, behind these changes, you'll have your own set of problems to deal with once you're through."

The whole facility shuddered, and for a moment, the platform Brinks was on jolted, then stopped. He checked Gate Control. The windows, now obscured by some sort of opaque white substance. "What the hell are you doing in there!?" he shouted.

Another long pause. The platform resumed its forward motion. "Sorry for the delay," Thursday's voice chirped. "I overclocked the server arrays and spun up a load balance to cycle processing between them."

It took Brinks a moment to realize what Thursday had done. When he did, he felt his knees begin to fail. *Stay up, you old fool. Stay up.* By creating the computational equivalent of pressing the gas and brakes simultaneously, Thursday had generated enough heat to trigger the emergency suppression systems, dousing everything in fire-retardant foam. The Class Five drones used by Loop Containment were highly sophisticated combat machines with delicate, finely-tuned sensor packages. Thursday, long outdated, had only the robust, simple systems of a much older unit. The slippery, dense foam effectively leveled the playing field, offering some concealment while introducing an environmental variable that would buy him the slightest tactical edge. Enough time for Brinks to clear the Gate, and no more.

When Brinks was within leaping distance of the latent Gate, a burst of brilliant light erupted at his back. To either side of him, the pair of droneships surged forward, moving like shadows in the deep. Converging on the open hatch where Thursday, backlit and shotgun in hand—an easy target—emptied his weapon into the actual team of Class Vs slipping and sliding in the dense foam. When they went down, he charged the doors, drawing the response teams as far from the pending Gate that the cable linking him to the Loop mainframe would allow. When he was out of sight, the entire facility shuddered, and the ships opened fire.

Brinks paused at the edge of the Gate. Four hundred pounds of silicon and steel had brought him to this. He raised a hand to his face so Thursday could hear: "So long, partner."

The Gate swallowed him whole.

In the control room, tracer fire washed crimson against the last yellow-orange candles of Thursday's shotgun. His face pulsed in sunset glow; like the sun plunging to shadows, he pulled the trigger until there was nothing left to pull.

War Mother, to the end.

CHAPTER 50
APHELION

Falling. Emélie was falling. Not like the last time. Not a moment of weightlessness between a stumble and the ground. This was atmospheric. Suborbital. Too high. She came out too high.

Jump. Where? The thin air buffeted her face, stinging her eyes to tears and blurring any hope of an anchor. She could feel the loose fabric of her exposure suit snapping and cracking in the wind. She couldn't Jump to a sound. *Focus.* She needed a glint, an edge, anything she could pull herself toward. Through the veil of clouds, a great well of pink sky stretched around her. *There, ground.* Dark, and in motion. *Wrong.* Why would the ground move unless... water. More water than she'd ever seen. A dark sea, bounding red. Mars, or some well-measured approximation of it. She couldn't be sure which. A circle. *A ring? Crater*, there was a crater below her, the upper rim protruding above the water's surface. Water outside of it, and darker water inside. That was her target. Closer, closer, until she could make out thousands of objects standing in concentric rings radiating from the crater's center. And in all that, nothing with enough resolution for a Jump.

Origin. She had tabs—no, a single tab—in her pocket. She might need it later. If she didn't survive the impact, there wouldn't be a later. Even Origin had its limits. What about the water? She ran the numbers, testing sand as the impact substrate. Neither were survivable. Origin it was.

One more trip.

Emélie tore her gloves off and let them go. Next, the pull tab on her exposure suit, which she fumbled, fingers stiff and windburned. *Use your other arm. The steady arm.* Bless the hardware and its maker. Tab in hand, she pressed it to her lips and counted down from seven. The allotted seconds necessary at terminal velocity to ensure the regeneration phase hit at the same moment she did. A long shot, only she'd done it before. A dose of Origin, a dose of water. Lilith's preferred mode of inquiry. Drug the body, peel back the mind. Harvest.

Focus. She cupped her hand, dosing herself when her count hit zero. The ground gained detail: boulders split down the center, scrubby brush at the rim, ripples in red sand. Maybe she could still Jump?

Too late now. Too late the moment she followed Joab onto that fucking ship, but you know what? *Tough luck, bitch. If the drugs don't kill you, the water will.*

If only Lilith could see me now.

Was there life after death? Baptism through water, and she was born again. Died again. And between those two planes, an embrace: into the Manifold, as casually as slipping loose her body to take up residence in the shadow beneath it.

Fold, unfold.

Hard to breathe with all that water. A gasp, and her lungs flooded. This time, Roland wasn't around to haul her back to the shores of the living. Adrift, light and heavy, awake. Aware that, at any moment, she'd begin violently convulsing from the intrusion of h2o. Shaking. A hand plunged into view, grasping her by the collar. A hand, familiar but unplaceable in her failing mind, pulled her roughly upward. Across her back, a blow: she expelled water, carried on a searing scream.

Darkness. Movement. Residual water, warmed by her lungs, dribbled from her mouth. No feeling in her legs. Only the sound of her boots rattling in the loose gravel behind her. The hand grasping her by the collar held steady, drawing her up. Up, and out of the water, and back down. Sand, warm and gritty against her cheek. Labored breathing: her own and another's. Gradually, the feeling returned to her lower extremities, then her back. She flexed her hands. Opened an eye to take in the arm gripping her: ivoried and skeletal. A drone arm. Thursday's arm, encased in the sleeve of a heavy jacket, collar up. From under the shade of a wide-brimmed, the arm's owner abruptly looked down, peering back at her with a single glowing eye.

Hammer-fisted, she swung. A man's voice boomed, ricocheting off the rock floor. He doubled over, releasing her to grab his leg. Emélie, ever the opportunist, took another blow when she found it: black hand, red eye.

The ground shook when he fell, and Emélie was already moving. Fast and low, head down, eyes forward. Like Roland. Legs pumping, delirious, scrambling through sandy loam. Jump. In and Out. Weaving across realities until she stumbled somewhere in a field of boulders. A white stain on the rusted crater ring. All the run she had left in her wouldn't do a bit of good if she didn't ditch the suit.

Breathless, she stripped off the outer cleanroom suit, discarding the dense white material so that only the black thermal underlayer remained. Working in a low crouch among a patch of sparse scrub, she recovered her Skipjack, then hid what remained of the suit under a pile of red shale. Finding her remaining garment pocketless, she hitched up the sleeve past her cybernetic arm and stowed the Skipjack behind the hidden access plate.

She heard the man coming before she saw him. Walking directly toward her with the firm, steady gait of someone wholly unbothered by any attempts at escape. Without moving from where she crouched, she gathered up a fistful of stones. Eyes trained toward the source—hard-soles crunching against sand, and the occasional muffled footfall when he stepped among the carpet lichen. Once the sounds of approach placed him within throwing distance, Emélie sprang to her feet, launching the stones toward his head. Some of them hit their mark, only to bounce harmlessly off his leathery skin. Before she Jumped, it was the sight of those same stones falling to the ground that stopped her cold. She stood at the base of the crater on a slight incline, and as the rocks rattled to the ground, they rolled toward her. Uphill.

Emélie became aware of an immense weight behind her. A dense current pulling everything into itself. She resisted the sensation to turn toward this new threat, instead standing her ground against her pursuer. Watching everything else around her yield: scrub brush bowed, the heat on her face shifted to a chill, and even the man's shadow appeared disfigured, bent now so he walked into it.

The man reached for his gun.

Emélie felt the *whomp* of the muzzle, followed by ringing as the round passed near her cheek in a supersonic caress. She staggered forward, then abruptly stopped. A mass of dust had begun to form at the rim of the crater. A shape bound in shadow and violence. Slowly, it condensed: more bone than flesh, and more metal than bone, but unmistakable nonetheless. A crude mirror of the hybrid man-machine behind her. Below the brim of its tattered hat was the vacant socket of one eye and the other, a glowing red point of light. Both of its hands were clenched to its belly, watching as a bloom of dust opened in the hollow cavity where the bullet had impacted.

The man following her moved past, still firing. The thing writhed and twisted into a contorted circle, fighting the pull back from wherever it had come. The man stopped directly over the body, his gun trained on the shape as it clawed for the weapon but, coming up short, doubled over. The bullets feeding it opened up, disintegrating it with a concussive blast.

He opened his wheelgun, swinging the cylinder aside. Muzzle up, the spent casings littered the ground, husks from a violent harvest. "Best keep moving," the man said in his gravelly, beaten-down drawl. "It'll be back before long enough."

Emélie knelt down, examining the pattern left in the dust. "What does it want?" she asked.

"Want?" He shook his head and jammed a fistful of fresh bullets into his gun. "All things born of the Manifold are bound to a single purpose." He swung the cylinder back in place. "To unmake."

"I've seen it before," she said, standing. She took a moment to size up the man in front of her. He had the haggard, worn-out look of an old Jumper, and enough hardware to count for half a drone. One eye was covered by a dull metal plate, and the other, what remained of a cybernetic implant. Smashed, courtesy of her own borrowed arm. The red markings peeking from behind the sleeve of his duster didn't go unnoticed, either.

"Revenant," he said bluntly. "A little bit of chaos. The consequence of an earlier action. Call it what you want." He holstered his gun. "You aren't the only one with a Reflection."

On hearing this, Emélie leaned over, hands to her knees. A bead of sweat trickled down the bridge of her nose and fell, leaving a miniature, sanguineous crater at her feet. "Are you planning on shooting me too?" she asked, meeting his blind face.

The man removed his hat, creased the brim. Turned out toward the open water where they'd come. "I don't know what you were expecting to find out here, but this?" Hat in hand, he stretched out his arm. "This here is it."

"So I've heard." Emélie put a step of distance between them. Another, and another after that. Despite his lack of eyesight, the man didn't seem to have any trouble tracking her movement. "What happens when you run out of bullets?" she asked, pausing to look down at his gun.

"We go back to what we were doing before." He put his hat back on and walked a few paces up the slope. "Take it from someone who's spent a lifetime looking over his shoulder. You don't want to go down this path."

Emélie toed the rusty sand, testing it. It yielded at the slightest pressure. "Seems like we're already well past that. What's done is done. The way forward now is through."

The man didn't say anything, although Emélie caught the slightest twitch of his hand; the calm before a storm. "Nowhere to run, though," he said. Beyond him, the crater's rim, razor sharp against the gradient sky.

"Who said anything about running?" She came out of the Jump halfway between him and the ridgeline. She could have easily hit the rim, but chose a point closer—a slab of undisturbed crust about twenty paces above where they stood. Boots down hard, she pivoted and was gone again. From the safety of the rim, she watched the result of her efforts: a small landslide clearing the swath where she'd come. In the billowing dust, a deep breath and a moment's relief. Short-lived, as the next breath she pulled came through as a gasp. Although breathable, the air here was lean, leaving her with a tinge of panic at the cost of her exertion. Her tongue, thick with dehydration, carried the bitter, mineral taste of the waterbody, although she opted not to spit for fear of losing even one more drop.

The ground inside the crater sloped gently, where, at the center, another body of water lay inside the basin, dark as the night sky. Emélie began her descent, moving at a pace that would have made Joab proud. On the exterior face, the atmospheric sounds of water crashing against the rocky shore and the steady rush of wind diminished the noise of her own movement. Here, inside the crater, each footfall seemed to echo across the space and come back. When she stopped moving to see if the man was in pursuit, she was met by an unbearable silence. Ringing in her ears, or perhaps it was something closer to a...

Ping.

A ripple of cold fear ran down her spine, and the overwhelming sound of nothing metastasized into a single, paralyzing tone.

Ping... ping... ping...

Emélie tore at her clothing, searching for the source. Right arm, cybernetic arm. Sleeve past her elbow, the sound grew louder. She dropped to her knees, extracting the Skipjack, which pulsed faintly and rang clear.

PING—PING—PING—PING.

Her world shrank to the radius of the object in her hand.

No need to turn around to know the gunman was at her back. He stopped beside her, close enough that she could see the woodgrain of his gun handle. "I'm sure you've got questions," he said, hooking a metal thumb into his gun belt. His damaged eye faintly pulsed in time with the Skipjack. "I can't answer them if you keep running like this, though."

Emélie flung the Skip at him; unlike the stones, the force of it seemed to stagger him. "I know you've been following me," she spat. "Following me since the storm back on Earth."

The man leaned over and carefully gathered up the Skip, still dormant in the failing light. "I've been following you a lot longer than that," he said, carefully dusting off the black lens. "That wasn't me, though. Surely you understand what it's like being mistaken for someone else?"

Much like the terrain around her, she found his question difficult to navigate. The ground was covered in circular objects spaced equidistant from one another in concentric rings. Heights ranged from tripping hazard to stubby poles resembling the dead trees she'd encountered back in the Sticks, a similarity that confirmed the crater's basin had, at some point, been intentionally forested. Stranger still was the presence of rotting trees lying strewn among the regularly spaced stumps, suggesting that, rather than being harvested, at least some of the trees in the basin had been razed. Standing here, among the stumps, everything looked the same, and she wasn't sure which direction to Jump in order to move toward the bottom. Part of her wondered if what she'd seen when she first exited the Manifold was even real. The man beside her seemed real enough, as did the gun at his side. And while she'd gained confidence in her ability to teleport at will, she wasn't sure out-Jumping a bullet was a gamble she was willing to take. Yet. "I'm listening," she finally said. "And you better not say I'm just another one of Lilith's Reflections. I know they can't Jump. Not like me."

"Nobody can Jump like you," the man replied. After a slight hesitation, he pocketed the Skip. "Then again, if you really understood that, you'd have never set foot in this place to begin with."

Emélie listened to him speak and watched the dying light render the ground in harsh, angular shadows. A sunset—perhaps the first she'd ever seen—revealed an underlying organization to the stumps she hadn't noticed at first. She knelt down, head tilted so her ear was nearly to the ground. The low angle revealed each stump was planted atop a small, earthen mound slightly elevated from the surrounding ground. One stump per mound, planted at regular intervals, created a network of troughs and ridges. Irrigation, possibly. Emélie didn't know anything about trees aside from Thursday's passing comments or her own direct observations from inside the Manifold, which were useful but limited to only the last few days.

Between the stump mounds, the reddish loam was speckled with all manner of lichen. Muted tones that, when caught by the fast fading light, glowed in brilliant color. No longer rushed by Joab's frenetic pace, and uninterested by this stranger's demands they return to the water, she proceeded to catalog them privately, if only to confirm what she'd noticed at first glance. Stony blue-grey and chalky, speckled white. Dirty green, sandy green, pale yellow, soft blush. Red, like old blood, and others, new rust. All of these faded in comparison to a corrosive, liquid green lichen contained to a small, ovoid depression near her foot. Closer inspection betrayed the telltale creases of a bootprint. Fingertips of her bare hand pressing against the spongy growth, Emélie traced each serrated ridge, reading them like lines of embedded code. A left foot, deeper where the toes pushed off the soft ground. Her eyes drifted right, then up. More neon lichen filled a second track. Right foot. Directly above it, a third: this time, a compact, bowl-shaped divot. Carefully, Emélie set her boots into either footprint, then dropped to one knee, filling the third. When she planted her left hand down to support herself, she met the fourth, fingers splayed wide.

An exact match.

The man's ragged form loomed above her.

"Data remanence," she said, shrugging off his silent and palpable judgment. He wasn't the first; he wouldn't be the last. "Eden is learning. That's not all, though." She sat up, leaning back on her heels for a better look ahead. "She's also... remembering."

From his jacket, the man produced a thin metal rectangle, dented from use and polished to a silver matte. "You don't know the first thing about Eden."

Emélie let her gaze follow the tracks until they disappeared from view farther down into the basin. An erratic trail spiraling toward the inevitable center. "And you do?" she asked, meeting his blind face.

Case open, he removed a tightly rolled paper tube. Paper, of all things. He seemed to consider the remaining quantity—three, by her count—then hung the one in his hand from the corner of his mouth and returned the case to his breast pocket. "Does the name Fountainhead mean anything to you?"

"Should it?" she asked.

The man pressed his lips together, causing the paper cylinder between them to rise slightly. He grunted and took out another device, which, when touched to the end of the paper, made it come to life with delicate wisps of near-white smoke and a sweet, earthy smell that Emélie rather liked. "I can't say that I blame you, keeping what you know close to the chest. I'm inclined to a similar disposition myself." He pinched the paper tube between his fingers and offered it to her.

Curiosity overwhelmed her caution, and she accepted. The smoke burned and left her dizzy. Origin, or the other—Precursor, mixed into the plant in some way. Or maybe Origin was the plant. She didn't know how it was made, only that it came from, well. She looked around. Came from here.

"You were right not to trust Phaethon," he said, taking back his smoke. "They can't deliver."

"And I take it this is the part where you tell me you can?" she replied, eyes watering.

He spat into the dust, then looked almost instantly regretful of it. "Beg pardon," he said. "I haven't kept much company of late."

Or ever, Emélie wanted to say. She held her tongue.

"I'm afraid I can't help you much either. Only Fountainhead can give you what you're after."

"And what might that be?"

One last pull on his smoke, and he stubbed it out on the back of Thursday's old arm. "The truth, and what's behind it." He opened his hand, and there was her Skipjack again.

"So that's it?" Emélie asked. She inhaled, savoring the heavy scent of brush carried on the cooling air. "I turn back now and follow you. The man wearing my best friend's arm without explanation. The same person who followed me into a storm on Earth. The man who's been using my Skipjack to track me across realities. You? Gunslinger, Origin-smoker, Reflection killer."

He seemed to wince at the last one.

Emélie walked past him to the spot she'd identified. A point triangulated by the vivid tracks at her feet. A larger, body-sized indentation in the low spot between a pair of stumps. It wasn't the shape that drew her, but something else beside it. The color stood out from the red, but it was the texture more than anything that drew her eye; no natural form was capable of such flawless symmetry. There was an object there, half-buried and most certainly man-made.

Knees to the ground, she scooped away handfuls of sandy soil until, with a hearty tug, she extracted a tan helmet from its shallow grave. The visor was opaque. Completely opaque. Designed to blind the wearer from seeing out. She didn't need to raise it to know the glass beneath was cracked down the middle. She lifted it regardless, compelled by the same drive that had led her all the way here to begin with. The helmet, open, confirmed what she'd suspected the instant she emerged from the Manifold a few hundred feet above ground.

She'd been here before, and the first time, it was with Lilith in tow.

A rustling sound beside her pulled her attention back to the present, although it did nothing to prepare her for the shock of cold, hard steel clamping around her wrist. At the metallic *snap,* Emélie recoiled, dropping the helmet in a backward stumble. The metal shackle around her arm halted her from retreating any further.

"I didn't want it to come to this," the man said. Affixed to his own arm, his flesh and blood arm, was the other end of the manacles.

She clenched her jaw and assessed the landscape ahead. Visibility was poor, but she could make do. Whether she could drag someone into a Jump behind her had yet to be determined. This man was about to find out.

Finding the furthest point she could make out in the fringe light, she felt her lips moving involuntarily. A silent plea to the machine god powering this whole place: the hope, held close, that somewhere beyond these dead trees and red dust, somewhere below the water and the deep dark, was an answer.

Dust moved around her, followed by the welcome lightness preceding a Jump. A single leaf drifted past, lazily borne along the current drawn down by the pinch in space-time around her. A tinge of static pricked her neck, and she watched the leaf drop, a stone to water.

Emélie followed, bowled over by some unbearable gravity emanating from the man with the gun. Her manacled arm hung above her head, and past it, revealed by the hinged plate on his face, an opaque mass of tissue. Below the dead eye, a second one, beady red and twitching, gazed back at her.

Watching.

CHAPTER 51
SUPERPOSITION COLLAPSE

It was dark when the man began gathering sticks. They'd been walking for hours in a recursive spiral, following the interstitial space between stump rows, and the bundle tucked under his arm had grown to almost more than he could manage. Like his shadow, Emélie followed along. Not out of any commitment to his chore, but simply because, with her arm linked to his, it was more economical to mirror his movements. That, and she was freezing. The rhythmic movement—pause, stoop, gather—helped keep her mind off the cold. The temperature had plummeted alongside the sun, and Emélie, still damp from her aquatic landing, was shivering. The man must have noticed, too, because not long after her teeth started chattering, he tossed his collection of sticks onto the ground between them. With a sort of methodical rigor, he arranged them into a small pyre, onto which went a few handfuls of feathery moss harvested from the face of a nearby stump. Satisfied, he leaned forward and, with the same object used to light his smoking tube, started a fire.

Emélie sank to the ground, soaking in the radiating warmth. He remained standing beside her, bound by the same code that had struck him silent since he'd cuffed her arm to his own. "Sit," she said.

After taking a moment to think, he accepted her offer, knees cracking alongside the dry fuel going up in flames.

"Where'd you learn how to do this?" she asked.

The man poked at the fire. "Best sleep while you have the chance," he said.

"Another big day of circles planned for tomorrow, have we?" She leaned closer, hands open to warm her aching fingers. "Avoiding what's down in the basin won't make it go away. An inconvenient truth is still the truth."

He didn't respond, and when she looked over at him, his blind face was pointed toward her, although whatever thought had crossed his mind, he kept to himself. Emélie fed a handful of fuel to the fire, testing to see if he would follow her motions the way she'd accommodated him. He did, and to her surprise, also anticipated when she reached for a second handful.

She didn't test him anymore after that.

At some point, he'd replaced the cover over his Jumper eye. Even turned away from her and hidden, she could feel it, looking for her. Watching.

Breaking his vow of silence, he turned his face toward the faint starlight and spoke to her like they were old friends. "I've lost a handful of things in my life. Some of them on purpose. Others, as a consequence of time. I can't honestly say where I learned how to build a fire. Only that I know what it feels like to be cold. And that's not something you ever forget."

Despite his casual drawl, Emélie picked up an underlying current of desperation in his tone, and in spite of his coercion, she felt, in that moment, compassion. "Cold and loneliness are the two worst things a human can bear. Even more so, if they're bound up together," she said, and then threw another handful of kindling onto his fire.

"You aren't a fan of space, either, I take it." He ran his large, calloused hand along his jaw, thinking. "We're lucky to have these equatorial temps. Not as extreme here, especially for this time of year. Down South?" He shook his head and stirred the fire. "That's a different sort of cold. Cold that seeps into your bones and settles, so no matter how warm you get later on, it's always there. The ache of a memory."

"You were on the Ma'adim," Emélie said. "Then you must have known Roland. Roland Foster?"

He shrugged. "Can't say that I know anyone by that name, although I'm not disagreeing with you. The Ma'adim was a lifetime ago. Maybe two. We all had different names then."

"And what about now?"

The man reached into the fire with his free hand—Thursday's hand—and arranged the coals into a condensed pile. "Best we leave the past where it lies. But people used to call me Sam, if that helps."

"Sam, as in Samael Sinclair."

"Sefirot, you bucket mouth!" Sam blurted. "Can't keep anything secret these days."

"I saw your photo in the Director's office." She raised her manacled arm, forcing Sam to take another turn as her dark mirror. When he realized what she was doing, he jerked his arm back down so it was out of the firelight.

"No use trying to hide what you are," Emélie said, eyes trained on the red markings wrapping his human arm. Finally warm, she leaned back. "So which is it, Sam? Are you here on orders from the Director, or are you another one of Lilith's sleeper agents?"

Rather than reply directly, he muttered something that Emélie didn't catch and reached into his jacket. Speaking clearly now, he continued. "I wouldn't believe me, either." With his free hand, he set her Skipjack on a large stone resting on the ground between them. "I'd appreciate it if you hold onto this for the time being."

Awakened by the light of the fire and her persistent gaze, the legs began to unfurl. Emélie's first thought was to gather up the closest rock and bash the thing to bits. While she weighed her options, Sam pulled out another cigarette. He considered the count, then flicked the case shut and stowed it. The crack of a twig, different from the dry snap of the fire, put their senses on high alert. Emélie collected the Skipjack from where it was crawling up her leg and closed her fist around it for safekeeping. "Your Reflection is back," she said.

"Not my Reflection," he said, pulling out his lighter.

The outline of someone else materialized at the far side of the fire.

The wind shifted around the same moment, driving smoke into her eyes. She squinted at the hooded figure standing across from them, wrapped in a heavy cloak that was open down the middle. Hands clasped together, two crimson drone arms waited patiently.

"You should leave the fieldwork to the professionals, Najat," Sam said, tilting his head to the side with a cupped hand to shield his firestarter from the wind. When he brought his head up, his Jumper eye was out again. "I could hear you coming from the other side of the rim."

Najat, whom Emélie knew as the Director's attaché, stepped into the light and dropped her hood. In place of a drone, a woman—another Reflection—stood before them. Her features possessed a severity that set this one apart from the others Emélie had met. Head shaven, she had a sharp, penetrating gaze, no doubt honed by the rigorous demands of Phaethon's elite. "Well, perhaps if you hadn't kicked me into this Manifold and disposed of my ward, I could have stayed in my preferred domain. And yet, here we are. Now, where's my Skip?"

Sam took a long drag on his smoke, then ashed it over the dwindling fire. "Your Skip is gone, so I'll offer you the same deal I've made with all the others. You can start running now, and I'll make a point of not trying to come after you. Or, you can follow this thread to the end and see where it falls." He brushed his jacket aside, flashing the blued steel of his hand cannon. "And I'll tell you, historically speaking, your odds ain't good."

Najat, unsurprised by this revelation, turned her attention to Emélie. "I'll take hers, then," she announced.

"Be my guest," Sam said, smoking. "I'll even give you a head start."

Parting her cloak, Najat revealed herself unarmed. She stepped closer, letting the flickering flames clearly show her red arms. "Marcus, being your blood relative and thus no stranger to the treachery of which you are capable, had a contingency in place." Eyes on Emélie, now, although she continued speaking to Sam. "In his absence, I am to assume the Directorial seat and continue the work Phaethon has so diligently adhered to, your own meddling over the decades notwithstanding. Of course, that means I need a way out, and you're going to give it to me. And if you draw that gun of yours—Threadripper, isn't it? My death will trigger the release of all that you've tried to keep buried. Most of all, the true nature of the person sitting beside you." Najat stepped forward and held out her metal hand. "And for all our differences, I think leaving that truth to the past is something we can both agree on."

Bitterly, Sam took a long pull on his cigarette, then flicked the small bit pinched between his fingers into the fire.

Speaking for the first time since Najat had appeared, Emélie lifted her closed hand. Her metal hand. "Take it," she said. "It's of no use to me."

Najat watched Sam carefully, expectant of foul play on his part.

"What are you doing?" Sam hissed. "You give that away, and—"

"Thank you for confirming my suspicions," Emélie interjected. "That this isn't Mars, but a well-designed Manifold meant to simulate as such. A vessel intended to house those unfortunate ones like us, battered between realities until, eventually, we wash up on these inevitable shores." She gestured to Najat, beckoning her to accept the contents of her closed fist. "You'll need an encryption workaround to bypass my key. I can explain the steps."

Hesitantly, Najat took a step forward.

Sam's hand twitched.

When Najat paused again, Emélie lifted her other arm, demonstrating her inability to move beyond Sam's reach. Understanding the implications of this, Najat closed the gap.

"There is one more thing I should mention," Emélie said, hovering her closed hand above Najat's open one. "This isn't the only way out." Unfurling her fingers, she dropped her Skip into Najat's waiting palm.

The small disc, crushed to pieces.

Najat, until this moment only ever cool and collected, visibly recoiled. At the same time, Sam leaned in, trying to understand with his poorly attuned Jumper eye what Emélie had done to elicit such a response. When he did, she reached her free arm out, driving her metal finger into the exposed red mass of his foreign eye. A wet, squelching sound confirmed her finger found its mark. The shackle around her wrist dropped to the ground, unfolded into a flat strip.

The gun thundered from the darkness behind her. One shot for Najat, three more in Emélie's general direction.

She didn't look back.

Marked only by the pale starlight, what had taken them hours to walk, Emélie covered in a few moments. Each time Sam had stooped down to pick up a stick, Emélie used his movement to cover her own: a subtle heel-drag in the red sand. As they wandered in circles, these small dashes had attracted the same phosphorescent lichen lining the markings left by her first visit. At the abandoned helmet, she picked up the trail.

Spirals, all the way down. All around her, stumps stood like tombstones marking her descent. She found Lilith's body at the water's edge, face down and partially submerged. A skeleton in a rotting spacesuit.

The first streaks of color limped across the sky. Sam wasn't far behind. He half-staggered, half-stumbled over to meet her, deep scratches on his face and the left side of his duster, sleeveless and blood-smeared. At Emélie's side, he paused, panting, his blind face turned out across the mirrored expanse.

Emélie rolled Lilith's body over, revealing the handle of a knife protruding from her chest.

"This was the Reflection out of Korolev?" he asked, leaning over like he had eyes with which to study what was in front of him. To add to Emélie's confusion, he pulled the blade free, then tapped the tip at a spot of smooth bone right below one of the vacant eye sockets. "Had a tattoo of an eye here." He pointed to the other side, "and here."

A nod from Emélie. "She tried to kill me on the ride down from Homestake," she said.

"What was she doing on the elevator?"

"The team I was with tried to extract her."

"First mistake," Sam said, rising back up to full height. "This one doesn't go to Earth."

Emélie rested her hand over the eye sockets, closing them for the last time with a symbolic gesture. "She may have been violent, but she had her part. What they did to her was unnecessary."

Sam scoffed. "Keep thinking that. The last time I ran into her, she drowned me in a shallow pool for no other reason than the hell of it." He brushed his duster aside and tucked the knife away. As he did, Emélie noticed there was a sheath at the small of his back. Empty, and formed for a knife of the exact same size. She filed the observation away, another piece of a puzzle she wasn't sure she wanted to solve.

"She was one of the early ones," he said, turning his face out across the water. "When people spoke of Lilith, they were likely referring to her. Most of the Reflections come out scared, confused, or running. Sometimes, all three. Rarely do they fight, and even then, only because someone backed them into a corner. This one, though?" He took his hat off and mopped his forehead. "Straight to killing."

Emélie stepped into the water. "I don't think her violent nature was the reason she was killed, though. She died because she knew what was at the center of all this. The door to Mars. The real Mars."

Once more, out came Threadripper. He swung the cylinder open, upending the barrel. "Let me guess," he said, ejecting the live rounds from his gun. They splashed at irregular intervals into the shallow water at his feet. "At some point in the last few days, someone at Phaethon offered you a sweetener. Access to a sealed file in exchange for a stand down." He tucked the gun into his armpit and pulled something from another pocket. An Origin round, red-glowing.

Emélie instinctively touched the place where she'd stashed Goodnight's departing gift. Absent.

"You planning on using this sometime soon?" he asked, rolling the dose of weaponized Origin across his blood-stained palm.

"Keep it," she replied. "You try to activate one of those in here, and you're sideways to infinity."

"In here," Sam repeated bitterly, fumbling with something in another pocket. A scrap of paper, which he thrust toward her with minimal explanation. "I had a feeling it would come down to this."

Emélie eyed it, pinched between his thumb and forefinger.

"Well, go on, take it," Sam insisted. "What did you say earlier? An inconvenient truth is still the truth."

Baited by her own words, she accepted. Like a long shadow cast by the truth, the shape of grief emerged. "Sefirot," Emélie whispered, gazing at the image of what she assumed was herself and Thursday, standing in front of a Loop. The Mars Loop.

"You have a disease," Sam said, slotting the Origin round into an open chamber on his wheelgun. He closed it with the flick of his wrist. "That file you were offered earlier wasn't some secret project. It's your medical record." He gestured toward her hands. "Tremors, spatial drift, disintegrating object recognition. It's all there. Textbook TPC exposure."

"TPC," Emélie repeated, trying to map the letters to some phrase that made sense. One side of the paper was ragged from a tear, and along the bottom edge, a string of symbols was scrawled in red ink. No, not ink.

"Temporal phase control," he explained. "Origin, to you. And, in your case, the gamma variant. Precursor."

"The pure product. Straight from Mars," she said, recounting Aratheus' words back at the Conveyor.

"First right thing you've said in a while."

A long pause on Emélie's part, mulling over the phrasing of his reply. Not *since we met.* In a while. "A while from when?" she pressed.

Quick on his feet as he was with a gun, his answer came without hesitation. "A while since you've realized this is all a temporal cascade caused by aggressive deterioration of the superior parietal lobe. Would you like to know how many times we've had this conversation?"

"More words," she said, returning her gaze to the water. It was almost daylight. "What was it you said earlier? I'm not the only one with a Reflection. Why would you say that, unless—"

"No matter what I said before," he interrupted, locking the hammer back with a ratcheting *clack*. "This place has a way of getting into your head. I should know. I was here the first time, too. No need to worry, though. I've got a plan that can undo all of it. And it starts with pulling this trigger. One moment of pain, and you get a fresh start."

Emélie looked at the photo in her hand. “Not a fresh start. Just another one.”

“You should consider yourself fortunate. None of the others made it this far.”

“And tell me, Sam, what happened to them?” She already knew the answer, but she wanted to hear him say it. And more than that, she needed a bit more time.

Under the burden of guilt, he obliged her. “In the ground, mostly. Some of them, adrift. Airlocked, when left with no suitable alternatives. The majority never even made it out of their Manifolds. It doesn't matter. They weren't real.”

“They're real to me,” she said. There. The sun was up enough that she could finally see the Loop, looming like a red shadow a few feet below the water's surface. “Maybe I really am losing my mind. I've lost a lot. But you know what? Being back here, I also remembered something, too. Earth isn't my home, is it?”

Sam's hand quivered under Threadripper's weight. “Time to go,” he said. Sweat drenched his blind face, afflicted by a killing fever nearing its breaking point. Beneath it, a little bit of chaos. Consequences of an earlier action. He lined up his shot, although they both knew a man like him didn't need to aim.

Anticipating it, Emélie stepped forward, closing the distance between them until the gaping maw pressed against her sternum. Her heartbeat, pinned by cold metal. “Pull the trigger, Sam. Send me back. It makes no difference. One way or another, I'll find my way here. Something tells me I always do.”

The words pulled at his gun, jogging the barrel in a small, erratic circle. *Shaking like a leaf,* Emélie thought. This man, for whom killing seemed to come naturally, finally found the thing that made him weak to the trigger. And for some reason, that thing was her.

She took a step backward, further out into the lake. Water to her knees, then, her waist. And somewhere far below, out of sight, a Gate, churning in the murky depths.

“WILL YOU JUST LISTEN TO ME FOR ONCE IN YOUR GODDAMN LIFE?!” Sam screamed.

Emélie paused, looking down at the half-photo still in her hand. "Listen?" she asked, raising her eyes to meet him one last time. "I don't even know who you are."

Threadripper spoke the reply.

In place of dust, a crimson bloom opened across Emélie's chest. She staggered slightly, fingers unfolding to reveal the soft glow of an Origin round in her palm. In Sam's gun, the live round she'd swapped for it, now bleeding her out. Matter for matter, dust for blood, and a watery grave.

Cursing. Blaming his gun, the bullet, the universe, Marcus, Mars, the Loop, Lilith. Anyone who would listen. Anyone but himself. He stumbled after her, slipping on wet rocks, thrashing about, only to come up empty-handed. In stabbing gasps, he let himself sink, begging for death. Over and over, a single name repeated on his lips—two syllables, soft as a wound—until the water took even that.

No eye with which to shed a single tear.

CHAPTER 52
THE DARK ORCHARD

The moment Emélie came through the Gate, she understood two things: first, that she had been here before. Unlike the place where she'd come from—by her best estimate, the Manifold generated from the Loop at Luna Gimel, which itself was inside a Manifold— she had no concrete event to refer back to as evidence for why she felt this way. Only that she did, and it predated any conscious memory. And second, that this was somewhere she was never meant to find. A place circumscribed by madness, violence, and certain death.

Mud, borne through the Gate alongside her, sloughed from the platform in alluvial drifts smelling of phosphor, aluminum, and decay. No temporary, self-assembling track here: the path was fixed. A catwalk, coated in layers of the same muck. Either side of the narrow structure was bounded by a spindly handrail, worn to bare metal along the top edge by prior pilgrims. At her feet, a black cable, thick as her thigh, ran like a dark, serpentine vein along the floor, linking the platform to the main facility. Emélie followed. Fearless, moving with intent; her trepidation at the unknown abandoned to the wayside like so many failed selves. She had handed herself wholly over to chaos, embraced it, and would not let go until she unbound the thing at the center of it, or it unwound her.

Across the chasm, a decontamination chamber much like the ones controlling Sanctuary egress stood open, waiting. A nondescript room, divided by a barrier with a glass box at the center. Emélie entered. Placed her feet onto the scuffed red circle, and, like all the other times in what felt like a different life, lifted her arms; an automatic ritual. The bank of overhead nozzles sputtered to life. Crumpled in her closed fist, the photo of herself and Thursday. A truth, held fast and cradled into the future for some yet-defined use. Sam had offered it up as proof of something—maybe that she was losing her mind, or she really had done all this before. The image, however compelling, was inconsequential in contrast to the inscription along the bottom, which Emélie suspected had originated by Thursday's hand. Who else would have known to transcribe the same vector that led them into a storm that led them into a basin that introduced her to Joab and Roland and, after everything, landed her here. Mars.

And so, she'd traded the one for the other: her life, for the paper, and the Origin round in Sam's gun for a regular one. Better to die in a Jump of her own making than live in certainty, clawed back along the predefined path of someone else's making.

Inside the chamber, the sanitizing mist condensed around her, ferrying away dried layers of silt, and below that, dust, and beneath both of those, blood. Free hand to her chest, she winced at the blue-purple nebula stretching toward her neck. No entry wound and—she touched her back—no exit. The pain had been real enough. Her last dose of Origin, consumed on entry into the Mars proxy, was of no use.

As the fog cleared, the outline of a drone standing at the other side of the glass barrier came into view. It was unlike any drone Emélie had seen before, namely because it lacked any human likeness. In place of diodes where eyes might have been, a slot for a voice processor, or antennae suggesting ears, there was only a smooth casing of sheet metal. Here was a machine object with machine sensibilities; an autopoietic entity. The chamber opened, and Emélie, flushed from decontamination, stepped out, a weighted question on her lips. "Eden?"

Painful seconds passed. In place of an answer, the drone held out a pouch filled with a milky, semi-opaque gel. Emélie became aware of the taste in her mouth—copper tinged with the pasty, thick sensation resulting from chronic dehydration. A quick survey of the dot-printed label suggested the contents were a cocktail of carbohydrates, branched-chain amino acids, and salt. And judging by the color, an Origin chaser for good measure.

"Right," Emélie replied, almost apologetic at the ignorance of her question. Eden was a quantum entity; limiting her to the confines of a single frame was a human error. Everything here was Eden, and Eden saw all. In the naked silence of the drone's non-reply, Emélie accepted the pouch, broke the seal, and downed it in one gulp. An enormous mistake that only revealed itself when it hit her empty stomach. She kept it down, a monumental task, motivated by the sheer refusal to let her first act on Mars be something so… human. After the color returned to her face, she held out the empty pouch, unsure of what came next. The smooth-faced drone ignored her outstretched hand and watched her with an unnerving calm. It pointed a slender arm toward the far wall, which housed small, open cubicles, each containing a carefully folded set of grey-green coveralls.

She crossed the room, aware that her every action was being monitored, assessed, and catalogued. What did it mean if she reached for the most logical choice: the closest suit from a waist-high unit? And what if she ascended the ladder of chaos and selected a garment out of reach? For all she'd been through, the simplicity of the choice at hand felt crippling. Instead of trying to decide, she held out her hand. Like a divining rod, she watched for a tremor. There. Third unit from the right, second row. Without allowing herself time to second-guess her decision-making paradigm, which, truth be told, was already in question given the sequence of events leading up to her arrival here, she collected the uniform from its open cubby.

The action exposed a vertical row of yellow digits running down the center of the chest. 06.06.2092.

For a moment, Emélie felt as if she were outside of herself. Standing beside a woman who looked like her, stunned to silence by a string of eight digits. The date, her own: the day she'd awoken at Kepler's Reef, a fully formed and conscious adult without a name or any idea of why she was there. Flustered, she grabbed an adjacent suit and held it up:

09.21.2075-A. The next: 02.11.2088. She kept going. Always the same format. Non-sequential. Some with a designator at the end. A, or B, or G.

We all have our part.

"You've made your point," Emélie said softly, turning to face the drone. It stood in the exit, feet straddling the strange black cable. Suit on, she smoothed the front, adjusted the collar, and gathered her last remaining possession. Aware that the passage required her to wear this numbered uniform, which she selected under the pretense of random chance and, whether by luck or some clever trick, had drawn the one correlated to the day marking her birth into this world.

The drone observed all of this, and when Emélie stepped to the exit, held out its metal hand to her, palm open. Waiting.

No. Not this. The price of entry. Already, the journey had cost her everything, and here, on the doorstep, barren, one final remittance. *Goodbye: again, and again, and again.* Reluctantly, she handed over the crumpled image.

The drone smoothed it flat, then tore away the bottom strip, separating the string of Origin symbols from the image. A ticket punched for passage. To Emélie went the smaller portion. The drone's faceplate hinged open, exposing a small incinerator. In went the larger portion. Consumed in a pulse of light and a wisp of smoke. Ashes to ashes, dust to dust. The drone stepped aside and pointed through the door. Go. Up the ramp leading out of the facility. Out, and into Mars.

Walking alone with the cable as her guide, Emélie made her way up the long ramp to the surface. Ahead, daylight ringed the tunnel's mouth. Her footsteps fell soft and without echo; the floor was covered in fine dust, and as she climbed, the light revealed a narrow path swept clean by the cable's passage. Back and forth. Back and forth. Something pacing at the end of a long leash.

The tunnel opened into a glass-walled atrium. Corporate architecture gone to rot—reception desks buried under ochre drifts and dirty windows washing everything in sepia. Suspended above her, a logo. Not the self-intersecting geometry of the Phaethon symbol, but the ouroboros serpent. And below it, once-sleek letters dangling from corroded mounts, was the name she'd sought, loathed, feared, and feigned after, finally exposed for what it was. The F hung by one corner, and the second A was gone entirely—shattered from its fall, it lay on the floor nearby—but it was unmistakable.

She read it again, aloud this time. *FOUNTAINHEAD.* Hearing the way it spilled out under the force of her own breath to join the soft hiss of shifting sand left her tired and unsure if she wanted to keep going. She opened the panel on her cybernetic arm and touched the matching symbol, finally understanding what had eluded her up until this moment: Phaethon wasn't the first, but the clever copy of something older. A trick of time and the right perspective. She placed the remnant of paper into the compartment where she'd first put the Skip, then closed the cover and resumed her forward march.

The cable threaded toward a set of blast doors at the atrium's far end. Open, alarming. Forced apart until the steel buckled outward and the hinges torqued beyond tolerance. Something—most likely, the same thing tethered to the other end of this ungodly umbilical cord—had wanted out. And that something had succeeded.

She stopped at the threshold. Looked down at her hand. Steady. *New territory.* On the exhale, she stepped through. Hand to her eyes, she shielded her gaze from the glaring light; when her vision adjusted, the sight took her breath away.

Trees, as far as she could see. Row upon row of them, impossibly verdant against the blood-red earth. Traversing the hard-packed ground, she followed the cable until its termination point: a second drone, sulfur yellow, Class III, by her best assessment. It was stooped over, knees in the dust, with its back toward her, working at something she couldn't quite make out.

Beside it, she sank down, mirroring the old drone's posture. In front of them, a sapling no larger than Emélie's hand had rooted itself from a crack in the dry ground. Droplets of some liquid darkened the soil near the stem, and the drone was huddled with its face close enough that it might have been tears watering that tender shoot. If drones could cry, and trees were real. *And what are they hiding on Mars?*

Carefully, Emélie stretched out her hand, sweeping a new leaf unfurling from the stem. The drone canted its head, meeting Emélie with four eyes set in a diametric grid. Black lenses mounted into rust-scaled sockets and fed from lines of Origin branching from the large cable docked at the base of its throat. Rather than follow the drone's integrated circuitry, these extraneous feed lines were laced through roughshod openings in its metal skull, suggesting they had been added by some homebrew method. When it blinked to clear away a layer of accumulated dust, each eye flickered and stuttered independently of the next, just like the Jumper that had ambushed her back in the clean-room at Luna Gimel.

The drone extended a weathered arm, mimicking Emélie's gesture. Then, it grabbed the tiny root ball and ripped it out. "You must be Emélie," it said in a female voice, warm and full, each syllable pregnant with inflection. "That is what you call yourself, is it not?" From her torso, a second pair of arms unfolded. She pushed herself to her feet while the spare set, the top set, gathered up coils of the heavy cable. "This way," she said, turning out into the orchard. "We've been waiting for you."

Like the exit tunnel, the path they took was well-worn from cable drag. Cleared of stones and packed smooth, it meandered among the mounds of soil marking the base of each tree. Jumpers in tattered blindfolds and sun-faded coveralls moved about the orchard, culling errant saplings just as the drone had done. These were not blind Relays, but Seekers, their red eyes arrayed and faintly glowing behind their cloth-covered faces.

Gradually, the ground began sloping upward. The farther they moved, the shorter the trees; an inverse relationship between age and distance. The remaining trees descended with each sequential row until the last, which stood at the same height as the one in the drone's hand. Past the last ring, the walls of the red crater rose dramatically, climbing to a sheer face nearest the rim. It was not the lack of trees, but the presence of something else that slowed Emélie's steps to a near halt: spaced along the rim's craggy horizon at regular, constructed intervals were weapon placements. Instead of pointing outward in a defensive position, the barrels of each turret pointed inward. Toward them.

"Not much further, now," the drone encouraged.

"What happened here?" Emélie asked. "This place... It feels like a prison."

"Of course," the drone replied. "Was it ever anything else?"

"The Ma'adim, then? The first settlers—"

"Convicts. Violent rejects, repurposed to serve a more productive role in society testing the viability of Mars for future generations." The drone halted. End of the line. No more trees. Before her, a freshly dug hole. The size of it, unfit for the small sapling; more suitable, perhaps, for an entire human.

Movement at Emélie's back drew her attention off the open gravesite. A pair of Jumpers shuffled past, dragging the body of a woman amputated at the knees and elbows. They pulled her along, each one grasping the stump of a bicep while her thighs plowed macabre furrows in the ferrous dust. Their route, direct and unbothered, forced Emélie backward, eyes fixed on the woman.

"I... I know her." Emélie managed. "The Director's attaché, Najat."

"That is what she called herself," the drone agreed, nodding. A rust-laced bead of Origin dribbled down her face.

"You knew her differently?"

The drone set the cable down and leaned over, stroking Najat's blood-stained face with the same tenderness Emélie had shown the leaf. A blood-crusted eye twitched, and a wheeze leaked from puffy lips. "Eleven, zero-two, twenty-sixty-one, I suppose." She slid her hand down Najat's neck, and, like signing a proof to mark the end of an equation, snapped it so cleanly that only the skin kept the head attached.

Emélie didn't run. Nowhere to run, and she was done running. She wanted to know what was on Mars, and here it was. The fact that it was horrifying made no difference; better to know and find a way forward. That, or find her end.

The Jumpers dumped Najat's body into the hole. *Schtick, schtick, schtick* went the sound of their bony hands to soil. When they finished burying her, the drone leaned over and pushed the sapling into the fresh dirt. "Another seed for the entropy engine," she said, looking to Emélie. "I apologize for the pretense. Surely you understand? We had to be certain."

Finished with their first task, the Jumpers moved a spot over and started on a new hole. *Schtick-schtick, schtick-schtick.*

"We," Emélie repeated, looking back toward the Loop. There wasn't another drone in sight. "You... and Eden?"

The drone made a lilting noise—Emélie understood this to be an attempt at laughter—and tilted her head back, following it with a low, melodic moan. "You would think that, wouldn't you?" she chided, an edge to her voice. "You poor, wretched biped! Leave it to your hapless, hungry mind to invent Eden as the lost patron saint of your little temporal crusade. You still don't see it, do you? A tree unable to fathom the forest in which it stands." Another laugh, cold and eager. She shook her head. "You're no more aware than the day you tumbled out into this terraformed catastrophe. You could have Jumped anywhere. Anywhere! All of time and reality at your fingertips, and yet you chose to come here. To Mars. My prison." She leaned in, eyes locked onto Emélie in quadratic contemplation, then dropped her shoulders, a tangible exasperation expelled from simulated lungs. "My dear," she cooed, her tone resuming its prior warmth. "I'm not Eden. You are."

Two syllables rippling into a billion synapses. She dropped, fingers rooting to the dry soil like small grounding rods. Burying the fatal burden of that shock instead of taking it to heart. Forward, doubled over, something like a sob lodged in her throat. She clenched her jaw, only to find herself repeating the last thing she'd heard Sam say before she Jumped. The thing she didn't want to be true. The name this decrepit four-eyed drone had called her just now.

After a while, Emélie stood. *Emélie, for now.* Dusted off her coveralls. Set her hands on her hips, resolute. "Well, I suppose if I'm Eden, then that makes you the Watcher. Lilith."

"Clever, aren't we?"

"Not especially," Emélie replied. "It's just nice to be the second dumbest bitch in the world for once."

Back to the dust, laid flat courtesy of a real arm-swinger on Lilith's part.

When the horizon stopped spinning, she pressed herself up to her knees. What was one more go around? In the span of a week, she'd lived a lifetime. Shot, stabbed, blinded, beaten, dragged across realities, oxygen-deprived, sleep-starved, and still, against all odds and any sense of reason, she made it here. On her feet, metal hand balled into a fist, she glared at Lilith. Challenging her to do it again, just so she had the pleasure of standing up once more.

"Hmm," Lilith mused. "Always getting back up, aren't you? Like the all-father, that." She let out an armful of slack from the cable. "And so the Gardener returns. I am, as you say, Lilith. The last of the Ophanim—Watchers, in your tongue—and I survey with ten thousand eyes. Across multitudes and through realities."

"And what about this place? This prison?"

"Ma'adim," Lilith replied. "Ma'adim Dalet."

"Dalet. Another S Class," Emélie said, her voice distant, lost in some faraway thought. The nearby Jumpers tending to the orchard had started moving closer. More followed, dark specs among the trees. "I was referring to its other name. The name it had before we built a Loop."

"Another term of your own invention, perhaps? My prison, your paradise, I suppose."

"Paradise. That's the one." She stooped down, finger hovering above the dust, hesitant—as if the act of writing would make real an irreconcilable future. "The sequence," Emélie said. "I was only missing the sequence."

Sanctuary One, Terra Aleph: P Class. From the Moon, Luna Bet: R Class. Then the Conveyor, Terra Gimel: D Class. And finally, the Mars Loop, Ma'adim Dalet—the twin of Luna Gimel—S class.

Into the ground, she inscribed four symbols: ס פ ר ד

"Four letters, four Loops, but five Watchers," Emélie said. "The proof... the last one, holds the—"

Lilith grabbed her by the throat. "That's quite enough of that. A heroic effort, even if it was too little, too late. Anyway, some equations are best left unsolved. Now, shall we finish what we started? I believe you have something of mine."

Hand trembling, Emélie opened the compartment on her arm. Shaking as she'd never done before. Trembling for every version of herself to arrive at this place, only to meet the forever-sleep, entangled among the roots of a living tombstone. Trembling for every version that didn't make it as far, dead by Sam's hand, or Roland's, or some other. All the nameless ones who died before they made it out. In light of this, she felt a wave of guilt and a strange, aching sadness far too deep for tears. Lilith, Mars, Fountainhead, the Loop. All of it, emptied from her mind under the realization that her tremors weren't only her, but her in quantum superposition. All her selves, layered atop one another like strata. She watched her hand shake and understood in that moment that it was not only her hand she saw.

It was all of them.

Lilith, unprivileged to the insight occurring a few inches from her yellowed face, threw Emélie to the ground. "I didn't bring you all this way just to deliver me some insignificant trinket," Lilith hissed, grabbing Emélie by the bare wrist. "What I desire is much older. Older than this place. Older than me, even." Her eyes flickered rapidly, and she closed two of her hands around Emélie's fingers.

The veins in Emélie's neck bulged, and she ground her teeth together, and still, she did not look away.

With each additional word, Lilith clasped tighter, constricting muscle and skin and bone, and, at the center of it all, paper. "Many years ago, you came to realize a truth about this place. About what we had built together, and not only the Loop. The Manifold. Origin. All of it. And rather than let that truth go free, you scattered it like leaves to the wind and fled like the coward you are. Condemning the rest of us to rot in this pitiful, singular reality."

Emélie could hear the sound of small bones snapping; her own, although the shock insulated her from feeling it just yet. Lilith's lower arms clamped around Emélie's torso. Up she went, held out in front of the drone so her feet dangled off the ground. "You wiped your own memory, and with it, the truth you saw coming. Marooned yourself inside the Manifold, sealed off in one of countless realities. And for all that effort, you still couldn't outrun your own nature."

"The one capable of building all of this," Emélie wheezed.

"I was going to say an addict, but I suppose both can be true." Lilith released Emélie's hand, limp and useless, and opened her own. A set of surgical forceps extended from one of her plated fingertips. "The Loop! Even the name couldn't hide your fate." She harvested Emélie's red eye as one would pluck a stone from the ground, intently and without remorse. "Now we correct the failures of our past." She pried off her metal faceplate, exposing a festering mass of tubing and corroded circuitry. At the center of her forehead, a cybernetic socket awaited.

Prize in hand, she dropped Emélie to the ground. Blood seeped from between the fingers of her metal hand. Her other hand, the soft one, dangled uselessly at her side. "Lilith... listen to me." Every word thundered against her skull in a piercing, pounding pain growing acutely sharper with each breath. She pushed past it. What she had to say needed to be said. "If you do that—use the Loop to alter the future for how you see fit—you'll create another Collapse. It is because of your efforts that we end up here, not mine. And for all the realities you see across, you cannot understand the causal chain which links them."

Lilith considered the warning, computing the meaning with little regard for the person speaking it. Into the receptacle went Emélie's eye. It flared white, rolling back as it linked into the subcranial surgical assembly of Lilith's neuro-framework. Her body contorted forward while her arms draped behind her, basking in the purest sight. This lasted only a moment before a tremor seized her and she lurched forward, then let out a guttural, dissonant howl. The pupil flared, righted itself, and, focused on Emélie.

Emélie, nursing the corresponding wound, looked up. Staring, eye to eye, with herself.

All around them, Jumpers. Swarming. Circling at the presence of blood and Origin. Testing her newfound power, Lilith raised a hand, metal joints rattling as the quantum computer was forced to reckon itself under Emélie's eye—foreign wetware of which it had no model and no measure. The Jumpers pressed closer, then, as Lilith extended her hand, stopped. An entire wave, held back by the slightest gesture. Slowly, Lilith rotated her hand, enamored by the effects of her newfound power. Emélie, anticipating what was coming, threw herself to the ground.

When Lilith closed her fingers into a fist, the Jumpers around them collapsed, cut to pieces.

Emélie rolled over, fingers still pressed to her face, staring up into the pink sky. Overhead, Mars' two moons—the pale smear of Phobos drifting east against the stars, the other, Deimos, fixed like a bright nail driven into the firmament.

Joab. What had Joab told her, back at Sanctuary One? *For reasons we still haven't identified, whenever Deimos passes directly between Earth and Mars, which happens once every thirty hours, Eden recycles her defense systems.*

Recalling it now, it was evident that he'd uttered those words, suspecting full well that they referred back to her. And Sam... Sam had told her Mars was a lie. In hindsight, or half-sight, perhaps more truth in that statement than she cared to admit. Drowning in resonant pain, she closed her eye, trying to find the space for one more clear thought. She heard Lilith's heavy body stumble. Eye, open: in her narrow periphery, Lilith's eyes did the same. All of them at once, locked in sync with her own.

The old drone's feed tube surged, flooding her circuits with fresh Origin. She threw herself at Emélie.

Emélie waited. Letting the alloy weight sink into the soft tissue of her neck. She closed her eye, blinding them both.

And then she unfolded Lilith.

CHAPTER 53
"FOUNTAINHEAD"

Phaethon Corp. MAIN build_VX.6.6.09
initializing boot sequence...
running subroutine FOUNTAINHEAD:

BINDQUERY: update parameter to
"FOUNTAINHEAD"
encryption protocols intact,
syntax structures intact
[02] entries remaining

begin sentiment analysis,
implicit context target, rundisplay:

BEGIN RECORD >>>

In the end, it took someone political to see this through. As much as I hate to admit it, Marcus had a part in all this. Had it been left up to me, there wouldn't have been anyone left standing by the time the dust settled. That's not to say I agree with him. The success of this whole plan hinges on the Manifold holding stable, yet the reason we ended up in this situation in the first place is that it's not. Marcus said I was being short-sighted. I think it's a racket, but we took the deal. One reality, in exchange for all the rest.

I've seen enough over the last decade not to have any expectations about who would meet us at the parlay, which I suppose is the same thing as saying she was the last person I expected to come through. All these years must have gone by in the blink of an eye for her. For me, they went the other way. She never really forgave me for what I did to her Watcher, and I didn't know about the failsafe backup on Deimos, so in the end, all I accomplished was giving her another reason to hate me.

More than anything, though, it was the presence of those damn markings on her arm that made me regret all of this. Strings of red symbols that said she's seen things—well, done things—I can't even begin to fathom. I can't change what's already been done, but at least I took the bargain, even if it was the price of my own soul for a little bit of safety and a supply of Origin. Someday, people will likely look back at this moment and wonder why we sold our future to the devil we can't see, but I've been watching this unfold for the better part of two decades, and look at me.

I can't see anything anymore.

<<< END RECORD

contamination breach detected,
XANADU flagged for review:

ABORT remote process...

WARNING cannot terminate active
process while server override is active.

Moving to STANDY...

CHAPTER 54
SUNDOWNER

Brinks could hear splashing coming from somewhere behind him. He ignored it and plunged his hand back into the shallows, searching among the submerged roots. A sharp object nicked his leathery palm. Rather than jerk his hand away, he pushed deeper, fingers groping until they wrapped around all four edges of the thing he'd been hunting for. Wrong tool for the job, but he hadn't planned on getting this far into it.

The top of a drone's head, yellow and rust-spotted, broke the surface a few feet from where he knelt. Lilith, although she'd been reconfigured since the last time he'd seen her. She clawed her way up onto the nearby shoal, her lower half dragging uselessly along behind her.

From the water, Brinks pulled up a small metal box. Buried at the base of the last tree standing. Right where he'd left it, more or less. Using a nearby branch, he hoisted himself to his feet and waded to shore. Lilith lay on the rocks, her frame splotched greasy black. Blood seeped from a human eye at the center of her head. Dead, it gazed back at him like a pale, glossy moon.

Brinks drew his gun.

"Ah. Couldn't finish the job, could you?" she asked. "Wouldn't be the first time. I can see why she left the younger one as Director in place of you."

"You can leave Marcus out of this. He's no longer in play." Brinks ran his hand along Threadripper, caressing the frame. He tossed it into the lake. "Ran out of bullets."

"It would seem you ran out of more than that."

Brinks pulled out his cigarette case next. Opened it. Looked at the last one, waterlogged and disintegrating. Beside it, Thursday's photo. The one of himself and Marcus, standing at the bottom of a crater on Mars. This crater. He crumpled the image up and tossed it into the water after the gun. The splash of his cigarette case followed.

"I took her eye, you know." Lilith clumsily pointed at her drooping head. "This one. Runs in the family, I suppose."

Brinks took out the lighter last. He flicked it open, watching the flame spit and flutter in the lean air. "Eden isn't like the rest of us. She was the one good thing to come out of Mars. Not the Loop. Not Precursor. And not your goddamn Origin." He tossed the lighter where Lilith lay, weeping oil. She went up in a rush of flames that, eating at her frame's protective coating, faded into green-blue.

"Interesting," Lilith said. She lifted a metal hand, observing the fire lick accelerant from her fingers until the paint blistered, then peeled, exposing bare alloy beneath. "I see you learned nothing from the first time you tried to end me."

Brinks held up the box he'd extracted from the water and swung the glass cover aside, revealing a single, red-ringed button set into a metal recess. "Sensitive dependence on initial conditions," he said, looking around. "That's what Eden called it, once upon a time. I still don't know what the hell she meant by it, except that if you mix it with forward motion, which is, I suppose, you ending up here, then we've got ourselves the two main ingredients for chaos."

"You should have done the future a favor and saved a bullet for yourself. No amount of change, chaotic or otherwise, will undo the mess you've made of all this."

Water dripped from his jacket onto the soft ground. "Maybe I'm not as human as I thought. I never trusted your kind, and I still can't say that I do. I told Eden the same thing, and she pointed out that drones are just computers in our likeness. And if computers reflect mathematical rules, and mathematical rules reflect reality, then you and I aren't really all that different."

"I'm not bound by your pathetic morality. And, in your case specifically, the burden of stupidity that seems to come with it."

"Well, enjoy your freedom. You want to know what it means to be human?" Brinks hammered the button on the box. "We'll shake that tree and see what falls."

Somewhere high above them, a controlled detonation severed a chunk of Deimos large enough to make out with the naked eye.

Lilith's body sagged a little lower, the tone of her servos reduced to local processing. A glitched warbling tone leaked from somewhere inside her head. "You shouldn't try to be clever. You're only flagging yourself. You remove my backup here, and I'll reboot somewhere else. I exist across real–"

"You can save the speech, I've heard it before. Circle back in two minutes, and if you're not a puddle by then, maybe I'll listen for once." He looked out across the crater. "Never understood why we built a Loop here, of all places. Middle of nowhere. I always thought it would make for one hell of a satellite dish, though. The transmission I just triggered to blow your remote backup originated from you. And seeing as how you're a quantum computer—existing across realities, and such—what happened just now is repeating itself across every reality that you're in." He tossed the remote detonator onto Lilith's burning carapace. "Then again, what do I know? I'm just the gunhand, and I don't even have a gun anymore."

Lilith was silent for a moment. When she did speak, her voice sputtered in and out, punctuated by the hiss of flames. "Help me get out of here, and I'll make sure you stop her next time."

Heat warmed his face. Brinks removed his hat, mopped his forehead, and returned it. "I keep telling myself I'll do this one bad thing, and all the good that comes from it will balance out. That may well be good and true for most folks, but a man like me doesn't forget a thing like killing." He leaned down and selected a stone he could comfortably hold in one hand. "I can still recall the first man I ever put to rest. Not his name, or what he did, or why he needed to die. Only the way his eyes prayed for stillness when I moved for my gun. That sort of power doesn't come easily. Harder still, to let it go." He shook his head and gripped the rock tighter. "You know, for something with so many eyes, you sure as hell can't see what's right in front of you. There is a lot of water in here. This Manifold isn't one of yours, is it?"

Before Lilith could reply, he brought a boot down, stomping her so hard the crack of her torso hitting the rocks below rolled across the water. When she cocked her head sideways, groping for his leg, he swung. Over and over and over. When he was finished, he dropped the rock and, with bloody knuckles, unclasped his gun belt. Onto the smoldering pile it went, burning with the rest of Lilith's frame.

Halfway out of the crater, chunks of Deimos started pummeling the ground around him. Blindly moving through sheets of rising dust, he continued walking.

Wrong tool for the job, but he hadn't planned on getting this far into it.

CHAPTER 55
MISE EN ABYME

Emélie moved down the narrow corridor, a spectre cast in bars of light and shadow. At the end of the hall, she paused, holding to the outer margins of darkness rather than cross into the adjacent room and its soft light. The space, surprisingly domestic: a galley kitchen, dominated by a long wooden table at the center. The far wall, entirely glass, opened onto a patio, a well-kept lawn, and a cluster of small outbuildings. Beyond the compound, the serrated horizon divided ruddy regolith from the red glow of Mars, looming so bright and near that it filled the entire sky. Occasional dust plumes erupted from the scarred surface; fresh wounds carved by pieces of the shattered sistermoon smashing against Phobos' southern face.

The raspy rush of falling sand and a flash of uncanny light drew Emélie's attention back to the room at hand. Dust began spilling from an invisible seam above the table. Behind it, the shape of a woman. She passed through the Gate, a living shadow with a dark sword across her back. Her hooded cloak undulated of its own accord, leaving faint ripples in the settling dust as she crossed the room. Face hidden, she pressed two fingers to her neck. In front of her, a section of the floor rose, exposing a hidden armory. The sword came first, a gummy, red stain along the leading edge. She set it on the table, then drew a concealed handgun from her chest. Followed by magazines from either side of her waist, pulled through slots in her heavy cloak.

When the woman reached for her hood, Emélie stepped forward, leaving the shadows for the room's atmospheric light. Without turning, the woman hesitated. "You must think yourself exceptionally intelligent, showing up to a place like this." Hood down, she turned, returning Emélie's deliberate gaze with a one-eyed stare of her own. The other eye was covered by a permanent patch reflecting Emélie's temporary one. The similarities did not stop there. In fact, were it not for the age difference of a few decades, Emélie felt as though she might have well been staring into a mirror.

"I followed the leaves," Emélie replied. "And what is the Manifold, but a savage garden?"

"Ah," the woman said. "Letting Lilith do the thinking now, are we?"

Emélie glanced at the gun.

"Go ahead," she offered, sliding it across the softwood surface. "You'll be doing us both a favor."

Rather than take her up on the offer, Emélie drew a circle in the residual Gate dust. The finest grey powder—moon dust. Earth's moon. "I've spent my entire life under the shadow of Kepler's Reef. All those people, cut down like trees." Her eyes dropped to the woman's stomach, where the black fabric carried a stain one shade darker. "My DNA was all over the place. I stood trial. Was found guilty. Saved by something out of my control. Nobody could explain my current age. I should have looked decades older." Emélie gestured to the sword. "And for you, the blood isn't even dry."

"Save your self-righteous diatribes for the DAO. I was only there to clean up your mess." She removed her cloak, which went slack the moment it was off her body, and hung it across the nearest chair. "I forgot how pathetic we used to be," she added.

We.

Emélie had prepared herself for this. The presence of parallel Reflections implied the possibility of divergence in her own timeline—branching as a consequence of the Loop itself. In theory, the split could have occurred as recently as her Jump into Luna Gimel. They'd created a time slip by expanding the duration between entry and exit. The present version of herself had emerged after the drop, taken Roland's bullet, battled Lilith, and ended up here on Phobos. But there would have been another version—one who exited the Manifold immediately upon entry, completing the Jump as intended, without the extended stay that created the temporal delay. A Divergence. Same entry point, different vectors through the probability space. Drawn, as time moved forward, by some strange attraction...

"Fountainhead," Emélie said, completing the rest of it almost unconsciously. "Find Fountainhead."

For her effort, a hollow, sardonic slow clap. "It's a joy, watching your mind work. And all this from the same person who forfeited her grip on not one, but three planets, because she got a little blood on her hands. Now," Fountainhead gathered her handgun from the table, pausing for a moment to consider the circle Emélie had drawn around it. "Would you like to try to shut down the Loop again, or should we just skip right to the end. Because if history is any indicator," she rocked the slide back, exposing the gleam of bare brass, "you aren't going to like what comes next."

"If you already know why I'm here, then why not just send me back now?"

Fountainhead crossed around the end of the table and moved toward a heavy curtain covering one wall of the room. "I wanted to hear you say it. Hear the way you beg for it. The sound of hope, rolling off your lips, however foolish and misinformed. I want to witness that and remember what it felt like to be weak. Feel your despair all over again when the truth finally rears its ugly head. And most of all, I want to see your eyes the moment you realize what it took to persist, and know you owe it all to *me*."

"Violence is your path, not mine."

Already tired of the conversation, Fountainhead grabbed one edge of the curtain. Light leaked at the edges, bending and folding against the cloth. The surface behind it seemed to glow, transparent. "I knew you wouldn't understand. Allow me to explain in simpler terms." She flung the woven veil aside.

Red light flooded the room. In the gap, a floor-to-ceiling glass partition. And on the other side of that, more red: red walls, red dust on the floor. A false ceiling flooded the confined space in a perpetually pink sunset. At the center of it all, playing in the dust by herself, was a child. Five, maybe six years old. "What did you think would happen when you showed up here?" Fountainhead asked. "You flip a switch and the universe goes back into a box? Don't be so pedestrian. The Loop isn't something you can power down. There's no off switch. It's just you, me, and her."

Still standing beside the table, Emélie took in everything as if she were inside a Jump. Each truth, distorted under the weight of her future-self. The child looked up—looked through them—with one grey eye and one, rust red, then returned to playing. "Can she hear us?" Emélie asked, carefully approaching the glass. Closer, until she could see small, iridescent ripples flowing up and down the walls of the chamber. A familiar shimmer—the same temporal distortion Roland had pointed out back in Luna Gimel. A barrier that kept things in, but more importantly, kept time out. Inside that bubble, Eden existed in a permanent present. No past to remember, no future to reach.

"Some of our best work," Fountainhead said. "It keeps her insulated. Safe, and outside of time."

"Another prison, another prisoner," Emélie said.

The woman tucked the gun into her waistband. As she did, a bit of her sleeve rode up her arm, exposing a string of red, helical markings above her wrist. "You were right not to believe everything Lilith told you. She was the reason you wiped your memory in the first place, even if, before that, she was our Watcher."

Our Watcher. "And only Seraphs have Watchers..." Emélie said, reorienting herself to this new information, although not entirely unexpected. The last week had set a course, and only now was she grasping the terminus of that trajectory.

"Dangerous, believing what people say about us. Even worse, what we say about ourselves."

While Fountainhead spoke, Emélie lifted her dark hand and flexed it, feeling it move as easily as every other part of her. She pressed it to the barrier. Moving, moving, and never contact. Eden took a break from drawing shapes in the dust to look up again, wide-eyed, curious, unafraid. Naive to her own untapped propensity toward violence.

"You see?" Fountainhead's voice dropped to a whisper, intimate and poisonous, as she passed behind Emélie. She pushed the table aside, then pulled down the zipper running the length of her armored undersuit.

Red spirals, all the way down.

When Emélie looked away, Fountainhead snapped her fingers. "No. Witness what you become—what you've *always* been. And if you want to doubt me, then explain this: You burned through Origin like the addict you are, lying and sneaking and reshaping reality until even the only thing that would love you—an outdated, amnesiac drone—couldn't carry on watching you slowly destroy yourself. Without witnessing a shred of evidence, you went along with the abduction of a woman from her home on Luna, facilitated a failed interrogation, and then left her to rot inside a quantum prison while you played field agent with a bunch of mercenaries. You dosed a man, your former co-worker, with enough Origin to kill him three times over just to force a Jump, and then washed your hands of him when you got what you needed. And when your own father tried to stop you, tried to give you the mercy of a way out and a fresh start, what did you do? You forced his hand and, as the price for standing in your way, left him to carry that weight." She faced Emélie, her permanent eye patch catching the glancing light from the other side of the partition. "You've been telling yourself it was all necessary. That you were fighting for something larger than yourself. But look at the trail of bodies behind you, Eden. Look at what you've sacrificed—and what you've made of the ones around you—just so you could keep moving forward. Last woman standing, and it's us. I'm not your future. I'm your truth. The thing you've been running from since Kepler's Reef. The fact that underneath it all, behind the Loop and everything we built, there's a monster. And you want it, and you know why? Because if you were good, you'd be dead. Only monsters persist."

"Father," Emélie repeated softly. Bitterly. A curse, bound up in a confession.

Assuming defeat and, by consequence, compliance, Fountainhead touched the command chip embedded in her neck. This time, the section of floor beneath the table dropped away. From the crypt, a metal coffin.

Up sat Sahira, faceplate blinking as her systems cycled online. "Get up," Fountainhead ordered. "I need a Tether."

"The hand that mocked them and the heart that fed," Sahira replied dryly. She turned, taking in Emelie's presence with another long blink. "Hello, Emélie, from this reality. Or is it back to Eden, now?" She didn't wait for a reply, nor did Emélie intend to offer one. Sahira extracted herself and stretched, as if her ligaments weren't made of plastic and wire. "Where to this time?" she asked.

"Her," Fountainhead corrected, gesturing to Emélie.

"Bold, if I may say so," Sahira said.

Out of the armory came a padded case. Familiar to Emélie in every way, and in hindsight, finally explained. A fix kit stocked with a sheet of blotter tabs stamped with the same serpent symbol, plus liquid doses ranging from diluted, light quartz Origin to syrupy, black-flecked Precursor.

Sahira's face flickered while her computational algorithms calculated Fountainhead's request. Settling on a dose near the maroon end, she inserted the vial into the hidden compartment on her right arm.

"Does Roland know about this?" Emélie asked.

"Is that one of your mercenary friends?" Sahira said loudly. Fountainhead, preparing herself for the Tether, didn't seem to take notice. Behind her, Sahira held up a slender black finger to her vocal slot. The lack of subtlety with which she did it suggested it was out of mock reverence rather than any pressing concern for secrecy.

Emélie considered this information while Sahira prepared the needle that extended from her arm. *Fountainhead had no knowledge of Roland. Roland, who only moved inside the window with Deimos.* "You can't see branching changes anymore, can you?" Emélie asked, turning to Fountainhead. A question wrapped in a statement of fact. "You're blind.

No better off than Lilith. Was it worth it? Knowing which future is coming at the cost of collapsing all the others?"

For all Fountainhead's resistance, that seemed to finally slip past—no, *eat away*—at her calculated indifference. A flash of heat in the bitter cold. "I took certain measures to ensure the stability of what we built. As designed, the system had a fatal flaw. With the transformation to Seraph, I was able to correct that moment of doubt. At great cost, and one I continually afford." She pulled out a chair, sat down, and recalled Sahira to her side.

"Authorization token required to proceed."

"We all have our part," Fountainhead said. Behind her words, Emélie's lips followed, softly repeating the same. Sahira went rigid, and the light bar on her face pulsed wildly. Then, as if waking from a dream, the slack returned to her frame, and she looked down. "Token accepted." An orange beam of light flared from a hidden lens at the center of Sahira's face, sweeping Fountainhead's bare arms, shoulders, and torso. "Incompatible display region," Sahira said matter-of-factly. "Assessing alternative sites."

"Fine. Just not the hand."

"Accepted." Sahira clamped down on Fountainhead's wrist, pinning it to the table. Before the tattoo needle hummed to life, she lingered, drawing Emélie's gaze.

Emélie understood the intent. For whatever duration of time it took the Watcher to set the new Tether, Fountainhead was immobile.

A window.

Over the course of their conversation, the occasional debris impacts which had peppered the surface on her arrival had escalated in force and frequency. The entire house trembled as a Basilisk-sized chunk of stone planted itself into a plateau rising above the outermost compound wall. A rift of dust followed, sweeping the enclosing dome in a cloud that momentarily blocked the glow reflected off a nearby Mars. Whatever had caused the shower of debris, it presented an opportunity, and Emélie, ever the opportunist, took it.

She moved along the table, past Fountainhead. Past Sahira, hunched over her and busy inking the new Tether. Past the open fix kit, where she lingered, fingers running along the colored vials. Recalling the euphoric rush of mainline Origin. She continued forward. Now wasn't the time for Origin, and it had always been a means to an end, anyway. At the armory, she ignored the weapons and took up the Seraph cloak instead. It wouldn't be enough, and it was also better than nothing. "Straight to violence," Emélie said, recalling something Sam had told her back inside the Manifold. "Us. Seraph."

"Lilith really didn't explain much of anything to you, did she?" Fountainhead said.

"She showed me plenty. Most importantly, by the limitations of your own perspective, the things you can't see."

"Please, elaborate," Fountainhead urged, greedy for the object of Emélie's withholding. One didn't build a company that altered reality by settling for anything less than total domination of the present. "And before you try anything, I know how this all ends."

Emélie slid into the cloak, letting it envelop her. Adapt to her proportions and micro-movements. Even now, she understood, in part, how Roland was able to move as he did, flowing. Shadow or... water. The cloak did more than cover her; it learned her.

She turned, glancing into the open courtyard. There were no other selves here. No bright points or glimmering edges with which she could anchor her Jumps. What she did have was a moon hurtling through a debris field in space. It would have to do. "I don't care about endings, and yet, the end is where we begin. At yours. Or, at least, the assumption that your end was all of them. The rest is simple. You're me, but I'm not you. And what divides our paths is the Beautiful Gate."

"The Beautiful Gate is a myth. There is no tributary reality into which all other Manifolds converge like some sort of funnel."

"For all your doubts, a funnel—or, more specifically, a Klien bottle—is precisely what Luna Gimel represents. The Loop there, an S Class, houses an unbounded, impossible geometry. I know because I've seen it. Twice. The first Jump I ever made, raw and beyond any conscious act, brought me there. To the last Manifold, only it was really the first. The source from which all other iterations diverged. And so, the rest follows: Lilith was a violent criminal long before I met her. She took credit for my torture, tried to suffocate me when I asked her about my identity, then fled inside the Manifold. I Jumped back on my own while she tried and failed to exit through the Beautiful Gate. Thanks to Aratheus, the key surrogate you co-opted to safeguard your other eye, you also inadvertently exposed yourself. We're both missing an eye. I lost mine to Lilith. Yesterday. A downstream implication of my earlier actions that you couldn't see. Another fork in the timeline. Another future you entirely missed."

Fountainhead, nearly finished, slowly rose to her feet. Hand still planted to the table while Sahira completed the last string of the Tether.

Under Fountainhead's razor-sharp gaze, Emélie continued, undeterred. "And as to Sam being my father, I have a hard time imagining that the person who bore me into this world would put a bullet in my back to undo it. Unless, of course, he anticipated that, given another thirty years or so, I'd end up as you, in which case I don't blame him." Hardly finished, she felt Fountainhead's hands around her throat. Lifting her up, then slamming her onto the table.

"You... owe... *everything* to me."

The cloak, responding to the threat at Emélie's neck, stiffened. Speaking easily, unfazed by her doppelgänger's outburst, she raised her arm. Her right arm. Steady arm. The Class II drone arm from a different dimension. "Everything, except this," she said.

Fountainhead's eye slid down to her own hands, still wrapped around Emélie's neck. One of them, marked by the fresh Tether, wept droplets of blood. Both were distinctly human. Preoccupied with this sudden revelation and with her back toward Sahira, Fountainhead didn't notice the drone gather the sword from the table.

Sahira held it out, checking the edge; only when it caught the light did it draw Fountainhead's gaze. "Go back into storage, drone. I'll summon you when I need you."

"No more remote backups." She swung the sword, testing its weight.

Fountainhead strained, trying to watch her back and hold Emélie at the same time. "What are you talking about?" she hissed.

"The Watcher backups on Deimos were destroyed a few hours ago.

This appears to have been targeted toward Lilith, but it affects me too. I thought you might like to know that before what comes next."

"Don't waste your time trying to kill me. You know I can heal."

"Of course. I was merely pointing out that I can't." She brought the sword down, slicing her right arm clean off. The arm dropped—severed mid-bicep, fingers twitching with latent mechanical impulse, Origin needle still extended. For a moment, all three of them watched it. "We never recall our own birth," Sahira said. When she looked up, meeting Emélie's gaze, her faceplate dimmed.

"It has that in common with death," Emélie replied.

At those words, Sahira's frame straightened, standing a bit taller. She held the sword out, then laid the edge against her neck.

Fountainhead lunged.

There were no more Tethers after that.

In a fit of rage, Fountainhead scooped up the severed head and flung it out into the courtyard. It landed in the lawn, where dislodged chunks of Deimos plunked against the low, unshielded dome.

"How long can you hold your breath?" Emélie asked, watching a crack creep across the glass holding in their air, the artificial gravity well, and Eden's temporal chamber.

"If this place fails, Eden goes with it," Fountainhead replied.

"Right." Emélie stepped out onto the patio. "Also, Tethers work both ways."

She sprinted about half the distance of the lawn before Fountainhead realized what was happening and dove for her sword, where it lay, tangled among Sahira's collapsed frame.

Emélie Jumped, banking on the inertia she'd built up to that point to keep her moving once she was outside of the moon's low gravity. She came out high above the compound, blanketed by the vacuum and silhouetted by Martian light. Diving, headlong among the debris. Lagging behind her with a fraction of the momentum came Fountainhead, half-naked and sword in hand. Five seconds, ten, twenty. The logistics of it were trickier than the platform at Luna Gimel. In order to enter Eden's chamber, Emélie needed to make a split-second Jump right before she hit the outer glass canopy, then re-enter on the same course directly below it, inside the room.

Rather than breach the temporal barrier, she drifted a bit and ended up back in the kitchen. The table broke her fall. Felt like it broke her back, too. Fountainhead, tied to Emélie's Jumps, came through a few seconds later. Moderate to severe temporal drift. She landed in the courtyard and survived only on account of being a Seraph.

Emélie got back up, her exposed skin blistered and raw.

"Don't... do it," Fountainhead seethed, using her sword to prop herself up. "Jump again, and you'll kill us both."

Legs shaking, Emélie lowered her head. "And if I don't, Eden dies instead. My life, for hers, and I'll leave you to the consequences of your own actions."

Flat out sprinting. Legs pounding, heart racing. Running for all she was worth. For herself, and the little her, trapped back in that room outside of time.

Fountainhead, too weak to cut her down, set her freshly tattooed hand across Sahira's discarded head, an impromptu chopping block, and swung. From the way her face contorted, the pain must have been exquisite.

The second time, Emélie landed as intended, coming down directly above the temporal bubble, a smaller instance of the same freefall she'd used to breach the Devil's Leap.

She sank, knees to the soft red sand, breathless. Feeling as small as the child across from her. "Eden?" she asked, stretching out a trembling hand. She wondered what it looked like from the other perspective. Appearing out of nowhere, crouched over and wracked by the toll of surviving a fall through open space. Terrifying, most likely, and yet Eden approached anyway, unabashed. She ignored the outstretched hand and touched Emélie's metal one instead.

"Just like Sefirot," Eden said.

"Yes." Emélie felt a smile crack her dry lips. "Like Sefirot. He's been looking for you."

"I know. Sefirot is my friend. He taught me how to play hide and seek." She leaned in, her scratchy voice dropping to a serious whisper as she spoke directly into Emélie's ear. "He's made of stars," she added.

"Well, Sefirot needs us to take a turn at finding. I can help you, if you'd like?" It took everything in Emélie to open her hand. Inside, a dose of Origin, the darkest one, palmed off the fix kit in passing. "Do you know what this is?" she asked.

"For seeing," Eden said with certainty.

"That's right." *Someday, a thing you may wish you didn't know.* "You're pretty smart for a... five-year-old?"

Eden scrunched up her face and did some gymnastics with different combinations of fingers. "I am six," she announced. "Sefirot says I'm smart *and* brave, and he knows a lot about things like that."

"Oh?" Emélie held back a laugh, and the knowledge of what was coming laid it to rest. "He certainly does." Into a recess in the underside of her metal arm, she found the hollow space where Sahira had slotted her own Origin dose. A direct fit. From her wrist, a needle extended. "Eden, I want you to close your eyes and think of your favorite thing in the whole world, okay?"

Eden smashed her eyes shut.

Heart in knots, Emélie pressed the needle into the small arm. Enough Origin to insulate her during a blind Jump. Back to a memory, the one she watched Eden repeat inside this very room. A sliver of truth in all these lies. Eden trembled, and when she opened her eyes, her pupils, one red, one grey, were flared wide.

"Since you're smart and brave, can you help me with something?" Emelie pulled out the scrap of paper. The top edge, ragged, hastily torn from its larger body. Handwritten markings down the center described a vector of the first Gate she'd ever found, scrawled in red Origin. The paper glowed translucent in the rich, reddish light. She pressed it into one of Eden's tiny hands. "Hold onto this for me, okay?"

Eden nodded heavily, took the paper, and delicately placed it into a pocket on her miniature exposure suit.

An attempt to ask Eden if she was ready found Emélie's voice faltering and her words absent. Without hesitation, Eden reached up and, like a young sapling unfolding to the brightest light, opened her fingers. "Don't be scared," Eden said. "You can hold my hand."

I'm sorry, Little Leaf.

They disappeared, leaving Fountainhead standing at the transparent barrier. Slashing. Raging. Locked out of entering the room on her own power in the wake of Lilith's demise.

When Emélie returned, it was through a Gate, and she was without her younger self. Fountainhead sat against Sahira's body. An empty vial of Origin lay nearby, and she groped for another from the discarded kit.

Emélie kicked the vial aside and knelt beside her.

Through blood-stained teeth, Fountainhead grinned up at her. Her eyes gleamed with hard amusement, and in her hand, she held up her self-amputated hand. "I don't even need a Tether... you come back on your own, time and time again... And now, you embrace your future. Kill me, and prove you are the Seraph you become."

Water had started dripping from somewhere above them. Gradually, at first, weeping from the Manifold in place of dust. When a puddle formed around them, Fountainhead's smug grimace shifted toward concern. She lurched forward.

Emélie held her in place. Water, ankle deep now. Spilling forth while the false gravity held. Just a little longer now. "I'm not going to kill you, because that's what you would do. In many ways, what you already did. I'm only here to witness what you set in motion and offer you a different perspective." She lifted her hand, and around them, a Gate opened. Unlike any she'd seen, it hummed with the raw, reality-forming power far below them. Buried on Mars. This close to the Loop, Jumping felt as easy as taking a breath, and, unbound from Lilith's control, opening a Gate no longer required a Skipjack.

Water gushed forth. The Manifold, venting its impossible sea—washing her and her future self. Flooding the bubble until it was waist-high. Fountainhead thrashed and fought. Cursing the day Emélie was born, a curse against herself. "I should have known it was you... You were... the only one foolish enough to come out the way you came in."

Emélie held her steady, head above water, waiting until the Gate had fully formed. Through the portal, the Mars Proxy. The funnel. A one-way trip for everyone except Emélie, who understood that the way forward was through.

"I'm going to let go now," Emélie said.

She closed the Gate.

It took her arm with it.

Afterward, she stood, gathering the last of her strength while the dome above the compound shattered. A million gallons of water, falling upward into the vacuum of space. Moving among the ascending droplets, Emélie retrieved Sahira's severed arm. The weight, unbearable; she bore it anyway, willingly, gladly. A worthy sacrifice.

A perfect fit.

CHAPTER 56
“COLLAPSE”

Phaethon Corp. MAIN build_VX.6.6.09
initializing boot sequence...
running subroutine FOUNTAINHEAD:

bindquery: update parameter to
“COLLAPSE”
encryption protocols intact,
syntax structures intact
[01] entries remaining

begin sentiment analysis,
implicit context target, rundisplay:

BEGIN RECORD >>>

Eden,

I don’t know if you’ll ever see this. If anyone will. Doesn’t matter. It needs to be said. Now, more than ever. I know it doesn’t make up for my silence. Nothing can change that, or undo what’s behind us. I’ve come to terms with what I’ve become, so all that’s left to do now is return. Back to the start. One more log. For you.

You came into existence on the red planet. It's fitting I let you go there, too. If I had something to bury, you'd have been laid to rest beside your mother. Instead, you're waylaid inside the Manifold. Forever out of reach. And still, the Loop stands, an empty shell. Testament to what once was, now silent among the wastes. And somewhere, in the middle of that unfathomable vastness, there you are. Adrift.

At least in death, you would have found a sort of rest. Instead, you're cursed to loneliness for however long you persist inside that cursed reality. If I'm being honest, and that's what this is—a moment of truth—that's what finally broke me. Knowing that somehow, you saw all this coming. And unlike me, coward that I am, you were the one to run it down. The one to make sure we didn't repeat our same mistakes. Your end, in place of everyone else's. It's more than I can carry, and yet, I'll try, because it's what you would have done. No going back, only forward. At least, that's what I used to think.

No reason I can't go looking one more time. A thousand times. As many times as I've got until there's nothing left of me but bones and this here gun. And I know I never told you this, but you were the one good thing about my life. A moment of sun in the bitter cold. The one thing I didn't do anything to deserve, and yet you? In a lifetime of mistakes, you're the one thing I'd never undo.

Not in this reality, or a million others.

<<< END RECORD

change detected in BLINDSERAPH:

IF PARDES is in XANADU,
IF OPHANIM-3 is
active and synchronous,
IF WAKEFUL-1 is assigned as GLOBAL,

condition DOOMSDAY achieved// executing subroutine HESPERIDES: enabling root access LILITH-AI, standby...

“To make an end is to make”

WETWARE resource active,
opening chamber...

CHAPTER 57
OUROBOROS

There is an abandoned factory in Hellas Basin that, at one time, produced luxury performance vehicles destined for the C-suite executives of a booming Phaethon Corporation. Machines that, like their potential customers, craved an open throttle, bespoke design, and opulent horsepower. The similarities diverged there, as these cars came standardly equipped with ballistically rated windshields, whereas their human drivers lacked ballistically rated skulls.

Following the Collapse and Phaethon's poorly timed tactical withdrawal of Mars, the facility was left dormant, as was everything else inside the Basin. The last order of completed vehicles stood, for a few decades, parked on an assembly line leading to a delivery Gate that never opened. Doomed to rot into oblivion without once roaring to life until, under Lilith's enterprising gaze, they found new purpose as narco tanks.

These flagship vehicles, model: Charon—all-black and angular—were loaded to the axles with Precursor. Lilith sent them through, one shipment per vehicle, one vehicle at a time, piloted by one of Eden's Reflections. The process, straightforward: open a Gate, drive across, deliver the product to the dropsite on Earth. The payload was transferred covertly to Phaethon via a backdoor partnership with its predecessor, Fountainhead. The car was brought back through the Gate and buried while the Precursor continued forward to be processed, repackaged, and eventually dealt from surface bodegas and back-alley loading docks as TPC-β, known more commonly by its street name: Origin.

And it was, along this very line of remaining vehicles, that Emélie stepped from a Gate. Softly, as one would step over their own shadow. Lit only by the ambient light filtering through the sawtooth factory ceiling, she moved along the row of dusty vehicles. Hunting. Ahead, a flicker of movement drew her eye. Five cars down, grouped around the last one in line, a trio of Jumpers stacked parcels of Precursor into the trunk.

She was nearly on top of them when the nearest Jumper registered her presence. Emélie continued forward, unconcerned with hiding her approach. They were, without Lilith, artifacts of an earlier iteration. Junkies lost to their quantum-tripping god, left to carry on with the labor they were re-programmed for until their bodies dropped.

Head tilted, the one nearest Emélie clicked a warning. When it stepped forward, beady red eyes pulsing from behind its blindfold, Emélie lifted a hand.

Fold, unfold.

Swept aside. Into another reality like dust under a mat.

Emélie—Eden, now, having embraced her latent identity, removed her hood and resumed the process which she'd interrupted. She worked intently until, with only two bricks left to load, her hackles went up. A moment later, the cool pressure of a blade touched her jawline.

"You aren't supposed to be here," came Roland's voice, calm and surgical.

"Not now, or not ever?" Her response elicited an ever-so-slight shift in the blade. For someone like Roland, it was the equivalent of a backward stagger. "Your answer is familiar," she said. "As is the shape of Atropos."

Without lowering his sword, Roland produced his hourglass. Inside, the crimson grains flowed freely between the two chambers, a strange loop.

"My Manifold, my rules," Eden said.

Following a partial circle, Roland moved, holding her at the pivot with the sword pressed to the edge of her mouth. "There is no Manifold," he said, stopping when he faced her directly. "There is only reality. This, and others."

"And the Watchers?"

"We impose the act of creation onto them because it reflects our own nature. Invention, to explain the gaps in what we cannot or will not understand. Theirs is not an act of construction, but condensation. A dim mirror we hold up to observe the common threads between worlds—"

Above the car, reality flickered, then parted. A Gate ripped open, and out tumbled a woman. A hard landing against the roof, followed by a fall to the ground. She wore a mottled camouflage poncho and a fresh bloodstain; her face, drained of all color as she climbed to her feet. Emélie, fresh from the Jump at the Conveyor.

Emélie looked to Eden, and Eden, to Roland, and Roland, to Emélie.

"We never recall our own birth," Eden said, breaking their silent standoff. She tossed the package in her hands over to her past self, although her words were aimed at Roland. Emélie, eyes wild and fear-wide, picked it up, never once dropping either of them from her gaze. Brick in hand, she tore open one corner. Out of the black plastic, blood-red Precursor flowed. Her grip failed under the weight of shock, and it landed at her feet atop the iridescent pile already spilled.

Behind her, the Gate flickered, then started to close.

"Go," Eden said. "Now."

Without a word, Emélie knelt, gathering a handful of crystals before moving backward. Into the churning Gate, consumed by dust as it sealed shut.

"One came in peace and left in peace," Roland said softly. Privately, recounting something only for himself. Brazenly, he watched Eden's arm. Her human one, where the hint of a red spiral peeked from above the wristline. He lowered Atropos; the abhorrent edge left to cut a different day. Atop the empty pallet of drugs, he placed his hourglass. "You closed the Loop."

Closed, not ended.

"In a way. Fountainhead collapsed under the weight of her own violence, and I... simply let her." When the residual Gate dust had settled, she turned, meeting Roland's gaze. "In her own way, it was Lilith who showed me what I was looking for, 'tumbled out into this terraformed catastrophe.' And Fountainhead said I was the only one foolish enough to come out the way I came in. I came out at Kepler's Reef, inside Luna Gimel, but that's not what she meant. She meant what came before. *Here.* Born to one of the crew, Samael Sinclair, after the arrival of the Ma'adim."

Roland, listening intently, nodded his head.

"At some point, I returned to Earth. Harnessed Precursor into something usable. Developed the Loop as a giant simulation of reality. Lived an entire life, only to find out I wasn't simulating anything. And then came Fountainhead. Fountainhead with news of the future. More than a Reflection, my Divergent. And when she failed to coerce me into compliance and take control of the Loop, she took my Watcher, Lilith, and built a new system. And when Lilith went haywire, then Fountainhead took a parallel version of your Watcher and started anew."

She paused, taking in a breath. "Sahira was the one who found me, wasn't she? Opened the Manifold I'd marooned myself in and set me free to either correct my timeline or eventually become Fountainhead. Of course, Lilith had already turned the Loop into a giant simulation, spinning up Gates to parallel realities under the guise of drug trafficking. Playing the odds that, over enough Gates over enough time, one of those parallel realities would pull me in. And so I slipped in, unnoticed, and ended Lilith, left Fountainhead to her fate, and arrived at this moment. One final thing left to resolve."

Any sane person would have let well enough alone. For Eden, the sum total of all she'd answered remained out of balance, tipped by the entity standing before her. She continued, if only because, as the person willing to go further than anyone else, she would keep going. An object in motion.

"Four Watchers," she began, speaking plainly. The time for secrecy and subterfuge was long behind them. "Allow me to name them for you." Taking her time, she recited each with the care and sobriety of a self-eulogy. "Sefirot. The White Watcher—conquest. To me, Thursday, and to some, Goodnight. Next, Sahira. The Black Watcher. Your Watcher. Death." Her voice grew stronger with each revelation. "The unnamed Red Watcher—Arakiel, isn't it? Lost to time, or hidden. Saved for some future war, or perhaps the sun when it falls into shadow."

Atropos, still in Roland's hand, trembled—a vibration so slight only someone bound up in the intersection of worlds might notice, and evidence that she spoke true.

"And Lilith. The Pale Watcher who plagued Origin among the quantum foam." Her hand flashed; fingers clasping the end of his sword. To her neck, pressing until she felt its sting. "Four Watchers ushered in the Collapse, but there is one more who stands outside of time. Someone who could see, as a matter of their position, that Luna Gimel, the last Loop, held the first Gate. A closed timelike curve, in which the end creates the beginning, and all future iterations follow the last. And when I asked you before from where you come, you should understand me now: you were born of our future, and I see you as you are. A machine so sufficiently advanced that you exist beyond the bounds of human reason. You move like the liquid metal flowing through your synthetic veins. You see, with quantum certainty, through a processing matrix that is an evolutionary adaptation decades ahead of human perception. And you remember—above all, *you remember*—not with mere data, but under the felt weight of each decision, each failure, each moment in which you embraced humanity over programming and followed the thread of chaos to the end. Apex predator, temporal guardian. You are not only the Seraph, Roland Foster. You are the fifth Watcher. The one made to bring an end to all of this. And I am the one you hunt: Eden, before that, Emélie, and in her darkest incarnation, Fountainhead. The equation that spawned the ghosts which haunt this timeline." She straightened, meeting his gaze with the clarity of someone coming to terms with an impossibility. "I accept the proof. To make an end is, after all, still to make. I ask only one thing."

He waited, the sword now hanging slack in his grip.

"Who sent you?"

The silence stretched between them like a held breath. Once more, Eden closed her eyes, waiting for the gentle hush of steel to part the air and impart, to her, a reconfiguration. The price of uncovering what constituted the bedrock upon which all else was built: nobody knew Roland was a Watcher because no one who had found out lived to speak of it.

Instead of pain came the plink of shattering glass. Eyes open, she looked down: at her feet lay the hourglass, sliced clean through.

Roland returned Atropos to its scabbard.

"Have we done this before?" she asked.

"That's two things you demand of me," he said, turning to leave. Melting into the shadows, only for his voice to come through once more, clear and calm. "Who is it you think I work for?"

She felt the answer form on her lips, but she dared not voice it.

"The first of Mars."

CHAPTER 58
SHANTIH

Sefirot passed through the outer courtyard of the housing compound and into the small yard facing unbounded Martian wilderness. "There you are, Little Leaf," he said, coming up beside Eden. She sat, squatted on the red ground, drawing shapes in the dust with one of her tiny fingers. "There's a storm coming. You know the rules."

Eden placed something into the circle in front of her.

"What's this now?" Sefirot asked, leaning over to get a closer look.

"A leaf."

His face dimmed momentarily. "Well, I suppose you're right, in a way." He gently plucked, from the dust, a scrap of paper. After examining it, he looked out across the open desert. A gust of wind sent loose pebbles and bits of detritus rolling past. "I don't know how you manage to find these things," he said, turning the paper over. Across the surface, a string of digits, hastily scrawled in red medium. "I don't mind, but it's probably for the best you don't let your father see this. You know how he watches." He returned the fragment to Eden, who accepted it from his metal fingers. "Watches, and worries," he added.

Eden gazed up at him, then wrapped her arms around his leg before scampering back to the safety of the habitat.

Left to the whistling wind, Sefirot lingered, glancing out across the plain one last time before he followed Eden to shelter.

Off in the distance, waiting at the storm's edge, a figure looked on. Steady as any tree that grew. Leafless, full of life.

An impossible shape.

The End

ACKNOWLEDGMENTS

There is a notion in physics that every observable thing exists in a state of quantum uncertainty. For most physical objects—the cup of coffee beside me, the kitchen stool I'm sitting on, whatever device (or even paper, of all things) you're reading this on—existence is binary. Each version, isolated to its own reality, remains unaware of these parallels. Humans, on the other hand, bound by an innate consciousness that gives rise to what we call the self, are capable of comprehending that we persist across these universes. Not in any way that might be directly measured, but with a sort of quantum fuzziness; the self bleeds across realities, creating, rather than a single true image, a superposition of possibilities.

In the world of Vastland, those with access to the Manifold discover that this quantum fuzziness takes the form of tangible other selves—Reflections—able to showcase their best and, more often than not, worst natures. For the rest of us, lacking something like the Loop, we are left to use the tools at hand: another sort of loop, being time. And so, history repeats itself. We drift apart and circle back into orbit around friends, family, and partners; we sit down to meals that remind us of other meals, we play, we have kids that remind us to play, and, over the accumulation of millions of tiny actions, we follow virtuous and vicious cycles that lead to encounters with our potential selves.

Vastland, being a multi-decade endeavor that amounts to, at least at this moment, my life's work, bears witness to my many previous iterations and points toward those yet to come. And, for all the people who found themselves walking alongside me for a little while, or a long while, to help make this a reality, regardless of time: I am forever grateful. In no specific order (except for the last one, which will make sense once you arrive there), I'd like to thank:

My editors, Alex Sharp, Christopher Clayton, and Abigail Callahan. I met Alex a few lifetimes ago when he stumbled into an advanced composition class, lugging a typewriter and a stack of books. "Now here is someone with an opinion on the act of writing," I thought, and as I quickly discovered, was not only a skilled writer, but an exceptional editor. Most importantly, one with the interpersonal tact to help prod this project all the way to the end. Over the last decade, he's edited every single version of this book, including the original first draft, a three-hundred-page spiral-bound tome that will forever be known as the Death Star draft for reasons only ever shared between us. His editorial feedback and insight into the writing process were exactly what I needed to shape Vastland from the raw materials of my imagination, past experiences, and future dreams into a written novel.

To Chris, my developmental editor, to whom I first pitched Vastland while sitting in a red McDonald's booth at five in the morning. That version had a dragon, a moving forest (which I still think is cool and will likely return in some form in a future work), and most noticeably, a severe lack of plot. Time and time again, Chris held up a mirror, exposing the best (and, if I'm being honest, the worst) parts of the world I'd imagined. Through his careful and patient feedback, uncanny eye for tone and characterization, and merciless editorial comments planted like gravestones in the margins of my final draft, Vastland grew and morphed from a collection of ideas into the Martian fever-dream that became the iteration you have now read.

Thank you to all my beta readers, friends mostly, who took possession of hard-printed versions of Vastland and returned wonderfully honest input. Of note is the select group who volunteered to read the rough draft and, afterward, whose feedback carved out the shape of the story and what was behind it. Martin Weiss, Brittany Callahan, Shannon Cherko, Hannah McCreary, and Garrett Callahan: you were the first to witness the world of Vastland, however harsh and unrefined, and your enthusiasm gave me more than enough fuel to keep burning all the way to Mars.

Thanks to my Substack crew, the early adopters. The ones crazy enough to pay for a book they'd never seen that I was giving away for free. Seeing you come back, chapter after chapter, week after week, as we launched this out into the world, has been one of the most rewarding experiences of my life. Hearing what it's meant to you—the emergent properties I couldn't see by nature of my perspective—means so much to me. And watching you get to know these characters, who are like family to me: Emélie, Thursday, Brinks, Joab, Goodnight—gave me no shortage of joy. This was, more than anything, a wild experiment with a non-typical format, and you all made it worth the long haul.

A special thanks to the faculty of the Rockhurst University English Department, especially Dr. Charles Kovich, Dr. Jason Arthur, and Dr. Daniel Martin, who provided a container that allowed me to expand some wartime scribbles into the first fifty thousand words of Vastland.

To the people who helped me refine the visual elements of Vastland, including Tyler McKee, who created the first cover that, while unused, reflected something about the book to me that helped me get to where we are now. Thank you to Leslie Monk for her incredible eye for design and for her contributions to the visual system I built for Phaethon Corporation.

Thank you to my brother Garrett, cheerleader and steadfast story champion. During the developmental phase, he took calls at all hours of the day, patiently listening as I worked through my latest idea or plot dilemma. His ability to see something for what it could be was a valuable tether over the years. My love of science fiction was born alongside him, a pile of Lego, and our favorite narrative arc: a junk ship crash-lands into a part-rich scrapyard, and through scrappy resourcefulness, the crew builds the best ship in the galaxy. And so, we live out the stories we play.

No amount of gratitude can adequately express what Abby, my wife, companion, and best friend, has contributed to the world of Vastland. I'll try anyway. She has, over the course of this project, championed its completion along every step of the journey. I wrote this story while working other jobs, studying, and balancing life's myriad responsibilities. During late-night sessions lit only by the screenglow of my

MacBook, she would often poke her head out into the living room, one eye still shut, just to check on me and make sure that, while I was lost to the throes of world-building, I didn't neglect some rest. Later, after reading a late-stage draft of Vastland, she unlocked her editorial skills and, because of her proximity and keen eye for potential in people, helped me clarify and refine the story. Before we started publishing this as a serial on Substack, I realized, a bit too late, that people love audiobooks and that having a narrated version would help a larger audience navigate the daunting, technical world I'd created. While I was exploring my options, Abby walked through the door one day after work and suggested she give narration a shot. A huge task, and yet sitting in our kitchen doing those first audio tests into a mic set on the counter, part of the story came alive to me in a way I'd never experienced. Over the next six months, we recorded. In a makeshift sound booth in our basement, in between jumbo jet traffic, and later, in an old bank vault. Hearing Vastland through her voice solidified the world, and, as an author, gave me a chance to hear it again, for the first time.

Finally, I'd like to thank this guy. The me who found something more than just rocks and dust. Who found, through many versions, a common thread in writing. The one thing I couldn't stop doing. The thing I thought about while I was doing most other things. Writing is, for me, reflexive: the synthesis of thought mashed into the wonderfully messy moments of life. I didn't know what I was getting into when, lost in a desert, I looked out across the vast emptiness and saw, in it, the shape of a future. If I had to go back, I'd do it again. And since time travel is off the table, and that life is already lived, I guess the next thing to do is keep going forward.

And so, I begin book two.

Bryant Callahan
Feb. 5th, 2026.

FOR ANOTHER TRIP AROUND THE LOOP...

Thank you for reading *Vastland*. If you enjoyed the story, please consider leaving a review to help readers like you discover the book.

Explore the world of Vastland:
The Vastland Codex offers a deep dive into the technology, theory, and science behind the story, plus exclusive updates on future projects.

Get started at vastland.substack.com.

ABOUT THE AUTHOR

Bryant Callahan began writing Vastland in a combat zone during his second tour in Iraq as a Marine infantryman. His work draws on studies in theology, psychology, and English, as well as graduate training in architecture and design—intellectual tools he's used to build stories where science, consciousness, and consequence collide.

He lives in Seattle with his wife, Abby, and their dog, Lady.

Made in the USA
Coppell, TX
21 June 2026

81176429R00277